FEROCIOUS

Also by Paula Stokes

Vicarious

Ferocious

FEROCIOUS

PAULA STOKES

TOR
TEEN

A Tom Doherty Associates Book
New York

FEROCIOUS

Copyright © 2017 by Paula Stokes

A Tor Teen Book
Published by Tom Doherty Associates
175 Fifth Avenue
New York, NY 10010

www.tor-forge.com

Tor® is a registered trademark of Macmillan Publishing Group, LLC.

The Library of Congress Cataloging-in-Publication Data
is available upon request.

ISBN 978-0-7653-8096-8 (hardcover)
ISBN 978-1-4668-7621-7 (ebook)

Our books may be purchased in bulk for promotional, educational, or business
use. Please contact your local bookseller or the Macmillan Corporate and
Premium Sales Department at 1-800-221-7945, extension 5442, or
by email at MacmillanSpecialMarkets@macmillan.com.

First Edition: August 2017

Printed in the United States of America

0 9 8 7 6 5 4 3 2 1

To Christina,
my books and my life are both so much better because of you

FEROCIOUS

CHAPTER 1

My name is Winter Kim. Today I killed a man. Soon I hope to kill another.

As the MetroLink train shimmies along its metal tracks, I repeat those words over and over in my head. I recently found out my sister, Rose, was murdered. Her ex-boyfriend, Gideon Seung, suggested we attend a bereavement support group together. But before I could even think about that, Gideon was killed too. And then I killed his killer.

I close my eyes and envision telling a room full of strangers that the only two people I loved were both murdered. There would be the obligatory sympathetic cooing and perhaps a gasp of shock. Then I'd tell them I'm a killer too and I'm not finished yet. The expressions of bland disinterest would twist into disgust. The woman who comes mostly for the free food would choke on her coffee cake.

You're a monster, she'd whisper, before quickly averting her eyes.

Maybe I am a monster.

As far as I know, there's no support group for that.

The train hisses slightly as it pulls into the next station. Snowflakes batter the windows, sticking fast to the cold glass in tiny deformed clumps. Beyond the platform, the streets of St. Louis stretch out empty and cold. And dark. It's only six P.M., but it might as well be midnight.

A man pushing a metal cart ducks through the open doors, the wheels leaving trails of grayish sludge on the patterned floor of the train. He takes a seat across from me and folds back the lid to his trolley, exposing items for sale—perfume, neckties, designer purses. The strange combinations of what people sell on the train remind me of the subway stations back in Seoul. You could buy almost anything there.

The train starts moving again. The man steps out into the aisle and begins pushing his trolley toward the front of the car, stopping occasionally to address specific passengers. Turning toward the window, I pull an envelope out of the center pocket of my hoodie. My name is written on the front in black ink. My eyes water as I consider Gideon's neatly printed capital letters. I'll never see that handwriting again.

I run my thumb along the flap of the envelope and the paper slices into my flesh, leaving behind a thin trail of red. I lift my hand to my lips and taste the metallic flavor of blood. My fingers brush against the rose pendant that hangs in the hollow of my throat. The necklace used to belong to my sister.

I wrap my fingers around it, grip it so tight that the metal cuts into my palm. Rose died so that I could escape our past.

And now I am free.

But alone.

Vengeance is all that I have left.

Monster, a voice hisses from inside my brain.

Monsters don't get happy endings.

The train reaches the end of the line—the airport—and I stay tucked in my seat as the other passengers disembark. A pair of security agents passes by in their navy uniforms, followed by two teens in NFL parkas. After them, a group of people wheel suitcases up the wet floor, most of them looking down at their phones as they trudge along. Finally it's just me and the man with the trolley. He gestures at me and I slide out of my seat. Behind me, his wet, metal wheels bump into the back of my ankles. The man grunts an apology. I nod an acknowledgment without looking back.

Outside, the sharp air cuts through my hoodie and the T-shirt beneath. I exhale a puff of white, half expecting the droplets of my breath to freeze and fall to the ground like a tiny ice storm.

"Cold, huh?" Trolley Guy says as he slides past me. A dark red necktie dangles from the top of his rolling cart.

"Yes." My voice is barely audible. My eyes home in on the red slash of fabric. I am thinking about the man who took everyone I love away from me. Kyung. His name is a knife blade, but I'm done being stabbed by it. It's my turn to inflict the damage.

The red tie vanishes from sight as Trolley Guy disappears behind a pillar. Kyung wore a tie that color the first time I met him. Rose and I stood side by side in the center of a room while he evaluated us like we were farm animals. *Not exactly what I was hoping for, but I guess they'll do.* My sister's face burned with shame as he circled us, touching her hair, lifting her skirt to examine her legs. I didn't understand what was happening yet, but she did.

A set of sliding glass doors opens and the stream of people funnels me into the airport and up a set of narrow escalators. I glance back at the MetroLink tracks through a wall of glass windows. It was probably foolish of me to come here. I don't even have any luggage—no place to check my knives and hide my spare IDs.

I couldn't go to my therapist appointment, though. If I had, I would've broken down and told Dr. Abrams everything. She would have been obligated to put me in a psychiatric facility and warn Kyung that I had threatened his life. Plus, she would've gone to the police and they probably would have figured out what really happened in the penthouse.

What really happened is this: Kyung sent a man named Sung Jin to coerce Gideon into giving up the ViSE technology.

Gideon tried to refuse and Sung Jin killed him. Sung Jin also shot my friend Jesse Ramirez and Gideon's head of security, Baz Faber.

And then I killed Sung Jin.

I should probably feel something when I think about that, when I think about pulling the trigger on the gun. When I think about his sharp, mercenary eyes turning to black glass. It's no small thing—ending someone else's life. There should be some sort of gravity to that, shouldn't there? My insides are heavy, but it has nothing to do with what I did. It is only about what I have lost.

I take a seat in the ticketing and departures lobby and watch travelers mill back and forth, their suitcases trailing behind them like obedient toddlers. A cell phone buzzes in my pocket. Sung Jin's phone—it's a text from Kyung.

Kyung: Should I arrange for a car to pick you up at LAX tomorrow?

Me: Tomorrow is too soon. Gideon told you the ViSE technology was stolen, right? I know who has it but reacquiring it will take time.

I actually have both the neural editor and recorder headset that Kyung wants me to bring him. Gideon lied to Kyung and said they were stolen to try to buy more time to figure out how to protect the technology. I'm hoping I can use his lie to my advantage.

Kyung: Two more days.

Me: That's not enough. I need a week.

Kyung: Five days. Bring the tech to me at UsuMed by Wednesday, or else.

Kyung and I have struck a deal of sorts. He claims I have a younger brother, Jun, who works for him, and that if I turn over Gideon's ViSE technology, he'll introduce us. ViSEs, or Vicarious Sensory Experiences, are neural recordings that allow a person to experience an activity via someone else's brain—all the thrills of rock climbing or bungee jumping or running from the police with none of the risk. I don't know what Kyung wants with the tech, but he wants it badly enough that he's threatened to kill Jun if I don't hand it over.

I hate that I'm risking my brother's life—assuming he's real—by not turning over the tech immediately, but I'm fairly certain Kyung is just trying to intimidate me. He won't really hurt my brother, as long as I don't push him too far. If he does, then he'll never get what he wants.

I switch to a browser window and do a search for "Jun Song" in Los Angeles. There are several screens of results, but none of them seem like they could be my brother. I try "Jun Song" and "UsuMed," but there's no overlap as far as I can tell.

I call up an airline website and search for flights to L.A. But then I get a better idea. Kyung is expecting me to fly into LAX or perhaps one of the local Orange County airports. I don't know how powerful he is, whether he might have men looking for me there. I clear the search box and search for flights to San Diego instead. I can drive up to Los Angeles. That way I'll have the element of surprise on my side.

There are open spots on two flights that are leaving later tonight, but my mind wanders back to the envelope from Gideon. I flipped through the contents but I didn't read all the documents. I should find somewhere to go through them in detail. There's no need for me to get to L.A. tonight. It makes more sense to find a place to stay, to make a plan.

I book myself on a flight leaving late tomorrow morning, using a fake name on one of the IDs Gideon left for me. Then I take the escalators down two floors to the baggage and ground transportation area. I try not to focus on all of the people down there reuniting with loved ones, but when a group of men—boys, most of them—in tan camouflage stroll past with green duffels slung over their shoulders, my legs go wobbly beneath me. Jesse was one of these guys once, so proud to be a soldier, so sure that he could make a real difference.

I pause for a moment, lean back against the cool concrete of the airport wall and close my eyes. "Please don't let Jesse die," I whisper.

Focus, Winter.

Right. Jesse is in the hospital being taken care of by doctors and nurses. I need to take care of myself.

I take a cab to one of the motels that is just across the highway, a run-down, seedy sort of place where a girl who just killed someone can be invisible. I check in under an alias and dead-bolt the door. Then, I lay out everything that was in the envelope from Gideon onto the bed:

A bundle of hundred-dollar bills.

Three sets of fake ID.

Bank statements from multiple bank accounts in both of our names. Just the money in these accounts would be enough for me to go to college and buy a small house—to live a life.

A business card from a lawyer who undoubtedly has additional paperwork for Gideon's business and personal assets.

And then something I'm not expecting: a blue memory card with my name on it.

It's a ViSE recording. It can't be of my sister, because she died before Gideon ever developed the technology. So it has to be a message from him to me. Which means that he must have known this day might come.

I pull in a deep breath and then let it out in fluttery little gasps. Retrieving my headset, I unfold the lightweight metal apparatus, slip the recording into the slot on the back, and adjust the prongs over my neural access points. I lie back on the mattress and press PLAY.

Gideon is sitting at the desk in his study, his laptop open in front of him. His black hair is slicked back like he just got out of the shower. He smiles slightly and a lump rises up in my throat. My eyes burn with tears.

I pause the recording. Sometimes when you're vising, you

can't distinguish what you're feeling from what the recorder is feeling. The lump, the tears—are they mine or someone else's? I lift a hand to my cheek. My fingers come away wet.

Crying is difficult for me. Dr. Abrams says that it takes more courage to express emotions than to hide them away, but it's hard to feel brave in this moment. I'm split between desperately needing Gideon and knowing that a ViSE of him won't be enough. It'll be like standing outside in a frigid St. Louis winter with nothing but a picture of a coat to keep me warm.

I give up and remove the headset. I'm not ready to play this recording. Dr. Abrams also used to tell me that love strengthened people. Right now my love for Gideon feels like a weakness, just like my tears.

I set the headset down on the bed and remove the memory card. As I slip everything back into the envelope, my fingertips brush against something cold. There's a thin metal chain at the very bottom that I missed when I dumped out the contents. I loop my finger around it and hold it up to the light. It's a necklace with a snowflake pendant. Why would Gideon buy me this? It's pretty, but everything else in this envelope is essential.

As my fingers trace the snowflake's detailed prongs, I notice there's a crack in the middle. Not a crack—a seam. The pendant pulls apart to expose a micro flash drive. My mind whirls as I turn the tiny storage device over in my hands. What sort of information could be so crucial that Gideon felt the need to disguise it in jewelry?

CHAPTER 2

I'll have to wait to find out. I don't dare turn on my phone in case the police are looking for me, and I left my tablet computer back at the penthouse. I won't be able to access the information on this drive until I can buy a new one.

I tuck all of the items back into the envelope and slip it into the motel room safe. Then I make a list of things I'm going to need in Los Angeles and have the front desk clerk call me a cab to a nearby shopping mall.

The taxi ride takes about fifteen minutes. Inside the mall, I duck into an electronics store to purchase a new tablet and two disposable burner phones. I debate buying more, but I figure that might stand out as suspicious, especially since I'm paying in cash. At the last second, I add in a few micro memory cards—just in case I need to record something.

"One for each boyfriend, huh?" the sales clerk jokes as he rings up the phones.

I want to ignore him, but I have a mission now. A purpose. One that's going to require me to act normal. I might as well start practicing.

I paint what I hope is a crafty smile on my face. "Our little secret, though, right?" I say.

He chuckles awkwardly and I realize he took my words as flirty.

That's because they sounded provocative, more like Rose than me.

Not my dead sister—a different Rose who lives inside of me. I have dissociative identity disorder and my alter persona calls herself Rose. Sometimes she takes over completely and I end up with blackouts and lost hours, but other times I just hear her in my head, encouraging me, calming me. And every once in a while, my words come out feeling like hers, like maybe she just stepped in for a few seconds.

I don't know what's actually possible when it comes to DID. I should do some research on my condition, but right now I'm still learning to accept that this is who I am.

I reach out and gently pat the sales clerk's arm—another Rose-like maneuver.

Are you helping? I think.

No response. She doesn't generally answer me—it isn't like we can have a conversation at will—but she's responded to direct questions in the past. At least I think she has. I guess her responses could have been hallucinations—I'm no stranger to those either. Sometimes I wonder if *everything* is a hallucination, if I'm really some other girl in some other world, and I've created this complex reality of murder and multiple personalities because it's somehow better than the life I actually lead.

A man coughs behind me. Another customer, whose patience is wearing thin. The salesclerk has pressed my receipt into my hand. He's staring strangely at me.

"Thank you for your help," I say quickly.

I hurry out of the store, but not before I hear the guy who was behind me mutter something about kids all being on drugs these days.

Next I visit a clothing store and head directly for a rack of hoodies in gray and black. And then I remember I'm going to Southern California where it's about seventy degrees. And also that I want somewhat of a disguise. I don't know what Kyung knows, whether Sung Jin might have followed me or researched me while he was in St. Louis, but it's better if the girl who shows up in L.A. can pass for someone else.

I allow myself one hoodie and a pair of jeans for times when I can be myself, as well as some sweatpants and a T-shirt to wear as pajamas. Then I reluctantly cross the store to a rack of dresses and pick out a couple that are modest but look like nothing I would ever wear. I buy some tights and boots to go with them.

I buy a coat and a purse, two more things that feel normal to most people but foreign to me. Then I leave the shop and stroll the mall's wide marble promenade, stopping in a drugstore where I buy makeup and a pair of nonprescription reading glasses, and a luggage store for a new backpack and a small suitcase. On my way out, I visit a brightly lit shop filled with beauty products. I pick up a couple of wigs—one long and black with a fringe of choppy bangs and one reddish blond with waves that will make me look different, but won't stand out on the streets of L.A. I had no idea how many things I would need to become someone else.

Back at the motel, I organize my purchases and pack them into my suitcase. I pull the tablet computer from the box and plug it in to charge. There is a sheet of instructions about the fastest way to connect to the Internet, but right now I just want to access the flash drive.

When the screen lights up, I plug the drive into a port on the side of the computer. A password box appears on the screen. It reads, *Three failed attempts to input the correct password will result in all information on this drive being destroyed.*

Standard Gideon. The password is probably on the ViSE.

I bite my lip as I consider going to sleep and dealing with things in the morning. But it won't be any easier then. It is never going to be easy to see Gideon again, to hear him and feel him after watching him die. If I am going to find my brother and kill Kyung, I cannot be afraid of sensory impulses on a ViSE. I cannot be afraid of my own feelings.

It's all right to be scared.

"It's not all right," I mumble under my breath. "It's not helpful, anyway." I grab my headset out of the safe and relax on the bed. I breathe in and out a couple of times, try to empty my mind of all thoughts, and press PLAY.

"Winter," Gideon says. "If you're watching this, then something bad has happened to me. I have many things to tell you, some of which I should have told you a long time ago. I don't know the exact set of circumstances that led you here, so you'll have to excuse me if you know some of this information already.

"Your sister is dead. She died when we were leaving Los Angeles. She died protecting you—protecting both of us. I blame myself. I was so focused on getting the three of us to safety that I took you in the elevator because it was fastest. We should have used the stairs. Perhaps then . . ." He swallows hard. "One of Kyung's men caught us leaving. When your sister tried to resist him, he stabbed her." Gideon blinks rapidly and looks down at the desk. "I hope you were aware of the details surrounding her death, because I would hate the thought of you going through that realization alone. If you need someone, Jesse and Sebastian have both promised they'll look out for you. And Dr. Abrams—you can always call her. Please don't try to get through this by yourself."

He goes on to tell me the things he told me when he returned from his business trip, about how he realized I was both hallucinating and dissociating as my sister and why he allowed me to live in a fantasy world for so long.

He holds up a brochure. "There are clinics for people with dissociative disorders where you can get special help. Dr. Abrams seemed fond of this one in Arizona. I know you won't want to go— that you think you have to fix all your problems yourself—but Winter, Ha Neul, some things are too big for any of us to handle alone."

My eyes water. I always get choked up when Gideon calls

me Ha Neul. I shed that name when we left L.A., like a moth shaking off the broken confines of its cocoon as it sees light for the first time. But it tethers me to my past, and to my sister, who never got a chance to fly.

I know he's right too, about doing this on my own. Gideon wouldn't want me to risk my life by going after Kyung. He wouldn't want me to skip out on my therapy sessions. But he doesn't know about my brother. It's not just my own well-being I have to consider. If I have a younger brother, then I need to look out for him, much the same way Rose needed to look out for me. Where I come from, the older siblings take care of the younger. That's how it is—how it always has been.

Next Gideon discusses the flash drive.

"The password has been coded to change every day at midnight Central Time, assuming Daylight Savings is not in effect. The first part of it is constant, the word sky, *with the* s *and* k *in lowercase letters and the* Y *capitalized. Then insert an underscore."*

I swallow hard. My real name means "sky" in Korean.

"The second part of the password is a numerical sequence. Start with your date of birth in US format—two digits for the day, two for the month, four for the year. Subtract your sister's birthday in the same format and then add the numbers for yesterday's day only. Be careful with your attempts because this drive cannot be copied and you are only given three tries in each twenty-four-hour period before the data will be destroyed."

Gideon clears his throat before continuing. "There are three things of importance on the drive. First is a folder with additional legal documents in it. There's my will, which has both your real and assumed name on it. My attorney has copies of all of this and knows that your identification paperwork was lost, but he has your picture and you'll be the only one able to answer the questions he'll ask to verify your ID. There is also the paperwork for Escape, the building, the ViSE technology, and some other assets. All of it is passing over to you.

"The next folder on the drive is my research. The flash drive

contains all of the notes I took from UsuMed and the ones I made when I was creating the ViSE technology. I disabled the neural editor when I removed it from Escape and hid it in the penthouse, just in case Kyung sent someone to steal it, but an engineer could re-build the missing components using my notes. I'm not sure why Kyung wants the tech so badly, but I suspect it's about more than mass production of headsets and streaming across platforms. Still, if he comes after you for it, just give it to him. I know better than anyone what Kyung is capable of. The tech isn't worth dying for. I want you to live a long and happy life. I know it might not feel like it now, but you can be happy. I promise.

"The final folder is full of pictures of your sister, and a few of you." Gideon turns his laptop around. There is a picture of my sister on the screen.

A sob bursts from my lips. I've never seen this picture of Rose. Gideon must have taken it of her in Los Angeles before we tried to escape. Our lives were hell there—Kyung's men selling us to strangers every night—but Rose's eyes are bright and her smile is wide, openmouthed, like she is laughing. I am so glad she had Gideon to keep her spirits from breaking. She had him and I had her, and because of them both, I'm still alive.

Gideon taps the screen and the image changes. It's a picture of me when I was younger, asleep on the penthouse sofa. A blanket is draped neatly over my slender body. "You weren't much for pic-tures when we first moved here," he explains. "I had to sneak them from time to time." Gideon closes the laptop.

He walks across the room, reaches out, holds my face in his hands. His touch manages to be both firm and soft at the same time. He leans in and gently kisses me on the forehead.

Tears roll down my cheeks. As I concentrate on the sensa-tion of him touching me, I wonder who recorded this. How strange it must have been for Gideon to talk to someone else—to touch another person—as if they were me.

"Always remember that I am proud of you," Gideon finishes.

"That I love you. I hope that you will play this recording any time you are feeling alone."

Another sob escapes me, this one from deep in my gut. For once, I embrace the pain instead of trying to lock it away. I am so grateful for this recording. At least now I won't forget how it feels to be loved.

I lie staring up at the ceiling of the motel room for a few minutes. Then I dry my tears with the sleeve of my hoodie and reach for the tablet computer. I work out the answer to the password in my head and enter it. A series of folders pops up.

I skim through the legal documents to assure myself there's nothing that needs to be taken care of immediately. I recognize a durable power of attorney for health care and a page with requests to be cremated in case of death. This causes another wave of tears to spill forth, and I'm not even sure why. Perhaps it's just the idea of Gideon sitting down at his desk and trying to think of everything he could do to make his death easier for me.

Next I open some of the research files, but most of them are incomprehensible to me. I have no idea what to do with Gideon's notes. Maybe I could share these files with a university or research team who might be able to use his findings for good. All I know is I don't want Kyung to have them.

I skip to the folder marked *Photos*—there are pictures of Rose with Gideon, Rose with me, Rose by herself. There are even selfies of Gideon and me that I have no recollection of posing for—most likely because I was dissociating at the time.

By the time I get to the last picture, I am crying uncontrollably. So many memories have come flooding back. I can't take the pain.

I trace the cross-shaped scar on my palm with one finger. I cut myself the first day of working for Kyung. I promised my sister I would never do it again, but sometimes it's hard to resist the temptation. I lift one of my throwing knives from the nightstand and consider the blade's edge. It's not very sharp.

The point is, though. I touch it to the skin of my palm, trace the scar once more. My hand tightens around the hilt until my knuckles blanch white.

Pain is not the answer.

I used to think the voices in my head were just my conscience, or perhaps my id and superego arguing things out the way you see angels and devils do in cartoons. After finding out about my DID, I have no idea who's telling me what. I guess I'm fortunate that the advice is usually good. This voice is right. I can't hurt myself—not now. There's too much to do.

I turn the blade of the knife away from myself and plunge it into one of the pillows. I exhale deeply and then pull the knife out and stab the pillow again. Bits of filling float through the air.

Hopping to my feet, I pull the mattress off my bed and lean it against the wall. I stand at the far side of the room and fling my knives, one after the next. They both hit the center of the mattress. I retrieve my knives and throw them again.

And again.

And again.

I throw them until my hands have stopped shaking.

Then I drop to the floor and start doing push-ups. Twenty. Thirty. Forty. The blood races from my head and heart to my muscles as they ache in protest. I collapse to the floor after the fiftieth push-up. My breath whistles in and out of my chest. "Weak," I tell myself.

You're strong.

"I need to be stronger." I grit through another twenty push-ups and then head for the shower. I love the feel of hot water pouring over me. It's the only time when I feel completely clean.

After about twenty minutes, I hop out and change into sweatpants and a T-shirt. I place both throwing knives on my nightstand for easy access. Frowning at the holes in the mattress, I slide the damaged side down onto the bed frame and replace the sheets, even though I seriously doubt I'm going to get much sleep tonight.

And then I remember my DID. What if my alter takes over after I fall asleep? I don't think she would do anything to hurt me—so far most of her actions seem to have been to try to help me or protect me—but I slip my headset over my ears and start recording just in case. I can review the footage in the morning, make sure Rose doesn't make my already bad situation even worse. Each memory card can hold two hours of recording time. I set an alarm on one of the burner cell phones to wake me up just before the card will run out. It's not ideal as far as sleep and restfulness go, but I'm done wondering about the things I do when I'm out of my mind.

CHAPTER 3

I wake to my alarm at twelve, two, and four, and then decide to get up at six a.m., even though my plane to San Diego doesn't leave until almost eleven. The first thing I do is skim back through the footage I recorded last night while I was sleeping. There is nothing but quiet blackness. *Thank you,* I think.

I remove the headset and go to the window. For a few moments, I watch flakes of snow flutter down and cling to the motel's black asphalt parking lot. It's like being trapped in a snow globe. I collect snow globes, or at least I used to. Lately all I seem to collect is death.

I pack everything up into my luggage except for what I'm going to wear. Slipping into one of the dresses, I study myself in the mirror. I look wan, washed out, my hair flat and stringy. I also look too much like me.

I don the reading glasses and the wig with the bangs and apply a little blush before taking another look in the mirror. Better. The girl who stares back at me manages to resemble my ID, yet still look like a stranger.

I go in search of breakfast, but all I find is coffee, orange juice, a few bruised apples, and a scattering of packaged pastries spread across a counter in the motel lobby. I fix myself a cup of coffee while the housecleaning staff huddles outside in the cold, smoking cigarettes before they come on shift. I should eat something, but I can't. My stomach feels like it's full of rocks.

After I finish my coffee, I fetch my bags from the room and call a cab. When the taxi driver arrives, I ask him to take me to St. Louis Medical Center, the hospital where Jesse and Baz were both transported to yesterday. When the driver puts the car into park about twenty minutes later and looks back expectantly at me, I stare through the smudgy side window for a few seconds, watching swirls of snow dance in the early morning sunlight.

"Can you leave the meter running and wait for me?" I ask. "I just need to say good-bye to someone before I head to the airport."

The driver nods. "I'll have to find a parking spot, but I'll watch for you."

"Thanks." I slide out of the car and shut the door gently behind me. I cross the sidewalk, stepping gingerly over a patch of ice. As I enter the hospital's main lobby, the heat envelops me like a breath of warm air. I wipe my feet on the damp rug just inside the doors and then stride purposefully up to the information desk. I flick bits of snow from the sleeves of my coat.

"Can I help you?" a woman wearing a dark blazer asks.

"My . . . friend got admitted through the ER last night." I keep my voice level, maintaining eye contact as she clicks her mouse. "Jesse Ramirez? I'm not sure what room they moved him to." Normally getting a patient's room number is a simple process, but since he came in with gunshot wounds, there's a chance his information might be restricted.

The clerk clicks her mouse and scrolls down a couple of screens. "He's in 5612," she says. "That's the cardiothoracic ICU. It's on the fifth floor of the Southwest Tower. You'll want to follow the signs to the ER and then continue past until you see the SWT elevator."

"Thank you." Cardiothoracic ICU. That doesn't sound good. I find the elevator she indicated and then hunt around until I find a door that leads to a narrow set of stairs.

I take the stairs to the fifth floor and follow the signs marked

CTICU. I end up in a small waiting room decorated in outdated earth tones. There's a desk at one end of it, but whoever is supposed to be manning it either hasn't arrived for the day or has stepped away momentarily. A square metal plate is mounted on one of the side walls next to a set of heavy fire doors. I press it and they open.

The inside of the ICU is bright white and pale green, with lights shining everywhere. Nurses and doctors stride past without even glancing at me. The rooms are numbered in order, so finding Jesse in number 12 is easy. The front of his room is a wall of glass with a sliding door that's currently open. I glance furtively around as I enter the room, but again no one is paying me any attention. I swallow back a little gasp as I approach the bed. Jesse's body is covered in plain white hospital blankets and he's breathing through an oxygen mask that covers most of his face. His hearing aid is in a plastic medicine cup that sits on the bedside table. An IV pump stands next to the bed, three different bags of clear fluid infusing him simultaneously.

My eyes flick to a flat-screen monitor mounted above his bed. There are numbers for heart rate, blood pressure, and something called SpO2.

"Hey," a female voice says sharply. I spin around to find a tall, dark-skinned girl in scrubs studying me curiously. She doesn't look much older than I am. "Did you check in at the desk?"

"There was no one there when I arrived," I say. "I'm sorry." I turn back to Jesse. "Is he going to be all right?"

"I think so," she says. "I'm Kendra, his nurse. Are you Winter?"

I should lie, but my curiosity gets the better of me. "How did you know that?"

"He kept saying your name over and over when we weaned him from the ventilator. Everyone else thought he was just talking crazy from the narcotics, but somehow I could tell he didn't mean the season."

I wonder what it was like for Jesse, waking up in the hospital on a breathing machine. I should have been there for him. "Do you know if anyone called his parents? They live in New Mexico. The number might be in his phone."

"He gave someone in the ER his cousin's phone number. Miguel, maybe? He was here last night. I think Jesse's parents are going to be arriving today."

"Good." My eyes go to the monitor again.

"His numbers aren't bad," Kendra says. "The surgeon was up here earlier and said he's recovering as expected."

I nod. "Jesse came in with a friend. They both got shot. Sebastian Faber. You don't know about him, do you?"

Kendra chuckles. "Oh, Mr. Faber. Now there's a piece of work."

This sounds like something someone might say about Baz. I try to imagine him in a backless hospital gown, a nurse spooning Jell-O into his mouth. I don't really see that happening. "So Baz is all right?"

"If by all right you mean a complete pain in the ass, then sure," she says. "Getting up without calling for help, eating and drinking when he's not supposed to, trying to say he's ready to go home when he can barely walk. Do you know if *he* has any family we can call? Maybe a parent or stern older sister who can keep him in line?"

"I'm not sure," I say. "I've never heard him talk about family, but I only know him from my job."

"Well, I'm not supposed to discuss his medical condition, but I can tell you he was up here on a monitor last night for a couple hours, but we already moved him to the step-down." She rolls her eyes. "Thankfully."

"Step-down?"

"It's a step down from ICU care," she explains. "For patients in better condition. He didn't need the same kind of surgery as Jesse."

"Oh." I look back at Jesse, at the tubes running from his arms to the IV pumps, at the clear plastic mask over his face.

"His stats dropped when we gave him pain medicine," she says. "That's why he's on the oxygen. We'll wean him later today."

It's still hard to believe this is Jesse. His normally tanned skin looks paler than mine. The bruises from where I punched him are a blackish-purple color and the blue veins at his temples stand out.

"I'll give you some time," Kendra says. "Sign in on your way out, if you don't mind."

"All right," I say, even though I'm not going to do it. I shouldn't have told her my name. Now she might tell the police. But it won't matter. After this it's back to the airport, where I will become someone other than Winter Kim. I'll be gone before they can track me down.

I take one of Jesse's hands in both of mine. The monitor above his head blips and I glance up to see his heart rate jump from sixty to eighty beats per minute. "You know I'm here," I say. "I wonder if you can hear me."

Eighty-five beats per minute.

Jesse stirs beneath his blankets but doesn't open his eyes.

"God, Jesse. I don't even know where to start," I whisper. "Thank you, I guess, for risking your life for me. I wish you hadn't done it, but I understand why you did. I'm so grateful for everything you've done for me." Leaning in close to him, I run a hand through his thick, brown hair. I trace the ridge of scar tissue that runs from his left temple to his jawline, my fingers pausing on a darkened area of skin, the bruising and swelling caused by me. "I'm sorry I blew up at you. That I . . . hit you. I was really angry, but I see now that my rage was misplaced. What you and Gideon did was wrong, but I know you did it for the right reasons."

Ninety beats per minute.

"I need to go take care of some things," I say. "Family things. But I'll see you soon, if everything works out as planned." I don't tell him the chances of that are slim. Somewhere beneath the hospital blankets and the soft cloak of sedatives, he knows.

Jesse stirs again. This time his fingers twitch. As much as I want to see him open his eyes, I can't be here for that. It'll make leaving him too hard. I turn toward the doorway and I'm outside in the main room of the ICU when I hear his weakened voice say, "Winter?"

I hurry back to the waiting area. Hopefully he'll think he dreamed me.

Maybe he did. Sometimes I feel like I'm not even real anymore.

CHAPTER 4

When I arrive in San Diego, I grab my suitcase from baggage claim and head to the ground transportation area. Even though Jesse, Gideon, and I traveled quite a bit, I've never arranged for a ride before. It hits me that I've never done a lot of things I'm going to need to figure out on my own. I pause in front of the first desk with no line. I clear my throat and the clerk looks up at me.

"I need to get to Los Angeles. What do you recommend?"

"Depends on what you want to pay and how patient you are." The clerk pulls out a brochure from beneath the counter. "We have this rideshare shuttle, which leaves from here four times a day. It's cheap but crowded. Or you can buy an Amtrak ticket. Or, if you prefer to ride in style, you can charter your own car and driver and get up to L.A. much quicker for a few hundred bucks." He points across the lobby at a booth called Executive VIP.

Money feels like the only thing I have at the moment, and time is definitely of the essence. Executive VIP it is.

"Thanks," I tell the guy. "You've been a big help."

I cross the lobby to the executive limo place, where the guy behind the counter sniffs and plucks an imaginary piece of lint from his starched collar. "Can I help you . . . miss?" he asks.

"I need to get to Los Angeles." I slap my fake ID on the counter. "The sooner the better."

"The fee is five hundred dollars," he says. I pay in cash. The man checks the authenticity of the bills with some sort of marker and then smiles tightly. "We can leave whenever you're ready."

I adjust the straps of my backpack. "Now would be good."

The man at the counter disappears into the back room for a few seconds and returns with a second man dressed in a black uniform with gleaming silver buttons. This man takes the handle of my suitcase and starts wheeling it toward the parking garage. "Where in L.A. would you like to be dropped off?"

I give him the name of a business-class hotel in Koreatown, but I'm not actually going to stay there. It's the kind of place where they'll be expecting me to pay by credit card. Instead, I'll find a smaller hotel or guesthouse, owned by Koreans. A place where I can be anonymous. A place where I can disappear without leaving a trail if I need to.

I follow my driver down a darkened row of the airport parking garage. We stop in front of a big black car. It's not quite a limousine, but it's close. The driver holds open the door and I slide into the plush backseat. The windows are tinted. The driver starts telling me something about Wi-Fi and showing me a minibar full of water and snacks, but I'm kind of zoning out. It's only lunchtime here, but it's already been a long day for me.

It's about three p.m. when we enter the area of Los Angeles known as Koreatown. K-Town is a mix of skyscrapers and strip malls, of BMWs and homeless people. I remember living in an apartment on the outskirts of this area with Rose and two other girls who worked for Kyung. I spent most of my days trying to sleep away the previous night. That or with my face pressed to the window, watching the Korean and Hispanic shopkeepers chatter to each other as they hosed down their sidewalks in the morning. Watching the sun rise hot and the tall palm trees sway in the wind. Wondering how California could be so beautiful during the day but so ugly at night.

The driver drops me off at the hotel I mentioned to him. I

slide out, tip him, and then head into the air-conditioned lobby with my luggage. A dark-haired woman behind the registration desk looks up as the door swings closed, but she quickly averts her eyes when I don't stride directly toward her. I step out of the main traffic path and make a point of pulling a phone from my purse, looking down at it as if I'm planning on meeting someone. The airport car pulls away from the street in front of the hotel. I count to ten and then head back out into the warm sun.

This block is packed with Korean businesses—restaurants, hair salons, and minimarkets selling kimchi and fresh seafood. It's comforting being surrounded by Hangul after years in St. Louis, where there are fewer Korean businesses and most of them have English signs. I turn off the main street and find what I'm looking for a few blocks away—a small guesthouse with a vacancy sign in both English and Hangul. There's a bright red-and-gold mural of a *haechi*—a mythical creature known for exacting justice and eating fire—painted on the side of the house.

Inside, a Korean woman with a round face and a tight perm is curled up in a wicker chair reading a book. She licks her index finger and turns a page.

"*Jeogiyo*," I say. Excuse me. The woman doesn't look up. I clear my throat. "*Ajumma?*" It's a common way to address an older woman.

She turns to face me, her book falling closed around one hand. She cocks her head to the side, the skin at the corner of her eyes crinkling as she smiles. We exchange greetings in Korean and then she tells me the house is empty right now except for one other boarder, so she can give me a good price.

I pay in cash and scribble a fake name in her guesthouse registry. She goes to a desk at the far corner of the room and fetches a key from a drawer. It's an actual metal key on a big wooden keychain, a duck carved from what looks like gingko wood.

I drag my suitcase and backpack into the back hallway of the guesthouse. At my room I have to jiggle the doorknob a couple of times, but the key finally turns in the lock and the door swings open. It's just a small square room with basic furniture. A doorway in the corner leads to a bathroom with a toilet and a shower. A set of taller doors along one side of the room opens into a wardrobe. I go to the window and peek out the blinds. The sun shines brightly on a deserted alley, empty except for a couple of derelict cars up on blocks and a roll of discarded carpet tossed to the side of a Dumpster.

Turning away, I explore the rest of my cramped quarters. A painting of the Seoul skyline hangs over the bed. My eyes are drawn to the strip of shiny reflective buildings, to the mountain, Namsan, in the background and its distinctive tower that looks out over the city.

Rose and I used to talk about going to the top of the mountain. Supposedly there's a sculpture where couples place padlocks to symbolize their unending love. Rose used to say we'd go there and place a lock for the two of us. Sisters, forever.

Who knew forever could be so short?

My chest goes tight as the enormity of what I'm trying to do crashes down on me. I could barely charter a car service. How am I supposed to rescue my brother without Kyung finding me first? How am I supposed to kill Kyung? Even if I'm willing to die to accomplish these goals—and I am—they still suddenly seem completely unreachable, like a fantasy. I'm not even sure I'll be able to face Kyung without falling to pieces. What if I start to cry? What if I run away? I hate that such a horrible man has so much power over me.

But that's what happens when someone owns you, literally and figuratively.

If my sister were here, rescuing Jun and killing Kyung would still be a massive undertaking, but at least it would feel possible. If she were here, she'd be telling me that very thing right this moment. I glance up at the painting again.

"I'm going to do it," I say. "For you. For both of us. He took away our forever. I'm going to take away his."

CHAPTER 5

After the sun begins to set, I ask the woman who owns the guesthouse where to get some decent Korean food and she gives me directions to a restaurant a few blocks away. I order food and bring it back to the room, where I settle cross-legged on the floor. Most Korean meals come with several side dishes, or *banchan,* and in addition to my sesame chicken, this restaurant packed me five little to-go cups filled with kimchi, bean sprouts, potato salad, fishcake, and anchovies. I haven't eaten anything all day, and I quickly devour most of the food, even the crunchy anchovies, some of which still have their tiny eyeballs intact.

After I finish eating, I pace back and forth in the cramped room for a few minutes, threading and unthreading my fingers in front of my body. I need answers, or at least to feel like I'm actually accomplishing something. I slip on my ViSE headset and secure the blond wig on top of it. I might as well check out UsuMed tonight. I know there's no hope of finding Jun in the dark on a Saturday, but I can at least get a feel for the area.

UsuMed's Los Angeles headquarters is actually located in Santa Monica, just outside of the city proper. It takes me a short walk, two Metro trains, and a bus to get there, but about an hour and fifteen minutes later, I step out into the warm night just in front of the main gate.

The corporate campus takes up several blocks and is surrounded by a six-foot-tall brick wall. I walk a loop around the entire complex, scanning for security cameras and recording everything I see. It's about eight p.m., and the streets and sidewalks are full of people.

I can only see into the UsuMed grounds through the main gate and a second, smaller gate located on the opposite side of the campus. There are several shorter buildings arranged to the left and right of a round glass tower. Beyond the round tower is a long, flat industrial-looking structure—almost like an airplane hangar. I walk another lap, noting the presence of several small cameras mounted along the top of the wall. Security definitely seems to be tight, but if there are only two ways to get in and out, I should be able to find Jun coming or going through one of the gates. Now all I need is a place with good visibility.

I scan the area directly across the street from the main entrance. A pastel-pink apartment building looks over a strip mall full of cafés and coffee shops in front of it. A couple of the coffee shops aren't horrible choices, but they're all one story, and I'll be able to see better if I can get up higher. I loiter around the entrance to the apartment building, pretending to be texting someone, until the door to the secure lobby opens and a lady dressed in hospital scrubs heads toward the parking lot.

I catch the door as she hurries by without even glancing at me. Slipping inside, I pass right by the elevator and find a door at the end of the hall that leads into a dingy stairwell. I ascend the stairs to the top floor, checking both ends of the main hallway for roof access. There's only one door that isn't numbered like an apartment, but it's locked. I dig in my purse for something I can use to pick the lock and come up empty. Then I remember my wig. Reaching up, I pull two bobby pins out of my hair and bite the plastic nubs off the ends. It only takes me about a minute to get the door open.

It turns out to be an elevator machinery room, the gears cranking and clanking as I scoot around them. My hands shake a little. I have a phobia of elevators. Just thinking about them makes me a little nauseated. Averting my eyes from the boxy controller, I head to the far side of the room where a door leads out onto the roof, just as I hoped. I open the camera function on my phone and zoom in. I'm four stories up and the angle is just right to monitor the UsuMed main gate. I'll have a perfect view of the driver's side of cars entering the campus.

I have four days before Kyung's deadline runs out. I hope that it's enough time to find my brother.

Back at the guesthouse, I imagine coming face-to-face with Jun. Will my mother have told him about me? Will he feel guilty about her giving Rose and me away? I can't blame him for my mother abandoning us. He didn't ask to be born. He didn't ask to be male. He didn't ask to be born male in a country that prizes boy children over girl children.

Sometimes things just are what they are.

I pull off my wig and adjust the prongs of my headset. Curling onto my side, I pull the sheet up to my chin and try to get some rest. But all I can do is think about what it's going to be like to meet the brother I didn't even know I had. What if he doesn't know anything about me either? What if he doesn't want to be part of my life? Or worse, what if it's all a trick and he doesn't even exist? Then I'll be alone again.

You're not alone.

"You don't count," I mutter. The voices in my head might give good advice, but they come and go as they please. I can't rely on them. For a second I debate calling Dr. Abrams. I can rely on her, sort of. Maybe she'd be willing to do a phone session with me. Then I remember it's Saturday night, and two hours later in St. Louis than it is here. Even if she were willing to talk to me, she's probably asleep already.

You can rely on Jesse.

It's true. I dig a burner phone out of my purse and stare at it for a few seconds. Then I dial Jesse's cell phone. I'm not expecting him to answer. I just want to hear his voice mail message, the friendly greeting of someone who will always want to be part of my life.

I am surprised when after three rings he comes on the line. "Hello?" His voice is hoarse.

My heart catches in my throat, rendering me mute, my own words trapped somewhere in my chest.

"Winter?" Jesse asks. "Is that you?"

I still can't respond, but I exhale a long, shaky breath.

"We're okay," Jesse continues. "Baz and me. He's going home tomorrow and I should be out of here soon too. The cops came around this afternoon but I was still kind of out of it so I didn't say much. I didn't get the feeling they were looking to arrest me, though. I think they'll see it for what it was— Gideon's employees protecting themselves against a home invader who killed their boss."

Another shaky sigh from me. I hadn't realized how worried I was about what the police might do to Jesse and Baz. An anxiety farther down the list than what Kyung might do to my brother, but no less real.

"I'm worried about you, Winter," Jesse says.

A tiny sob sneaks out without warning. Stupid body. Stupid emotions.

"Please let us know you're okay too. You can call back now if you want and I won't answer. That way you could leave a message."

The tone of his voice rises just slightly. I know that sound— it's hope. It cuts me, but I can't leave a message, just in case Jesse is wrong about the cops and their investigation. Messages are forever. This call record is forever. I need to hang up.

But I can't. I can't even move. I am paralyzed by Jesse's voice. By his hope.

"You came by my room, right?" he continues. "When I woke up, I thought it was a dream, but my nurse told me it was real."

"It was real," I whisper. I pull my knees up toward my chin, tuck my body into the fetal position.

"Winter!" Jesse struggles to clear his throat. "I am so glad to hear from you. Where are you?"

"It's better if I don't say."

"Better for who?"

"For both of us."

"Come home," Jesse says.

"I will, once I've taken care of some things," I say softly. "I'm sorry for what I did to you, Jesse." I think of the bruises on his face, and worse, the injuries I can't see. The ones caused by the cruel things I said.

"Winter, you don't have to—"

"I should hang up now."

I disconnect the call before Jesse can tell me I don't have to apologize for attacking him. I was out of my mind when I did it, but that's a reason, not an excuse. I turn the phone off and slide it back into my purse.

I try once more to go to sleep. But as soon as I close my eyes, my head is flooded with images of my sister—Rose smiling, Rose laughing, Rose bleeding, Rose dying. I hate that these memories are just fragments, moments out of order, snapshots out of context. Tears leak into the softness of my pillow. "I want to remember all of you," I whisper. "I want the pieces to fit."

The voices in my head are quiet for once. Eventually the night is kind, stealing me into its dreamworld, where I get a momentary reprieve from the pain of not knowing.

Until I wake up the next day, and I'm not in my bed.

My breath sticks in my throat as my eyes flicker open. The surface beneath me is wet and cold, the lights bright but hazy. A soft pattering echoes in my ear like raindrops on pavement.

I blink hard as I lift myself to a seated position. I'm in the bathroom, on the floor of the shower.

Struggling to my feet, I reach out and turn the water off. Shivering violently, I reach for the nearest towel and wrap it around my naked body. That's when I see the message on the mirror. Dark red letters: WE HAD TO SEE IT.

CHAPTER 6

My heart thrums in my chest. At first I think the message is written in blood, but as I get closer I see one of the tubes of lipstick I bought back in St. Louis sitting on the edge of the sink. My recorder headset sits next to it.

"See what, Rose?" I murmur. "What did you do?" I take the headset back into the main room and quickly pull on sweatpants and a T-shirt. I double-check that the door and windows are locked. Then I recline back on my bed and play the ViSE. I fast forward through about an hour of peaceful darkness before I get to the start of the action.

I sit up in bed, my feet sliding around to land on the hardwood floor. I go to the wardrobe and change from my pajamas into one of the dresses I bought at the mall. The soft fabric caresses my skin. I grab the blond wig and go to the bathroom. Flicking on the lights, I slip the wig on over my headset. I study myself in the mirror for a couple of moments and then reach for my bag of toiletries. I fish out a tube of lipstick and an eyeliner pencil.

"Seriously, Rose?" I mutter. "I'm not sure now is the time to be going out clubbing."

After applying a bit of makeup, I grab my purse and keys from the dresser and head for the door. Outside, the night air is surprisingly chilly on my bare legs. The branches of a nearby plum tree swish against each other in the wind, casting wavering shadows on the pavement.

I cross the street and turn left at the corner, swearing under my breath as the heel of my boot gets caught in a sidewalk crack. The sound of a car braking cuts across the night, startling me. My heart accelerates in my chest. I pause, looking back over my shoulder, looking left, looking right. There is only silence and the overlapping darkness of houses and shops stacked close to one another. I start walking again, heading for a larger intersection a couple of blocks away.

I have no idea where Rose is going, but I'm not surprised where she ends up.

A red-and-green gazebo rises up before me, illuminated slightly by streetlights. The painted latticework blurs before my eyes. Beyond it, a steel-and-glass hotel stands twelve stories high. No one is coming or going at this time, but light emanates from the first-floor lobby and I can see the movement of staff or guests beyond the wall of glass.

My heart sinks low in my stomach. I should fast-forward this. I've already remembered my sister's death. I watched Sung Jin stab Rose like it was happening. I killed him for it. I don't need to go back to that place. I should put it all behind me.

But my alter is right. I have to see the elevator.

I cross the street in front of the hotel, pausing in the middle for a car to go past. It's black and sleek. The kid behind the wheel doesn't look much older than me. Our eyes meet for a fraction of a second and then he looks away. I turn my attention back to the hotel.

I can't help but wonder if there are girls inside this hotel doing what I used to do. The thought sickens me.

I step into the revolving door and out into the lobby. My boots make a soft clicking noise against the marble floor tiles. I stride right past the desk clerk as if I already have a key. There are two elevators located at the back of the building.

I can't remember which one it happened in. Both of them make my heart climb into my throat. Both of them make me think of tombs. For years I've been afraid of elevators, but I only recently realized why—because I watched my sister stabbed to death in one.

I press the button to summon the elevators, backing away slightly as the red numbers count down toward one. When the first one opens, it's the same size as I remember, but different paneling, different floor tile. Even different buttons. I wait for the second elevator, but it's also been remodeled. I stand still for a moment. Then I turn and head back out into the night.

As Rose retraces her steps back to the guesthouse, a wave of emotions rushes through me—relief followed by confusion followed by despair. I don't know exactly what my alter wanted, if some part of me was hoping to actually stand in the place where my sister stood. See things through her eyes. Feel her pain. But whatever I went looking for, I left without it.

There were no answers.

There is no closure.

It's like a part of my history has been erased.

On Monday, I wake up early so I can take special care disguising myself before returning to UsuMed. My blood courses with anxiety as I work my legs into a pair of panty hose, my fingers shaking as I affix my headset to my skull and clamp it tight. I slide the reddish-blond wig over the top and adjust tendrils of hair around my face until everything looks natural. Heading into the bathroom, I apply some pale pressed powder, eyeliner, mascara, and lipstick. I blink at my reflection. Even I can barely recognize myself.

This level of disguise is probably unnecessary, but in the unlikely event I cross paths with Kyung or someone from my past, I want to be certain they don't recognize me. Cold fingers rake down my spine at the thought of coming face-to-face with the man who bought me like a slave and sold me like a product, the man who was responsible for Rose's and Gideon's deaths.

I take a taxi to a coffee shop two blocks away from UsuMed,

arriving just in time to see the sun start to rise over the city. I pay the driver and slip into the shop, buying a small green tea to soothe my nerves and a ham-and-cheese sandwich to eat later.

After I've relaxed a little, I duck out of the shop and head for the apartment building where I'll be keeping watch. I loiter outside again, pretending to be looking something up on my phone until I'm able to slip into the building when a resident leaves. I pick the lock to the elevator machine room and find the spot on the roof where I have the best view of the UsuMed main gate.

Traffic into the campus picks up around seven thirty a.m., and the cars come in steady for the next two hours. There is also a stream of employees entering on foot, most of whom come off the bus that stops right in front of the gate. Additional people enter the grounds sporadically until around ten. Then there's no action at all for the better part of an hour. I pull my wrapped sandwich out of my purse and choke it down without a drink. It manages to be both soggy and dry at the same time.

Around eleven thirty, a few cars start to pull out, probably to go to lunch. Clusters of people walk through the gate on foot as well. No Jun. I grow restless as the afternoon drags on, doing some stretching and push-ups during the slow period. I'm trying to ignore the possibility that he's not employed here, that maybe he works for Kyung in some other capacity, like as a landscaper or delivery boy, or helping out with his human trafficking side business. If I can't find Jun by staking out UsuMed, I'm going to have to meet with Kyung, give him the disabled ViSE tech, and go from there.

But I know sometimes laborers work twelve-hour shifts, so I'm not giving up yet. I pull Sung Jin's phone out of my purse and skim through the pictures Kyung sent to me once again.

Movement on the street below attracts my attention. A dark-haired woman is walking down the sidewalk, the fingers of a school-aged girl clutched in her hand. My eyes trace the curve of the woman's pregnant belly and a memory flits into my head.

I'm sitting on the hardwood floor of a small house, holding a wrapped package. In the background, Christmas music is playing. My mother walks into the room with my sister beside her. I flip my gaze to my mother's stomach as my sister says something about a baby. My mom smiles and pats her belly.

I look back at the pregnant lady on the street, trying to decide if the memory is real or fake. She and her daughter step inside the coffee shop. I wonder if I ever went to a coffee shop with my mother. Why don't I know more about my childhood? If I have a brother, I should remember him, shouldn't I?

There is a mass exodus from UsuMed around six p.m. and then a few more cars start to trickle out between seven and seven thirty. Just as I'm starting to think about leaving, a bus pulls up to the stop just down from the main entrance. A few people get off and start heading in various directions. I don't pay them any attention until I notice one of them approaching the UsuMed gate. It's him—the boy from the picture.

CHAPTER 7

Maybe he's on the night shift, sorting mail or working as a janitor. If he's really my brother, he's only sixteen, or barely seventeen at most, so there aren't too many jobs he could be working at in a place like this. I watch him until he disappears from view, trying to see myself or my sister inside his stocky build.

If he starts work at eight p.m., he might get off as early as four, or as late as eight the next morning. I make a plan to return around three thirty a.m. tomorrow so I definitely won't miss him.

With a start, I realize my cheeks are wet.

Blotting my tears with the back of my hand, I abandon my spot on the roof and return to the sidewalk below. I catch a cab to the Metro station and take the train back to K-Town. I lie on the bed in my little rented room and replay the footage. I watch Jun get off the bus and enter the UsuMed campus over and over. Could he *really* be my brother? If he is, it would change everything. It would give me a reason to try to heal myself.

It would give me a reason to live.

Tuesday, I rise before the sun and dress in the closest I can come to jogging apparel—sweatpants and a hoodie—because I feel like exercising is one of the least conspicuous things a person might be up doing before sunrise. I take a cab to the same coffee shop as yesterday and then jog toward the campus right at four.

I pause just past the bus stop, like I'm catching my breath. It's still pitch-black and I can feel the UsuMed gate guard's eyes on me. I take off running again, down to the end of the block where I'm out of sight. I linger in that area, pretending to be sending a text message. Then I go for another short jog and turn back the way I came, checking the bus stop in front of the main gate regularly for any sign of Jun. At seven thirty, things get crowded at the gate again. As the moments tick down to eight a.m., I worry that somehow I missed him.

But then, at 8:06, he comes strolling through the main gate, stopping just outside to check his phone. He takes a seat at the bus stop.

I wait until I see the bus approaching from down the block and then cross the street. I stand a few feet away, peeking at him out of the corner of my eye. It's definitely the same boy from the photos that Kyung sent to me, but is he really my brother? I feel like that's the sort of thing I should know intuitively. Then again, I felt that way about Rose being dead, and I could not have been more wrong. The only way I'm going to know for sure if this boy is my brother is to talk to him.

But not here.

When the bus arrives, I get on after Jun, flailing in my pocket for cash as he ambles down the aisle. He leans back in his seat, crossing his legs at the ankles. I pass by him and take a seat in the very back.

When I see him reach up to pull the stop-request cord that runs along the windows, I follow him off the bus. On the sidewalk, I let a couple people get between us to reduce the chances he'll realize I'm following him.

It turns out I don't need to worry. The only time Jun looks anywhere but straight ahead is when he pauses to stare into a store window for a few seconds. I glance over as I pass by. It's a music shop with a couple of electric guitars and a drum set displayed.

Jun lives in a run-down three-story brick building. I follow him inside, pausing by the mailboxes to check out the names of the building inhabitants. There are only six units. Five of the mailboxes are labeled, one with the name Song—my real last name.

My heart starts pounding against my ribs. Song isn't a common surname like Lee or Kim, and the boy looks the right age. I race up a flight of stairs to his apartment. He doesn't answer the door when I knock. I stand in plain view of the peephole and knock again. And again.

Finally, a sleepy voice calls, "Who is it?"

"I just moved into the next building," I say, hoping the next building is apartments and not a nail salon or a car wash. I was so excited while I was following him that I forgot to pay attention to my surroundings. "I think I have some of your mail."

The boy opens the door and peeks out. He sees my empty hands and a look of confusion crosses his face.

"I need to talk to you," I say. "Inside."

And now he looks suspicious, like he thinks I'm a tax auditor or an undercover cop. He starts to close the door.

I jam my foot into the crack before he can finish. Lowering my voice, I say, "Please. It's an emergency. It's about your family."

The boy blinks rapidly and his jaw drops a little. He opens the door wide enough for me to stride past him into his apartment. Then he pushes the door closed behind me and affixes a dead bolt and chain lock. I glance around, wondering what he has that he's so diligent in protecting, but all I see is a sparsely furnished studio apartment with fast-food wrappers and dirty laundry strewn about.

He stands awkwardly in the center of the room. "What about my family? Did something happen?"

"Are you Jun Song?" My eyes search the clutter for some clue that we might be related.

He doesn't say anything. Then he nods slowly. "Yeah. That's me."

"Where were you born?"

"Taebaek," he says. "But I grew up in Seoul. Why?"

I can't imagine my mother living in the city. Maybe she went there to be close to us, so she could still see us from time to time, even though she couldn't care for us.

"Do you have any brothers or sisters?" My eyes do a second lap around the room, looking for family photographs. There is a picture of a Korean girl tucked into the side of his dresser mirror—a girlfriend, probably—but that's all.

He pauses for a moment. "Who did you say you were again?"

"I didn't say. Brothers or sisters—just tell me." My voice is pleading.

"I know I had two older sisters. My mother was forced to give them up for adoption after our father died."

I have no memories of my father. Growing up, I wasn't even sure if Rose and I had the same dad. She never liked to speak of the past, encouraging me instead to focus on the possibilities of the future. Easier said than done.

I focus all of my attention on Jun, on the way his hands are folded in his lap, on the sound of his voice, the frequency of his blinking. "What are your sisters' names?"

"Min Ji and Ha Neul."

A tremor races through my body at the sound of my real name from this boy's lips, but I'm still afraid to believe. "Let me see something with your name on it," I demand. I swallow a lump in my throat.

Shrugging, Jun removes a California provisional driver's license from his wallet and holds it out toward me. A tear leaks out of my eye as I rub one finger across the black printing. "I can't believe it's really you. I am Ha Neul."

"What?" Jun's voice rises in pitch. "Seriously?"

I nod. "I'm your sister." I finger the snowflake pendant that hangs against my throat. "I don't have ID with me, but I can show you some legal documents. Papers with my full name."

"Nuna?" Jun's eyes widen as he addresses me by the polite title for elder sister. "This is—I mean—I can't believe it's really you." He glances down at the floor, his cheeks coloring slightly.

I step forward to hug him, flinching from the heat of his skin. I'm still not used to touching people. But this is my brother, my family. My blood. I wrap my arms around the middle of his back and give him a gentle squeeze. "I'm sorry I didn't find you sooner."

Jun pats me awkwardly on the shoulder and then disentangles himself from my embrace. "Sorry. I think I'm a little in shock. How did you end up in the States?"

I lean back against the wall. "It's a long story. What about you? How did you end up here? Do you still live with . . . our mother?" There is no sign of a female presence in this apartment beyond the picture of the girl in the mirror.

Jun pauses for a moment, an uncomfortable look flashing across his face. "I'm sorry, nuna. Our mother committed suicide shortly after I was born. I was actually raised by my—our—aunt."

"Suicide," I repeat. "Why?" Perhaps my mother was depressed. Perhaps some of my own psychological issues stem not from the things that happened to me when I was younger, but from genetics.

"I don't know," Jun says. "I was just a baby and our *imo* doesn't like to talk about it."

"I don't remember my mother having a sister." I know I should feel some kind of sadness at learning my mother is dead, but she's been gone from my life for so many years, in a way I think I have already grieved for her.

"Imo is ten years older. I believe the two of them were estranged for quite a bit of time." Jun cocks his head to the side to study me and there's something so Rose-like about his gaze that my lips slant into a half smile despite hearing that my mother is dead. "What brings you to L.A.?" he asks.

I've become so giddy at the thought of having family again that I almost forget the reason I've been looking for him in the first place. "I came here to find you to warn you that you're in danger. You need to stop working for UsuMed."

"I don't understand." Jun sits on the edge of the bed and gestures at a chair tucked under a desk in the corner of the room. He taps one foot nervously. "I need that job to pay for school."

I pull the chair close to Jun, take a seat, and lean in to him. "What school?"

"I'm starting at UCLA in the fall."

"How can you be starting college when you're not even old enough to have finished high school?"

"I got my GED back in Seoul and then came here to go to college, but I need to establish residency and save up some money for living expenses first."

It's an ambitious plan. I'm impressed that he's younger than I am but so much closer to living a normal life. "All right, but there are plenty of other jobs. Can you find something besides UsuMed? One of the executives there threatened your safety. I have something he believes belongs to him. If I don't give it to him, he might hurt you."

"What do you have?" Jun asks.

"A type of technology, developed by a friend of mine. A friend who is now dead, thanks to UsuMed."

"My superiors have been nothing but supportive and kind," Jun says. "UsuMed is one of the biggest employers in Southern California. I find it hard to believe they would hurt anyone in the way that you're saying. Are you all right, nuna? You have had a long journey to get here, perhaps?" Jun's eyes flick toward the door and then back to me, like maybe he's thinking of making a run for it.

This is not the reunion I was hoping for. I suppose I should have considered how my story would sound to a stranger—he thinks I'm crazy. "I'm fine," I say. "But you're in danger. Kyung Cho is a very dangerous man." I give him a quick summary of the ViSE tech and how Kyung wants it bad enough that he had Gideon killed.

"But you say this Sung Jin killed your boss, not Mr. Cho. And if the technology was stolen from UsuMed, maybe you should just give it back."

"I can't," I say. "Kyung is not going through all this trouble to obtain the ViSE tech to license it for entertainment purposes. If he's willing to kill for it, he's going to use it for something horrible."

"Like what?"

"I don't know." I lean my forearms on my thighs, tug at the ends of my wig.

"It's not that I don't believe you, but you're asking me to quit my job. Do you know how expensive it is to live here? If I lose my position at UsuMed . . ."

"I can help you with money," I say. "For as long as you need—if in return, you'll hide out for a couple of weeks until I can clear up this matter with Kyung."

"Where would I go?"

"Have you ever been to St. Louis?" Jesse said Baz was getting released from the hospital. Even if he's not in shape to protect anyone, he probably knows someone who could watch out for Jun for the right price.

Jun makes a face like he's not exactly thrilled by the idea. "No, and I—"

I keep talking before he can object. "I have friends there who could keep you safe." I try to ignore the fact that Baz couldn't keep Gideon safe. That was different. Baz didn't know Gideon was in real danger until it was too late.

"This is all very sudden and a lot to consider," Jun says. "This technology you're talking about—maybe if I understood it better, I'd be able to see why you're so worried. Do you have it with you?"

I shake my head. "No, but if you come back to my guest-house with me, I have some recordings that you can view. I know you're probably tired, but it won't take long."

Jun shrugs. "I'm a little tired, but mostly I'm just shocked that you're here. I wasn't sure we'd ever meet. Of course I'll go with you." He grabs his keys and we head for the door.

I'm not convinced vising will persuade Jun that Kyung is dangerous, but the longer I keep him with me, the longer I can guarantee his safety.

Back at the guesthouse, I load the shark-dive recording into my ViSE headset for Jun. I tell him to lie on my bed and slip the headset on him. After giving him basic instructions on how to minimize external stimulation, I press PLAY. It's fun watching his involuntary body movements, the way he relaxes at certain moments and goes rigid at others.

Jun finishes the recording and removes the headset. "Don't get me wrong, it's cool technology, but why would UsuMed want this?"

"I'm not sure," I admit. "But Kyung Cho threatened to hurt you if he didn't get it. Will you *please* go to St. Louis, just until I can talk to him and we can come to some sort of agreement? Tell your boss your grandmother died or something." I bite my lip. "I just found you. I don't want anything bad to happen to you."

Jun exhales. "If it means that much to you, nuna, I guess I can go. But if I lose my job, I'm going to take you up on that offer to help me with expenses."

"Done." I power on my tablet and start to book my brother a flight to St. Louis leaving later today.

"No, no. Not today," Jun says. "I have a few things I need to take care of first. What about first thing tomorrow morning?"

I start to argue but then think better of it. I don't have to meet Kyung until tomorrow, so as long as Jun is gone before then, he should be safe. "What about seven a.m.?"

Jun nods. "That'll work." He gives me his ID and I book the ticket for him. Then I call him a cab. "I'll have someone waiting for you in St. Louis."

"Who?"

"Probably a man named Sebastian, but I'm not sure yet. I'll call you with more information as soon as I have it."

"Okay."

I give Jun another hug. He tenses slightly and it occurs to me that he's like I am—not comfortable with being touched. "Be careful," I tell him.

He nods. "You too, nuna. I'll talk to you soon."

After Jun leaves, I call Sebastian from a burner phone. He picks up but doesn't say anything.

"Hi," I say. "It's me."

"Hey," he says. "You can come home, you know? The cops bought my and Jesse's story about what went down in the penthouse."

"I'm glad you're not getting arrested." I sit on the edge of the bed, my free hand plucking aimlessly at the blanket's pilling balls of lint.

"No one is getting arrested," Baz says. "It's all good."

If only that were true. "I need a favor."

"Oh yeah? What are we talking about?"

"I'm sending someone to you tomorrow morning. I need you to keep him safe." I scoop all the lint balls into a little mountain.

"Because I've done such a great job of that lately," Baz says wryly. "I'm not quite back on my game yet."

There's a clatter from the alley outside my room. I leap up from the bed, scattering the balls of lint across the blanket. I spread the slats of the blinds apart with one hand so I can peer out the dirty glass. Three boys who look about twelve or thirteen are kicking a soccer ball around. A trash can lies on its side.

"It doesn't have to be you," I tell Baz. "It can be a friend or just someone you trust. But you're the only one I have to ask," I say. "Please. It's my brother."

There's a long beat of silence. "I didn't know you had a brother."

"I didn't either, until recently."

"I can probably find someone who will keep an eye on him."

"Thank you." I pace back and forth as I relay the flight information to Sebastian, still edgy from the noise outside.

"Who's keeping *you* safe, Winter?" he asks.

"I am."

"You know Ramirez is supposed to come home soon."

"Good," I say.

"It'd be good if you were here. He might need someone to look in on him for a couple of days."

"I don't think I'm the right person to be taking care of anyone else. I have to figure out how to take care of myself first."

"Maybe you could take care of each other," Baz suggests. And then, "Have you talked to your therapist since you found out the truth about everything?"

"I was going to, but then I found out I had a brother and that took precedence." I stop pacing in front of the mirror. I look for pieces of Jun in my reflection.

"You're not doing anything stupid, are you? Like going after Kyung?"

"What would make you think that?" I try to keep my voice light.

Sebastian chuckles. "Gideon installed a tracking device in the neural editor, just in case someone ever stole it. I know you're in Los Angeles. If you're going after Kyung, hold off for a couple of days until I get back in top form. You're going to need my help."

"Why would you help me?"

Another long pause. "I lied to you for years and helped Gideon trick you. Maybe I think I owe you."

"Come on, Baz. You would've put a bullet in my brain if he'd asked you to. We both know you don't feel indebted to me."

He sighs deeply, but he doesn't deny it. "Maybe I owe Gideon."

"Why?"

"None of your business why."

I don't actually know how Gideon and Baz met, whether they were friends before we left Los Angeles or not. I just remember Sebastian being there in St. Louis from the very beginning, advising and looking out for Gideon, occasionally watching me when Gideon was working. "I'll reach out to you if I need help," I say. "But right now I just need to get my brother to safety."

"I'll make sure he's taken care of," Baz says.

"Thanks."

"Take care of yourself, okay? And call me if you need anything."

"I will." I meant what I said about Baz not feeling like he owes me, but there's something beyond obligation in his voice. Maybe he's not as cold and emotionless as I thought.

I hang up and call Jun. He doesn't answer, so I leave a message telling him that a man named Sebastian will pick him up at the airport in St. Louis.

Next I call Kyung.

"Ha Neul." His voice is a mixture of oil and poison. My stomach curls at the sound of him speaking my name. An image flashes through my brain—my sister in that elevator, blood spurting from a gash in her side. I wish I had the knife that stabbed her. I wish I could use it to cut out his tongue. "Do you have what I want?" he asks.

"I do," I say, my mind still slicing and dicing him. I struggle to keep the violence from bleeding into my voice. "I just arrived in Los Angeles. I can bring you the tech tomorrow morning."

"Splendid. I have time to meet you at eight a.m. sharp," he says. "I trust you can find your way to the UsuMed campus? Once you're there, just tell the guard at the gate that you have a meeting with me and he'll call my office. I'll send someone down to retrieve you."

"Thank you, *ajussi*," I say, forcing myself to address him politely. It's important that he think of me as weak, as under his control. It'll be much easier to kill him if he doesn't view me as a threat.

"No, thank *you*. I look forward to our reunion."

I flinch. I have no idea what will happen when I come face-to-face with this man. "What assurances can you give me that my brother won't be harmed?"

"You have my word. As long as you have kept your part of the bargain, I will keep mine."

"And if your word doesn't mean much to me?"

"I've already started the paperwork to give Jun a promotion. No more sweeping floors for him. I'm moving him to a night security position. Better pay and he'll still have days off to attend university. You are doing a great service for your brother," Kyung says.

"And what are you going to do with the tech?"

"Turn it over to Phantasm," Kyung says. "Or perhaps UsuTech. I am not an expert in such things as Ki Hyun was. I am merely obeying the orders of my superiors."

I don't believe him, but there's really nothing else to say. Tomorrow, once Jun is safely on a plane to St. Louis, I'll meet with Kyung and give him the headset and disabled neural editor. He'll come after me once he realizes it doesn't work, so I'll either have to hide somewhere until I can figure out the best way to kill him or pretend I didn't know it was broken and offer to help him fix it.

A couple of days ago I would have just walked up to him

and stabbed him in the throat, even if that meant being gunned down by one of his men or being arrested. But meeting Jun has made me rethink that. I can't leave my brother right after I found him. He might need me, and even if he doesn't, I should be there for him just in case. Knowing Jesse is getting out of the hospital has changed things too. I'm not alone, like I thought I was. I have a brother and a friend. I could still have a life of sorts, if I can just figure out a way to kill Kyung and live.

CHAPTER 8

I awake in the middle of the night to the sound of breaking glass. There's a swishing noise and a soft thump. I reach instinctively for one of my throwing knives on the bedside table. My fingers close around the hilt just as someone else's hand clamps down over my mouth.

"Don't say a word, bitch," a harsh, guttural voice warns me.

Male, I think. *Twenties to thirties. Probable smoker.* I'm about to lash out with my knife when I feel the barrel of a gun jamming into my side.

"Drop the knife," a second male voice says.

I hesitate and one of the men plucks it out of my grasp. As my eyes adjust to the darkness, I realize both of the men have guns. I could probably subdue one of them, but multiple assailants with multiple weapons? That fight only lasts for more than a few seconds on television. In the real world, one unarmed girl usually loses.

"What do you want?" I ask, trying to make my voice sound fearful. It doesn't take a whole lot of effort.

The bathroom light buzzes to life and suddenly I can see their faces. It's a bad sign that they've chosen not to cover them. If they're not worried about me going to the cops with a description of them, then they're probably not planning on letting me live. My gaze flips back to their weapons. Both guns have silencers—another bad sign.

"Kyung sent us to collect the ViSE stuff," the shorter man says. He's Korean like me, with a buzz cut and a tattoo of a snake on his neck. "I'm guessing this is part of it." He lifts the headset off my head while it's still recording. A slight shock moves through me.

"Kyung and I had a deal," I say. "We're supposed to meet tomorrow."

"That deal did not involve you tracking down your brother and attempting to disappear him before Kyung even realizes you're in town." The taller assailant steps forward out of the shadows, his gun aimed. He's American, with broad shoulders and ice-blond hair that reminds me of a wig I used to wear.

I don't respond. Blondie holds his gun to my head while Snake Tattoo starts going through the drawers, which are all empty. He finds my suitcase under the bed, paws through clothes and wigs until at last at the bottom he finds the neural editor. My stomach clenches as I watch him hold it up so his pal can see. At least they didn't find the envelope of ViSEs and paperwork I have stashed under my mattress or the flash drive hidden in the snowflake necklace that I'm wearing.

"Is Jun okay?" My hands start to shake at the thought of something bad happening to him.

"He's not our concern," the Korean man says. "Right now, he's not yours either."

"How did you know where to find me?" I ask. "Did you follow me from UsuMed?" I want them to say yes. The alternative is that my brother is on Kyung's side—that he betrayed me. I cannot take any additional betrayal from men who are supposed to care about me.

"Mr. Cho knows where to find everyone," Snake Tattoo says. His eyes trace the length of my body. The sweatpants and T-shirt that I sleep in suddenly feel revealing. "He's looking forward to seeing you again."

Revulsion courses through me. "Well, I don't ever want to see *him* again. You have what you want. Now go."

Blondie gestures toward the window with his gun. "Our orders are to bring you with us."

"I'm not going anywhere with you."

He jams the gun back into my ribs. "We'll take you by force if we have to."

"Really?" I ask, struggling to hold my voice steady. "Are you going to shoot me? Because I don't think that's quite the reunion Kyung has in mind. I'm the only person left who understands the ViSE technology. If you shoot me, you'd better hope he doesn't have any questions."

The men exchange a glance and I know I'm right. If Kyung wants them to bring me in, it's because he thinks he might need me. The Korean man lashes out with no warning, backhanding me across the face with his gun. My head snaps sideways and I taste blood. The room goes a bit hazy as a piece of duct taped is secured over my mouth.

"Here's the thing," Snake Tattoo says. "You're right. We're not supposed to kill you. But I know enough about anatomy and first aid that I can shoot you multiple times without much danger of you dying. So if you enjoy the use of your hands and feet, you'll stop fighting us."

I consider my options as I struggle to take in a breath. I've never been shot. Jesse told me it was like being hit with a sledgehammer. I imagine that pain inflicted upon one of my feet. I can't go after Kyung if I can't walk. I exhale slowly, focusing on my hands, which are still trembling slightly. As my vision clears, I glance around the room again, looking for anything that might help me escape.

Blondie wriggles through the window and out into the night. He turns to reach back through the opening for my shoulders. Snake Tattoo has my feet. I am still stinging from the blow to the head, but I realize that the men are using both hands to pass me through the window, their guns temporarily holstered. I sense an opportunity. If I can get the man inside to let me go, I might be able to escape from the one outside.

We're only a few blocks away from a major street and I'm positive I can outrun these guys. They won't try to abduct me in a place with lots of potential witnesses.

I bend my knees and then kick hard. My left foot connects with Snake Tattoo's jaw and he reels backward into the center of the room. I try to rotate around, but the momentum pulls me downward and I fall back through the window into the guesthouse. Snake Tattoo has his gun out, but I push the weapon up and away from me. His hand hits the wall and the gun falls, skittering across the hardwood floor.

I slam my palm into his nose, hoping to disorient him enough that I can escape the room before the American man can maneuver his wide shoulders back through the window. But I'm too late. Blondie grabs me from behind as I reach for the door to the hallway. He yanks my hair so hard I see stars. He presses his gun to my kneecap and cocks the hammer. "On the ground," he says.

I pull the duct tape from my lips. "Why don't you just take the tech and leave?"

Blondie pushes me roughly to the floor. "All the way down. Lie on your stomach."

Snake Tattoo bends down to look me in the eye. Blood drips from his nose. "You're going to pay for that, you little bitch." He brings the butt of his gun down on the back of my head.

Pain rockets through me. I struggle to scan the floor for anything that might make a good weapon. From this vantage point, I can see beneath the bed, but there's nothing there except a couple of dust balls and a pair of shoes. One of my throwing knives is still on the nightstand, but that's on the other side of the bed and might as well be in a different county.

Snake Tattoo strides across the room and peeks out the window. "There's a couple people heading this way," he says. "We'd better wait a few minutes until the street clears."

Blondie has a knee jammed into the center of my back, his gun pressed against the outside of my leg. "I can think of a good way to kill a few minutes," he says suggestively, his free hand stroking the back of my neck.

Immediately my whole body goes tense. "I'd rather kill *you*." The words surprise me, not because they aren't true, but because I meant to say, "I'd rather die."

Snake Tattoo chuckles lightly. "Sounds like she's not that into you."

"Yeah well, she might feel differently once I'm into her."

He rolls me over and once again pins me to the floor with his knee. His eyes rake down the front of my body like claws.

Kill them, a voice whispers. *Kill them both.*

Rage stirs in my chest. Quiet first, then louder. It spreads to my extremities as Blondie runs his knuckles down the bruise on my face. "You're pretty when you're scared," he says.

"They're all pretty when they're scared," Snake Tattoo says. He affixes a new piece of duct tape over my mouth.

I squeeze my eyes shut, searching for a safe place in the dark. But it's like I can hear colors, and my brain is shrieking *RED! RED! RED!* Suddenly I am lashing out all over. The laughter and jeering of the men turn to swearing.

And then shouting.

And then silence.

CHAPTER 9

LILY

I am going to kill them both.

Repulsive.

Disgusting.

Winter thinks she's lost her humanity. She cries into her pillow. She calls herself a monster. These two are the monsters, not her.

My first punch breaks a nose. I hear the crunch as cartilage gives way beneath my knuckles. Blood coats my fingers. The yellow-haired man windmills backward. He points his gun at my legs and pulls the trigger, but his aim is off and his bullet ends up in the floor.

"You're dead, you little bitch," one of them says.

I can't tell who the voice comes from. I don't even care. I like the idea of being dead. That means I can do anything I want.

I want to kill these men.

I want to kill every man who has ever hurt us.

Yellow Hair aims his gun again but all it does is click when he tries to pull the trigger. The bullet must be jammed. Lucky me.

I lunge for him. He kicks me hard in the gut and I end up on my back on the bed. The other man slams the butt of his gun into the side of my head. Their blows should hurt, but they don't.

I am the one who doesn't feel the pain.

I reach for Winter's throwing knife. So black. So sleek.

Rearing back, I throw. The blade twists end over end through the air and then buries itself in the center of the yellow-haired man's chest with a slippery *thunk*.

His mouth gapes in surprise. Like a fish, I think. Only I'm not sure if I've ever seen a fish, for real. Winter has seen fish. Winter swims with sharks.

"Now look who's dead," I say.

Blood rises up and spills from his lips as he reaches down and grips the end of the knife. He's going to pull it out. I'm only thirteen and even I know better than that.

The man crumples to the ground, the handle of Winter's knife still protruding from his body. I look around for the other knife.

The man with the tattoo backs away from me like he thinks I might be rabid.

He might be right.

Are monsters afraid of other monsters?

Winter doesn't usually give herself to me like she does Rose. Only once, when she was dying. I stabbed a man for her. I would have killed him if he hadn't run away.

I might be younger, but I'm getting stronger. Winter should trust me. She needs me.

She needs me to do the monster things.

The man with the tattoo points the gun at my legs and squeezes off a shot. It grazes my shin, leaves a trail of wet heat.

But still no pain.

I reach for the nearest thing, which just happens to be a cheap painted vase, and throw it at him. As he bats it down with his free hand, I kick hard at the hand with the gun. It flies through the air and ends up somewhere on the other side of the bed.

I dive for it. My fingers close around the grip. I spin around, just as the man grabs something from the desk. He goes for the window, launching himself through it like he can fly.

I wish I could fly.

I lower the gun as his feet disappear from view.

I don't know what he took from Winter, but whatever it is, at least that's all she lost tonight. I look down at the man with the knife sticking out of his chest. He looks dead, but I don't know how to tell these things for sure. I should probably stab him a few more times, just to be safe. I don't want him or his friend to come after us. This is a thing I've learned about men. If you give them a chance to hurt you more than once, they will.

Setting the gun on the bed, I wrap my fingers around the hilt of the knife and pull it loose from his chest. The blade is wet with bright-red blood. The fabric of the man's shirt grows darker around the wound. I bury the knife into the flesh of his stomach, the soft tissues swallowing up the blade. I pull it out again. More blood. My eyes skim the muscle and tendons along the side of his throat.

Stop, a soft voice says. *Let me fix things.*

Rose. Big sister. It's good there is at least one of us who fixes things.

I am the one who destroys them.

CHAPTER 10

ROSE

"You shouldn't have, Lily," I chide. "Winter doesn't need more blood on her hands."

The younger girl thrashes around inside of me, trying to regain control, but I'm stronger than she is. I'm stronger than all of them. There are five of us, counting Winter, but she doesn't know that. She thinks it's just her and me, which means I'm going to get blamed for this.

Let me finish him, Lily hisses in my brain. *He deserves to die.*

I wonder if Winter hears Lily sometimes the way that I do. "You already finished him," I say. "And then some. You need to learn how to control it. One day you're going to get us all in trouble."

I pace back and forth across the floor. Winter is my responsibility. I feel her beneath our skin, reaching for the surface, emerging from some murky pool. I push her down, focus on me, Rose. The helper. The protector. I am going to take care of this. It's my fault, in a way. I'm the one who watches Lily. I work hard to control her—she can be so rash.

It's my turn to be rash.

CHAPTER 11

I open my eyes, disoriented by the harsh fluorescent lighting. Something cold and wet pings off my body. Damn it. I'm in the shower again. I'm curled in the fetal position, my back and neck pressed awkwardly against the glass door. Glancing around, I realize with a sickening dread that some of the tiles are pink.

"What did you do, Rose?" I lift a hand to my head and then glance around the tiny bathroom. There's no note this time, and there's also no headset on the sink. As I turn toward the doorway, the attack rushes back to me. The blond man and the man with the snake tattoo, sent by Kyung to steal the technology. I remember them holstering their guns when they tried to take me out the window. I kicked at one of them, fought back, but didn't manage to escape. Then what? I think one of them made some sort of comment about touching me and it made me feel sick inside. That's all I remember.

I shut off the water and struggle to my feet, wincing in pain. I look down at my legs. There's a line of missing flesh on my right calf where my skin looks like it got seared off, like maybe a bullet grazed me. The tissue is red and meaty like raw hamburger. My stomach lurches and I look away. There are bruises forming on my torso and ribs from a fight I don't remember having. I dry my body on a threadbare bath towel.

As I step out of the enclosure, I notice my bloodstained

clothes on the bathroom floor. Shit. All of that did not come from my leg.

"What did you do?" I repeat.

No response. I tie a hand towel around my calf to keep the wound clean, even though it's mostly stopped bleeding.

Tucking the bath towel around my body as best I can, I open the bathroom door a crack and look out. Light filters through the open window, but there's no movement. I press my ear to the crack. No sounds. I open the door a little wider. That's when I see the feet.

They're connected to a body. Shit, shit, shit. A man with bright-blond hair.

I bend down and test for a pulse, even though I can tell right away that he's dead. One of my throwing knives lies next to his stomach, the blade crusted over with dried blood. Stepping past the body, I check the dead bolt and the chain on the door—both secure. At least there's no danger of a maid stumbling in here before I can figure out what to do. But then, how did the men get in? I glance around the room and find the open window, one pane broken in order to undo the lock. Balmy air wraps around me as I pull the window shut. If anyone had heard the commotion, they would have been banging on the door by now. Still, there's no way to fix it. I can't stay here. I'm not safe.

My suitcase is empty, the contents strewn across the floor. I grab a clean set of clothes and get dressed, noticing that it's after eight in the morning. I have no idea what happened since the men broke in, probably around one or two a.m.

I sit on the edge of the bed and try to calm myself. But it's hard to be calm when a dead body lurks in your peripheral vision. I decide to drag him into the bathroom where I won't have to look at him.

I bend down and grab the collar of his shirt and give him a tug. The fabric rips. Swearing, I try again, this time grabbing onto the meaty parts of his upper arms. I manage to move him a few inches. He must weigh two hundred pounds or more.

I quickly abandon that plan and instead sit cross-legged on the floor, the bed serving as a barrier between me and the blond man. How did they say they had found me? *Mr. Cho knows where to find everyone.* Could they have followed me from Jun's? Maybe Kyung suspected I might try to trick him. Maybe someone was watching Jun's apartment.

I grab my phone and call him, but then I remember he should be on a flight to St. Louis right now. All I can do is pray that he made it to the airport.

I need to get moving. I start wiping down the room. I'm not exactly sure what to do about the body. I'm fairly certain I killed him and that it was self-defense. Still, I have no desire to get police involved. There are no cameras in the guesthouse lobby. The ajumma didn't make me give her any identification. Therefore, there isn't much evidence here that the police could use to track me down.

I need to deal with the body and find a new place to hide until I can figure out my next move. I grab my suitcase from the floor and start stuffing my clothes and wigs back into it. That's when I hear a knock at the door.

CHAPTER 12

Swearing under my breath, I peer out the peephole, expecting the owner of the guesthouse or perhaps the police. What I'm not expecting is Jesse. He's wearing track pants and an oversized hoodie. His brown hair is sticking up in places and flat in others. He's got a couple days' worth of dark beard stubble—more than I've ever seen him with before.

I open the door a crack. "What are you doing here?" I ask incredulously. "How did you find me?"

"It's a long story. Let me in so I can help you."

"I don't need your help," I hiss. "You shouldn't be here."

"You need someone's help." He glances from left to right. "And I'm the only one I see."

"Fine." I open the door just wide enough to admit Jesse and then close it again, putting on the chain and dead bolt.

Jesse whistles long and low as his eyes take in the scene. He pulls out a hat and a pair of gloves and slides them on. He goes to the body and does a perfunctory pulse check. He looks up at me. "Do you remember calling me?"

I furrow my brow. "You mean Saturday?"

"I mean last night, or I guess this morning for you."

"I didn't—"

"Check your phone."

I grab the burner phone from the dresser and check the call

record. Sure enough, I talked to Jesse from 1:31 to 1:37 this morning.

"You called yourself Rose," he says.

I sink to the mattress. I cradle my head in my hands as reality dawns on me. "So my alter did this, to protect me. And then called you for help."

"Maybe," Jesse says. "You said something about Lily."

"Lily is the name my alter used as an alias when she was recording."

Jesse kneels down so we're eye to eye. "I know. But you talked about Lily like she was a separate person. You told me not to be mad at her, that she was just a thirteen-year-old kid, that she didn't know any better."

I have no memory of any of this. "Did you come here just to remind me that I'm crazy?"

"I came because you asked for my help," Jesse says. "At least some part of you still trusts me. I started reading up on dissociative identity disorder on the plane. You know, it's common to have alters that are different ages."

Alters. As in more than one. My leg is pulsing with pain and now my head is throbbing too. "I can't think about any of that right now." I lift one hand, gesture around the room. "I don't suppose you know how to make all of this go away?"

"What name did you use to check in?" Jesse asks.

"A fake name."

"Different from the one you used to fly with?"

"Yes."

"Then I think we should just leave it," he says. "Leave the body. Leave his gun. Leave the room as is."

"But my fingerprints are everywhere."

"But they're not on file, are they? Were you ever arrested for . . ."

"Prostitution?" I finish, my voice sharpening into a hard edge. "No. Kyung's men were very careful about that sort of thing."

"So then it doesn't matter if they have your fingerprints. This guy is probably a known thug with an illegal weapon. From the state of the room, it's obvious there was a struggle here. I say we just make it look like you were attacked and you managed to get into the bathroom and lock the door and then you escaped."

I rub my temples with my fingertips. "But I've wiped away some of the evidence and . . ."

"It doesn't matter. Like I said, this guy was probably a loser. Was he alone?"

I shake my head. "There was one other man. He stole my headset and the neural editor."

"Well, that sucks, but he's not going to go to the cops and say you stabbed his friend while they were robbing you. If we set up a somewhat decent self-defense scenario, the cops will run with it."

I nod. It makes sense. "So what do I do?"

Jesse has me walk him through what I remember. He takes some coagulated blood from the dead guy and smears it on the furniture in a couple of places that I had started to clean.

"You should leave your suitcase and some of your stuff," he says, "so it looks like you really ran off in the middle of the night."

I pull my other knife, a wad of cash, and the envelope of items from Gideon out from beneath the mattress. I tuck the knives into my boots and the cash and envelope into my backpack. Then I also pull the wigs out of the suitcase.

Jesse arches an eyebrow.

"They're expensive," I say. "Plus, it might seem weird, a girl traveling with multiple wigs."

"Good point," he says.

I peel a few hundreds off the wad of cash and slide them back under the mattress. "That will at least pay for the damage to the room."

"Only you would worry about something like that right

now." Jesse coughs sharply. He winces as he presses one gloved palm against his chest.

"Are you all right?" Up until this moment he's been moving and acting like the Jesse I remember. I almost forgot he was bedridden and wearing an oxygen mask only a few days ago.

"Yeah. I'm just a little weak. I'm going to go outside and make sure there aren't any cameras pointed at your bathroom window. I'm also going to make sure no one else is around. Go into the bathroom, lock the bathroom door, and then sneak out the window once I give you the signal."

"Wait," I say. "How did you even get out of the hospital? Are you going to be all right?"

"I pulled out my IV and left," Jesse admits. "They can't keep me there if I don't want to be there."

"But you were taking antibiotics, right? What if one of your wounds gets infected?"

"Then I guess I'll have to go back to the hospital," he says. "I don't really deal in what-ifs anymore. I deal in whatever needs to be done now."

In the bathroom, Jesse has dried the tiles of the shower enclosure and smeared a bit of blood on the glass and the sink to make it look like I didn't stop to clean myself. My clothes and the towel I used are nowhere to be found. He's good at this, I admit grudgingly. I'm glad Rose called him.

His face appears outside the window. Through the smudged glass, his hazel eyes look monochromatic, but it's only been a few days since I stared into them affectionately, allowing myself to get drawn into an undertow of browns and golds and greens. That feels like another lifetime ago.

I miss it.

Jesse makes a "hurry up" motion with his hand and I slide open the window. I wriggle through the narrow opening and out onto the streets of K-Town.

I follow him to a rental car parked two blocks away. He unlocks it and I slide into the passenger seat. I don't even ask him where we're going. I'm just glad to be away from the man I killed.

Jesse slides behind the wheel and signals as he pulls out into the street. The area is deserted, except for one older woman watering the flowers in her front yard.

"How did you know what to do in the room?" I reach for the center console and turn the temperature gauge into the red. It's not a particularly cool morning, but for some reason I'm shivering.

He leans over and turns the heat on for me. "I asked Baz for help."

"Baz knows about this? Did you tell anyone else?"

"No." Jesse shakes his head. "It's not like Baz will rat you out. He wanted to come with me, but he's been helping Adebayo deal with Gideon's effects and keep the building and club running."

"I still can't believe you're here," I say. "I figured you'd be in the hospital for days."

"I'm mostly better. But it hurts when I cough or laugh, so try not to be too funny, okay?"

I snort. "I'll try, but you know me. Always cracking jokes . . . when I'm not blacking out and stabbing people. I guess we all have our special skills."

"What you did back there was self-defense," Jesse says. "The same goes for what you did in St. Louis. It doesn't make you a killer."

"Technically it does." I lean over and turn the heat down a notch.

"Fine. It doesn't make you a murderer."

"What if I told you I wanted to kill Kyung?" I say softly. I'm expecting Jesse to tell me that there's a difference between wanting to do something and actually doing it, that all of us have murderous impulses but that doesn't make us all murderers.

But all he says is, "Kyung deserves to die."

It's true. But what does it mean that I want to be the instrument of that death?

"You were limping," Jesse continues. "Where did you get hurt?"

"My leg. I'm not sure what happened. I think a bullet grazed my calf."

"You got shot? Jesus, Winter. Why didn't you say something?" Jesse looks over at me, his face a mixture of frustration and worry.

"I'm saying something now. It's just a flesh wound. Apparently, Ro—I cleaned it really well after I called you. I can clean it again when we stop." I glance around. "By the way, where are we going?"

"To a hotel."

"Why?"

"Because we'll be safe there. So we can make a plan. And you can get some sleep."

"I can't sleep, Jesse. I have to get the ViSE tech back. Plus, what if Kyung got Jun?"

Jesse looks left and right as he slows for a stop sign. "Who is Jun?"

"My brother. I'm surprised Baz didn't tell you." I quickly explain how Kyung sent me the pictures of Jun on Sung Jin's phone and how I tracked him down once I got here.

"What if this guy told Kyung where to find you?"

"He wouldn't do that. You don't betray your family."

Jesse sighs. "Winter. How do you know he's actually related to you? Maybe he's just some guy that Kyung hired."

I shake my head. "No. He can't be. I have a brother. I remember him, Jesse. I remember my mother with a baby. Jun showed me his ID. And he knew things. Family things." But even as I say this, a seed of doubt takes root in my brain. Fake ID isn't that hard to come by. And anyone can find out almost anything if they know where to look for it, can't they? Kyung somehow found those pictures of my mother. Maybe he did learn just enough personal information to be able to set me up. I wanted so much for Jun to be my brother. It's not like I quizzed him very hard.

"We'll go check out his place," Jesse says. "But first we really ought to drop your stuff off at the hotel and take a look at your leg."

"But Jess—"

"We're almost there," Jesse says. "And if Kyung took him, he's already gone. But hopefully you'll get a phone call with demands."

"You're right." I slouch down in the car seat, trying to ignore the throbbing pain in my calf and skull. Trying to ignore the reality that my brother might be dead, or that he might not be my brother after all.

The hotel Jesse booked online assigns us a room on the fourth floor. We limp up the stairs together. As I listen to Jesse's labored breathing, I wish more than ever that I could get over my fear of elevators. He sounds like he's going to die before we make it to his room.

"Let's rest for a few seconds," I say.

"I don't need to—"

"I need to," I lie.

Jesse and I both lean heavily against the wall of the stairwell. He doubles over. "Shit, I feel like an old man," he groans.

"You shouldn't have left the hospital," I chide.

"You sound like my mother."

"Well, she's right. You need rest, time to heal."

He doesn't respond, but I know his expression well. I've seen it on my own face—the look of someone who feels like no matter what they do, it's wrong.

"But I'm glad that you're here," I say. "Thank you for helping me."

"You're welcome." He pushes a couple sweaty tendrils of

hair away from his eyes and starts creeping up the stairs again. Eventually we reach the fourth floor.

The room has two beds and a kitchenette. I drop my backpack on the bed closest to the door and again find myself thinking about the last time Jesse and I were in a hotel room together. Things got a lot more intimate than we expected, or I expected anyway.

Jesse is apparently thinking the same thing. "Are you going to be okay sharing with me? I could book a second room."

"This is fine." I reach out and smooth a wrinkle from the bedspread.

"Okay." Jesse closes the door and dead-bolts it. He turns to me, his face deadly serious. "Let's take a look at your leg."

I go into the bathroom, sit on the edge of the bathtub, and roll up my pant leg. I peel away my makeshift bandage. Jesse starts the tap and adjusts the temperature so the water is warm without being scalding. Still, the shock of heat on my wound makes me gasp in pain.

Jesse squeezes my shoulder gently. "Hang in there," he says. "Just keep rinsing it. I don't have any triple antibiotic, so you want to make sure it's really clean." I nod. Neither of us speaks for a few seconds. Then he brushes my hair back from my face. I wince as his fingers find the spot where Snake Tattoo backhanded me. "That's going to be an impressive bruise."

I reach up to rub the spot, my fingers brushing against Jesse's. "I'm lucky he didn't break my jaw," I say. "He hit me on the back of the head too. Trying to knock me out because I wouldn't go willingly with them to see Kyung."

Jesse blinks hard, his eyes focused on our hands, which are still touching. I slide my fingers away from his and search for the tender spot on my scalp. There's a lump the size of a golf ball. I probe the rest of my skull gently and find a smaller lump on the side of my head. It must have happened while I was dissociating.

Jesse turns away from me. He grabs one of the hand towels

and uses a pocketknife to cut it into strips. "This'll have to work for a bandage for now."

"Thank you." Our eyes meet just for a second and I see so many emotions in Jesse's gaze. I wonder if he sees anything in mine or if I'm projecting nothing more than a dead, black stare.

"I'll, uh, give you some space," he mumbles. He leaves me alone in the bathroom.

I shake my head. Jesse has never been very good at giving me space. He's so convinced that he's what I need, that he can somehow love me back to normal. It's sweet. If only it were true.

After I finish rinsing my wound, I tie a strip of hand towel around my calf and knot it securely.

I find Jesse out in the main room. I hold up a clean, damp washcloth. "Your turn."

He turns and heads for the bathroom. "I can do it."

"I know." I follow him. "But it'll be easier if I do it, so let me help."

"Okay." Jesse works his hoodie and T-shirt over his shoulders. My pulse accelerates a little. He doesn't have the definition that some guys his age have, but he's solidly built, with broad shoulders and a muscular torso. He's got a long, straight bandage down the center of his chest, as well as pieces of gauze taped over his shoulder and ribs. "The big one is where they had to crack my chest," he says. "One of the bullets apparently ended up lodged in a weird place, so they couldn't get to it any other way. The smaller ones are the entry wounds."

"I still can't believe you got shot trying to protect me." I loosen the edges of the largest dressing on one side to expose the incision beneath. It's a smooth red line, crusted over, with tiny white pieces of tape perpendicular to the wound.

Jesse's eyelids flutter shut the moment I touch him. His face flushes slightly.

"Am I hurting you?" I ask.

"No."

I lift the washcloth up to his skin and start gently scrubbing away bits of dried blood. His heart pounds, robust and steady, beneath my fingertips. The rhythmic thumping grounds me, like it's my own heartbeat instead of his. A sigh escapes from his lips.

I stop scrubbing for a second. This is the first time Jesse and I have been close since I found out that he lied to me. I wasn't sure if I would ever feel the same way about him, and I still don't know if I will, but the pull of physical attraction is definitely still present. My eyes trace the lines of his tattoos—an eagle wrapped in a Mexican flag on his chest, an elaborately decorated skull on his right shoulder. Then lower on his arm, a military insignia and the initials of four friends who died in Afghanistan.

He swallows hard. "Winter."

There are so many different ways for someone to say your name. I'm not sure I ever realized that before I met Jesse. Prior to him, it was just Rose calling out to me with love and affection or Gideon relaying his quiet approval or disapproval. Crisp, clear notes. When Jesse says my name, it's a chord, a mash-up of several intense emotions all reflected in two syllables.

"Yes?" I say.

"I will never stop being sorry for what happened between us."

"I know." I'm hoping that this simple answer will be enough to silence him. Jesse and I slept together when I was dissociating. I know this because I found a ViSE of it that my alter recorded. I know he didn't mean to take advantage of me, but it's hard to think about how things are imbalanced between us now. He knows me intimately, but I don't even remember being with him. To be honest, I wish my mind would take back the memory of finding that ViSE and file it away somewhere in a dark, forgotten place so then we could be equal again.

"I still ask myself if somehow I might have known," he says. "I should have known, right?"

"Jesse." I pause for a second, trying to decode all of the notes beneath my usage of his name. Kindness. Forgiveness. Affection. "I didn't even know. How could *you* have known?"

He opens his eyes and looks down at me. "Okay, maybe not that you had DID. But that you weren't yourself that night. I think I did know and I just didn't acknowledge it because I wanted you so bad."

He looks away, toward the doorway. Gideon told me once that when people look at doors or windows it's because some part of them is trying to escape. When Jesse found out about my condition, he felt like he'd assaulted me. I felt like that too, at first. But the more I thought about it, the more I realized I couldn't have expected him not to be with me that night. He'd liked me for months. He'd been drinking. I was the one who instigated the physical contact. I was the one who talked him through all of his reservations.

I wipe the cloth along the other side of the incision. "You didn't do anything wrong." I turn his head back so he's facing me, so I'm looking into his beautiful hazel eyes. "I know I said—I did—terrible things to you, but I was in shock. Since then I've had time to think about everything and I don't blame you for being with me that night. I don't feel violated and I understand why you hid the truth. Let's just leave it in the past."

"Seriously?" he asks.

"Seriously." I pat his incision dry with the other side of the washcloth. "What are these little white pieces? Are they holding your chest together with tape?"

"The nurse called them sterile strips or something. Apparently they help keep the wound clean. They're supposed to dry up and fall off on their own."

I clear my throat. "Well, it looks good. No redness or swelling." I loosen the tape of the smaller bandages on his shoulder and rib cage and it's more of the same. Angry pink incisions, but no swelling, and minimal drainage. I wipe them down with the washcloth and then restick the tape as best I can since we have no gauze for fresh dressings.

Jesse's phone buzzes and he turns away from me, still shirtless, to retrieve it from the bedside table. I study the muscles in his back as he crosses the room. He lifts the phone to his ear and turns to face the big picture window that looks out on the neighborhood as he talks.

I can't make out what he's saying, but when he ends the call, he turns to face me. Flicking off the light in the bathroom, I step back into the main part of the hotel room and toss him his sweatshirt. "So was that Baz?"

"Yeah." Jesse pulls the hoodie back over his head.

"What did he have to say?"

"Unfortunately, as far as he knows, Jun never arrived in St. Louis."

CHAPTER 13

Jesse and I head immediately to Jun's apartment. My mind spins the whole way. My brother got taken by Kyung's men. My brother betrayed me to Kyung. My brother isn't really my brother after all. I can't decide which possibility is the worst, but it doesn't take us long to figure out which is true.

The first thing I notice is that the mailbox no longer says "Song." The label has been scraped off but not replaced.

"He's not my brother," I whisper, a lump rising up in my throat. "He tricked me."

"We don't know that for sure," Jesse says.

But I do. Why else would the name be gone? How could I have been so foolish?

Jesse and I ascend to the second floor and I let him knock on the door. No one answers. I pick the lock with a couple of bobby pins but the chain is also on the door.

"Kick it down," I bark.

Jesse gives me a look. "Maybe we don't need to go there just yet. I have an idea."

I follow him down the stairs and back outside. He heads around the back of the building and pulls down a rusty fire escape. We climb up to the second floor. The bedroom window is closed around a small air conditioner. Inside, Jun—if that's even his name—is sleeping.

Jesse pulls his gun and motions for me to lift the window

from the AC unit. Holding my breath, I slowly raise the window to Jun's bedroom. He stirs beneath his white sheet but doesn't open his eyes.

Jesse and I step over the air conditioner and slide through the opening one at a time. We approach the bed from opposite sides. Too late, Jun's eyes blink open. He looks from Jesse to me, his eyes taking in my bruised face before focusing on Jesse's gun.

"You're not my brother, are you?" I ask. I can tell immediately by his expression that he's not. Sadness stirs in my gut and I bite my lip to keep it from trembling. How could I have been so stupid?

"I'm sorry that I lied to you. I didn't know you were going to get hurt," the boy says. "They told me that you stole something from the company and they just wanted to know where you were staying so they could send the police to recover it." He glances nervously at Jesse and then back at his gun. "Please don't hurt me."

"Do I even have a brother?" I ask.

"I don't know. My name is Kevin. I moved here from Seoul with my family when I was eight years old. I've never even been to Taebaek. A couple of UsuMed execs told me that you might show up here. They gave me the fake ID and told me to play along. They said that I'd get promoted if I did well."

I sigh. "I want your badge. Call in sick tomorrow and you can tell them the next day that you lost it."

Kevin shrugs. "Okay, but it's just a janitor's badge. You can't get very far with it."

"How do I find Kyung?" I ask. "Which building is he in?"

"He has an office on the top floor of the round tower," Kevin says. "But I heard he's going to be out of town for a while, heading up a big project in Seoul."

"Of course he is," I mutter. It makes perfect sense that Kyung would take Gideon's tech out of the country to work on it. Korea is full of brilliant engineers. I'm betting he can find someone to fix the neural editor even without Gideon's notes. And even if I could claim some sort of patent violation, Gideon's patent on the technology is under a fake name and my papers are also fake. I'm not sure how all that would be resolved legally, but I know enough about the American justice system to know we'd be fighting court battles for years.

I don't want to fight Kyung in court. I want to stick my knives into his chest and watch him die, slowly. But first I want to regain control of the ViSE tech.

"Looks like I'm going to Seoul," I say.

Jesse and I head back to his hotel, where I call Sebastian.

"Hello?" he says.

"It's Winter. I need your help again."

"Yeah. Sorry about your brother. I checked in with a friend of mine who has access to passenger manifests and as far as he can tell, no one named Jun Song has gotten on a plane anywhere yesterday or today."

"That's because Kyung played me. His men had one of his employees pretend to be my brother."

"Shit, Winter. I'm sorry. Are you and Ramirez okay? Did you handle the hotel room?"

"I don't know about *handle*. We left it as is."

"Not as is," Jesse yells in the background. "I did everything you said."

"You guys should probably get out of Los Angeles," Baz says. "Just in case."

"Good idea. Can you GPS the neural editor?"

"Why?"

"Because the guy I didn't kill stole it."

Baz swears again. "Yeah, okay. Give me a second." He sets the phone down and I can hear him muttering under his breath. He comes back on the line. "That's weird," he says. "The chip is reading that it's in the middle of the Pacific Ocean."

"So, on a plane," I say. "On the way to Seoul."

"Possibly," Baz says. "I could make some calls and try to match it to a registered flight path, but it'll probably just be easier to wait and see where it stops moving, especially since whoever has it could switch onto a connecting flight."

"You're right," I say. "Can you check it later and give us a call?"

"Sure," Baz says. "I wouldn't panic. I'm pretty sure Gideon disabled the editor in case someone came after it. It'll be useless."

"He did disable it. He told me. Well, he left me a ViSE that told me. But Kyung will be able to find someone who can fix it, even without Gideon's notes."

"So he has the tech but not the notes?"

"Right. Gideon's research is . . . in a safe place." Sebastian loved Gideon and I want to trust him, but the fewer people who know about the flash drive built into my necklace, the better.

"Cool. Put Ramirez on for a minute."

I hand the phone to Jesse and lie back on the bed. He and Baz talk for a few minutes and then Jesse hangs up. "You should get some sleep," he says.

"I'm not sure if sleep is going to be easy for me to come by."

Jesse pulls a pill bottle out of his pocket. "I have some really good drugs that say otherwise."

I smile. "I'm not taking your painkillers."

"Then I guess you'll just have to be soothed by my natural calming presence." When I don't respond, he adds, "There's nothing we can do until we know for sure where the tech is. We might as well get some rest. You look exhausted."

"I am," I admit. "I've been sleeping in two-hour chunks so I can record myself in case I dissociate." I don't tell Jesse about going to see the elevator where my sister died. I don't want him to think I'm dissociating all the time or he'll try to convince me not to go to Seoul.

"God, Winter. I'm surprised you're not a total wreck. You

can't survive like that. Go to sleep. I'll watch you." Jesse pauses. "Sorry. I didn't mean that in a creepy way. I'll keep an eye on you while I watch some TV. I won't sit here and stare at you or—"

"It's fine. I know what you meant." I crawl beneath the sheet on the bed. "But aren't you tired too?"

"I am, but if we're going to Seoul, then I can sleep on the plane."

I stare up at the ceiling. "Are you sure you want to be involved in this? You were in the military. Your fingerprints are on file. You could end up going to jail just for helping me at the guesthouse."

"I didn't leave any fingerprints," Jesse says.

I swallow back a yawn. "What about DNA?"

"I tried not to leave much of that either, but either way I'm pretty sure the local police can't access the military DNA registry without probable cause," Jesse says. "Plus, it's a guesthouse. There's probably a hundred people's DNA in there."

"Good point," I say. "Just don't feel obligated to come with me. It could get . . . ugly."

"I know ugly," Jesse says. "I was miserable before I started working for Gideon. Each morning I got up and went to work in my aunt and uncle's Mexican restaurant. Every night I went to Krav Maga class, desperate to get out all of my anger in a nondestructive way. Desperate to keep my mind off the past. Working for Gideon made me feel strong again, like I wasn't worthless. Like I could be more than a victim. So yeah, he and I might not be related by blood, but he was my family and I don't want Kyung to have that tech any more than you do." Jesse pauses. "Whatever you're doing, wherever you're going, I'm with you, Winter, as long as it takes."

CHAPTER 14

A gentle knocking sound wakes me out of a deep and dreamless sleep. My eyes snap open and for a few seconds, nothing makes sense. Where am I? How did I get here?

Across the room, Jesse stands in a pair of plaid pajama pants and an army-green T-shirt. He's talking to someone in the hallway. As if he can sense that I'm awake, he glances back over his shoulder. "It's okay," he says. "It's just room service."

That's right. Jesse helped me escape the guesthouse in K-Town. He moved me to his hotel room. The soft sheets fall away from my body as I sit up in bed and rub my eyes. I run one hand through my hair. "What time is it?"

The door to the hallway closes with a heavy click. Jesse turns to me. He's holding a tray stacked with covered plates. "It's, uh, nine a.m."

Once again, it takes me a little longer to process that than I would like. "I slept for an entire day? Why didn't you wake me?" I lift a hand to the lump on the back of my head. I hope Kyung's goon didn't do any permanent damage.

"Because it seemed like you needed sleep, and it's not like we could do anything without knowing where the ViSE technology is, right?"

"And can I assume Baz called?"

"Yep," Jesse says with a smile. "It's in Seoul. He promised he'd call back if anything changes." Jesse sets the tray on my bed and sits down next to it. He starts pulling lids off plates. "I didn't know what you'd want, so I hope you like pancakes, French toast, yogurt, an omelet, or mixed fruit."

I'm ravenous after not eating for almost a whole day, but my stomach lurches at the combination of colors and smells. "I might just go out and see if I can find some *gimbap*."

Jesse's face falls a little. "You mean that sushi-looking stuff I've seen you eat before?"

"Yes," I say. "Same seaweed and rice, but no raw fish. It's what I normally eat in the morning."

Jesse looks down at the tray of food and back up at me, probably wondering what's wrong with someone who can't find something she likes among an entire breakfast buffet. "You probably should stay here in case Kyung's men or the police are looking for you. I could try to go get you some, if you tell me where to find it."

He's breathing kind of heavy, like maybe just carrying the room service tray to the bed was a workout for him. "No," I say. "Sorry. I didn't mean to sound ungrateful. Now that I think about it, fruit and yogurt sounds delicious. This whole room is really nice. I hope it's not costing you a fortune."

"It's fine. I have some money saved up."

I slide out from under the covers and pull out a wad of cash from my backpack. "Take this." I drop the money next to the tray.

Jesse hesitates. "You don't need to pay me for helping you, Winter."

"I'll be getting the building and the club in Gideon's will, not to mention some stocks, some bank accounts, and the technology if I can steal it back. Money is the one thing I have to offer right now, so please take it."

"Okay." Jesse grabs the wad of bills and shoves it in the pocket of his pajama pants. "But you have more than that to offer, all right?"

"If you say so." I spoon some of the cut-up fruit into the

bowl of vanilla yogurt and swirl it around with my spoon. Jesse attacks a plate of pancakes with the vigor of a starving man. For a few minutes, we sit next to each other, chewing quietly.

"I'm guessing you don't care if I eat the last pancake?" he asks.

I shake my head.

Jesse reaches for the remaining pancake, spoons some fruit and yogurt on top of it, drizzles a line of syrup down the middle, and then rolls it into a tube. Lifting it carefully, he takes a bite out of the end. He chews, swallows, blots his mouth with his free hand. "Now that's good eating."

My lips curl at the edges. It's comforting for some reason that he can find so much joy in little things. "How do you do that?"

"Do what? Pancake burrito? You just put the fruit and—"

"No, not pancake burrito. How do you make me smile when it seems like there's nothing in the whole world to smile about?"

His shoulders rotate down and back as his whole body seems to perk up in response to the comment. He flashes his teeth at me. "Like you said, we've all got our special skills."

After we finish eating, I make a list of things we're going to need for Seoul, and Jesse goes out to look for them. I decide to wait and buy more clothes once I get there. I'm not sure how the fashions have changed over the past few years, and it'll be easier to blend in if I'm dressed like a local. I take a long, hot shower and then grab my phone and call Dr. Abrams on her cell phone. It's about twelve thirty p.m. in St. Louis. Maybe I can catch her on her lunch break.

She picks up on the first ring.

"It's Winter Kim," I say.

"Winter!" When Dr. Abrams says my name, I also sense several different emotions, but mostly concern. "I'm so glad you called. Are you all right?"

"I'm fine. I had to go out of town to deal with some things.

I just wanted to apologize for missing my appointment. I didn't want you to worry."

"I heard what happened to Mr. Seung. I'm so sorry for your loss."

"Thank you," I say. "Do you have a few minutes? I just have one question."

"Sure. Go ahead."

"You said you never saw any alters in my sessions with you, right? Is there any way I can determine how many I have?"

Dr. Abrams clears her throat. "No. There's no magical way to see into your mind, I'm afraid. Some people have only one. Some people have twenty or more."

Twenty or more! I can't even bear the thought of sharing my body with some part of me who thinks she's my dead sister. I try to imagine what it would be like if there were twenty other alters competing with her. "Is there a reason one of them might be . . . violent?"

There's a long pause at the other end of the line and some paranoid part of me wonders if her office is full of government agents in black suits telling her to keep me on the line long enough to trace the call. "Dr. Abrams? Are you still there?"

"Why would you ask that, Winter? Did you have something to do with what happened to Mr. Seung?"

"I would never hurt Gideon," I say sharply. "But lately I feel like there's a . . . new darkness inside me. Another voice in my head." *You talked about Lily like she was a separate person.* I exhale deeply as I look toward the window. I hope Jesse returns soon. "Or maybe she's always been there, but she's louder now?"

"Given everything you've gone through, I don't think the awakening of violent urges or emotions would be out of the norm," Dr. Abrams says. "But it could be dangerous. You should get help, Winter. If not from me, then from someone wherever you are."

"Soon," I murmur. "I'll get help soon."

Honestly, I don't know if I'll be able to move forward after what I've learned. I'm caught in this endless loop where all I can think about is revenge and death. That's what happens when you lose your sister and the closest thing you've ever had to a father.

They were the glue that held together my pieces.

But I can't break. Not yet, anyway. There's work to be done.

CHAPTER 15

When Baz calls back later to say the location of the technology hasn't changed, I call the airport and book Jesse and me on a three p.m. flight to Seoul. Luckily I can afford to fly business class now, and the ticket agent rearranges a couple solo travelers so that Jesse and I can sit next to each other.

As the plane lifts off, we pass his cell phone back and forth, using the memo function to communicate without anyone else on the crowded plane hearing us.

Jesse: So what's the plan when we get there?

Me: Find a place to stay. Figure out if I really have a brother. Find Kyung. Figure out a way to infiltrate wherever he has the tech. Steal back the tech. Kill Kyung.

"Oh, is that all?" Jesse elbows me in the ribs as he deletes my words.

I wince inwardly. My whole body is sore from my fight with Kyung's men. I feel for the knot on the back of my head and am relieved to find the swelling has gone down. The bruise on my cheek is still visible, but I covered most of it with makeup. "I never said it was going to be easy," I tell him.

He taps out another message.

Jesse: Baz says he's going to rent us rooms in a hotel where he and I won't stand out as foreigners.

Me: I still can't believe Baz is coming to Seoul to help.

Jesse: Gideon was his family too. He doesn't want the ViSE tech used for anything evil.

Me: Do you trust him? I thought he scared you.

Jesse: He does scare me. But he got shot trying to protect Gideon, so he's obviously loyal. And apparently he has military contacts in Seoul. That could be useful . . .

Jesse doesn't have to finish that statement. He means guns. Handguns are almost impossible to get in Korea. All weapons are very tightly regulated. We had to stash his gun and my knives in a safe-deposit box in Los Angeles because bringing them into the country would have meant risking arrest.

I start typing out a message on the phone, but something outside the window catches my eye. Swatches of white against the previously endless blue sky. Clouds, thin like ribbons. The plane's wing cuts through them one after the next. Below us, there is only ocean for as far as I can see. So much blue. If the plane went down, the sea would swallow us whole. No one would ever find us. No one would probably even look for me.

I turn away from the great expanse of blue. "I can't believe he's gone."

"I can't either." Jesse scoots closer to me in his seat, our forearms almost but not quite touching on the armrest between our seats.

"Do you miss him?"

"Yeah," Jesse says. "He was this . . . consistent force in my life. I mean, he had these expectations for me, for all of his staff, and when we didn't meet them, we heard about it. He was always so strict, but fair. He never played favorites. Well, except for you."

I smile through my pain. So many men in Gideon's situation would have abandoned me. After Rose was killed, he could have left me in Los Angeles or at the airport or at the hospital. So what if he loved Rose? I was nothing like her. I was this confused, violent, broken little girl. He probably should've given me up.

But he didn't. He took care of me. He made me strong. And sure, he made a lot of mistakes along the way, but what parent doesn't? Especially if they never asked for a child in the first place.

"I wish I would have better appreciated the time I had with him," I say.

Jesse nods. "Me too."

I lower my voice. "He made me a ViSE, like a 'just in case something happens to me' message." A tear rolls down my cheek. It's on the side by the window and Jesse doesn't notice. I reach up and brush it away.

"He was good about preparing for all possibilities, wasn't he?" Jesse says.

"He was." I wonder if Gideon is looking down on me right now with dark, disapproving eyes. I wish to honor his memory, but part of that means making sure the ViSE technology he worked so hard on doesn't fall into the wrong hands. He would understand me going after the tech. He would be less accepting about me going after Kyung, but he can't possibly know what it's like to feel so violated by one human being. Like as long as Kyung walks the earth, I will always be a victim.

I turn to Jesse. "Thank you for coming with me."

"Thank you for letting me." Jesse smiles awkwardly and then reaches for the phone again.

Jesse: Do you think you really have a brother somewhere?

Me: I don't know. I still can't remember my sister ever mentioning him, but after Kyung sent me those pictures, I remembered my mom with a baby. And I think I remember her being pregnant too. I know my memory has tricked me, but only by blocking out the truth—not by manufacturing falsehoods.

I want my brother to be real. He has to be. Kyung couldn't have known about my memory gaps. He wouldn't have tried to trick me if he didn't have reasons to believe it would work.

Jesse: If he exists, we'll find him.

Me: Just promise me you'll be careful. I don't want you to get hurt for me.

Jesse: I think you're a little late there.

He winks at me to let me know he's kidding. Only Jesse could joke about getting shot. Our arms brush against each other as he turns away. A rush of heat moves through me. Part of me wants to extend the physical contact, reach for his hand. I miss being touched. I miss being held. Jesse would hold me if I asked him to. He'd put the armrest up and wrap his blanket around both of us, sheltering me against his chest. But it's not fair to use him like that. He wants more than the occasional close moment that happens on my terms—he wants a future, and right now all I can think about is the past.

Jesse and I spend most of the flight watching movies. Eventually he falls asleep and I watch the regular rise and fall of his chest, hoping that the stresses of high altitude and traveling so far away aren't going to delay his recovery.

We land at Incheon Airport just after nine p.m. local time the following day. The plane sits for a few minutes because our arrival gate is still occupied. I blink sleepily as I look around my seat and gather my things. Jesse has a red mark on his face from where his cheek was smashed against the headrest while he slept. I resist the urge to reach out and touch it.

"I can't believe we're here," he says.

"It's a long ride to the city," I remind him. "Plus, we still have to pass immigration and get our luggage." I'm not too worried about the immigration process. My fake passport should get me into the country fine, but I'm a lot less convinced it'll get me back to the US.

We exit the plane and follow the passengers in front of us through the wide passageways, around several corners, and down two flights of stairs to where a shuttle will take us from the arrivals terminal to the immigration area. Around us, most people are talking or texting on their phones while they wait.

Jesse's phone buzzes in his pocket. He fishes it out. "Baz texted me the address."

I glance at it. It's in a central part of the city called Itaewon—a neighborhood that caters to military guys and foreign English teachers. We shouldn't raise any suspicion there. "That will take us about an hour to get to."

Jesse doesn't respond. The shuttle is approaching and he's staring at it. "Whoa," he says.

The enclosure is full of people standing shoulder to shoulder, packed in tightly.

The glass doors open and the people disembark in a wave of black coats and carry-on luggage. Once everyone has gotten off, Jesse and I step into the shuttle. I find us an area in the back of the car where he can lean against the wall for support. People pile in behind us, and then keep piling.

"The perception of personal space here is different than in the US," I tell him. "The subway is sometimes like this too."

Jesse gives me a look as an old lady rolls her suitcase over his feet and then reaches across him to press her palm against the back of the shuttle. "I feel like I'm taking up way too much space."

I wink at him. "They're used to Americans taking up lots of space."

"How are you okay with this?" he asks. A bell rings. A few more people smash into the shuttle before the glass doors close with a hiss. "I thought you hated crowds."

"I'm not sure," I say. "Maybe it's because some part of me remembers taking crowded trains as a child. Plus, I have a purpose now. I can't be afraid of everything anymore."

Jesse leans down to talk in my ear. "You were never afraid of everything. And you had good reasons for the stuff that scared you."

The shuttle starts up with a jerk and we head for the next terminal. It feels weird being pressed against Jesse, but I'd be lying if I said I didn't like it, a little.

He coughs and his face contorts. He struggles in the crowded space to lift his hand to his chest.

"How are you doing?" I ask, leaning back away from him to give him space.

"I'm pretty sore, but not too bad, all things considered."

"That moment in the penthouse," I murmur. "I thought I might lose you."

"I assure you, I'm not that easy to get rid of," Jesse says lightly. But there's a seriousness in his hazel eyes that belies his casual tone. Jesse knows he could've died for me. He knows he still might.

CHAPTER 16

We hire a car to take us from the airport to Itaewon. Jesse spends the entire ride peering out his side window, his eyes taking in as much as he can in the dark. I scan the scenery on my side, wonder what has changed in the past six years. There seem to be more buildings and less green space, but we're still a ways outside of the city.

Digital billboards light up both sides of the road, advertising everything from cigarettes to cars. Beautiful models smile down, promising glamour and happiness if you'll just buy what they're selling.

"They use pretty girls to advertise everything, huh?"

"Pretty girls sell." I point out into the night. "You can't see them, but there are mountains over there, and over there."

Jesse squints. "All I see are little groups of tall buildings that look like high-rise apartments."

"That's how most people live here," I tell him. "Even the wealthy."

He turns back to his window. After a few seconds he says, "Aside from the signs and people, it doesn't look as different as I expected it to look."

"I remember thinking the same thing about California."

After about twenty minutes on the highway, our driver exits onto a small, congested road and we quickly end up mired in traffic. He says something about a shortcut and makes a couple of quick turns. We pass a vacant lot, a metallic crane peeping over the top of a fence of boards and orange netting. A giant banner hanging from the gate proclaims this as the latest construction project from UsuCon. In Korea, the biggest corporations, or *jaebeols*, don't just specialize in one thing. The same company might make cars and computers and operate hotels and department stores. I didn't realize how powerful the Usu jaebeol had become throughout the city. Going up against them, even just one segment, even just one *man*, isn't going to be easy.

We wind our way through the back streets of Seoul, our driver finding openings just big enough for us to slide through, occasionally coming close enough to a pedestrian to brush up against a purse or puffy winter coat. College kids and young professionals are out in droves. Girls saunter by in tall boots and short dresses. Men in suits drink from green soju bottles. Some of them are already intoxicated to the point of yelling and stumbling.

"Party central," Jesse says.

"I think the motto here is 'Work hard, play hard,'" I say.

Eventually, we turn onto the main street of Itaewon and pass a string of fast-food restaurants and bars, some of them with signs welcoming gay and transgender patrons. I'm not sure how socially progressive Seoul has become since I left, but I'm guessing Itaewon is probably a lot more accepting than other parts of the city. When the car finally slows to a stop in front of a tall cement building, Baz is waiting out in front. I almost don't recognize him. Instead of the dark suit and slicked-back hair I'm used to seeing on him, he's wearing jeans and a T-shirt, a baseball cap pulled low over his eyes. I pay the driver, who helps unload our bags from the trunk.

Baz gives Jesse a fist bump and turns to me with a half smile. "Flight okay?"

"Okay?" Jesse says. "They had like sixty different movies to pick from, including every *Star Wars*. It was awesome."

I smile. "It was fine." I glance up at the building. "What is this place?"

"I was going to book us rooms at one of the hotels the military guys usually use for their families, but then I saw a flyer for a flat rental. I figure we might as well have the space since paying for multiple hotel rooms will cost just as much. Plus, this way no one is monitoring our comings and goings."

"Good point," I say. The hotels probably all have security cameras. "Speaking of being monitored, you seem to have a fan club." A few feet away, two Korean girls with dyed hair and heavy makeup are eyeing Baz appraisingly.

He glances over his shoulder and snorts. "No regard for taste, I guess."

"Have you been able to GPS the tech since you got here?" I ask.

"Sure did. The signal only locates to within a radius of a couple of blocks, but the tech appears to be in Gangnam-gu, and guess what's right in the middle of that—the international headquarters for UsuMed."

"Imagine that."

Baz eyes my suitcase. "We're on the sixth floor. Stairs?"

"I can try the elevator," I say slowly.

"Cool," he says, like it's no big deal. But we all know that it is. I haven't taken an elevator in years. Well, except for the day Gideon died, when Sung Jin dragged me into the private penthouse elevator at gunpoint.

I struggle to breathe, my chest suddenly tight as we step inside the building and approach the shining steel doors.

Baz reaches out and presses the up arrow. It lights up red.

Red means stop, a voice whispers.

"You know what? You guys go ahead. I think I'll scope out the stairs, make sure I'm familiar with the escape routes just in case something happens."

"I'll take your bag up," Baz says.

"I'll come with you." Jesse leaves his luggage and starts to follow me.

"What am I? The bellhop?" Baz kicks at Jesse's suitcase. "Carry your own shit."

"I thought you said—"

"Her bag, not yours."

"Good to know chivalry isn't dead," I say weakly, but mostly I'm just grateful for the reprieve from lugging my suitcase up several flights of stairs. I'm fairly certain that's not even a possibility for Jesse right now, so I'm not surprised when I head for the stairwell and he doesn't follow me.

My leg is throbbing a little. I pause halfway up the stairs and pull back the tape on my bandage to make sure I'm not bleeding again. The wound looks a little inflamed, but the scab is holding.

Baz and Jesse are leaning against the hall outside of apartment 608 when I duck out of the stairwell. Baz glances down at his phone like he was timing me. "When did you get so slow?"

"After she got shot," Jesse says drily.

"Fair point, but try to step it up a little in the next few days. We're all going to need to be at the top of our game if we're going to steal back the ViSE tech without ending up in Korean prison." Baz turns to the apartment door and punches in a six-digit security code. I watch and memorize the string of numbers. He swings the heavy door inward.

The flat is nicer than I imagined based on the outside of the building. It has wooden floors with traditional Korean *on-dol* heating and all new appliances.

I stroll into the living room. "How many bedrooms?"

"Two." Baz looks back and forth from Jesse to me. "It was the best option I found on short notice. I figured Jesse and I could share one room and you could have the other."

"Or I could sleep on the sofa," I say.

The living room is small but furnished with a faux leather

sofa, a set of glass tables, and a flat-screen television. I wander through the room, to the big picture window that looks out onto the street. An older woman, her arms laden with packages, totters by. Behind her, a couple of dark-skinned guys with military haircuts are looking down at their phones. I watch all three of them disappear into the nearest entrance to the subway station at the end of the block.

Jesse joins me at the window. "You're not going to be able to function if you set your alarm to wake up every two hours. Let me or Baz sleep on the sofa. That way if you dissociate and try to leave the apartment, we'll wake up."

"I don't mind sleeping out here," Baz says. "I'm a light sleeper. I'll wake up if you try to go anywhere."

Jesse reaches out and touches a metal ring that's embedded in the wall next to the window. "What's this for?"

Baz chuckles. "That's part of the Korean fire escape." He looks around and locates a red metal basket in the far corner of the living room. Bending down, he retrieves a neatly coiled rope with a nylon harness attached and a folded piece of paper. "Just slip this around you, clip into the anchor ring, and follow these instructions on how to use the descender."

"You're shitting me, right?" Jesse grabs the paper out of Baz's hands. He scans the tiny print, his jaw tensing up as he reads. "Maximum weight a hundred kilograms? What if you're bigger than that?"

Baz slaps him lightly on the shoulder. "Then you die."

"No one is dying," I say firmly.

"Did I say die?" Baz asks innocently. "I meant *diet*. Yeah, that's it." He turns toward Jesse and claps his hands together. "Splat," he says under his breath.

"You're an ass," Jesse says.

Baz grins. "But I'm an ass who will survive a fire." He places the rope back into the red basket.

"I'm sure this rope could hold double the weight if it had to, but let's try not to start any fires, all right?" I turn to Baz.

"How do you know about Korean fire escapes? Have you been here before?"

"I used to live here."

"In Itaewon? When you were in the military?" I ask.

"Actually, after that," Baz says. "I did some contract work for the government."

Jesse arches an eyebrow. "Which government?"

Baz grins. "Whichever government was paying the best that week."

Jesse smirks. Something outside the window catches his eye. "What's a PC cyber zone?"

"A good thing for us," Baz says.

"We call them PC bangs. "Bang" means room. It's like an Internet café," I explain. "Mostly full of college kids playing RPGs."

"They're playing with rocket-propelled grenades?"

I'm fairly certain Jesse is joking, but I'm too tired to pretend to laugh so I explain anyway. "Role-playing games. Like some of the college kids like to do at Escape."

"Why do they pay for Internet access when everybody has it at home?"

"Camaraderie," I explain. "They like playing together."

"Also, some of the games are team oriented and others reward gamers with virtual currency when they log on from a cooperative gaming area," Baz says. "But we don't care about any of that. We just want to be able to use the Internet anonymously."

"You think they're anonymous?"

"More or less," Baz says. "They don't track who sits at which computer or ask for any sort of ID. I mean, they probably have cameras, but they're not going to be watching every tourist who stumbles in looking for a place to catch up on his e-mail cheaply. And there are certain people it's safer for me to contact from an outside terminal. I'll head over there and hit up my contacts in the area and see what I can do about procuring some equipment. You two should come with me."

"Why?" I ask.

"I don't know. So you stay out of trouble? You can try to look for information on your brother."

"You don't think I tried that?" I ask. "I've searched for Jun Song in Los Angeles and in Seoul and in Taebaek, where I was born. There are results everywhere, but no way to know if any of them are actually my brother. Kyung could have lied about me having a brother. Or maybe I have one but his name isn't Jun, or maybe it is but he has a different last name."

I'm still standing in front of the window. The dark corners of the nearby buildings cut into the sky. Beyond them, more buildings. Beyond them, still more. People hurry past on the sidewalk—one, two, ten, a thousand. Faceless, nameless shadows.

The absolute hopelessness of ever finding my brother threatens to drown me. How does someone find one boy in a sea of buildings and people, especially a boy who may or may not even exist?

CHAPTER 17

"Do you know your mom's full name and date of birth?" Baz asks. "Maybe there's a birth announcement or some sort of medical records."

I shake my head. "I remember that people called her Hyun, but that might have just been part of her name. And Song was my father's last name."

"You don't know your mother's surname?"

I turn to face Baz. "I was only two when she gave us up. How much do you remember from that age?"

"Dude," Jesse interjects. "Winter's had a hellish couple of days. Maybe go take care of your business and finish the interrogation tomorrow?"

"No. It's fine," I say. "I'll give you all the information I can, if you really think you might be able to find my . . . family. What do you want to know?" I sink to the sofa, pull my feet up onto the cushions and sit cross-legged. Could I have a brother *and* a mother? Perhaps even a father somewhere? I'm not sure how I feel about that. I know the boy Kyung hired in Los Angeles could have been lying about everything, but it was easy to believe that both my parents were dead. Comforting, even. If I have a mother and father who are still alive, it would hurt to think about how they didn't try to find me. I'm not even sure I'd want to meet them anytime soon. They might be ashamed of me, of the fact that I am mentally ill.

Jesse sits next to me. He looks back and forth as Baz and I talk.

"What happened to your dad?" Baz asks.

"I don't remember him at all. I don't know his first name. I don't even know if they were married."

"Then how do you know Song is his name?"

"Because that's how it's done here," I say sharply. But even as I'm insisting I'm right, I know that I could be wrong. My mother could have given Rose and me her name if she really wanted to.

"What was the name of the orphanage you lived at?"

"Singing Crane," I tell Baz. "In Songpa-gu." I hadn't thought to look up the Singing Crane again. I guess it's possible they might have information on my mother, assuming she actually talked to a representative and signed us into their custody. I never knew for sure if we were documented orphans or if she just left us there knowing that eventually someone would find us.

"That's not a ton of information to go on, but I'll see what I can find out."

I nod. "I appreciate it."

"However," Baz says. "Even if we can find your mom or brother, I think it might be best to hold off on contacting them until after we regain control of the ViSE technology."

"But—"

"Kyung's people could be watching them. If he sees you make contact, it could put them in danger. Plus, I know you want to trust your family, but it's always possible UsuMed has some sort of hold over them."

"You're saying my own family would betray me."

"I'm saying I don't know." Baz grabs a sweatshirt from the back of the sofa and pulls it over his head.

"Fine," I say. "But then there's no reason for me to go to a PC bang with you. Maybe I'll hop on the subway and go check out the UsuMed building, just get a feel for the layout."

"I'll come with you," Jesse says.

Baz shakes his head. "Before anyone goes to UsuMed, we need to make a plan."

"Says who?" I narrow my eyes at him.

"Says me."

"Who put you in charge?"

"I put me in charge." Baz crosses the living room to the entryway. He starts to slide back into his shoes.

I rise from the sofa to face him. "Well, I didn't even ask you to come to Seoul, so—"

"Winter." He holds up a hand. "Do you know why surgeons aren't supposed to operate on family members?"

"Because they're too emotionally invested?"

"Yes. I get that you are pissed because Kyung tricked you and stole the tech, and your blood is teeming with vengeance because of what he did in the past, but that does not make for a good mission, if you know what I mean. When any of us go to UsuMed, we need to be calm, focused, purposeful in our actions. That way we won't be conspicuous."

"All right." I shrug. "But just because you're an emotionless robot doesn't mean I can turn off all my feelings too."

"Exactly, which is why I put myself in charge." Baz drums his fingertips against his arm. "We need to have a meeting first, make a list of objectives, come up with a solid plan."

"Our objective is to find the tech, steal it back, and then kill Kyung. I don't think we need a meeting for that," I scoff.

"Oh, okay," Baz says. "Well, maybe you can just hang out in the lobby and wait for Kyung to stroll in. You can ask him if he has the tech in his pocket and if he says yes, snap his neck. I'll go ahead and book our tickets home."

"That is not what I—"

Baz leans against the inside of the front door. "I took a bullet for you, so how about we try it my way?"

"As I recall, you took a bullet for Gideon," I point out. "Jesse took a bullet for me."

"Damn right." Jesse loops an arm over my shoulder.

"Well, I hope you two are this detail oriented when you head off to UsuMed to do some recon." Baz smirks. "Tomorrow. Once you've gotten some sleep and we've all sat down together and talked about everything."

I sigh. It probably would be dumb to go running off to UsuMed tonight, but my muscles are twitching, my nerves humming. Even though it's getting late, I can't just go to bed.

Jesse's still got his arm on me. "We could eat?" he suggests hopefully.

I glance at the time. "We ate about three hours ago."

"I know!" he exclaims.

"Feed the bottomless pit," Baz says. "I'll be back in an hour or so."

I don't have the energy to explain Korean food to Jesse tonight, so I take him to a Kentucky Fried Chicken a couple blocks down from our building.

It has the same red-and-white layout as KFC back in the States, but the menu is in Korean and some of the food options are different. Jesse's eyes widen as he scans the choices.

"It's probably a little different from what you're used to back home," I say. "But the chicken should taste about the same."

"Does this sandwich seriously have chicken patties for the buns and a bacon cheeseburger center?" Jesse asks, pointing at something called a Double Down King.

"Looks like it," I say.

"That's a little much, even for me."

He ends up ordering a fried chicken sandwich combo meal and I get myself a side of fries and a drink. We take our food upstairs and sit in a booth next to a big glass window where we can look out at the night. Below us, people mill around on the streets, meandering in and out of bars and browsing the various shops. Something specific catches Jesse's eye and I follow his gaze. A couple of guys in jeans and winter jackets are standing in front of a pub. Their close-cropped haircuts give them away as US military, probably from the nearby base at Yongsan.

I glance over at Jesse. His thick hair is longer now, but it's not much of a stretch to imagine him standing next to these guys. "I'm sorry," I say. "I didn't think about how being in this neighborhood might remind you of things."

"It's okay." Jesse drags a trio of French fries through a puddle of ketchup. "It's not like I'll ever forget, or that I even want to forget. Being in the military was a big part of my life. Just because it's over now doesn't make it any less meaningful to me."

I nod. I want to reach out and touch him, but that doesn't feel right. Instead, we finish our food in silence and head back to the apartment. Seoul is a city of layers and Jesse peels them back with his penetrating gaze, taking in the glitzy Western bars, the alleys sloping upward into cramped housing developments, the doorways leading to dark hallways that lead to offices and noodle shops the casual observer would never even know existed.

I unlock the front door to our building and turn toward the stairwell. Jesse follows me without question. We're both pretty slow on the stairs.

"How are you feeling?" I ask.

"Still sore, but I'm a little better each day."

"Good."

"Thanks for asking."

"You're welcome."

Jesse reaches out and grabs my arm. I pause on the third-floor landing to look back at him. He's a step below me, so we're almost eye to eye. "What is it?" I ask.

"Is this how things are going to be between us now?" he asks. "This awkward sort of politeness?"

I swallow hard. Jesse's eyes have always been my undoing.

The swirls of color, the depth, the warmth. "Are you asking me to be rude?"

He drags his hand down my arm. With one finger he traces the cross-shaped scar on my palm. "I'm asking you to be you."

"Oh." I force a smile. "I'm still figuring out who that is."

"Okay," Jesse says. "But I'm hoping someday we can find our way back to being friends at least."

"We're friends, aren't we?"

Jesse flares his nostrils. "Friends don't bullshit each other."

I cross my arms. "Don't they? Because I'm thinking the idea of you wanting to be my *friend* is kind of bullshit." I'm not normally the one to bring up Jesse's feelings for me, but he doesn't get to stand here and accuse me of being a liar when he's doing the same thing.

"I said 'at least,'" he points out. "I'm not trying to hide how I feel. I'm just trying not to throw it in your face, because I know it makes you uncomfortable."

"I'm sorry." It's not really an answer to anything, but it's all I have. Sometimes those words make people feel better, and I don't want Jesse to feel bad. I turn back to the stairs, focusing on each individual step like if I ascend enough of them, the solutions to all of my problems will be waiting at the top.

Jesse is right about his feelings making me uncomfortable, but he doesn't know the whole reason why. He thinks I don't want to be with him anymore because he slept with me when I was dissociating. That or because I found out he lied to me and helped Gideon trick me. That did—still does, when I think about it—make me angry, but I understand why they did it. I understand it was an impossible situation. I might even have done the same thing in their position.

But my feelings for Jesse are more complicated than that. I still struggle with the idea that he could really love me after finding out about my sex-trade past and current mental issues. I am not even in control of the person I am. I traveled thousands of miles to get here so I could kill someone. What about that is lovable? Maybe he just wants to save me because he's got the initials of four army buddies that he couldn't save inked onto his wrist. Maybe I'm just a penance for him and one day he'll decide he's atoned enough. If I give in and let myself love him, what happens if he leaves? I lost Rose and went crazy. I lost Gideon and became a killer. My sanity, my humanity—both gone.

I can't lose anyone else.

I don't have anything left to give.

I pass by the landing to the sixth floor. "I'm going to check out the roof."

"Why?"

"I don't know. Most apartment buildings and hotels here have roof access. Sometimes they have gardens or even mini-cafés."

"Cool. I'll come with you," Jesse says.

Of course he will. I almost ask him to go back to the apartment, to give me some space. But the thought of one day pushing him away for good crushes down on my chest. I need air. I need the cavernous expanse of night. But I need Jesse too, at least the possibility of him.

We exit out onto a wide, flat roof. There's a small area along the building with an overhang, where forgotten herbs and plants sit in various states of decomposition. The frigid night air stings my nasal passages and blows tendrils of my hair forward into my eyes.

"There's enough room to spar up here," I muse. It's only been a few days, but already my mind and body are suffering from the lack of exercise.

Jesse groans slightly. "Not sure I'm ready to go one-on-one with you yet."

I stride across the concrete to the roof's edge. The railing is only waist high. It occurs to me this is probably why Jesse didn't want me up here alone. I scared him once when I was in St. Louis. For all I know, I've scared him multiple times but blocked some of them out. I'm not suicidal, at least I don't think I am, but it's hard not to think about death sometimes, especially when I've repeatedly witnessed it up close and personal.

Jesse comes to stand next to me at the railing. "Does it feel weird being back here?"

"I don't think it's really sunk in yet," I say. "Other than hearing people speak Korean, I don't feel any differently from how I did in Los Angeles or St. Louis."

"Were you happy here?"

It's an interesting question. You would probably think that growing up in a city orphanage after your mother abandoned you would make for an unhappy childhood. It didn't, though—perhaps because I was surrounded by other girls who were all in the same circumstances as I was, or maybe just because my sister did such a good job of looking out for me.

"Yes," I say. "My situation wasn't ideal, but whose is? I have a lot of fond memories from here."

"I'm glad," Jesse says. His phone buzzes before I can think of anything else to say. He fishes it out of his pocket and looks at the screen. "Sebastian's back. He says it's time to make a plan."

CHAPTER 18

Baz and Jesse take seats on the sofa and I sit across from them on the floor. Jesse offers to scoot over so we can all fit, but I shake my head. I'm still chilled from being on the roof, and the heat coming up through the floor is warming my bones.

"I downloaded all the specs I could find on the UsuMed building onto my tablet. I also set a meet with two of my local contacts," Baz starts. "One is going to get me some supplies and weapons. The other is going to make sure we all have fake documents in case we need them to get out of the country."

"You're already making arrangements for leaving?" Jesse asks.

Baz shrugs. "I'm a big believer in contingency plans."

"You two can do what you want, but I'm not leaving without the tech," I say. "And not until I find Kyung."

"And by find, you mean . . ." Baz waits for me to fill in the blank.

I lick my lips and swallow hard. "It's like you said back in St. Louis. Sometimes the only way to end something completely is to end it completely."

Baz rubs at his chin, at the stubble of his blond beard. "Gideon left you plenty of money. We could hire someone to take care of Kyung."

It's a smart plan. Baz probably knows assassins we could

trust. But I want Kyung to know it was me. I want my face to be the last thing he ever sees. "What if I want to do it?"

"Killing someone is different in practice than it is in theory," Baz says quietly. "There are factors you can't prepare for, feelings in the moment where you'll question everything you thought you knew about yourself, other feelings that might follow you long after the deed is done."

"I killed Sung Jin," I say. "And some guy in Los Angeles."

"Did you enjoy it?" Baz asks.

Yes.

Apparently, part of me did.

"No, but I don't feel bad about it."

"Those were self-defense," Baz says. "Executing someone is different."

I know he's right. To be honest, it still bothers me that I'm not feeling any kind of remorse about killing Sung Jin or the man at the guesthouse. Maybe I'm still in shock, or maybe I feel like what I did was right. Those men were trying to hurt me, but no one has hurt me more than Kyung. "It's hard to explain, but this feels like self-defense too."

Jesse sits quietly through these exchanges, his jaw tense, hazel eyes flicking back and forth from Baz to me. I wonder what he's thinking.

"Believe me, I understand," Baz says. "I've executed multiple people in the name of defense. Sometimes the best defense is a good offense. But prioritize it for me. What matters more to you—regaining possession of the ViSE technology or killing Kyung?"

"Stealing back the tech," I say, even though the real answer is that I won't rest until I do both. But recovering the ViSE technology feels like something I'm doing for Gideon, and for anyone Kyung might hurt with the technology. Killing Kyung is more personal.

"Then let's talk about the technology first," Baz says. "And later we can talk about killing."

"Any idea how we can get inside UsuMed?" Jesse asks.

Baz pulls up a map of the city on his tablet and turns it so Jesse and I can see. I take note of some new subway stops and an entirely new line that's been built in the past few years.

"I don't think we want to just go in guns blazing," Baz says. "We need to be smart about it, figure out how to gain access in the middle of the night when we only have to evade a couple of security guards. But that building has twenty floors. We could spend all night looking and still not find what we want. We need to figure out exactly where the neural editor and headset are located. First, we need to do some recon. Once we see things, we'll have a better idea of what we're dealing with."

"Jesse and I can do that while you meet up with your spy friends," I say.

"Well, only one of them can meet me tomorrow, but I see no point in all three of us going to UsuMed, so if you two want to go, that's fine."

"What, specifically, are we looking for?" Jesse asks.

Baz clears his throat. "Let's start with photos and/or ViSE footage of the front of the building, the front doors, the locks on the front doors, the lobby, the elevators, the back doors, a door to the parking garage, and the elevator in the parking garage. Also get footage of the buildings directly next door to UsuMed as well as across the street—just general images so we know how tall they are and what kind of businesses are in them." Baz rubs at his beard stubble again. "If they won't be able to fix the neural editor without help, we should have some time to come up with a workable plan." He turns to me. "Are you sure no one can access Gideon's notes?"

"I'm sure," I say. The snowflake necklace feels heavy around my neck. "What if they can fix the neural editor without them, though?" I ask. "Or what if all they really wanted was the recorder headset?"

"Then we're probably screwed," Baz says. "But I prefer not to get distracted by worst-case scenarios. Gideon was the smartest guy I knew. If he was worried about the ViSE tech being stolen, whatever he did is probably not going to be easy to fix."

"All right." I lift myself up from the floor. "I'm going to get some sleep. It sounds like tomorrow is going to be a busy day."

"That reminds me." Baz hops up and pulls a small amber bottle from one of the kitchen cabinets. "I went by the penthouse before I left St. Louis and made sure Gideon's valuables were secure. I grabbed a couple of recorder headsets and some blank memory cards just in case we need them. I saw these while I was there." He tosses me the bottle. "I figured you might want them to help you sleep or whatever."

It's the antianxiety medicine I sometimes take when I feel a panic attack coming on. I try not to take them unless it's an emergency. I like the way they make me feel—blunted, cocooned—but right now I need to stay sharp.

"Thanks," I say.

"And I'm supposed to ask if you're keeping up with your studies," Baz adds.

I make a face at him. "You're joking, right?"

"I promised Gideon I would look out for you."

The way he says it makes me wonder if he was the one who recorded the ViSE Gideon left me, but I can't bring myself to ask. It feels too personal, like it's not my business whether he let Gideon talk to him and touch him so intimately.

"I haven't logged into my virtual classroom for several days, so I'm going to fail this session, but once we deal with things here, I'll reregister for classes." I roll my eyes. "That all right with you, Dad?"

A funny look flits across Baz's face, so quickly I might have imagined it, but it makes me wonder about who he really is, and how he ended up working for Gideon. "I guess it'll have to do," he says.

As I head for my room, I think about the seemingly impossible task of locating the ViSE tech in a twenty-story building.

Kyung said he wanted the technology to turn it over to one of Usu's tech companies, but I don't believe that's all it is. He might be evil, but he's also a shrewd businessman. I can't believe he'd go through the trouble of hiring someone to pretend to be my brother and sending men to my guesthouse to abduct me just to gain access to technology and pass it along to a sister company.

No, Kyung wants the headsets and neural editor for some other reason. A personal one. But what could it be?

CHAPTER 19

The next morning we're all awake early, thanks to a combination of jet lag and nervous energy. Jesse and I head to the nearest subway station. The lobby level is quiet at this hour on a Saturday; the small shops located inside it are closed. It's funny how different subway stations look during rush hour, when some of them almost feel like small cities. I buy each of us a T-money card and add 20,000 won to them.

"How much is that?" he asks.

"Around twenty dollars, depending on the exchange rate. The subway is fairly cheap, though, so it should last awhile."

We take two long escalators down to the platform level. An LCD board shows that our train will be arriving shortly. To Jesse's relief, it's not very crowded. We step into the gray-and-white car and take seats just inside the sliding glass doors. Most of the people in our car seem to be wearing the same white earbuds attached to the newest Samsung phone. They're fixated on their screens; no one is talking or paying attention to anyone else. I study the clothes they're wearing so I can figure out what to buy myself.

As we pull into the next station, more people get on, but not so many that anyone has to stand. An older woman holding hands with a boy about five or six steps into our car wearing a paper surgical mask over her mouth and nose. She sits next to me.

The boy stands in the aisle, secure between her knees. The bottoms of his shoes light up as he stamps his feet. *"Eomma,"* he exclaims. The Korean word for "mommy." He points at something in the station as the train starts to move. "Eomma," he says again. The woman shushes him and he falls silent. He looks over at me with sad, dark eyes. I give him a tiny smile.

"Why are there people wearing masks?" Jesse asks me in a low voice. "Is there some sort of flu going around?"

I shake my head. "Most people don't take sick days here unless they can't get out of bed, so they wear the masks in order not to infect others."

"A third of the people on this train are sick?" Jesse asks dubiously.

I glance around. I hadn't realized how many people were wearing masks. This was fairly common even when I was little, so it doesn't stand out to me. "They wear them for other reasons too, like to block out the pollution or keep their faces warm. I've heard that girls wear them when they don't feel like putting on makeup or sometimes just because."

A pair of high school girls holding hands and wearing matching Hello Kitty masks get on at the next stop. "Wow, they even have them in designs," Jesse says.

"Koreans are a fashionable people," I say with a grin.

When we arrive at Gangnam Station, Jesse is astounded by the main level. Corridors snake off in several directions, filled with shops selling clothes and shoes and souvenirs and all types of food.

"It's like an entire underground shopping mall," he says.

"More or less."

We make our way through the long rows of shops and eateries—a sprinkling of which have opened for business—and exit the subway tunnels. As we walk past the front of the UsuMed building, I slow down and look around, being sure to capture ViSE footage like Baz instructed. Jesse snaps some photos with his cell phone, like he's a tourist out for an early morning stroll.

We cross the street to a red-and-gray building called Shinsa Tower. Inside, there's a coffee shop with a banner in the window advertising something called honey bread. It smells delicious. I pull Jesse over to a corner and we stand next to a giant potted plant, scanning the doors and the lobby. While Jesse pretends to be checking something on his phone, I record as much information about this building as I can without arousing the suspicion of the security guard who stands next to the alcove where the elevators are located.

Jesse and I repeat this pattern at the buildings on either side of UsuMed, pausing in the Hyundai building to buy coffee and the lobby of the Woori Bank to use the ATMs. All we have left to do is gather info on the actual UsuMed building. I stride up the steps, pause for just a second in front of the main entrance, glancing down to capture whatever information Baz is hoping to get about the door locks. There's a coffee shop in here too, located next to the back entrance. I stride toward the elevators, where a couple men in rumpled suits are clutching cups of coffee. They look less than thrilled to be working on a Saturday. Jesse hangs back near the entrance to the building—probably trying to get some pictures of the different doors.

I pretend to be studying the directory of what businesses are in the building—all the floors seem to be owned exclusively by UsuMed except for the main floor, which has a restaurant in addition to the coffee shop. The directory tells which departments are located on which floors. I notice floors B1 and B2 are marked private, with B3 being the first of two levels designated for parking.

The elevator dings and the men move forward, one of them giving me a quizzical look as I step away. I motion for Jesse to join me and we exit out the back of the building, him taking a few pictures and me looking everywhere to capture as much as possible on the ViSE.

"What now?" Jesse exhales a puff of mist into the chilly air.

"Feel like doing a little shopping? I need to get some clothes, and we might as well pick up some things for the apartment while we're out."

"I'm up for whatever," he says. "Should we hit up the shops at the subway station?"

"We could." I adjust my wig to cover my ears. It's eerie how the weather here is exactly like the weather back in St. Louis. "But if you don't mind shopping outside, how about we check out the most popular market in the city?"

"Sounds good to me," Jesse says. "Lead the way."

Namdaemun Market is both the oldest and largest market in all of Korea. Jesse rests one hand on my back as we exit the subway station and head toward the nearest gate. Tall buildings, both traditional and modern, line the busy streets. Vendors crowd the sidewalk selling dumplings, noodles, and dried fish. Korean flags, with their bright red-and-blue yin-yangs, flap in the breeze above their carts.

We reach Gate Five and turn in to the market proper. Tibetan prayer flags hang from wires that stretch across the path. Saturday is a prime shopping day and people are streaming in and out. It's chaos, but at least the crush of bodies provides a little shelter from the cold. I take Jesse's hand so he doesn't get swept up in the quick-moving shoppers. He scans the rows of market stalls selling everything from squid jerky to T-shirts to electronics.

"This place is huge," he says.

"Better selection than the subway station, and the prices are good." I pause just inside a stall while Jesse checks out some military surplus gear. There are displays of camouflage pants and tops along with duffel bags and other army items—

most of it American. I wonder if the soldiers sell their excess stuff before they get discharged.

The vendor hurries over and speaks to me in Korean. I tell him Jesse is just looking but then ask him if he sells knives. I need to replace the ones I left in Los Angeles.

"Only these." He leads me over to a case of folding pocketknives, most of them small enough to fit on keychains. "Anything else requires a permit."

Jesse comes up behind me. "Looking for new knives?"

"Yes, but they only sell pocketknives here. Bigger knives require a permit."

"Baz can probably hook you up."

"True," I say, but I'm only half listening. Across the crowded market aisle, in a booth selling pots and pans, a woman wearing a black wool jacket and a green scarf seems to be staring at me. She's also wearing a pair of wide sunglasses and a paper surgical mask, making it impossible to determine what she looks like. My heart starts pounding and I have to tuck my hands into my pockets to hide the fact that they're shaking. What if she works for Kyung? What if he already knows that we're here?

"Winter?" Jesse has picked up on my sudden change of mood. "You okay?"

"Come on." I keep my eyes trained on the woman as Jesse and I leave the stall, but she turns her attention to a display of rice cookers and makes no move to follow us. I toss a glance back over my shoulder as we turn the corner onto a main aisle of the market, but the woman has disappeared from view. Stopping at some large square bins that run down the middle of the market rows, I quickly pick out some clothing to replace the stuff I left behind in Los Angeles.

As the clerk is putting my purchases in a plain black bag, I feel a prickling sensation. Sure enough, I catch a glimpse of a splash of green in my peripheral vision. I turn, ever so slightly. It's the same woman. She's looking down at her phone as she stands in line at a food cart, but I swear I felt her eyes on me a second ago.

"I think we're being watched," I murmur, just loud enough for Jesse to hear.

"What?" He furrows his brow. "By who?"

"There's a woman down the row, at the food cart with the gray-and-white tarp roof."

"There's a lot of women at that stand." Jesse starts to move closer for a better look but I grab his hand.

"Don't," I say. "It's the one with the green scarf. If she doesn't know we're onto her, we can follow her. Maybe she'll lead us right to Kyung."

"I thought we were going to find Kyung at UsuMed," Jesse says softly, but he turns his focus back to me. I pull out my phone and pretend to be showing Jesse something on the screen. Slowly I lift the phone so I can snap a picture of the mysterious woman. The ViSE I'm recording might be helpful, but I need a photo if I want to zoom in.

The woman is still wearing sunglasses but I feel our eyes meet for a split second. Without warning, she steps out of line and starts hurrying away from the cart. The back of her scarf sparkles in the sun. It must have some sort of reflective threads woven into it.

"Damn it." I loop my shopping bag around my wrist and start to push through the crowd after her.

"Winter!" Jesse is trying to follow me but he's too big to navigate the crush of people.

I don't look back. I can't. I'm focused on the green of the woman's scarf. She turns down a row that leads out to the main road and I follow. The woman ducks through the gate and out onto the street. I elbow my way past clusters of old men who are huddled around the food carts, slurping noodles or spearing steamed dumplings on their silver chopsticks.

The woman quickens her pace as she heads for a covered set of stairs. At first I think she's heading for the subway, but then I realize it's just an underground arcade—a pass-through for people to cross the street, probably connected to a network of shops that links back to the market itself. A cell phone falls from her hand as she hits the top of the stairs. She bends down quickly to retrieve it and the sleeve of her coat rides up, exposing a black tattoo on the inside of her forearm. I squint, but I'm too far away to see what it is—a bird, maybe.

"Winter!" Jesse grabs my hand from behind and I stumble, accidentally bumping into a man with a cart of persimmons and sending a handful of them to the gray sidewalk. Swearing under my breath, I kneel down to retrieve the bright-orange fruit.

"Sorry." Jesse looks chagrined as he bends down to help me. "But what are you—"

"Not now. Come on." I mutter an apology to the persimmon vendor and hurry down the stairs after the woman. At the bottom, the tunnel predictably leads in multiple directions. She could have gone right back up to the same sidewalk or crossed under the street and continued in either direction. There is no one around except for a homeless man sitting with his back against the brick wall, his eyes closed. There's a stone bowl set in front of him, a few crumpled paper bills tucked into it with a smattering of coins.

"*Ajussi*," I say. The man stirs but doesn't look at me. "The woman with the green scarf. Did you see which way she went?" I ask in Korean, a trace of impatience creeping into my voice.

His eyelids flick open revealing milky, sightless eyes. "I was sleeping," he mutters.

"Sorry." My shoulders slump forward as I exhale deeply. Wherever she went, she's gone by now.

Jesse rests a hand on my shoulder. "What were you going to do if you caught up with her?"

"I don't know." I dig into my purse and drop a few thousand won in the old man's bowl. "Ask her why she was watching us?"

I turn back to the stairs. "If you don't know for sure she was watching us then why would she run?"

"She didn't really run, that I saw. She just turned and left the marketplace . . . Maybe she got a text from someone."

"So you think I'm paranoid, then?" I call up the photo I took and zoom in on the woman's face as we head back up to the sidewalk. It's impossible to even gauge how old she is behind the sunglasses and surgical mask.

"I don't know," Jesse says. "I just don't see any way Kyung could possibly know we're here already, and I didn't see that woman at UsuMed. Did you?"

"No, but I was focused on getting in and out of the buildings without arousing suspicion."

"I definitely didn't see her. Maybe she just took off because she thought *you* were watching *her.*"

I lift my gaze to meet Jesse's. Concern flickers in his hazel eyes. "Maybe," I admit reluctantly. But inside I'm not convinced.

When we get back to the apartment, I replay the ViSE footage, looking for any clues I might have missed. I focus on the woman with the green scarf, but there's nothing familiar about her. And Jesse's right: what I thought was her running away was really just her walking quickly.

I pull off the ViSE headset and check out the cell phone picture again, swiping the screen to enlarge the photo.

"What are you looking at?" Baz leans over my shoulder.

"I thought this woman was following Jesse and me at the market today," I say. "Do you recognize her?"

"Not much to recognize," Baz says. "Did she approach you?"

"No, but when she caught me looking at her, she left in a hurry."

Baz shrugs. "Probably just a coincidence, don't you think?"

"I guess." I've definitely been on edge since being attacked

in Koreatown. Maybe my brain is seeing threats where are none.

On Monday, Jesse and I return to UsuMed in the early mo[rn]ing to see if we can catch a glimpse of Kyung. We arrive arou[nd] seven a.m. but there's no one coming and going yet.

I buy a coffee for Jesse and a tea for me and then scan the area, looking for a place we can loiter without being conspicuous. I decide upon a bench in front of the Shinsa Tower building across the street. There's a metal sculpture here that looks to be a fountain, but there's no water spraying, just a thin coating of ice in the basin at the bottom.

I sip my drink and try to make it seem like I'm looking past the UsuMed entrance, not directly at it. An old woman with a broom and dustpan is sweeping up bits of trash in front of the building.

"How are you ever going to recognize anyone from this far away?" Jesse asks.

The prongs of my recorder headset feel cool beneath my wig. "We can move closer once there are more people out on the street and we won't be as conspicuous, but something tells me I'll be able to identify Kyung from this distance."

Jesse doesn't respond and I wonder if he's thinking about the fact that I'm so eager to end the life of another human being. What kind of person has the means and money to hire a competent hit man and says, "I want to do it myself"?

An insane person.

A brave person.

Who cares what kind of person?

I let the voices in my head argue it out for a few more minutes. Finally they grow quiet, but there's still not anyone showing up for work.

To pass the time, Jesse points out unfamiliar things and asks me to explain them. "Why are there so many guys in skinny jeans?" he asks. "And scarves?"

I grin. "Like I told you, we are a fashionable people."

He scans the sidewalk as a wave of people who probably all got off the same subway train pass in front of us and move down the street. "So many more scarves than hats or gloves. Do they really keep you warm? Maybe I should try one."

"I could've bought you a Hello Kitty scarf from the market." I wink. "Miso would've approved."

"Moo!" Jesse exclaims. "I miss that little guy. What's the first thing we should do for him when we get home?"

"Promise never to call him Moo again?"

"You know he likes it." Jesse kicks at my boot with one of his own. "Do you suppose by the time we get back he'll have fallen in love with Natalie and forgotten us?"

"Me, maybe," I say. "Not you. He loves you."

Jesse grins. "He has good taste."

The first wave of employees starts to trickle into UsuMed just before eight A.M. They're mostly blue-collar types in service clothes or women in secretarial garb. Another half an hour passes and I see a group of men and women in dark suits approaching from the direction of the subway.

"Executives probably start at nine," I murmur. "Let's get closer." We cross the street to the front of the building. Some of the employees hurrying up the steps are wearing laminated badges on lanyards. I break away from Jesse for a second in order to bump into one of them. I want to get close enough to get a good visual of what the badges look like, just in case there might be some way to manufacture a duplicate.

Suddenly I see a flash of green out of the corner of my eye. There's a girl across the street standing just behind the bench where Jesse and I were sitting a few minutes ago. Is it the same girl from Namdaemun Market? Was she eavesdropping on us? I can't be sure.

The girl catches me looking at her and ducks her chin to her chest. She turns and hurries off down the sidewalk, the sun reflecting off silvery threads in her green scarf.

Instinctively, I dart out into the street to try to follow her. A horn blares. A bright orange taxicab slams on the brakes, the bumper just inches from my legs. My heart thuds in my chest. *Get back on the sidewalk.* A truck in the next lane swerves slightly as it screeches past. A couple men on the sidewalk point at me and frown. The cabdriver leans his head out the window and hollers at me.

"Winter, what are you doing?" Jesse rushes to the curb.

I look from him to the other side of the street. More cars are coming. It's not safe to cross. I hold up a hand to apologize to the cabdriver and turn back to the sidewalk in front of UsuMed. "Sorry," I mumble, as I reach Jesse's side. "But try not to yell my name like that."

"You're right." He shakes his head. "That was stupid on my part. I just saw you out in the street and panicked."

"I thought I saw the girl from Namdaemun Market. The one who was watching us." Across the street, a steady stream of people moves down the sidewalk, but I don't see the girl with the green scarf anywhere. "But if I did, she's gone now."

Before Jesse can respond, a trio of big black cars pulls up in front of the building. My heart starts to race again. Inside me, something pulls, dark and angry, urging me to rush forward, to rip open the back doors and force the inhabitants out onto the cold street.

I think of Rose calling Jesse for help, of a possible second alter named Lily. A thirteen-year-old girl in my brain, a thirteen-year-old killer. It seems like the stuff of fantasy, but so many impossible things have recently shown themselves to be true.

I'm real.

"Shh," I say to her, or to whatever might be rising up beneath my skin. "Calm down."

One at a time, the drivers get out and open the back doors for the passengers.

"Can you get pictures of those license plates?" I ask Jesse, my voice wavering slightly. A man with the bulk of a private security guard emerges from the first car. He scans the sidewalk and then gestures at the vehicle. Two men in dark suits and black woolen coats emerge from inside. The hair on the back of my neck pricks up.

"I can get two of them at least." Jesse snaps a couple of images.

More men exit the other vehicles, but there's something about one of the men from the first car that has me on edge. My eyes cling to him as he steps to the side of the revolving door to take a phone call. Just a hint of a dark red tie is visible above the top button of his coat.

My mind flashes back to that day in Los Angeles. *Not exactly what I was hoping for, but I guess they'll do.*

It's him. It's Kyung.

CHAPTER 20

The darkness thrashes around inside of me, an angry raven beating its wings against the bars of a tiny cage.

"Let's get out of here," I mutter, turning and hurrying for the subway station. Jesse follows me as I race down the stairs.

"What happened?" he asks.

"Kyung." I slap my T-money card on the reader and pass through the turnstile.

"For sure?"

"For sure." I bite my lip and then turn toward the subway platform that will take us back to Itaewon. I pace back and forth on the platform, counting the tiles beneath my feet, doing my best to slow my breath and heart rate. "I felt Lily in me. Or something."

"What?" Jesse says. He adjusts his hearing aid and it whistles sharply for a second.

I start to repeat what I said, but my voice is lost as a train roars into the station. "Never mind."

The Plexiglas doors open and a sea of people pours out into the station. I push my way onto the train with Jesse behind me. We stand close together in the aisle, the car crammed with morning commuters in their sharp suits, their woolen hats and coats.

The car jolts on the tracks and I pitch forward. Jesse reaches out to steady me, one hand landing on my waist. He braces me with his body as the car continues to shimmy and shake.

For once I let myself enjoy the feeling of him against me—solid, muscular. Warm. I drink in the sensation of human touch, trying not to think about the way I felt when I saw Kyung.

Back at the apartment, I jump in the shower while Jesse makes breakfast. I stand under the hot water, suddenly longing for the hard pressure of the showers back in St. Louis. This one is barely a trickle and seeing Kyung has left me feeling filthy.

There's a gentle knock on the door. "Win, you okay?" Jesse asks.

It occurs to me I have no idea how long I've been in here.

A long time, apparently, because by the time I dry off and change into clean clothes, Sebastian is back from his meeting and Jesse is remaking breakfast because his first attempt got cold.

He gestures at a pot of something gummy and white that probably resembled rice at some point. He's making pancakes and bacon in another pan. I've never been a fan of bacon, but right now it smells amazing.

Baz is sitting on the sofa in the living room scanning something on his tablet. He's dressed in jeans and a baseball cap again. I peek over his shoulder, but he swipes at the screen and the tablet goes dark. He makes a big point of stretching. "Are you going to be done making that breakfast soon?" he asks Jesse. "It's almost time for lunch."

"Funny," Jesse says. "I don't see you offering to cook."

Baz strolls into the kitchen. "My idea of cooking is calling for delivery."

I stir the gummy rice, trying not to smile at the way it congeals to the spoon and doesn't want to let go. "That bacon is actually looking pretty good," I say. "Maybe I'll have an unhealthy American breakfast today."

"My rice is terrible, isn't it?" Jesse asks.

"That's rice?" Baz says. "I thought maybe it was grits or some weird Mexican shit."

I can't help it. I start giggling. "Don't feel bad. Rice is really hard to cook. A lot of Koreans use a rice cooker." I lift my eyes to Jesse's and give him a small smile. "Thank you for trying."

"You're welcome," he says, turning to glare at Baz. "I'll show you weird Mexican shit," he mumbles under his breath.

I rest a hand on Jesse's arm. "The pancakes and bacon look amazing."

He looks down at the pan. "They do, don't they?"

"Not to interrupt this tender moment, but how did your intel gathering go?" Baz asks, as he scoops a couple of pancakes off a serving plate and drizzles them with honey.

I give him a summary of when the UsuMed employees go to work and then hand over the headset and recording so he can see for himself. He heads for the living room couch with Jesse and me following with our plates. We eat quietly while he vises, not wanting to create overlay, additional sensory experiences from the real world that can cause nausea and disorientation.

Baz pauses halfway through the recording. "Here's something interesting. When you bumped that guy to get a close-up of his badge, you also got a shot of two girls behind him. Their badges are different. 'Cheonma Staffing Agency.' "

"Meaning they're temps." I remember how Gideon was able to get Natalie, another of his recorders, hired as a temp for Phantasm.

"Yep," Baz says. "Could be useful."

He finishes the recordings, seemingly unfazed by the rush of anger I felt when I saw Kyung. Next he skims through Jesse's photographs. "Nice job getting these license plates. I'll get them run by tomorrow at the latest. If one of these cars belongs to Kyung, hopefully it'll be registered to him. In the meantime, I'm going to see if I can track down a hacker."

"A hacker? Why?"

"Some of these access points have card readers." He points to a picture Jesse took in the elevator and another one of the back doors to the building. "We're going to need a list of UsuMed employees. Preferably ones with all-access badges."

Baz doesn't know any hackers, but it only takes him about an hour to track down a friend of a friend who was actually trained in cyber warfare by the Korean government.

I'm sitting on the floor of the living room, my back against the wall. "The government is training hackers?"

"Absolutely." Baz taps out a short reply to someone on his phone. "Ever since the North Korean cyber attacks on government and banking websites about ten years back. Some people don't really think of North Korea as a threat the way they do certain other countries, but make no mistake: the North Koreans are a lot more sophisticated and ambitious than most of us realize."

"So he can help us?" Jesse asks.

"He's willing to meet with us," Baz says. "I suggested the PC bang, but I'm waiting for a confirmation. If he agrees, I think you should come with me, Winter."

"Why me?" I ask. "I don't know anything about hacking."

"This kid just finished his mandatory military service, which means he's probably not much older than you. A hot girl could come in handy if he needs a little extra persuading."

"I'm not in the persuasion business," I say pointedly.

"Yeah," Jesse tacks on, clearly not liking where this conversation is headed.

Baz snorts. "Jesus. I just meant like some flirting or something."

My turn to snort. "If you knew me at all, you'd know I'm not exactly good at that."

"Part of you is," he says. "You forget that I've seen you in action."

I did forget that. Or maybe I conveniently chose not to remember it. Baz was following me for Gideon when I was dissociating and going out as Rose. He's probably seen me do all sorts of things. "Fine. I'll play nice with him, but I can't dissociate on command, so apologies in advance if my *flirting* does more harm than good."

"I'll come too," Jesse says. "I can hang back in the corner or outside, just in case you guys need help."

"No," Baz says. "You'll be too conspicuous. It'll look like we brought an American soldier for backup. I get that you want to protect Winter, but I assure you we'll be fine."

Jesse sighs. "Well, what do you want me to do then?"

Baz glances over at the kitchen area. "Dishes?"

Jesse's eyes narrow and I jump in quickly. "Maybe you can go over the schematics for UsuMed that Baz downloaded the other night? See if you can optimize the different ways we might be able to access the building once we know for certain where the tech is kept?" It's a busywork assignment, since the location of the tech will most likely be the deciding factor in where we should break in, but hopefully it'll at least make Jesse feel useful.

"Fine." He gives me a look and I know he's not fooled, but at least I'm not treating him like a maid.

"Here we go." Baz holds up one finger as he clicks on a new text message with the other one. "He says he can meet me in two hours, but not here. We're supposed to take the subway to a station across town and leave via exit 5. There's a PC bang a couple blocks past the exit he says is safe for a meeting."

South Korean PC bangs aren't much like the Internet cafés back in the United States. This one is in the basement of a building that also houses a nail salon and a noodle shop. At first I think it must be closed—how can anyone be running a business in such dim lighting—but when I press the button, the glass door slides open. I step inside where I'm immediately assaulted by the scent of smoke. I cough, wishing I had one of the surgical masks so many people are wearing to block out part of the noxious fumes hanging in the air.

Baz gives me a look. "Suck it up."

"Why would he suggest this place?" I ask. "It's not exactly private."

There are about one hundred computers from what I can see, arranged in horseshoe-shaped clusters to facilitate cooperative game play. Each computer station has its own headset and is separated from the next user by small fiberglass walls on either side of the widescreen monitor.

"It is anonymous, though," Baz murmurs. He pays for an hour of time and a bag of crispy squid snacks. The guy behind the desk gives him a card with a generic login ID and tells him he can sit at any computer he wants.

"Tasty," I say, gesturing to the small foil bag in his hand.

"I was told to buy them," Baz says. "He's probably going to use them to make a positive ID."

"I see."

Baz scans the clusters of terminals. "We're supposed to sit at computer ninety-three."

"I can't see anything in this light," I grumble.

We wander from cluster to cluster until we find computer ninety-three, which thankfully is unoccupied. Baz slides into the leather executive chair and I pull a chair over from the next computer and squeeze in next to him. Baz flips on the computer and the letters on the keyboard light up blue. He logs in with the information given to him.

Behind us, a cheer goes up from a group of college boys in headsets. They seem to all be attacking some kind of mutated zombie that's wreaking havoc on what looks like a military base. Their winter coats and messenger bags are draped all over. I can't help but think about how easy it would be to steal from them while they're so engrossed in their virtual pursuits.

I turn back to what Baz is doing. Our computer screen has a shortcut for Google and Daum, a popular Korean web portal. The wallpaper is a group of sexy anime girls in provocative positions.

"If this kid is into girls who look like that, I'm not sure any amount of flirting I do is going to be helpful," I say.

"Don't sell yourself short," Baz says. "You're hot in a 'she might bite your head off after sex' kind of way."

"Nice. Make fun of a girl with mental illness."

"Oh, I wasn't talking about your murderous alter," he says with a wink. "Lighten up and learn to take a compliment."

"Learn to give one," I snap back.

Baz smiles. "You remind me so much of Gideon sometimes. So serious and intense until someone starts pushing your buttons."

"And then?"

"Sharp, witty. Possibly even fun." He opens a window for Google mail. "Look away," he tells me.

I scan the other side of the room while Baz inputs his password. There's a second cluster of college boys playing the same zombie game as the kids behind us and then a pair of older men playing some kind of strategy game with tanks. Pictures of superheroes—some printed and some painted—hang above each workstation.

"I never really thought of Gideon as fun," I say.

"Yeah. It was a side he didn't let out too often." Baz pauses. "I know some of the things he and I did were pretty messed up, but you know he loved you like a daughter, right? If you believe anything about him, believe that."

"I do," I say softly.

"Good." Baz's eyes are still focused on the screen.

A new message pops up in his inbox. As Baz clicks on it, a guy in a hoodie and a baseball cap pulled low approaches. He grabs a chair from an empty station and positions it on the other side of Baz. But he doesn't sit. I can't really make out any features in the dim lighting, but Baz is right about him looking young.

"Who's this?" He gestures toward me.

"She's a friend you can trust. Are you Chung?"

"Some people call me that." The kid gives me a long look. "Do I need to pat her down?"

"I wouldn't. She doesn't like to be touched. Besides, if anyone needs to worry about recording devices, it's me."

Apparently this satisfies Chung. He lowers his body into the chair next to Baz. "What's up?" he asks.

"I'm looking for some technical support," Baz says.

"Is that so? What happened?"

I listen quietly, impressed by Chung's fluent English and almost perfect American accent. I wonder if he spent time studying overseas.

"I got locked out of my work account," Baz says.

"Where do you work?" Chung asks.

Baz drops his voice. "UsuMed."

Chung whistles. "That's unfortunate. I'm not sure I can help with that."

"What about Cheonma Staffing? My, uh, friend here works for them."

"Hi," I say, in what I hope is a flirty voice.

Chung grunts an acknowledgment to me. "That I can probably help with." He nudges Baz with his elbow and Baz scoots his chair over so the guy is in front of the screen.

I hop up from my chair. "I'm going to step outside for—"

"Stay," Baz commands.

"Actually," Chung says, "can you grab me a coffee? I've been up for a day and a half and I'm starting to crash."

Baz grins at me. "Be a dear and get us each a coffee, will you? I'll take a latte."

"Americano for me." Chung is completely focused on the screen. I might as well be a robot or an old ajumma.

Muttering under my breath, I make my way up to the front counter and order Baz and his new friend each a coffee. Now I know how Jesse feels about being told to do the dishes while everyone else handles the "real work."

While the drinks are being made, I scope out the entirety

of the PC bang. The room has filled up some since Baz and I arrived. Besides me, there is only one girl in the whole place and she's hanging out in a little glass booth in the center of the room that I think is supposed to be a smoking area. Maybe it's there just so people won't get ash all over the keyboards, but it's definitely not preventing mass inhalation of second-hand smoke. I feel like I've smoked a half-dozen cigarettes since we arrived.

Beyond the glass booth is a hallway with a sign hanging from the ceiling. I squint and can just barely make out the word *bathrooms*.

The kid behind the counter hands me the drinks and I return to our computer, where Baz and Chung are copying files to a flash drive.

"Are we finding what we need?" I ask, giving them their coffees.

"It's a start, anyway," Baz says, pulling a sealed envelope out of his jacket pocket. "There's more where that came from if you're able to help with my other problem."

Chung slips the envelope into his messenger bag. He polishes his glasses on his shirt and then looks back and forth from Baz to me. "Are you guys a couple?" he asks suddenly.

"What?" I snap, a little more sharply than I intended. "No. Not at all."

Baz chuckles. "She's a little uptight for my tastes."

Chung drops his voice. "So then is there any chance you might want to hang out with me some night?"

I am so surprised by this turn of events that I almost spill Baz's coffee all over the keyboard. At no point did Chung even look at me except when he was trying to decide if this was all a setup and I was wearing a wire. "I guess I could," I say hesitantly. "Depending on what you mean by 'hang out.'"

Chung laughs, like a full belly laugh. His face reddens a little. "Not you." He turns to Baz. "You."

I suck in a sharp breath. Does this kid seriously think

Sebastian is gay? I glance nervously around the PC bang as Baz's jaw goes tight. I hope he doesn't make a scene.

Baz grabs Chung by the scruff of his shirt and lifts him from his chair. "Let's have a quick chat, shall we?" He pushes Chung in the direction of the back hallway that leads to the bathrooms.

"Sebastian," I say. "Don't forget we have to focus on the mission. Not let our emotions get in the way. All of those things you told me."

"Oh, I'm very focused," Baz says. "I just need to clarify something for our new friend."

One of the boys from the zombie game cluster has noticed the situation. "Is he going to kill him?"

"Hopefully not," I say.

As the minutes tick by, I start to worry. I rise from my chair and try to decide if I should go intervene. But maybe they're just talking. Baz didn't look mad, exactly, when he pulled Chung toward the bathroom. It's possible everything is fine. I transfer my weight from one foot to the other. Just as I'm about to go see what's happening, Baz strides out of the bathroom. There's no immediate sign of Chung and I'm wondering if trusting Baz was the best idea after all. But then the door to the bathroom opens again, slowly, and Chung emerges. His shirt is a bit rumpled and he looks a little dazed, but there are no obvious wounds.

I grab my coat and purse. "We should probably go, right?"

Before Baz can respond, Chung makes his way back to us. "I'll do my best to get you the rest of your information." He nods as he tugs the brim of his hat low over his face.

"Sounds good," Baz says. "I'll call you." He's logging off the terminal now. He's focused on the screen, not looking at me or Chung.

Chung exits through the back door of the PC bang. The kids behind the counter who rent out the machines probably never even knew he was here.

"What just happened?" I say. "I was afraid you were going to kill that kid."

"Why? Do I look like a homophobic asshole to you?"

"If we're being honest, kind of?"

"Well, I'm not," Baz says wryly. "Let's get out of here."

I slide my coat back on and train my eyes on the floor as we make our way back to the counter. We leave the PC bang and turn toward the subway station.

Outside, the bright sun takes the edge off another blustery winter day. I tuck my hands deep into my pockets. "Seriously. What happened in there?" I ask again.

Baz chuckles. "You don't want to know."

Chung is standing outside the subway station smoking a cigarette. He doesn't say a word, but the look he gives Baz as we walk by is impossible to confuse.

"Wait a second." I start down the subway stairs right behind Baz. "Did the two of you . . . please tell me you didn't hook up with a strange guy just to get information about UsuMed. I'm not sure what Gideon told you about my past but—"

"I know about your past," Baz says. "Look. If I tell you I didn't mind, will you drop it?"

"All right." *I didn't mind?* What does that even mean? We pass through the station turnstiles and find the escalator that leads down to our platform. I pace back and forth for a few seconds but I can't stop wondering. "So you're . . . gay?" I whisper.

"That is not dropping it," Baz says.

"Sorry. I guess I'm just surprised."

"You should probably stop judging people by their looks, then." He pauses. "And I'm bi, not gay."

I've never met a bisexual person, or for that matter a gay person. It suddenly strikes me how tiny and isolated my world has been. "Is that why you quit working for the government?"

Baz laughs out loud. "Are you kidding me? If my employers had known, I'm quite certain they would've put that particular attribute to very good use. But like you, I prefer to make my own choices about who I sleep with, so I didn't exactly advertise my preferences."

The train roars into the station. "I still can't believe you . . . So you *like* him?" I press. I don't know why I'm so fascinated by this turn of events. Maybe it's seeing cold and mercenary Sebastian Faber as a human, with feelings, for the first time.

"I don't know. He seems cool," Baz says, as the doors open and a swarm of passengers disembarks. "But we're done here. I'm not your sister. I'm not your girlfriend. We're not going to talk about boys, all right?"

"Fine." But I can't resist giving Baz a little poke as we squeeze into the already crowded subway car. "You like him," I hiss.

"Shut up, Winter," he says. But his lips twitch at the corners like he's fighting back a smile.

Two stops later, we hop off the train at the Itaewon station. We take the escalators up to the street level. Baz gets a phone call as we're exiting the subway. I listen to his end of the conversation but can't get a feel for who's on the other end of the line.

"I have another job for the two of us," he says. "Turns out those license plates Ramirez photographed are from a local car hire service. Chances are Kyung uses the same company every day. You think he's still at work?"

I check the time. It's only a few minutes after four p.m. "Almost definitely," I say. "Koreans usually work late and then sometimes go out for food and drink with colleagues before returning home."

"Let's grab Ramirez and stake out UsuMed, then. We can't bug Kyung's car since the service might not always pick him up in the same vehicle, but maybe we can follow it and see where he's staying."

"Follow it how?" I ask. "You mean rent a car ourselves?"

"Oh, I forgot to tell you what I did when you guys were at UsuMed this morning. I rented something better than a car." Baz walks past the front of the apartment building and around to the side where a dark, sloping ramp leads down into a parking garage beneath the building. Parked in one of the front spots is a sleek blue-and-silver motorcycle, with two black helmets looped over one of the mirrors.

"I don't think we're all going to fit," I say.

"Yeah. We're going to have to split up again. Ramirez can take the subway."

"He's going to love that."

As predicted, Jesse is less than thrilled about separating again, but even he admits there's no way for all three of us to fit on one motorcycle. And since Baz is the only one with an international driver's license, he's going to be the one driving the bike.

Baz calls up the UsuMed building on his tablet computer and switches to street view. "Ramirez, you're going to take the subway, leave via exit 7, and buy yourself a coffee at the shop inside the UsuMed building. Winter and I will be across the street at this restaurant." He swipes at his tablet and the screen changes. "Between Ramirez and us, we should be able to see everyone as they leave the building, regardless of which exit they use." He turns to Jesse. "If you see him going out the back, you need to let us know right away, okay? You also need to get up from your seat and follow him through the doors so you can see if he gets into a car or goes somewhere on foot."

"Got it," Jesse says. "What are you guys going to do if you follow him to the hotel?"

"We're going to try to determine which room he's in so we can come back tomorrow and install surveillance equipment," Baz says. "If we're going to figure out exactly where Kyung is keeping the tech, and what he plans to do with it, we're going to need access to some of his conversations."

A rush of excitement moves through my veins. I know that what we did earlier today at UsuMed and the PC bang was also working toward my goals, but this feels more like action, like instead of just gathering information that may or may not be helpful, we're finally going after the actual target.

CHAPTER 21

Jesse heads for the subway station and I climb onto the motorcycle behind Baz. "You're not going to kill me, are you?" I ask dubiously as I slide on my helmet.

He looks back over his shoulder. "Probably not."

"Very comforting."

He turns the key in the ignition and the engine of the bike roars to life. "I guarantee you that riding with me is less dangerous than jumping off a bridge or trying to beat a train in the middle of a high-speed chase." He kicks up the kickstand. "You might want to hold on."

I wrap my arms around his waist. He's leaner than Jesse, but muscular, his abs firm beneath my fingertips. Touching him like this feels strange. I've known him for years but we've never so much as hugged.

When he takes off up the ramp of the parking garage and hops up over the corner of the sidewalk on his way to the street, I quickly get a lot less shy.

He laughs. "I hope you're recording this," he calls back over his shoulder. "Riding a motorcycle might not be too exciting in the US, but it's a whole different story in Seoul. This could be a great ViSE."

Unfortunately, I know exactly what he means. Motorcycles here are supposed to follow the same rules as cars and trucks, but in reality they seem to function as hybrid cars/bicycles, shooting up the middle between crowded lanes to avoid traffic and making flexible use of sidewalks and public plazas when it suits them.

Baz accelerates as we turn onto a major street, and the bike's engine whines. My helmet has a face shield, but the cold air funnels itself down the front of my coat and threatens to freeze the skin of my neck and chest. My eyes start to water. I hunker down and try to use Baz's back as a shield against the wind. The pedals beneath my feet vibrate heavily. Riding a motorcycle is not nearly as fun as it looks in beer commercials.

We shoot across the Han River, and the cold air gets even colder. My eyes gravitate toward the dark, twisting water. We reach the other side and turn sharply onto one of the main streets of Gangnam-gu. We pass the Buddhist temple Bonge-unsa, its traditional architecture in stark contrast to the jungle of glass and concrete of the surrounding business district. The Hyundai Department Store comes up on my right and then I can see the UsuMed building on the horizon, the giant *U* on top of it backlit by the setting sun. Jesse is probably still en route unless he managed to catch the trains at the exact right moment. Subways in Seoul are kind of like the traffic lights back in St. Louis. You have to deal with several of them to get where you're going, and some days it seems like everything is timed just right to get you to your destination, while other days you end up waiting at every possible spot.

We turn down a side street before we pass UsuMed, and Baz finds a place to park the bike. He puts down the kickstand and then glances back expectantly at me. I realize he's waiting for me to get off first. Resting my hands lightly on his shoulders for balance, I dismount the bike. I give the helmet to him and then button the top button of my coat, pulling the collar up to my chin. "Now I see why everyone is wearing a scarf."

Baz slides off the motorcycle and loops both helmets over one of the bike's mirrors. "Fix your hair," he says.

"You're not really my date," I remind him. "You don't get to critique my appearance."

He rolls his eyes. "Well, I would hope your actual dates don't critique your appearance either. But your headset is showing."

"Oh." I quickly reach up and feel for the base of my wig, which was pulled to the side when I removed the helmet. I straighten it as best I can and then use the reverse camera on my phone to double-check that everything is covered.

A blast of warm air hits me in the face as we step inside the restaurant. Baz rests a hand on my lower back as we approach the hostess and ask for a booth by the window. I know it makes sense for him to pretend to be my boyfriend—plenty of Korean girls date foreigners who are older—but I'm still a little uncomfortable with it. Then again, it would be worse to be here with Jesse, because that would feel like a real date and I'd have to struggle with all the distractions that come along with it.

I glance out the window at the UsuMed building across the street. My phone buzzes with a text. It's Jesse letting us know he's in place. Baz orders us appetizers and a bottle of soju—a vodka-like liquor that almost all Koreans drink. He pours us each a shot, but I'm definitely not going to drink it and I'm hoping he's not either if I have to get back on that motorcycle with him.

"I just figured with a soju bottle on the table, we'd blend in better," he murmurs.

I nod. My phone buzzes again.

Jesse: Are you guys having a nice date?

Me: Jealous?

Jesse: Is it lame if I say yes?

Me: Kind of.

Jesse: I guess I'm lame, then.

Me: Kind of. ;)

"What are you laughing about?" Baz asks.

"Nothing." I set my phone next to me on the table.

"Nothing? What's going on with you and Ramirez, anyway?"

"What do you mean?"

"Are you into him or not?"

The server arrives with our appetizers. She averts her eyes from both of us as she sets the dishes on the table.

"Oh, look. Our food is here," I say loudly.

Baz ordered us two of Korea's most popular appetizers, a dish of stir-fried tofu and kimchi and a *pajeon*, a savory pancake filled with vegetables.

"So," Baz says, helping himself to some of the tofu stir-fry. "Does your lack of answer mean that you *are* into him?"

"God, Baz. How is that your business? I thought we weren't sisters or girlfriends. We're not going to talk about boys, remember?"

"Like most people, I change the rules when it suits me." He grins. When I don't answer, he continues, "I just want to know where your head is at. This whole thing could go sideways really quickly if you're not on your game."

"I'm focused," I say. "I swear to you. I won't let Jesse distract me." I glance over at my phone, just making sure there are no new messages. "Now can we change the subject?"

"What do you want to talk about?"

"Let's just eat." I glance down at my phone again. Jesse's last message is still on the screen. *I wish I were with you instead,* I type.

And then I erase it. I've established actual boundaries with Jesse here. I shouldn't be sending him flirty text messages, especially not five seconds after I promised Baz I was focused.

We pick at our food for a few minutes. It's delicious, but my stomach feels like it's full of spiders, and every mouthful I manage to swallow threatens to crawl its way back up. I keep peeking out the window, looking for Kyung.

"Oh," Baz says. "I found out about the Singing Crane.

They closed down a year and a half ago. Lost their government funding due to bookkeeping issues. No one seems to know where the paperwork went."

"Where'd the kids go?" I ask, thinking of the girls I grew up with.

"Spread out to different group homes throughout the city." Baz lifts a slippery chunk of tofu to his mouth with his chopsticks and chews thoughtfully.

My phone buzzes again.

Jessie: He's heading your way.

I glance up from my phone and out the window. A long, black car has just pulled up to the front of the UsuMed building. A man emerges from the central revolving door.

Kyung is on the move.

CHAPTER 22

"Let's go." Baz drops a couple bills on the table and heads for the door. This is not normal behavior in Korea, but since he's a foreigner and it's more than enough money, he'll probably get away without being stopped.

We push back out into the chilly evening and I tug the helmet over my head as Baz pulls away from the curb. I fumble with my phone and manage to send Jesse a short text:

On the move.

We follow Kyung's driver through the streets of Seoul, staying a couple of cars away from him in order not to be spotted. Our face shields are tinted, so even if he noticed us, he wouldn't recognize me, but neither of us wants to raise his suspicions. Kyung no longer has a way to contact me since Sung Jin's burner phone doesn't work here, and I'm hoping he thinks I just gave up and let him win.

The driver slows and then signals to pull into a parking garage less than two miles from the UsuMed building. I glance up at the glitzy glass hotel. It's the Seoul SkyTower, one of the city's most exclusive business hotels.

Baz turns at the street past the hotel and pulls his bike over in front of a noodle shop.

"Now what?" Once again, I use Baz's shoulders for balance as I somewhat clumsily dismount from the bike.

"Now you stay with the bike and keep the helmet on so

you don't end up on a security camera. I'm going to head inside and see if I can at least figure out what floor he's staying on."

"Makes sense. You'd better hurry."

Baz heads toward the front of the SkyTower at a fast clip. I check my phone. Jesse has left several messages:

Jesse: On the move where?

Jesse: Should I meet you guys somewhere?

Jesse: Are you okay?

Me: We'll meet you back at the apartment. We're fine.

At least I hope we're fine. I tap one foot nervously against the cracked asphalt while I wait. It feels like forever. A man saunters past me walking a fat bulldog. Two girls come behind him, both in short dresses and thick woolen tights. Finally I see Baz emerge through the glass doors of the hotel. He jogs across the street and over to the bike. "His room is on the twentieth floor," he says.

"You got in the elevator with him?"

"No, I waited until he was moving and watched where it stopped," Baz says.

"Smart. So how do we narrow down which room?"

"Luckily, the twentieth floor is the penthouse and there are only two units up there. Guess who's in the other one?"

"I don't know. Who?"

Baz pulls a hotel keycard from his pants pocket. "Me."

"You rented a penthouse?"

"Well, I didn't want anyone else to rent it. And I think the only way we'll be able to access the twentieth floor with our keycards is if we actually have a room up there."

I glance up at the top of the SkyTower Hotel. The roof is lined with white lights. "You are a big spender."

He arches his eyebrows. "Revenge and international corporate theft don't come cheaply. You'll get a detailed report of my expenses once we're back in St. Louis. I will be expecting reimbursement."

"Fair enough," I say. "Money feels like the only thing I have right now."

"Well, that puts you ahead of a lot of people." Baz slips his helmet back on.

"I guess. What's the plan for tomorrow?"

"The keycard will activate the elevator." He pauses. "Or in your case, let you into the stairwell. The maids won't start cleaning until at least eight A.M. because they won't want to wake anyone up. So we'll come back here around seven thirty and wait until we hear the maid in Kyung's suite. Then one of us gets to engage her in a short conversation so we can clone her keycard."

"Clone it how?"

"I have a badge cloner. It takes thirty seconds to record the information and then a simple swipe will copy that info onto a new card. All we'll have to do is wait for her to finish cleaning and we'll have access to Kyung's suite."

"Sebastian. You are brilliant!" I say.

"Nah. I just have a lot of cool toys."

He smirks at me and I return it with a tentative smile. He definitely has access to a lot of resources that Jesse and I wouldn't have on our own.

Back at the apartment, Jesse is flipping through our TV channels. "Look! I found a channel that plays English movies."

I squint at the screen. An elderly Chinese man is telling a guy with awkward hair not to feed something furry after midnight. "From what decade?"

"Eighties? Nineties? Better than nothing. So what happened?"

"We followed him to a fancy business hotel. He's in a penthouse suite. Baz and I are going to plant cameras and listening devices while he's at work." I give Jesse a rundown of following Kyung to the Seoul SkyTower and our plans for tomorrow.

"I'm surprised you didn't just stay there tonight," he says.

"We were afraid you might miss us," Baz says with a grin. "Or be unable to find food without Winter's help."

"Oh, I've figured out how to order food here." Jesse mimics like he's pointing at different things and nods vigorously. "I had a sandwich on something called honey bread at the coffee shop, and it was delicious." He turns to me. "You still owe me actual Korean food at some point, though."

"I know," I say. "We've only been here for three days." Even as I say it, it's hard to believe. I've accomplished more than I ever would have thought possible. I'm really glad Jesse and Baz are with me.

Jesse coughs, and I watch him lift one hand to brace his chest from the pressure.

"Do you want help changing your dressings?"

He shrugs. "Either way. How is your leg?"

"Not bad," I say. "It's been aching a bit today, but no bleeding."

"I'll grab the first-aid stuff from my suitcase and meet you in the bathroom," Jesse says.

When I duck into the bathroom a few minutes later, Jesse has laid out squares of gauze, a roll of tape, and a tube of antibiotic ointment on the little ledge above the sink. He shrugs his T-shirt over his shoulders and I do my best to ignore the little rush of desire that floods through me. Some of the tiny strips of adhesive are drying up and falling off the incision that runs down the middle of his chest. All of his wounds appear to be healing nicely. I apply antibiotic ointment and tape fresh dressings on them.

Next Jesse helps me. My own wound on my leg is looking a little puffy, but the pain is just sort of gnawing and dull. I sit on the closed toilet while Jesse uses the shower nozzle to give my leg a really good rinsing.

"Is the water too hot?" he asks.

"It hurts a little, but it feels good, you know?" I watch the skin around my scab turn pink. "I can tell it's really cleaning things."

Jesse shuts the shower off and I blot my leg dry with a towel. I squeeze a bunch of antibiotic ointment on top of the scab and smear it around a little with a piece of gauze. I hold the new gauze in place while Jesse tapes around each of the edges.

"Thanks," I say.

"What are you going to do now?" he asks.

"I don't know. Why?" Having free time is not something I'm accustomed to. Gideon used to curate my days very carefully, filling them with what he thought was the optimal mix of academic study and physical exercise.

"There's another movie from before we were born getting ready to start. I think it's called *Labyrinth*."

"What's it about?"

"A girl who has to make her way through a labyrinth in order to save her little brother from a goblin king."

I used to have dreams about being separated from my sister and trapped in a maze. It makes me wonder if I've already seen this movie and don't remember it.

"Or we could find something else to watch," Jesse offers. "You could explain one of those Korean dramas to me. I tried to watch something earlier today with a lot of crying and yelling and sad music, but I never did figure out what the actors were so upset about."

I smile. It would be fun to relax on the sofa, explaining K-dramas to Jesse. It would be like a date.

And then I remember those boundaries I set. I'm not here for dates. "I'm actually feeling sort of tired," I say. "I should probably just get some sleep."

"Okay. I guess I'll see you in the morning, then." Jesse manages to hold a neutral expression, but it's impossible not to see the light fade from his eyes.

CHAPTER 23

The next day, Baz and I are up by six a.m. to prepare for our mission. The two of us move quietly through the darkened apartment, taking turns in the bathroom and slipping into our winter weather gear. I resist the urge to send Jesse a text as we head out into the cold, figuring the buzz of the phone might wake him.

I climb on the back of Baz's motorcycle and we zip through the streets of the city. It's kind of beautiful right now—the pollution and grime disguised by the purple sky, the neon lights melding together in a blur of color as we speed past. We take the same path as last night—the Han River, the Buddhist temple—but everything feels more peaceful. Even the wind isn't quite as brutal, Korean flags hanging like sashes in front of the banks and post offices.

A digital billboard displaying two pretty girls out at a club promises yet another new phone from Samsung and then flicks to an advertisement for UsuTech's newest tablet computer—this one with pretty girls in a conference room. Soon, the SkyTower hotel looms on the horizon. It's taller than the other buildings around it, a silvery spike stabbing into the fading night.

"I wonder why Kyung doesn't stay at a family home," I muse, as we slow to a stop at an intersection.

Baz rests his boots against the frosty pavement. "Maybe he doesn't have any family here. Or perhaps they're estranged."

"Is that what it is with you?" I ask.

"Maybe."

"I was just wondering. Jesse's nurse asked me if you had any family, but I had to tell her I wasn't sure."

Baz chuckles. "Let me guess. Kendra?"

"Yes," I say, surprised. Jesse probably had at least three or four different nurses in the hospital. "How did you know that?"

The light turns green and the bike's engine whines as Baz accelerates sharply. He turns his head for a second as we lean into a curve on the road. "That girl loved me."

I snort. "She seemed to have strong feelings, but I don't know if love is the best description."

Baz laughs again but doesn't respond. We cut across three lanes of traffic and hop up onto the corner of the wide city sidewalk in order to avoid a snarl of delivery trucks that are clogging up one lane of the road.

"I thought you weren't going to kill me." My teeth click together as the bike drops from the sidewalk back to street level.

"If I wanted to kill you, you'd be dead." Baz pulls the bike in a sharp angle and cuts through a narrow alley. I cling to him as he navigates the steep, twisting pavement with ease. About three minutes and three more close calls later, he slows to a stop in front of the parking garage for the Seoul SkyTower. The parking attendant steps forward in his navy uniform, collar zipped up to his eyes to protect his face from the cold. Baz flashes a keycard at him and he ushers us into the garage.

We pull into the first open space we see and Baz cuts the engine. I hop off the bike and gingerly remove my helmet, reaching a hand up to make sure my wig is still in place.

Baz secures our helmets to the bike. "You know, it's going to look odd that you're using the stairs when we're staying on the twentieth floor."

"I know, but it would also look odd if I have a panic attack in the elevator," I say. "I'm sure there's a camera in there."

"I'm just saying you should probably work on at least being

able to survive a few seconds in an elevator. At some point it might end up being the thing that makes it possible for us to escape."

I mull that thought over as we walk toward the entrance together. I imagine Jesse, Baz, and myself at UsuMed finding the stolen technology in some top-floor office and then getting caught just as we're leaving. I see us all running down twenty flights of stairs because I'm scared of the elevator. I know who would lose that race, and it isn't me. Baz might leave us and escape on his own, but Jesse would end up sticking by me and getting caught. "You're right. I'll start working on it once we're through here."

"Maybe Ramirez can help you. I get the idea he's feeling a little left out."

"True. And probably isolated since both of us are somewhat familiar with the area."

Baz nods. "This can be a tough place to get used to. Everything moves at such a fast pace." He gives me a keycard. "See you on the other side."

I head for the stairs. It takes me longer than usual to go twenty floors. I'm sweaty and out of breath by the time I make it to the top, where Baz is waiting for me. He looks me up and down as I close the door to the stairwell, but doesn't comment on my condition.

We slip into the penthouse suite together. The heavy door closes behind us with a soft click.

"Wow," I say. The entryway is made of black marble tiles inlaid with gold. It opens into a large living area with a vaulted ceiling and a set of glass doors that lead out onto a wide balcony. The walls are done in silver-and-white textured wallpaper and the black L-shaped sofa is buried in embroidered pillows. This is one of the most beautiful rooms I've ever seen, but by far the most impressive thing in the room is the huge TV screen built into the wall.

"It's a smart suite," Baz says. "You download an app and

control everything from your phone—the TV, the lights, the heat, even the coffeemaker."

"Where are you going to hide the cameras?" I ask.

"Good question." Baz ducks into the master bedroom and I follow him. There's another TV in here, a flat screen sitting on the dresser. A black-and-white photograph of a skyline I don't recognize hangs on the wall above the bed.

"It's Kuala Lumpur." Baz lifts the frame from the wall and peers at the back of it. "I can hide a listening device here, and behind one of the paintings in the living room, but the cameras are going to be more tricky." He strolls back into the main room, a focused look on his face. "Got it." He points up toward the ceiling. Several sprinkler heads are embedded between the noise-dampening ceiling tiles. "We can put cameras up there. It's not an ideal angle for spying, but there's no way he'll notice them."

"And so now we just wait for the maid and then one of us needs to talk to her?" I ask.

"I'll talk to her. The front desk attendants have already seen my face. The fewer people who see you the better."

"All right." I flop down on the living room sofa and Baz sits in a chair across from me.

"So," he says.

"So," I repeat.

"Back to Ramirez. If you're not into him, why do you keep stringing him along?"

"This again? I don't do that," I say. At least I've been trying really hard to keep from doing that.

"Even I can see that you totally send him mixed signals."

I pull my legs up on the sofa and fold them behind me. "What do you mean?"

"You two were inseparable in St. Louis. Now you're acting more like cousins who've just met for the first time."

"It's complicated." I run the tip of my index finger along the edge of the sofa, hoping that maid shows up sooner rather than later. "I have sent him mixed signals, but some of that is because of my condition. It's hard to send the same signals if you're not always being the same person."

"Ah," Baz says. "Right. I almost forgot that the two of you—"

"Don't," I say through clenched teeth. "Don't say it."

Baz holds his hands up in self-defense. "Sorry. I didn't mean anything by it."

"Why do you care, anyway?" I ask. "It's not like you're friends. You treat him like a pet."

"That's a little extreme."

I arch an eyebrow. "Is it?"

Baz stretches his legs out in front of him and crosses them at the ankle. "When I was his age, I was a lot . . . harder than he is, so maybe I don't always take him seriously. But that's why I have to look out for him. He's the sensitive type. I don't want to see you rip out his heart and toss it in front of a packed express train."

"Now who's being extreme?" I pick at a loose thread on the sofa. "I'm not messing with him. I do care about him. I'm just not sure how to reconcile that with who I am."

"Who are you?"

"I'm broken," I say. "And I don't know if there's a way to fix me. Why would he want to be with someone so screwed up instead of a normal girl?"

"No one is normal." Baz makes air quotes around the word. "Sometimes love is about finding a person you connect with to a degree where you don't mind putting up with their issues." He pauses. "But you just found out about your condition. Don't write yourself off as unfixable before you even try."

"Good point," I say, touched by Baz's words. "I've been meaning to do some research about DID, but I can't focus on anything else right now. Still, even if I could get better someday, I came here to kill someone. That should feel wrong, but it doesn't. It's like I'm . . . blinded by hate." I grab a throw pillow from the back of the sofa and hug it to my chest. I rest my chin on the edge of it. "I don't feel very lovable. Sometimes I don't even feel human anymore."

"Hate is a very human emotion," Baz says quietly.

I blink back tears. "All I know is that it will never go away unless I kill Kyung. Unless I stand over his body and say, 'This is for my sister, this is for Gideon, this is for every girl whose life you destroyed, this is for me.' Needing to kill someone like that makes me feel like a monster. Monsters can't love, can they?"

There's a clattering noise from the hallway. Baz rises from his chair and strides quickly over to the door. I follow. We hear the maid humming softly as she pushes her cart past our door.

"Ready?" He slips the cloning device into his pocket. "I'll be right back."

He pauses to grab the towels from the bathroom. Then he opens the door to slip out into the hallway. Just before it closes behind him, he looks back at me, his gray eyes deadly serious. "For what it's worth, I don't think monsters spend a lot of time worrying about whether they're monsters."

I ponder the words while I wait. Baz told me once that he was a terrible person, and he was fine with it. Is he trying to say the two of us are different, that it's *not* wrong for me to want to kill someone? That I can have both vengeance and love? It seems like too much for any one heart to handle.

"Ajumma," Baz says. I press my ear to the door so I can listen to him.

"You need towel? I clean next," the woman says haltingly.

"Um . . . no need to clean," Baz says. "Just new towels?"

"Clean later?"

"That's okay. Just towels," he repeats. The hallway is silent for a couple of moments and I envision the maid giving Baz some new towels. I'm not sure if it's been thirty seconds yet.

"Thank you," he says. "Ah, one more question. Phone works for heat?"

"Phone for everything," the woman says.

"Can I show you this?" Baz asks.

There's another pause. Then the maid says, "You ask front desk. They explain."

"Ah, okay," Baz says. "Thank you. *Gamsahamnida*."

"*Ne, gamsahamnida,*" the maid responds.

A few seconds later Baz keycards himself back into the room. He gives me a thumbs-up as he shuts the door behind him. He pulls the cloning device from his pocket. He swipes one of the keycards he got for our suite and the light on the machine turns green. "And we're in business."

After the maid has left Kyung's suite, we wait another ten minutes just to be safe. Then we each don a pair of rubber gloves and let ourselves in.

"It's a little scary how easy that was for you," I say, slipping out of my boots in the entryway.

"It's a little scary to me the way people put so much faith in random technology." Baz places his boots next to mine. "Electronic locks, mobile banking, backing up documents to *the cloud*. I would never trust any of that. Trusting tech means trusting the people who created it, and not all of those people are good. And even the good ones can make a mistake."

I lift a hand to the back of my skull and press RECORD on my headset. While Baz installs the surveillance equipment, I'm going to go through Kyung's personal belongings to see if there's anything useful. We don't want to spend too much time in here, so I'm just going to scan everything and then review the recording later.

Baz grabs a chair from the dining area and positions it under one of the sprinkler heads in the living room. I head for the bedroom, a sick sense of dread pooling in my gut as I think about being so close to where Kyung sleeps.

The shades are lowered completely and I have to flip on the

lights to be able to see my way around. The room is set up just like our master bedroom next door—though the décor isn't quite the same. The photograph hanging behind the bed is of a different city; the bed itself is dressed in navy blue sheets and a dark duvet with gold trim.

There are no obvious signs of Kyung here. I'm not sure what I was expecting, but this could be anyone's room. A few scattered papers are strewn across the dresser. When I look at them, I see it's just the boarding pass stub from his plane ticket and a few receipts from purchases. Nothing interesting—mostly food and drink. Set back against the wall is a small satellite alarm clock and a black circle that looks like a coaster—a wireless phone charger.

I pull open each of the drawers one at a time. The top one has a few bills and a handful of loose coins in it, as well as a paperback novel. I don't recognize the title and can't resist the urge to flip it over and see what it's about. Apparently it's the latest techno-thriller from one of Korea's up-and-coming authors. It's strange to me, imagining Kyung reading novels like a regular person. For so long he has been this almost mythical source of evil in my life. But here, now, it occurs to me that he's just one man. Fallible. Mortal.

A chill crawls up my spine at the thought of coming face-to-face with him after all these years. Once again I question my ability to follow through with my plan. What if I freeze up?

We won't let you fail.

Goosebumps rise up on my skin. I don't want one of my alters to kill Kyung. I need to do it. I need to look into his eyes as the life bleeds out of him.

I hear Baz moving around in the living room and force myself to focus. The second drawer is full of socks and underwear. The thought of touching Kyung's intimate apparel even while wearing gloves makes me cringe. I quickly check the rest of the drawers—empty. I turn away and go to the side wall, pulling open the accordion-folded door to reveal a long closet.

Four suits hang in a neat row; beyond them are several button-up shirts and a hanger full of ties, most of them red.

For a second, the slashes of crimson fabric seem to come to life, writhing and twisting like a knot of bloody snakes. I shudder. *Not real*, I tell myself. I start going through the pockets of Kyung's suits. I'm not expecting to find anything, but on the third suit I get lucky. There's a scrap of paper in the coat pocket with three names on it: *Cristian Rojas, Nai Khaing, Erich Cross.* None of those names is familiar to me.

Baz peeks his head in the door. "Find anything?"

"Maybe." I hand him the scrap of paper. "Have you heard of any of these people?"

"I don't think so, but I'll check them all out." Baz pulls his phone from his pocket and snaps a photo before handing the scrap of paper back to me. "Be sure to put it back exactly where you got it."

I slip the scrap of paper back into the pocket of the third suit. Baz pats down the rest of the suit pockets and then kneels down to look in each of Kyung's shiny dress shoes.

"Any luck?" I ask.

"Nope." Baz pulls Kyung's empty suitcases back from the corner of the closet to expose a small safe. "Chances are, anything good is in there."

"Can we get in?"

"Not without him knowing." Baz hops up on the neatly made bed and inserts one of the minicameras into a sprinkler head right over the center of the room. Then he tucks the listening device behind the photograph. "Hong Kong," he tells me.

"You're quite the traveler," I say.

"Yeah. I spent a lot of time searching for a place that felt like home."

"Did you ever find it?"

"I'm not sure." Baz smiles slightly. "Man, this room is freezing, huh? We should probably get going, unless there's something else you want to check out in here."

It is cold. I thought it was just my nerves, but now I realize this room feels cooler than the rest of the penthouse. Quickly, I peek under Kyung's mattress and then do a quick check of the kitchen and bathroom. Baz is right. If there's anything here worth checking out, it's tucked away in the hotel safe.

We head back to our suite, on the other side of the top floor. I remove my wig and stop recording.

"Now to see if they work." Baz pulls up a program on his tablet and Kyung's bedroom appears in slightly blurry gray-scale. He taps at the screen and it splits into four different feeds—living room, dining room, master bedroom, second bedroom. "There are four listening devices as well." He taps the screen again and it flips to audio surveillance.

"Good job," I say. "Can we put this on my tablet too?"

"Sure. No problem. Hopefully we'll get lucky."

"What if we don't?"

"I've got Chung Hee working on a couple things. I might have some other ideas after I meet up with him tonight."

"For a *date*?" I say, biting back a smile.

"You just aren't going to let it go, are you? Don't make me tell you all the things Ramirez says about you when you aren't around."

My eyes narrow. "What kinds of things?"

"'I am so whipped it's not even funny' types of things." Baz grins at me. "What's it like to have someone in your life who will do absolutely anything for you?"

"I don't think he would've agreed to a date with Chung Hee," I shoot back.

"Touché," Baz says. "There you go again, reminding me of Gideon."

I perch on the arm of the sofa. "How did you two become friends?"

Baz goes to the glass doors that lead out onto the balcony. He stares off into the distance. "That's not a good story."

"Did you know him before you worked security for him?"

"Yes." Baz turns away from the glass. "We should probably head back soon, before Ramirez wakes up and decides to destroy more pots and pans."

"Do you miss him?" I blurt out. "Gideon?"

Baz stops short. His gray eyes shine in the sunlight. "I miss him every single day."

And just like that, the two of us end up in an awkward embrace. I'm not even sure which of us instigated the hug. All I know is one second we're looking at each other and the next Baz's blond beard is scraping against my left temple, the muscles of his chest firm beneath my face.

"Thank you for helping me." My words are mostly swallowed up by the fabric of his T-shirt, but he hears them anyway.

"Any day, kid," he says. One hand rubs my back for a few seconds. Then he pulls back. "We'd better get going. Your boyfriend is probably getting lonely."

Baz and I head back to Itaewon, where Jesse is once again making breakfast. Or has taken charge of breakfast, anyway. There's a pot of freshly brewed tea on the stove and a platter of gimbap and scrambled eggs on the counter. Bacon sizzles in a pan on the stove.

"Did you make this?" Baz asks.

I grab a piece of gimbap and pop it in my mouth. The rice is moist, the vegetables crisp. "No," I say.

"Hey," Jesse says. And then to Baz, "I went out for a run and a lady was selling it on the street."

"A run, huh? How far did you get?"

"Not far," Jesse admits. "But at least I can go up and down stairs without huffing and puffing now."

My leg is feeling better too. The scab is kind of crusty and ugly, but the pain is mostly gone and it's not affecting my movement much anymore. "Ready for some rooftop sparring?"

Jesse brightens. "Maybe, if you go easy on me. But we don't have any protective gear."

"We won't have any if we have to fight our way out of UsuMed either," I point out. "Perhaps it's time I learn to fight the way it's really done."

Jesse exchanges a glance with Baz, who shrugs. "Just don't go overboard."

"I won't." Jesse scoops some scrambled eggs onto his plate. "I'm still kind of beat-up from—"

"I wasn't talking about you." Baz winks at me. "Seriously. Go easy on him. He's not much, but he's all the backup we've got."

"Hey," Jesse says again.

"Ignore him," I tell Jesse, reaching for more of the gimbap. "If it weren't for you, I might still be sitting in that K-Town guesthouse, trying to figure out what to do next. You saved me that day, you know it?"

"Glad I could help." Jesse squeezes my shoulder gently.

We eat our breakfast in the living room, Jesse and Baz on the sofa and me on the floor again. Baz and I fill Jesse in on bugging Kyung's room, and Baz shows Jesse how to access the recordings on his tablet.

"Oh good," Jesse says. "I can make myself useful and go through these while you two are cruising around the city doing the real work."

"We're not leaving you behind on purpose," Baz says. "But renting a car would be useless since we'd be constantly stuck in traffic."

"Actually, I was wondering if you would help me get over my elevator phobia," I say, thinking back to the conversation Baz and I had earlier.

"What could I do?" Jesse asks.

I look up at him. "Just be with me."

His cheeks redden slightly. "Sure. If you think having me there will help."

"Great," Baz says. "While you two work on that, I'm going to meet with a guy about scoring some weapons, and then later I'm meeting up with Chung Hee."

Jesse turns to me. "What should we do first? Sparring or elevator?"

I think about the last time I was in an elevator. I remember crying and begging Sung Jin not to pull me into the cramped compartment. I remember fighting, my bones rattling beneath my skin as the older man pummeled me.

And then I shot him. At least I think it was me. There were multiple voices in my head that day. *You don't have to kill him. Yes, you do.* Lily . . . the name haunts me. I grow a little dizzy at the thought that I might have some rogue alter who kills people on my behalf. How many parts do I have? What happens if we all go to war against one another?

CHAPTER 24

I opt for the physical pain of sparring over the emotional pain of the elevator, and ten minutes later, I'm standing in the center of the roof, crouched low but ready to strike. Jesse stands about ten feet away from me. He rolls his head in a circle and then lifts his fists to protect his face and chest. Behind him, the city stretches out, people bustling in and out of buildings and shops, mountains on the horizon looking so out of place they might as well be mirages.

The last time Jesse and I fought, it was inside the penthouse, in my bedroom to be exact. I had just found out everything—that Rose had died years earlier, that Gideon, Jesse, and Baz had joined forces to trick me into accepting the fact that she was gone. Jesse tried to justify it by saying he truly believed Gideon could heal me.

I did not feel healed.

I felt severed, adrift, betrayed by the only people I trusted.

I was out of control that day. And even though I know this moment is different, I'm a little afraid of what might happen when Jesse actually strikes me.

I blink and he's standing less than two feet away. He snaps his fingers in front of my face. "I could have knocked you out. What are you thinking about so hard?"

"Lily," I say. "That day in the penthouse when I attacked you. I'm wondering if part of it was her." I pause. "I didn't black out or anything, but I remember feeling . . . powerless. Like I knew I should stop but couldn't."

"It's okay," Jesse says.

"It's not okay, though. It's not okay to attack someone who isn't fighting back. It's not okay to hurt you the way that I did." I blink back tears. "It's like I want an excuse for that day. But then even if somehow it was all Lily, she's just a piece of me, you know? She's me. It was me. Some part of me is capable of terrible things."

"Winter." Jesse cups my shoulders in both hands. "We're all capable of terrible things in the right combination of circumstances. We all have days we want excuses for. I thought we agreed to let this go. I messed up. You messed up. I understand and I forgive you."

"What if I need someone not to forgive me?"

"Seems like you got yourself for that," Jesse says softly.

"I just worry that I don't know what brings her out. What if you land a good hit and she emerges from some dark place inside of me and tries to push you off the roof?"

"That won't happen," Jesse says. "I've landed plenty of good hits against you in practice and you've never snapped on me."

"What if I do?"

"I can handle myself," Jesse says. "Even with Lily."

I think of the guy with the blond hair lying dead on the floor of the guesthouse and I'm not so sure, but Jesse's right about the fact that we've sparred against each other for over a year without incident. The same goes for Gideon. I've never lost it any time while working out with him, never exploded into psychotic rage. I'm just being paranoid.

"So are we good here?" Jesse asks. "Because if not, the elevator awaits us."

"We're good."

Jesse steps back and then resumes his ready stance. Our eyes lock. We dance around an imaginary perimeter. I realize he's going to wait for me to strike, so I move in and lunge at him. He ducks back, sidesteps, tries to attack me from an angle.

The edge of his hand makes contact with my jaw, but I can feel the energy stop as he pulls back. Rage sparks inside me. I need to be hard and focused, and Jesse is babying me. I attack full force and land him on his back on the cold concrete in a handful of moves.

His breath leaves his mouth in a puff of mist. His eyes widen. Clearly I surprised him by going for an early takedown. He lashes out with one leg, hooking it behind my ankle and making me stumble. Leaping to his feet, he kicks me in the midsection. I flail backward, but the attack leaves Jesse off balance. We both land in a pile on the roof, his body on top of mine, his face just inches away.

"Sorry," he mutters.

There was a time that the weight of Jesse's body, of any man's body, would have terrified and repelled me. But all I can think about is how warm he feels, like a blanket protecting me from the cold.

I don't want protecting.

I roll out from under him. "Again," I say. "I know you're going easy on me."

"What?"

"You heard me."

"I really didn't." He points at his ear. "I took my hearing aid out, so I'm half-deaf."

"Sorry," I tell him. "I said I know you're going easy on me."

Jesse snorts. "I'm going easy on *me*. I'm recovering from major surgery, remember?"

"No. I feel you pulling back when you make contact. Like you don't want to hurt me."

"Um . . . that's because I *don't* want to hurt you." He clambers back to his feet and assumes an offensive stance.

"I know, but you have to actually go for takedowns. Otherwise this is pointless." I advance on him, my fists raised.

"Sorry." His chin drops a little. "I guess it's just hard for me to touch you. Even like this."

I stop, midattack. "Why?"

Jesse rakes his hands through his hair. "Because fighting can be . . . intimate. Touching you makes me want you," he says. "And that makes me feel shitty. And sad."

I've fought Jesse fifty times or more, and I've never really considered what that was like for him. "Why shitty?" I ask.

"Because I'm supposed to be helping you stay strong in case we need to fight our way out of a jam while we're here. Not getting all . . . whatever because I'm close to you." He looks away from me and sighs.

All . . . whatever. I remember the attraction I felt to Jesse when I was dressing his wounds, the way part of me wanted to reach for him on the plane. If it's difficult for me to resist those urges, it must be hell for him. "Why sad?" I reach out and touch his arm.

He turns back, his eyes locking onto mine. "Because I totally blew it with you."

His expression is neutral but his voice cracks open something inside of me. I think about the way Baz teased me earlier, how he wanted to know what it felt like to have someone who would do anything for me. Maybe it sounds comforting to know there is a person out there who would risk his life to protect you—a person who would back off when you asked and then come to you when you changed your mind. Especially when that person is as kind and decent as Jesse. The truth is, it's terrifying. It's just one more opportunity for me to be a monster.

I want to tell Jesse that he didn't blow it, that I just need time. That even if he can love me when I'm broken and full of hate, that I have to find peace with myself before I can find it with another person.

But what if I don't manage to kill Kyung? What if I never learn how to live with my DID? Or what if I do, but my feelings never grow into the same thing Jesse is feeling? Maybe I'm wasting his time. Maybe it's hurtful to give him hope. I don't know.

I turn away from our practice area and walk toward the edge of the roof. The sky is a rainbow of grays, thick brush-strokes layered on rough canvas. The wind grabs pieces of my hair, twists them up and out, away from my face. Even without looking, I can feel Jesse approaching. I can feel him hesitating behind me. "Come here," I say.

He comes to stand next to me. For a few seconds, we both stare out at the city. I want to do the right thing, but I have no idea what that is, so I decide to do the next best thing and tell the truth. I glance over at him. His eyes threaten to drown me. Maybe it'll be easier to say it to the sky.

I turn my head upward, look for secret messages in the clouds. There is no guidance. There is only Jesse and me on a rooftop, almost seven thousand miles from home. We might as well be aliens on another planet. "I have feelings for you," I say.

"Yeah, but not the same as I have for you." Now his voice is light, almost carefree, like his emotions threatened to spill out a few seconds ago but he's back in control. I hate that he thinks he has to hide his bitterness from me.

"Maybe not. I don't know," I admit. "Now seems like the wrong time to figure that out. But it's hard for me to touch you too, all right?"

"What do you mean?"

"Dressing your wounds, sitting next to you on the plane, even up here right now. These are more than just moments to me."

"I don't understand." Jesse moves his hand closer to mine on the railing.

Another surge of pain jolts through me. Before, he would've just taken my hand. Now he's afraid to. He needs for me to be the initiator. He needs for me to make even the tiniest moves, because otherwise he's going to feel like he's forcing himself on me.

I can't make all the moves. But I can make this one.

I take his hand, twine my fingers through his. "Let's just say you didn't totally blow it," I say. "I don't know how we're going to end up, but I still think about you . . . like that."

Admitting my feelings is like letting go of a dark secret, like popping a balloon that's been increasing in size, crushing my heart, blocking out the rest of my organs.

He loves you, Rose reminds me.

"But you've been acting so distant." Jesse stares down at our hands.

"That's because the way you feel is scary, Jesse. I don't want to hurt you worse than I already have. Even Baz pointed out that I've been sending you mixed messages."

Jesse rubs his thumb across the pointy bone in my wrist. "Baz is an idiot."

I smile. "Maybe, but he's right. We're like magnets, you know. Only I'm spinning, so I keep pulling you in and then pushing you away. I like you, but then you hurt me, so I run. I like you, but then something makes things feel impossible, so I turn away. And you. You're so constant. Your orientation never wavers. You feel what you feel and you want what you want without hesitation or doubt. God, I envy that. I feel like if someone stripped away my hesitation and doubt that there'd be nothing left."

Jesse tucks a lock of hair back behind my ear, his fingertips lingering on my jawbone for a second. "It's okay not to know what you want."

"I know what I want, Jesse. I remember thinking the night of the Phantasm break-in how if we were normal, that instead of gearing up for a heist we'd be ordering pizza and watching movies together. I would love to have that life. I just don't know if it's going to happen. I feel like you became more normal and

I've become less normal. Maybe we don't fit." My voice trembles. "I don't know if I'm supposed to fit with anyone."

"But you *want* to fit? With me?"

I look up at the sky again. "Yes."

"Come here." Jesse wraps me in a hug, pulling me in tight against his chest. His arms threaten to crack my ribs.

"You're squishing me," I say, my voice muted by the fabric of his sweatshirt.

"Sorry." He loosens his hold a little. "That just made me happy. You . . . make me happy."

"I wouldn't get accustomed to it," I say, my face still buried in his chest.

He kisses me on the forehead. "Do you believe that people can change?"

"Of course."

"Then maybe even if we don't fit right now, we will someday in the future."

"Assuming I have a future, you mean."

Jesse steps back and regards me seriously. "You don't really think you're going to die here, do you?"

"I don't know. When I left St. Louis, I was prepared to die. It's probably greedy to want to find my brother, recover the ViSE tech, kill Kyung, and also get to live."

"Any progress on finding your brother?"

"No. Baz said the Singing Crane Orphanage was closed down over a year ago and no one seems to know what happened to the paperwork. Right now he doesn't have any other leads."

"What about using social media to look for him?"

"I scanned through a lot of profiles for people named Jun Song, but I didn't find him. Maybe I can dig deeper after we steal back the tech. If my brother is out there, I don't want Kyung to find out I'm searching for him. No point in putting him in danger."

"You really think Kyung would hurt him?"

"I don't know," I say. "It's hard to speculate about the safety of a boy who might not even be real." I gesture back toward the center of the roof. "Let's go again."

This time Jesse attacks like I'm the enemy and I fight him back like he's the enemy. His hits are solid. My teeth rattle in my gums. My bones pulse with pain. My counterstrikes are fluid, graceful. I am Winter, trained by Gideon to survive in any situation. There is no Kyung, no Jun, no missing technology. I am not a girl in pieces set on revenge, not at this moment. I am a deadly ballerina, facing off against an adversary.

After about a half an hour, Jesse holds up his hands. "All right. I'm done. I'm going to be sore all over."

I lift up my hands in victory. "If you're quitting, then I win."

"You never would have quit, would you?"

"Probably not." I smile.

Baz is sitting in the living room of the flat when Jesse and I tumble back through the door, achy and bruised. He rises up from the sofa and comes to stand in front of me as I'm slipping out of my shoes. He lifts my chin, looks at both sides of my face, and then examines my arms individually.

"What are you doing?" I ask.

"Just making sure Ramirez didn't do too much damage."

"What does it matter?" Jesse asks.

"How is Winter going to be able to blend in at UsuMed if she looks like a domestic abuse victim?"

I furrow my brow. "Blend in at . . . what do you mean?"

Baz smiles triumphantly. "Let's just say I think I got you a job."

CHAPTER 25

"A JOB at UsuMed? How?"

"Chung managed to access a list of UsuMed security guards with full badge clearance, but he also found a list of new hires slated to start next week, several of whom were from Cheonma Staffing. He went back to the Cheonma database and made copies of the information for a girl who looks enough like you that you can fill in for her."

"But what about when that girl shows up for work too?"

"Chung sent her an e-mail from an official-looking Cheonma Staffing account apologizing for the mix-up but saying the position had already been filled. She also received a generous wire transfer payment to make up for the mistake."

"How can Winter work at UsuMed?" Jesse asks, slipping his hearing aid back in. "What if Kyung sees her?"

"It's a temporary customer service job because they just launched a new line of blood pressure medications. Winter will be fielding English inquiries from physicians and sales reps and connecting them to permanent staff who can answer specific technical questions, translating as needed. I seriously doubt an R and D executive like Kyung spends a lot of time in the bottom tier of customer service."

"Sebastian, you're a genius," I say.

"Doubtful," he says with a smile. "But try not to amass any black eyes or busted lips before Monday, because that's when you start." He pauses. "And you'd better get to work on over-coming that elevator phobia, if you haven't already."

Unfortunately, that is easier said than done. It takes me until nighttime to work up the nerve to try. And then, even with Jesse by my side, when I approach the elevator, my heart starts galloping and my throat closes up. I would honestly rather be waterboarded than let those shiny steel doors swallow me up.

"I think I need to talk to my therapist before I try this."

"Sounds like a plan," Jesse says. "We still have time."

I do a quick calculation as we both head back to the apartment. It's about ten p.m., which makes it about seven a.m. in St. Louis. Maybe I can catch Dr. Abrams before she starts her day.

I call her cell phone and she answers but says she's driving and that she's booked all morning. "I can do a phone session with you at three P.M., if you want."

I calculate the time difference. That's six a.m. Seoul time. "Sure, I can do that." I set my alarm for five forty-five.

When I wake up to the soft chiming sound, I open my bedroom door and peer out into the darkness of the apartment. Everyone else seems to be still asleep. Good. I pull the cover from my bed. I sit on the floor and wrap the blanket around me like a protective cocoon. Then, a couple minutes before six, I call Dr. Abrams.

She picks up right away. "Winter. How are you?"

"I'm good, but I need your help. I need to get over my phobia of elevators," I say. "I know why I'm afraid—my sister actually died in an elevator."

"So you remember that now."

"I do, but I still have a panic attack when I think of getting in one."

"Well, there's nothing wrong with you taking the stairs forever if you want, but if this is something important to you, you need to just take it a step at a time," she says. "First, just stand and look at an elevator. Next, just go in for a few seconds and get back out. Do you have your antianxiety medicine with you?"

My eyes flick to the amber pill bottle on my nightstand. "Yes."

"Good. Take one for this step if you need to. Then try riding one floor. Gradually work your way up to taking longer rides. And if at all possible, don't work on this by yourself."

"That's basically what I thought I should do. No other tips?"

"Sorry. No secret shortcuts," Dr. Abrams says. And then when I don't respond she adds, "So how are you *really*?"

I wrap my blanket even tighter around my body. Part of me wants to spew out the whole story—that I shot the guy who killed Rose and Gideon and then ran away to find my brother, that Kyung stole the tech and I'm here in Seoul trying to steal it back.

"Winter?" she probes. "Are you still there?"

"I'm here," I say. "I'm all right. But I'm struggling with the DID thing, with the idea of sharing my body with other parts of me."

"It's a lot to digest." Her voice is free of judgment. "Especially finding it out at the same time as learning the truth about your sister's death."

"Right. It's too much." I pull in a sharp breath. "Sometimes it's like I'm one realization away from exploding into shrapnel." My voice cracks. "I still can't believe you didn't tell me about your suspicions."

"Brains are funny things. Therapists have to be careful not to plant ideas. Otherwise sometimes we latch onto possibilities we are given, even though they're incorrect."

"That's sort of what Gideon did to me," I say. "He used

the ViSE technology to try to make me believe that my sister was dead."

"Are you still having hallucinations? Do you still see your sister?" she asks. I hear a shuffling sound on her end, like maybe she's organizing some papers.

"No. I can feel the alters, though. Is there any way to keep them from taking control? Some sort of medicine I can take?"

"I'm afraid there are no medicines to suppress alters, Winter." She pauses. "How do you know they're taking over?"

I'm not going to tell her about the guy I killed in Los Angeles. "I'm missing blocks of time. Not anything major, but enough to know something isn't right."

She clears her throat. "Let's back up a little. It's been so long since we've had a full session. Are you still making ViSEs?"

"Not right now," I hedge. "I'm not sure what's going to happen with the club now that Gideon is gone."

"Do you want to run it?"

I twist the corner of the blanket in my free hand. "I don't know anything about owning a business."

"You could take some classes at college, major in business if you wanted to."

"I would like to go to college," I say. "But I'm afraid. What if I dissociate in the middle of a class and make a scene?"

"I don't think that will happen. Try to remember that your alters aren't working against you, even if it sometimes seems like they are. It's not their job to humiliate you or make your life difficult. If they show up, it's because part of you truly needs them in that moment."

It's a good point. As far as I know, Rose never took over during the day unless I was in danger. "What you're saying makes sense. I guess I just worry. Will I ever be normal again?"

"There's a wide range of normal when it comes to DID. Some people eventually fully integrate while others only partially do, but they learn to function normally despite the presence of alters. The important thing here is that healing requires treatment."

"I know, but—"

"If you want a clinician with more experience, I can give you some names," she continues.

"It's not about experience, Dr. Abrams," I say. "Do you think I could improve with just outpatient sessions? My memories of the hospital are terrible—being sedated, being restrained. I don't want to go back to that."

"Those are crisis interventions, Winter. If you checked yourself into an inpatient setting, it wouldn't be like that. There's the place in Arizona—"

"Gideon told me about it. I know you're right. I know I need help. And I promise I'll make some decisions as soon as I get back home."

She sighs. "You're not alone, are you?"

"No. I'm staying with . . . friends."

"That's good." She asks me a few questions about where I am and what I'm doing that I answer as truthfully as possible. Then she asks, "Are you dating anyone?"

I pause. I don't even know how to answer that. "I wasn't expecting the questions to be this hard."

She laughs. "It's my job to challenge you. It's part of getting better."

"There is a guy. I like him, but I have a lot of questions about that too."

"Such as?"

"I got close to him once when I was dissociating. We did things I'm not sure I would've done as me. Will I ever be able to . . ."

"Enjoy intimacy?"

"Yes. Is that part of me broken forever? The part that loves?"

"There's nothing wrong with the part of you that loves," Dr. Abrams says. "It's the part of you that accepts love you need to work on. But don't push yourself. Eventually, it'll feel right."

"I hope so," I say.

"I know so," she says. "And if he's the right guy, he'll wait until it feels right."

"Oh, he'll wait. He'd probably wait forever. That's another problem I have. I feel guilty letting him wait when I'm not sure I'll ever be the girl that he wants."

"Have you told him this?"

"Yes. Recently, in fact."

"Does he know that you were trafficked as a child?"

"Yes."

"And he knows about your DID?"

"Right."

"Well, those are two very serious things. So if he hasn't left, then it sounds like you're already the girl he wants. Are you just worried you might not love him back?"

"Maybe," I whisper. "He told me he loved me, but I couldn't say it back. Is it cruel to let someone hang on if you don't feel the same way?"

"Winter. No relationship progresses at exactly the same speed for both parties. Granted, not a lot of men are willing to be that open. But you should respect that he is and let him decide if and when he needs to walk away. After all, you wouldn't want him to make that decision for you, would you? No one should choose for us when it's time to let go of someone that we love."

I think about how angry I was at both Jesse and Gideon for doing that very thing—making the decision to take Rose away from me. "You're right," I say. "Thank you so much."

"You're welcome. I'd love to see you back here when you return to town. Or if you're going to be gone for an extended period of time, we can continue to do phone sessions or possibly via the Internet?"

"I don't plan on staying here," I say. "I can make an appointment when I return to St. Louis." *If I return.*

"Well, good then. I look forward to hearing from you." She pauses again. "You'd tell me if you were in trouble, right? I could find someone to help you wherever you are."

"I know," I say. And then, "Good-bye."

I wish it were that simple, that I could just go home and let Dr. Abrams take care of me, forget about Rose and Gideon and Jun and the ViSE equipment. I wish I could just start over. But even as I think those thoughts, dark parts of me start pulsing and swirling. I can't start over until I finish what I came here to do. I can only hope there will still be something left of me to start over, once I'm done.

One more chance for rebirth. One more chance to finally do things right.

CHAPTER 26

Someone knocks gently on the door to my room.

"Come in," I say.

Jesse peeks his head in through a crack. "I thought I heard you talking in here."

"You did," I say. "I did a phone session with Dr. Abrams."

"Oh. Cool." He slips into the room and shuts the door behind him. "How'd that go?"

I don't answer for a second. I just study Jesse, from his rumpled hair and scarred face to his NFL T-shirt and pajama pants, to his bare feet. He is so comfortable in his own skin, comfortable sharing himself with me. Dr. Abrams was right when she said most men wouldn't be so open.

"Why are you looking at me like that?" He takes a step back toward the door.

"I'm just glad you're here," I say softly.

"Me too." His cheeks redden slightly. "Do you want me to try to make breakfast again?"

I shake my head. "How about I try this time?"

"Okay." When I make no move to crawl out from my covers, he points over his shoulder at the door. "I'm just going to go so you can get dressed or whatever."

"Thanks."

Jesse disappears into the hallway and I slide out of my blanket cocoon. I toss the cover back onto the bed and change into a pair of jeans and a sweatshirt. I pull my hair back into a ponytail.

Jesse is taking a shower, so I brush my teeth in the kitchen sink and splash a little water on my face.

"What did you do to him?" Baz asks from the living room.

"Nothing, why?"

Baz hops up from the sofa and goes to stand by the bathroom door. He motions for me to join him. "Because he's singing. That's why."

I press my ear close to the painted wood. Sure enough, I can hear Jesse's voice over the patter of the water. What's even funnier is the fact that he seems to be singing one of the recent K-pop hits. He must have heard it on TV.

"Sounds like he's ready for *noraebang*," I tell Baz. Noraebang is the Korean version of karaoke.

"I used to be quite the noraebanger myself," Baz says.

"You are just a constant string of surprises, Sebastian Faber."

Baz grins. "You've got to keep your audience guessing."

"Any news on Jun?"

"Sorry. Nothing yet," Baz says. "But I've put out a lot of feelers with my contacts in the area."

"I appreciate it. What about those names on that paper we found in Kyung's pocket?"

"I passed them along to a friend so he could run a deeper search," Baz says. "I Googled them myself and I think one might be the leader of a rebel group in Myanmar, but I'm not sure about the others."

"Myanmar. That's odd."

"It could just be a list of contacts for something else business related." Baz rubs at his beard. He hasn't shaved since we got here and it's getting quite thick.

Turning back to the kitchen, I look for the rice pot and realize it's still in the sink with Jesse's gluey burned rice stuck to the bottom. "I was going to make breakfast," I say. "But it might just be easier to go buy something."

Baz waves me over to where he's sitting on the sofa. He's skimming through recording footage of Kyung. "Speaking of lists of names, here are all the lead security guards with full building access." He hands me the tablet computer and the badge-cloning device. "If you see one of them, all you do is try to stay within three feet of him long enough for it to copy the clearance codes."

I skim the list of five men on the computer screen, memorizing their names and faces. Two of them are older, with streaks of gray in their hair. The others are younger, probably twenty-five to thirty-five. "Three feet is pretty close." I set the computer on the coffee table.

"Well, if it doesn't happen at UsuMed, we can try following them after they get off work. Maybe I can sit next to one of them at a bar or something." He swipes at the tablet. "Hey. Check this out."

I perch on the edge of the sofa and look down at the screen. Kyung is pacing back and forth in the living room with his phone, so the listening device behind the painting only picks up sporadic bursts of conversation. I hold the tablet up to my ear, closing my eyes to focus on Kyung's words. "Right now it doesn't work . . . I don't know . . . She's disappeared, but I can find—"

It doesn't work. He's probably talking about the neural editor. Do you think *she* is me? I can't hear the end of what he says. It's like he quits talking midsentence."

Baz flips the tablet back to the video feeds. "He stepped out on the balcony. I wish there was a way to get close enough to bug his actual phone."

"Can't you do it remotely, with spyware or something?"

"Not without him noticing changes to his phone, and I'd need to have his number to even try."

"Maybe one of us could sneak into his room while he's sleeping and plant a bug."

"Too dangerous," Baz says. "But I'll keep thinking on it."

When Jesse is finished in the shower, I fill him in on Kyung's phone call and then invite him to go with me to pick up some breakfast. We head around the corner to a convenience store that sells all kinds of food and drink. I pick out two cartons of noodles for Baz and me and a doughnut for Jesse. I find him in the refrigerated section admiring the triangle gimbap.

"Is it like a seaweed-and-rice sandwich?" he asks.

"Sort of. There's usually some kind of meat or fish in the middle with sauce and then rice around it, and then it's packaged so you just wrap the whole thing up in seaweed and hold it in your hand."

Jesse peers at the label, trying to figure out what flavor he's holding. "Can we get some for later?"

I smile at him. "We can get whatever you want."

Those might not have been the wisest words, because Jesse takes me up and down each of the aisles, asking me to explain the stuff he hasn't seen before. We end up with two bags of stuff, including triangle gimbap, hard-boiled eggs, spicy noodles, honey-flavored milk, cookies made from wheat flour, Japanese Pocky candy, and a couple cans of Chilsung Cider, a Korean version of Sprite.

As we walk back to the apartment, a scrawny cat darts across the alley in front of us. I immediately think of Miso.

Jesse can sense the change in my posture. He squeezes my hand. "I'm sure little Moo is doing just fine. I bet he misses you, though."

"I miss him too." I bend down and make a clicking sound with my tongue. The stray cat peers out from behind a trash can, its eyes winking orange in the morning light.

Jesse bends down next to me. "Here kitty, kitty," he says. He rustles one of the plastic bags with our food.

The cat cocks its ears forward. Its tail flicks back and forth.

"Give me that." I pull the bag out of Jesse's hand and tear open one of the packages of triangle gimbap. I break it into balls of rice and filling and toss bits toward the cat.

For a few seconds it just looks at me. Then it creeps over toward the nearest ball and sniffs at it.

"Holy crap, they eat rice?" Jesse says.

"Apparently so," I say, as the cat gobbles up the food.

I lower myself to a seated position. The cat inches its way closer to Jesse and me. As the cat eats another bite of rice and meat, my hands start to go numb from the cold. I blow on my fingers as I slide the partially unwrapped food back into the bag. "Sorry, that's all you get," I say apologetically.

Jesse stands up and reaches down to give me a hand. As he pulls me up, the cat rubs against my leg.

"Aww," I say. "Maybe you can have one more bite." I toss another bit of rice down onto the sidewalk before reluctantly turning away.

But the cat is interested in more than just food. As Jesse and I turn the corner onto our block, it trots beside us, its furry face contorted into what looks like a smile.

"Now look what you've done," Jesse says. "We're being stalked."

"Me? From what I've seen, you're the cat whisperer. I bet if we split up, it'll follow you."

Jesse laughs. "I almost want to try that just to see if you're right." He lowers his voice. "But I don't want to leave you."

Warmth radiates out from my center. *I don't want you to leave.* I can't quite spit the words out. I know Dr. Abrams is right. That Jesse is an adult and he can decide to walk away from me if he gets tired of waiting. But I still feel bad about the push-pull thing I do with him. I glance down at the sidewalk. There's a star beneath our feet that reads "Hej." This whole neighborhood is interspersed with sidewalk stars that say "Hello" in different languages.

"Sorry. I didn't mean to—"

I turn back to Jesse. "It's fine. I know what you meant."

The cat lets out a plaintive yowl as if to ask what's taking us so long. When we reach our building, I spend a few minutes scratching it behind the ears. "You can't come with us," I say sadly.

The cat blinks once and then flops down on its side as if it understands.

"See you around, Blackie," Jesse says.

I snort. "Blackie? You come up with the worst pet names ever."

"Whatever." Jesse holds the front door open for me and then heads for the stairwell.

I pause in front of the elevator, my eyes tracing the crack between the two doors, wondering.

"You ready to try?" Jesse asks.

"No, but I'm feeling reckless. Let's do this."

I tap one foot nervously as I wait for the doors to open. When they do, I step into the compartment and glance quickly around to make sure we're alone. Jesse follows me inside and presses the button for the sixth floor. As the doors slide shut, my breath sticks in my throat and I realize what a bad idea this is. I should be taking medication and doing it a little bit at a time like Dr. Abrams suggested. I lunge for the "door open" button but it's too late—we're already moving.

The second I feel the ground shift beneath my feet, the walls start to lose their shape. They go soft, almost liquid; they twist around me, pressing on my chest, pressing on my throat. I try to inhale through my nose but I can't get any air. When I exhale, all that comes out is a wheezing sound. I look desperately up at the red numbers. We're only to the third floor. That can't be right. I lunge for the button marked five, but

Jesse catches my hand before I can make contact. A strangled sound escapes from my lips.

"Breathe, Winter," Jesse says.

"Can't," I try to say, but if I open my mouth, I feel like the walls of the elevator will pour down my throat and drown me. I shake my head violently. Darkness creeps up on me. I'm either going to pass out or dissociate, and right now I don't care which. I reach for him, wrapping my arms around his neck and holding on.

"You're doing good." His hands gently twine together around my lower back. "Almost there."

I press myself against him harder. I blink back tears. Gradually the walls press back into their actual form. The doors open and all of my breath rushes out of me at once. Jesse supports me as I limp out into the hallway. I'm still clutching the plastic bag of food. I gripped it so hard that the plastic handle has actually broken the skin of my palm.

Jesse gently removes the bag from my hand. He looks down at me, lifts one hand to touch my cheek like maybe he's checking for a fever. "You did it," he says. "It'll get easier."

I am too drained to do more than just nod.

Baz is sitting on the sofa assembling something out of batteries and wires. He looks up as Jesse and I enter. "What happened?"

"She took the elevator," Jesse explains.

"Good," Baz says.

I am still shaking. I slip out of my shoes, one hand clinging to the bathroom doorway for support. I point at the mess of wires and components. "What's that?"

"Plan B."

"What's plan A?" Jesse starts to put the food we bought into the refrigerator.

"Plan A is where we can access the tech with nothing more than a cloned badge."

"And if we can't?" I ask.

"Then we find out where it's located and blow our way in. Unless of course you want to cut out some guy's eyeball and carry it around for a retinal scanner."

The nonchalant way Sebastian delivers this line makes me wonder if he'd be all right with that. A fist clenches and unclenches in my stomach as I watch him deftly manipulate the wires and components. Gideon trusted him, and so far he's given me no reason not to do the same. But what kind of person knows how to make bombs?

CHAPTER 27

I wake up early on Monday to prepare for my first day at UsuMed. We haven't learned much yet from surveilling Kyung's hotel room, so my goal is to get close enough to a security guard to clone his badge, and also to keep my eyes and ears open about any hints to where the ViSE tech is being kept.

My stomach churns as I crawl out of bed. My muscles twitch. I pull my hair back in a ponytail and drop to my hands and knees on the wooden floor. I do a set of twenty-five push-ups, but I still feel kind of edgy.

In the living room, Baz is sitting on the sofa, flipping through some files on his computer. "Oh hey, I got you something." He gestures at the coffee table. A set of two titanium throwing knives are laid out on the glass. "Jesse told me you left your knives in Los Angeles. I know how it feels to go undercover without any kind of weapon."

"Thank you." I go to the knives and lift one of them. The weight is almost the same as that of the knives I left behind, but the blade is sharper and stronger. "Where did you get them?"

Baz grins. "I know people who know people." He pulls something small and metallic out of his pocket. "Take one of these with you too."

"What is it?"

"Another listening device."

"What am I supposed to do with that? You're interested in

the inner workings of the UsuMed customer service department?"

"Maybe you'll run into Kyung."

"And if I do, you expect me to bug him? Just slide it into his pocket without him noticing or something?"

"I don't know. Maybe you can figure out what office he's working out of and pick the lock. Better to have and not need, right? Just in case an opportunity presents itself."

"I guess you're right," I say grudgingly. "Sorry. I'm just a little nervous."

He looks over, studying me with his gray eyes. "Are you going to be okay?"

"Yes. I was thinking I would run the stairs a few times."

"Maybe you should take the elevator a few times," he says.

"Good point."

I put the knives and listening device in my bedroom and then slip out into the hallway. I run up to the top floor and then take the elevator back to the lobby. Jesse and I spent the last few days practicing, and by the tenth time I was able to go by myself. By the fifteenth time I was able to go with a stranger.

But it's still not easy.

The bell dings and the doors open. I head for the stairwell again, my feet pounding the steps a second time. Before I know it, I'm back on the top floor. Now the calm is starting to move through me, my blood spreading out into my extremities instead of pooling in my chest and making my insides feel tight. I do two more laps, riding down and running back up. Then I ride the elevator down to the sixth floor.

Back in the apartment, I take a quick shower and then dress in a knee-length skirt, white button-up blouse, and gray blazer. Instead of nylons I wear a thick pair of black leggings, both to make me feel less exposed and to keep me warm. I slip one of the knives in each boot.

My next decision is the headset. If I get caught with it, Kyung will definitely find out that I'm there. It could wreck the whole plan. Or it could *make* the whole plan if I can record something helpful.

I decide to put it on. Like Baz said, the chance of running into Kyung when I'm working in the customer service offices is pretty slim. I pin the black wig with bangs over my headset and adjust the hair around my face until I'm certain everything looks natural.

Jesse wakes up while I'm in the kitchen nibbling on a hard-boiled egg and pacing back and forth. "You okay?" he asks. "Because if you don't want to do this, there's probably another—"

"I'm fine," I say quickly. There might be another way, but so far this is the best way.

On the subway, I stand in the middle of the car, one hand gripping a support beam and the other clutching my leather portfolio with copies of my work documents. Baz and his friend went through and made sure I had all of the identification paperwork I would need.

After I exit the train, I walk two blocks and then follow a scattering of people up the wide, flat stairs to the set of doors leading into the UsuMed building. Pressure builds in my chest as my heart and lungs decide to malfunction at the same time. *Focus, Winter.* I pause, pretending like I'm checking something on my phone. People swerve around me, their eyes glued to their own phones as they head inside. I take a deep breath like Dr. Abrams taught me, holding it in for four seconds before expelling it slowly and holding my breath for four more seconds.

Then I step through the glass doors and into the UsuMed lobby.

I approach the information desk and clear my throat. A man with dark, unfriendly eyes studies me for a few moments. Beneath my business-appropriate shirt and coat, my heart starts to accelerate. Why is he looking at me like that? Am I already about to be exposed as a fraud?

"You've got a bit of something on your collar," he says.

I angle my head and see a few drops of some kind of sauce standing out on the dark wool. Someone on the subway must have spilled something on me.

"Thank you." I pull a tissue out of my purse and dab at the spots. I take a deep breath, trying to slow the pounding in my chest. "I'm supposed to report to the Talent Acquisition Department. Can you tell me where that's located?"

"Fourteenth floor," the man says crisply.

"Thank you again." I turn away and wait in the lobby for an elevator. My heart revs up once more as a small crowd gathers and a couple of men with leather briefcases push in close to me. As much as Jesse and I practiced the elevator, we never did it with this many people. I bite down on my lip and visualize riding the car up to the fourteenth floor. *It'll only be about ten seconds,* I tell myself.

When the doors on the elevator finally open, it's like getting on the subway all over again. Everyone makes a mad dash and I just barely squeeze in before an older lady with deep scowl lines etched in her forehead presses the DOOR CLOSED button.

I turn toward the corner of the car as we begin to move, resisting the urge to close my eyes. I'm sure there's a camera somewhere and I don't want to call attention to myself. I hold my breath for most of the ride, flinching each time the car slows to a stop to let people on or off. I just want the ride to be over with.

When we make it to the fourteenth floor, I squeeze out of the elevator behind two men with briefcases. There's a set of restrooms here and I duck into the ladies' room to smooth the wrinkles from my skirt and catch my breath. Then I find the Talent Acquisition Department at the west end of the hallway. This entire wall of the building is made of glass and I pause outside the door for a moment to look down at the busy street below. A swarm of businesspeople emerge from one of the subway exits, many of them looking down at phones as they walk.

You can do this, I tell myself. *You're just one more worker. No one will pay you any special attention unless you give them a reason.*

Taking a deep breath, I open the door to the Talent Acquisition Department. There are three other girls milling about the waiting area. Two of them are chatting, and I realize they're new employees, like me. The third girl is glued to her phone, tapping out a text message. She's wearing silvery-gray tights with her black skirt. Sparkly silver ribbons are threaded down the middle of her wispy pigtails. I envy her carefree style. I wander the length of the room, pretending to be checking out the different notices on the walls, but really I'm trying to capture as much on my ViSE as possible.

A stern-looking woman in a dark pantsuit strides out from the back part of the office. Her eyes skim over the group of us. I try not to fidget or adjust my hair.

"I am the manager, Mrs. Kim Eun Young," she says in Korean. "Come. We have much to do today."

The other girls and I follow her back out into the hallway and into a deserted conference room where she has us all take seats around a plain fiberglass table. She removes four tablet computers from a locked cabinet and hands one to each of us. Then she gives us instructions on how to log in to the UsuMed network. For the next two hours, we complete new-hire paperwork on these computers. I have all the items Baz had printed for me, and I do my best not to arouse suspicion as I slowly complete the forms. I spent a couple of hours last night memorizing the basic information of the girl whose job I stole, so I wouldn't have to think if someone asked me something like my date of birth, year of graduation, or Korean ID number.

After we finish the forms, we're given a short ten-minute break. The girl in the gray tights says she's going to step outside for a few minutes. "Anyone want to come with me?" she asks.

"I'll go." I hop up from my chair. I figure she's probably going to smoke, but maybe I can get her chatting. I don't know what I can find out about UsuMed from her, but at this point the more information the better.

We walk down the hallway silently together. The girl punches the DOWN button on the elevator and I say a silent thank-you to Baz for forcing me to practice. "I'm Choi Yoo Mi," she says, clicking her tongue against the roof of her mouth. The elevator arrives and I try not to flinch as I enter it. A couple of men in suits are standing at the back of the car.

"I'm Lee Jae Hwa," I say as the elevator doors close with a soft swish.

We stand silently as the elevator carries us to the first floor. When the doors open, the men push past and hurry across the tile floor toward the coffee shop. We turn the other direction, ducking out through the revolving door into a clear but cold day. I follow Yoo Mi around to the smoking area.

She pulls a pack of cigarettes and a lighter out of her purse. She offers a cigarette to me.

I shake my head. "I just wanted to get some fresh air."

"Then you live in the wrong place," she says with a grin. "I actually don't smoke either. I just pretend to so I have an excuse to sneak out here. We're not going to meet many guys in the call center. My friend met her future husband in the smoking area." She gestures around us as she lights her cigarette. There are about fifteen people out here right now and eleven of them are men.

"You don't have a boyfriend?" I ask, surprised. I just met Yoo Mi, but she seems so confident, so comfortable in her own skin. She seems like the kind of girl guys would fight over. But maybe I'm thinking about American guys. Individuality is still somewhat frowned upon here.

"No. I had one in college but we broke up senior year. You?"

I have a strange urge to tell her about Jesse, even though he's not my boyfriend. But if I mention him, she's going to want to see pictures and she's going to wonder how I met a foreigner, and there are just too many potential questions I don't want to answer. So instead I lower my gaze to the ground. "Oh, I've never had a boyfriend."

"Surprising." Yoo Mi lights the cigarette and holds it down-wind of both of us. "You're really pretty."

My face reddens a little. "Thank you. So are you."

A gust of wind picks up, ruffling coattails and blowing bits of trash down the street. Yoo Mi watches a pair of guys in suits as they lean over their phones.

"How long did it take you to get this job?" I ask her.

"I've been in the Cheonma database for a couple of months," she says. "I had one other offer but I refused it because the commute would have been almost two hours each way."

Yoo Mi turns out to be the kind of girl who keeps talking once you get her started. She lives in one of the outermost areas of Seoul. She has to take a bus and two trains to get here, but it's worth it because the recruiter told her if she does a good job, there's a decent probability that UsuMed might hire her permanently, and then she can move to an apartment in the city.

Yoo Mi drops the cigarette to the ground and grinds it out under the toe of her leather boot. She places the butt into one of the marked receptacles and we turn back toward the lobby. We return to the same conference room, where Mrs. Kim starts a series of informational and legal videos on a projector screen.

After about twenty minutes of boring corporate history and policy, I realize the memory card in my recorder headset has run out. I ask Mrs. Kim if I may be excused to use the restroom.

Her eyes flick to the clock on the wall. I know she's wondering why I can't wait another hour for our official lunch break, but she's not going to ask me because she doesn't want to embarrass me. "You may, but please hurry. We have a lot to get through today."

I head down the long tiled hallway, duck into the bathroom, and swap out the cards in one of the stalls. "Most boring ViSE in the history of the world," I mutter as I slip the full one into my purse. "Maybe we can market you as a cure for insomnia."

On the way back to Talent Acquisition, I make an intentional wrong turn, hoping I can play the clueless new girl on day one without anyone holding it against me.

The sign near the fourteenth-floor elevator says that in addition to Talent Acquisition, this floor is also home to college recruitment and something called the Science Scholars Program. I make a loop around all the hallways, scanning both ways to record as much as I can, but nothing feels particularly helpful. I duck into the stairwell and try to swipe my badge to access the floor below, but the access light remains red and the door remains locked. I don't know if it's because the thirteenth floor is a restricted area or because the temporary agency badges aren't coded for stairwell access.

I head back up to the fourteenth floor and realize my mistake. That door also has a badge reader but my badge doesn't work. I've locked myself in the stairwell. I'm not sure how much time has passed, but probably enough for Mrs. Kim to wonder what I'm doing. Sighing, I descend all the way to the first floor, hoping it will be an unsecured door since it leads into the lobby.

The stairwell is empty, so I figure I might as well check out the lower levels while I'm down here. But all of them—B-1 to B-4—have card readers. At least I have all of this on a ViSE recording now.

I return to the first floor, which as I suspected has no card reader. I exit out into the lobby. As I'm waiting for the elevator to go back up, I catch sight of a security guard heading for the front exit. Damn it. He looks like one of the guys on Baz's list. He's probably going to smoke. If I hadn't wasted so much time, I could go out there too. I've got the badge-cloning device in my purse.

The elevator doors open while I'm still debating. Mrs. Kim steps out. She's got a wallet in her hand and appears to be heading for the coffee shop. I try to duck behind a potted plant, but I'm not quick enough.

"Jae Hwa, what are you doing?" Mrs. Kim's eyes narrow. "I thought you were going to the restroom."

"It was being cleaned," I say quickly, my breath catching in my throat. My heart pounds in my chest as I try to make the lie sound more believable. "The janitor recommended I use the bathroom on the floor below, and then I locked myself in the stairwell, so I had to come all the way down here."

"You took the stairs instead of the elevator?"

"Well, I thought I would only have to go one floor." I bite my lip, trying to look contrite. "And I've been trying to get more exercise."

Mrs. Kim purses her lips. I can tell she's not sure whether to believe me. "Come," she says finally. "I'll walk you back to the training room."

I know better than to protest. I scurry into the elevator behind her, my chin tucked low in what I hope looks like remorse. I stand at the back of the car, with Mrs. Kim to my right side. I can feel her eyes on me. I keep my own eyes trained carefully on the floor.

When the elevator arrives at the fourteenth floor, I mumble another apology to Mrs. Kim and hurry down the hallway. I slide back into the training room, where the other three girls are still watching orientation videos.

Yoo Mi glances over at me. "Everything all right?" she mouths.

I nod. She makes a face that I'm pretty certain is an imitation of Mrs. Kim. I swallow back a giggle. When I imagined coming to work at UsuMed, all I thought about was finding the tech and the possibility of running into Kyung. It didn't occur to me that I might actually make a friend.

At one o'clock, Mrs. Kim informs us that we have an hour for lunch, and the four of us decide to go to a local restaurant together. Many of the UsuMed staff eat in the coffee shop or restaurant located on the first floor, but there are at least a dozen other places within a two-block radius. Yoo Mi links arms with me and the other two girls hold hands as we head down the street to a nearby noodle shop.

Inside, the tables are crowded and packed close together, trapping the heat from the kitchen and keeping us warm. I order a bowl of *tteokguk*, which is a hot broth soup with leeks and slices of rice cake in it.

While we're waiting for the food to arrive, the four of us chatter about our first day at UsuMed. The other two girls are best friends who were roommates in college. Their names are Soo Jin and Min Hee, but they like to go by their Western names, Susan and Minnie.

"Where do you live?" Susan asks. She starts to pour a cup of water for each of us from a pitcher at the end of the table.

I hold my cup with both hands as she pours mine. "Gwangjin-gu." I give them the area of the city that is printed on my fake ID.

"Did you go to Sejong University?" Minnie takes the pitcher and pours Susan a cup.

I shake my head. "I went to Yonsei."

"Lucky," Minnie says. "I bet you'll be the first of us to be offered a permanent position."

"I don't know. Mrs. Kim already hates me."

Yoo Mi giggles. "Where did you go, anyway? Longest bathroom trip ever."

"I had to go to a different floor because the bathroom was being serviced, and then I got a little lost on my way back." I pause, do my best to look thoughtful. "This building is so huge. I wonder what's happening on all the other floors."

"There's a directory in the lobby," Susan says.

"Right, but some of the floors are marked private, like B-1 and B-2."

Yoo Mi's eyes light up. "Ooh. I wonder if that's where they do the top-secret stuff."

You and me both, I think. But how can I find out?

Our food arrives and I lapse into silence, realizing we have to be back to the conference room in less than thirty minutes. Yoo Mi focuses mainly on her phone. Susan and Minnie chatter about a K-pop sing-off that's supposed to happen on Thursday night, close to the office.

I'm dreading going back for a boring afternoon of more UsuMed corporate policy videos, but as the four of us approach the wide plaza in front of the building, things get more interesting. A long black car pulls up. *Kyung,* I think, even though I don't know for sure. A man with broad shoulders wearing dress pants and a fitted jacket steps out of the car. There's a telltale bulge in the small of his back—a gun. I bet the other girls don't even realize it because it's such a rare sight here. The man glances both ways and then gestures to someone still in the car.

A man in a suit slides out of the back.

It's not Kyung. This man is taller, younger, with hair that's just a little long for a Korean executive. He turns back to say something to the driver and I catch a glimpse of his face. I don't recognize him, but I know him from somewhere.

I'm certain of it.

I flip back through what's left of the memories of my past, looking for a match. *Who is he?*

A name comes to me, out of nowhere. *Alec.*

I don't know if it's real. I search my memories again. But then another man steps out of the car and something dark and damaged rustles beneath my skin. *Kill,* a voice whispers. *Finish it.*

It's Kyung. He doesn't even need to turn around for me to know. He strides up the steps in front of the building as if he owns the world.

He owns our world. Take it back.

Lily. Violent, impulsive Lily. I'm still not sure I believe in her.

Believe.

I tremble. My breath goes silent in my chest. The gray day gets even darker. My left hand drops to my side. The knife in my boot is so close. My eyes trace the path from my hand to Kyung's back. Clear shot.

No, I silently protest. *Not here, not now.*

Let me.

I still haven't taken a breath. My lungs are on fire. I feel the darkness sliding over me, my body slipping away. The scene before me starts to blur.

"No," I whisper.

Yoo Mi gives me a strange look. "Jae Hwa, are you all right?"

I contort my quivering lips into what I hope is a smile. "Fine. I just thought I might have left my phone at the restaurant." I hold up my phone so everyone can see everything is okay, but I'm not looking at them. Kyung and his mysterious colleague have taken a detour around to the smoking area and now all I see are their backs.

Kill.

"Sorry. I need to make a quick phone call," I tell Yoo Mi. "I'll see you guys back in the conference room." I turn and hurry toward a bench near the street before she can ask any follow-up questions. Pulling out my phone, I pretend like I'm calling someone when really all I'm doing is trying to stay in control. If I were calm—if I were healthy—I'd be over in the smoking area cloning Kyung's badge right now. But just the thought of that sends another storm of fury swirling beneath my skin. *Focus, Winter.* I bite down hard on my lower lip, fight the spreading darkness. "Everything is fine," I whisper. "Don't mess things up."

Kyung and his friend are chatting. *Alec.* Where do I know that name from? I study him from a safe distance, his lean frame, relaxed posture, the slight tint of auburn in his hair. I squeeze my eyes shut and probe the dark places of my memory. *Alec. Come on—help me out here.*

But my mind doesn't have the answer, or if it does, it's not ready to give it up.

Alec and Kyung flick the last bits of ash from their cigarettes and toss the butts into one of the marked receptacles. I hold my breath as I watch them walk from the smoking area to the revolving doors.

Lily is finally quiet, but I am still unsettled. If I go back into the building and run across Kyung grabbing a cup of coffee or chatting with the information desk attendant, I have no idea if I'll be able to stay in control. I rest my head in my hands, feel the pounding of my heart in my fingertips.

My first thought is to call Dr. Abrams, but I realize it's nighttime in St. Louis. She wouldn't pick up, or even if she did, she'd be worried about me.

With shaking fingers, I dial Jesse instead.

"Yeah?" he says in a drowsy voice.

"Did you go back to sleep?" I ask incredulously. "It's almost two!"

"I was trying to study Korean, but looking at all the foreign words made me tired," he mumbles.

The anger and rage coiled around my heart start to loosen. "No one expects you to learn Korean," I say softly. "It's not an easy language."

"I'm not doing it because someone expects it. I'm doing it because I want to. It'll be easier for me to help out with things if I know some basic terminology. Plus, your pal Kyung made two phone calls last night, and I thought maybe I could figure out some of what he said."

"Two calls? Has Baz listened to them yet?"

"No. He was gone somewhere before I got up."

"I'll check them out first thing when I get home." I peek at the time. I have two minutes before I need to be back inside. Even if I sprint and the elevator is waiting, I probably won't make it. "I should get going."

"Are you all right? Your voice sounds funny."

I rise from the bench and dust off the back of my skirt. "I saw him again," I whisper.

"Kyung?"

"Yes."

"Well, that's a good thing, right? If he's there all the time, that means the ViSE tech isn't going anywhere."

"I guess. I nearly lost it, though," I admit. "It was like I could feel a darker part of me trying to burst through my skin."

"Lily," Jesse breathes.

"Yes."

"Are you okay now? Because if not, maybe you can say you got sick and—"

"I'm fine," I tell him. "I called because I thought I might need you to talk me down, but just your voice helps a lot."

"You called me for *help*?" Jesse asks, his voice brightening.

I start to tell him I was going to call Dr. Abrams, but then I swallow back the words. He sounds so happy that I reached out to him. I should let him have that. "Of course," I say. "We've always been there for each other like that, right?"

"Yeah. And we always will be, okay? No matter what happens."

I hear someone yelling the name Jae Hwa. I glance up and see Yoo Mi's head sticking out of the conference room window. She holds out her arm and taps at her watch.

I call up to her in Korean, "I'm coming right now."

"I love listening to you speak Korean," Jesse says.

For some reason this makes my eyes water. I blink hard. "I'm glad that you love it. I really do have to hang up, though."

"Winter," Jesse says.

"Yes?"

"Stay safe."

"I will," I promise. But I think again of the knives in my boots. Of how close I came to attacking Kyung. We have to find the technology and find it quickly. Next time Lily might win.

CHAPTER 28

The rest of the day goes smoothly, but we've switched from legal and informational videos to building safety, which unfortunately is just as dull.

"If the fire alarm is activated, all of the badge-coded doors will unlock and all staff must immediately evacuate the building via the stairwells," a girl on the projector screen chirps.

"I dare one of you to go pull it right now," Yoo Mi murmurs.

"Seriously. Either that or I need a biohazard containment breach," Minnie adds. "I'm about to fall asleep."

"Is biohazard breach the one where you have to strip down and shower in the decontamination tent before being allowed back on the property?" Susan tries to swallow back a yawn and fails.

Immediately, the three of us yawn one after the next, which makes Susan yawn again. "I think we might have missed something important." Yoo Mi points at the projector screen. All of the actors on it are wearing gas masks while one person is lying on the floor having a spasm.

"I hope they have a bigger stock of those than they do in the subway stations," Minnie grumbles. "In the event of an airborne-contaminant emergency, the first fifty people should affix a mask to their face and run like hell so no one without a mask steals it."

We all laugh. For the rest of the afternoon, the four of us complete the training videos and help each other complete orientation modules and exams for each video. In between modules, I open a window to the UsuMed company directory and do a quick search for the three names that were on the paper in Kyung's pocket: Nai Khaing, Cristian Rojas, and Erich Cross. None of them is in the system.

At the end of the day, Yoo Mi and I push through the revolving door and exit into the dampening cold. A street vendor is selling *hotteok*—pancakes made with rice flour and stuffed with melted brown sugar—in front of the building. The tantalizing scent wafts across the wide sidewalk. I freeze up for a moment, hit by a memory of my sister and me as children—before we went to the US, back when we were still Min Ji and Ha Neul.

"Ha Neul, what is it?" My sister stopped next to me on the sidewalk, following my gaze to the little silver cart. A boy a couple of years older than her was frying balls of dough on a hot plate while an older woman—his mother, probably—took orders from a line of high school and college kids. "Hotteok? You know we have no money for that."

I nodded. But I couldn't pull myself away from the sweet smell, from the warmth of the hot plate. The boy smashed each of the balls flat. I closed my eyes and let the aroma wrap around me. I could almost taste the soft bread and melted brown sugar on my tongue.

My sister petted my hair and it made me think of our mother. It'd been eight years since she left us at the orphanage, and my memory of her had fallen away except for a few jagged pieces. "I have an idea," Min Ji said. "Wait here."

I stood at the edge of the sidewalk, watching my sister in line with the school kids, wondering what she might possibly trade for one of the warm, sweet pastries. When she got to the front, she whispered into the ear of the boy helping. His mother looked over in disapproval, but her attention was quickly drawn away by the next customer. My sister brushed her lips against the boy's cheek. He blushed and gestured with his head toward a little silver canister off to the side. Min Ji waited until his mother was focused on making change for a college girl with hair the color of honey and then reached into the silver canister, her dainty fingers closing around a circle with blackened edges. She glanced back at me and started heading down the block.

I pushed through the people on the sidewalk and caught up with her as we hit the corner. We took the stairs down into a subway station and leaned back against the wall, watching people stream past us. Min Ji took one bite of the hotteok and then pressed it into my fingers. "Eat fast," she said, "so no one can take it away from us."

Even though the edges were a little burnt and the melted insides had cooled and congealed, it was still delicious. I wolfed down the rest of it in a couple bites. Min Ji kissed me on the cheek, much like she kissed the boy. "Are you happy?" she asked.

I nodded shyly.

And in that moment I truly was.

"Do you want one?" Yoo Mi gestures at the cart. "You're staring like it's been years since you've had a hotteok."

"Yes, let's," I say. "I used to love them as a child."

Yoo Mi and I stand in line and each buy a hotteok. We step to the side of the cart and nibble at our treats. The brown sugar inside the soft bread is melted almost to the point of syrup, and I have to hold the treat carefully to keep from spilling it on myself.

Yoo Mi's phone buzzes with a text and she glances down at the screen. "Sorry. I need to get going."

"Me too."

She starts heading toward the subway station and I keep pace next to her. She steps in front of me as we reach the narrow escalator that feeds us down into the endless subway tunnels.

Yoo Mi heads for the silver turnstiles. I follow her through.

"I'm the other way from you," she says. "But it was nice to meet you. I'll see you tomorrow."

"Hmm?" It takes me a minute to remember that I told all of the girls at lunch I lived in Gwangjin-gu, which is actually the opposite direction from Itaewon. "Oh right." I give Yoo Mi a little wave and then take the stairs to the opposite platform.

Through the glass safety doors that prevent people from falling onto the tracks, I watch her insert a pair of white earphones into her ears. When her train pulls out of the station, I take the escalator back to the main level and cross over to the other platform. Glancing up at the LCD board, I see the express train is coming. Good. I'm eager to get back to the apartment and show Jesse and Baz everything that I learned today.

When I get home, Jesse is on the sofa watching K-dramas. I slip out of my boots, leaving my knives inside of them, and flop down next to him. "Still working on your Korean?"

"Is it weird that I can sort of understand what's happening even though I don't know what they're saying?" he asks.

"No. It's not like there's no picture to fill in the context for you. Plus, I find Korean people to be very expressive. You can usually tell how they're feeling just by their faces and tone of voice."

He turns to me. "I wish I could usually tell how you were feeling."

I smile. "I am an anomaly."

Jesse turns back to the TV. "I'm feeling kind of useless, you know? Baz speaks some Korean and knows how to get around the city. And he's good with computers and has hacker and spy friends. I don't have any of that."

I nudge him in the ribs with my elbow. "But you're our official cook."

He sighs. "I'm not even good at that. I'm like no help at all."

"You helped today," I remind him. "On the phone. And you

helped me get over my elevator phobia. Don't discount that kind of stuff just because it's not as flashy as hacking company servers or procuring weapons."

Jesse nods. "I just wish I could do more."

"You can. Show me these phone calls of Kyung's that we recorded."

Jesse grabs Baz's tablet and opens the recording app. He selects last night around eleven p.m. and then hands the tablet to me.

I turn the volume all the way up. I hear a soft buzzing sound and then Kyung answering the phone. His voice is low and I can't make out all of the words, but I hear him talk about "the project" and "diagnosing the problem," which has to be about repairing the neural editor. He also says something about bringing in a specialist from UsuTech to help. Unfortunately he doesn't mention anything about where the technology is located.

When he stops speaking, Jesse switches to the other call. This one is outgoing and turns out to be Kyung calling the hotel concierge to have his dry cleaning expedited.

"So nothing useful?" Jesse looks crestfallen.

"I didn't say that. It's not all the information we were hoping for—not yet—but it's good to have verification that he is here working on the problem and that he's planning to bring in a specialist. It means we still have time. Let's check in and see what he's doing right now."

I flip the camera feed back to present time, not really expecting Kyung to be back in his hotel suite, but to my surprise find him stretched out on his bed at seven P.M.

Jesse squints at the feed. "Is that . . . is he . . . wearing a headset?"

My breath catches in my throat as I realize what we're watching. Kyung is vising.

CHAPTER 29

"Zoom in," I say.

Jesse enlarges the screen, confirming what I was afraid of. "It's not the headset he stole from me," I say. "It's not one of Gideon's."

"Are you sure?"

"Look at the shape of the prongs." I point at the screen. "They're different."

"So he's managed to produce his own headset already? That's bad," Jesse mutters.

I flip through the different camera feeds, pausing on the one in the living room. I glance around the apartment. "Where's Baz?"

"Somewhere with Chung Hee, I think."

"Did he take the motorcycle?"

"I don't know. I haven't seen the keys anywhere. Why?"

I point at the computer screen. There's a black circle on the end table closest to the front door—a wireless phone charger. "Look. Kyung left his cell phone in the living room."

"So?"

"So if he's vising, maybe I can sneak in there and put this in it." I hold up the tiny bug Sebastian gave me to take to UsuMed.

"Too dangerous," Jesse says. "What if he hears you?"

"I'll be quiet," I say. "This whole plan is too dangerous, but the less information we have, the riskier it gets. Come on—you just said you wanted to do more." I get up and head for the door.

"Do more does not include getting us killed," Jesse grumbles but follows me. As I slide my boots back on, he tries again. "You know Baz would not approve of this plan."

"Baz would think this plan was brilliant," I lie, trying to ignore the fact that Baz said sneaking into Kyung's room when he was there was too risky. "He'd want to be the one who planted the bug."

"What if Kyung's finished vising before we even get there?"

"I'll bring my tablet so we can check in." I grab my coat from the closet and button it over my work clothes. I gesture impatiently at Jesse as he finishes lacing up his boots and grabs his knit cap.

"All right," Jesse says. "Let's do this."

I call up the train schedule on my phone as we head for the nearest subway station. "It's going to take us forever," I mutter.

"What about that?" Jesse points at a hot-pink moped with butterfly decals parked in the alley behind our building. It probably belongs to a college student.

"What about it? Did she leave her keys?"

"No, but I think I can get it going." Jesse glances furtively around and then hurries over to the bike. Quickly he pulls off a small panel by the speedometer and reaches inside. In less than a minute the moped sputters to life.

"And you said you weren't helpful." I give him a hug and we both pile onto the tiny bike. "Do you know how to drive one of these things?"

"Um, not really. But I can ride a bike so how hard can it be? I'll try to bring it back in one piece. Hopefully she won't even know it was gone."

The seat is barely big enough for the two of us, so I sit

pressed against him, my arms wrapped tightly around his middle. Luckily the moped is sturdy and manages to stay upright, even through a few sharp turns. Jesse doesn't try to ride it up and down curbs like Baz, so that helps a lot, as does the fact that the bike's speed seems to top out at about forty miles per hour.

"The subway might have been faster," I joke, as we pull up to a stoplight.

"True. But this is riding in style. All I need is one of those Hello Kitty facemasks."

"Remind me to buy you one of those for your birthday," I say.

About twenty minutes later, Jesse and I arrive at the Sky-Tower hotel. We pull around the corner and leave the bike parked on the side street, close to where I waited for Sebastian the other day. Keeping our heads down, we cross the street to the hotel's entrance, take the elevator to the top floor, and duck into the penthouse Baz rented to check on whether Kyung is still vising.

My skin crawls when I see that he's still in his room with the headset on, but now he's no longer alone. There's a girl on the bed with him who doesn't look much older than I am. They're kissing. In one smooth move he pulls her slinky dress over her head and drops it to the floor.

I turn away from Jesse, hurrying toward the bathroom where I lean over the sink, retching for a few seconds.

"Winter." Jesse places a protective hand on my lower back. "It isn't necessarily—"

"What?" I say, my head still hanging over the sink. "Prostitution? You think a girl that age wants to do those things to someone twenty years her senior? It makes me . . ." *It makes me wonder if Kyung assaulted me and I don't remember it.* "It makes me want to go over there and stab him right in front of her. At least that way she'd be free."

"I was going to say against her will," Jesse murmurs. "You

know what? Never mind. Why don't you stay here and I'll sneak in and plant the bug?"

My whole body goes tense. "Stay here and watch that? No, thanks."

"But what if—"

"I'm fine. I can do it," I say tersely. I stare at my reflection, willing myself to stay calm, stay in control. Jesse is right. I can't assume that girl is living the same existence I lived. And even if she is, there's nothing I can do to help her without blowing our entire plan.

It hits me that it's a bad idea for me to go in there looking like Jae Hwa, UsuMed customer service trainee. If Kyung catches me in his suite, he'll know I'm here and that I'm after the tech, but that doesn't mean he'll suspect I've infiltrated his company. I pull off my wig and shake out my natural hair. "Give me your hoodie," I say.

"What?"

"I should have changed. If something goes wrong, I don't want to blow my UsuMed cover."

Jesse shrugs and shucks off the sweatshirt. He's wearing a white T-shirt underneath. The angry red line that runs down the center of his chest is just barely visible through the thin fabric. He hands the hoodie to me. I start to unbutton my own shirt, for once not caring if Jesse sees me less than completely dressed. I'm not sure how much time I have or if I'll get another opportunity like this.

Jesse turns around and I yank off the shirt and slip into his sweatshirt. It's almost a dress on me. I slide out of my skirt and boots too so I'm just in leggings and Jesse's sweatshirt. I tuck my throwing knives into the center pocket of the hoodie, just in case. "Wish me luck," I mutter.

"Wait. I'm coming with you. What if you need backup?"

"Backup is supposed to wait until someone calls for help. Watch the cameras. You'll see if I get in trouble."

"But I won't be able to warn you if he, uh, finishes."

I shudder. "Fine. Text me if I'm in danger." I set my phone on silent and slip it into the pocket next to my knives.

"I think we should call—"

I reach up and give Jesse a quick kiss on the cheek and Baz's name disappears on his lips. "Everything is going to be all right. Thanks for the sweatshirt." I take one more look at the video feed to make sure Kyung is definitely still occupied. Then I duck out into the hall.

I slink around to the other side of the top floor. Glancing at my phone and seeing no messages, I tap the cloned house-keeping keycard against the reader and the door light turns green. Very slowly, I open the door and step onto the tiled area where shoes are left. I close the door quietly and creep up onto the hardwood floor. Another glance at my phone. No texts.

The door to Kyung's bedroom is closed, which is both help-ful and harmful. Helpful because it means the noises coming from it are muffled and indistinct. Harmful because as much as I don't want to listen to what's going on, if either of them get up and leaves the room, I won't hear it until it's too late to hide.

I check my phone again. So far so good.

Staying low, I tiptoe into the living area. I crouch down behind the sofa as I reach for Kyung's phone. I pause for a mo-ment to memorize exactly the way it's sitting on the charger. Then I lift it from the base. The screen lights up, asking me for a password. I turn the phone over and slide it out of its protective case. I use my fingernail to try to pry off the back-ing to the battery compartment. My nail breaks. The battery cover stays where it is.

I swear under my breath as I fish one of my throwing knives out of the pocket of Jesse's hoodie.

Jesse: What's taking you so long?

Ignoring the text, I use my knife to carefully pry the back-ing off the phone, and place the bug. I slip the phone back into its case and wipe my fingerprints off with the cuff of Jesse's sweatshirt. I replace it on the charger. I'm getting ready to head for the door when I hear a squeak.

Jesse: The girl is coming!

Damn it. Still completely naked, the girl crosses from the bedroom to the kitchen. Humming to herself, she opens a couple of cabinets. Then she begins to fill a teapot with water.

Me: I'm stuck.

Even if she makes tea and returns to Kyung's room, I can't get out without risking being seen unless they close the bedroom door again.

Jesse: I'm going to pull the fire alarm.

Me: Wait.

If Jesse pulls the fire alarm, there's a good chance Kyung will find me if he stops to grab his phone before evacuating. I inch toward the far end of the sofa, closest to the doors leading out onto the balcony. They're latched, but unlocked. If I time it just right . . .

The tea water starts to boil, the sounds of bubbling and whistling filling the entire room. I steal a glance at the girl. Her back is to me as she moves around in the kitchen. Hurriedly, I slip outside onto the balcony, leaving the door slightly ajar behind me so as not to make a noise.

The penthouse balcony takes up almost the entire north side of the hotel, which faces a small alley and the side of an office building made of brick. There's a set of chaise lounges with a small table between them, and long rectangular boxes at each end of the balcony that probably hold flowers during warmer months. I scoot toward one of the boxes and press my back against the wall of the hotel.

Me: Balcony. East side. Maybe I can climb up to the roof.

I reach out and test the decorative iron railing that runs the perimeter of the balcony. It feels sturdy, but also slippery and cold.

Jesse: Hang on. I have an idea.

Me: ?

Jesse doesn't respond immediately, but a couple of minutes later a new message blinks on the screen.

Jesse: Look up.

I look up. He's on the roof with the escape rope and harness from our suite. I give him a thumbs-up signal and he starts to lower the rope.

But then I see movement out of the corner of my eye.

The balcony door is opening.

Someone is coming out here.

CHAPTER 30

Almost without thinking, I vault over the edge of the railing, clinging to the cold iron for dear life, my fingers barely hidden behind one of the empty flower boxes. I climb partially underneath the base of the balcony, my hands wrapped tightly around the bottom of the metal bars, one foot propped precariously across a support beam. Below me is open space. Twenty floors of open space. When I look up, I can just barely see Jesse. He looks back at me in shock.

I shake my head no. I'm not sure who has come outside, but either Kyung or the girl is going to notice a rope with a harness being lowered. Gentle footfalls parade across the balcony. The scent of cigarette smoke stings my nose. Chances are it's the girl and she's just trying to sneak a couple of puffs before returning to Kyung. I can hold on for a few seconds. Everything will be fine.

Unless I fall.

Focus, Winter.

If only it were that easy. I've never wondered about the calming voice in my head—I guess I thought everyone had one of those, a sort of self-preservation alter ego that steps in to keep minds from overloading with anxiety. But now I'm not so sure. Maybe it's me, or maybe it's Rose. Or some other alter persona. I try to kick my other foot up so I'm supported by all four limbs, but my leg isn't quite long enough. *Save me,* I think. *Save me and I'll stop thinking of you as some liability, some disease I need to be cured of.*

I hear the girl's voice and for one horrible moment I worry I've spoken my thoughts aloud and that she's about to discover me. Or that maybe Kyung has stepped outside too, that both of them are going to watch me fall to my death. I crane my neck to look below me. There's nothing down there but a couple of trash cans and an old bicycle.

From above me, the girl laughs. I wait to hear Kyung respond, and when he doesn't, I realize she's talking on the phone.

The girl laughs again. She tells someone she finally has the money to pay off a debt. I hate that she had to sleep with Kyung for that. I hate how unequal, how unfair the world can be sometimes. I wish I had just stormed into his bedroom and killed him.

You're going to be all right.

The fingers of my left hand start to go numb in the frigid air. I make the mistake of looking down again. A boy shuffles past, his face focused on his phone. I imagine falling, crushing him, killing us both. He wouldn't even know what hit him.

Don't scream, I think. *If I fall, don't let me scream.* If I don't make a noise, maybe no one will know I was in Kyung's room. Maybe people will think I'm some random suicide and Jesse and Baz can continue on with the plan.

I look up at Jesse again, surprised by his expression. I expected him to be freaking out and falling apart, but he's just staring down at me with razor-sharp focus, ready to lower the harness the instant the girl goes back inside the penthouse.

Our eyes meet, and even from twenty feet away I see his gaze soften—I see that he loves me. He loves me so much he's managed to lock away his fear to focus on my safety. The thought should give me strength, but instead it makes me want to let go, to fall, to set him free. Sure, he would mourn me for a few months, but then he would move on, because he's sane and normal, and that's what normal people do. What if I'm never able to love him back like that?

I look away, back toward the pavement far below. Bits of cigarette ash swirl past me. Above me the girl walks from one end of the balcony to the other, her footsteps causing slight vibrations in the beam where I'm supporting my foot.

I wonder how quick it would be over. I wonder if the wind would sing songs to me as I fell.

Let go. See if you can fly.

My fingertips start to loosen.

No, don't let go.

The sliding door opens and then closes with a harsh click.

"Winter," Jesse hisses. He lowers the red escape rope toward me. I breathe a sigh of relief. But then, as I reach for it, my foot slips off the beam.

I'm dangling by the fingertips of one hand, twenty stories in the air.

CHAPTER 31

ROSE

I reach out with my free hand for the metal railing. I wrap both hands around the icy cold bars even tighter. Winter might be ready to give up, but I'm not giving up on her. My shoulders feel like they're coming out of their sockets. I flail with my legs and manage to get one foot back onto the support beam underneath the balcony, which takes a little bit of the pressure off my upper body.

I look up at Jesse. He widens his eyes at me and then he shakes his head. I can't imagine how scary it must have been for him to watch me almost fall. I inhale deeply, hold my breath for four counts, and then exhale. Winter breathes like this sometimes when she's anxious.

As I prepare to reach for the rope again, I catch sight of the ground. A dark, yearning voice whispers, *Just let go.*

That's another alter. I call her Black because she spends most of her time thinking about death. *It'll be okay,* I tell her. The fingers of my left hand close around the rope. I let go of the balcony and wrap my other hand just below the first one. The rope swings slightly and my leg bumps up against the side of the building, but my grip is secure. Jesse begins to pull me up toward the roof. In a few short seconds he's helping me over the railing.

Before I can utter a single word, he's got his arms wrapped

around me, his face buried in my hair. "Jesus Christ. I thought you were going to fall."

"You saved me." I look up at him. "Thank you."

He lifts one hand to my face and for a moment I think he's going to kiss me. For a moment, I want him to; I want to feel that kind of connection. But I shouldn't do that to Winter. I feel her inside me. She's curled up asleep, not fighting for control. She's probably still scared about almost falling. I should wake her, but maybe she needs to rest. Maybe she wouldn't care about one little kiss . . .

It turns out not to matter, because when Jesse locks eyes with me, his expression changes. His body tenses and he slowly removes his hand from my cheek. He blinks hard, as if he's not quite sure what he's seeing. "Rose?" he asks.

"Hmm?" I say, not wanting to lie to him but not quite willing to leave him yet.

He cradles my face in his hands and looks directly into my eyes. "Let me talk to Winter."

CHAPTER 32

I blink. Jesse has my face in his hands. Somehow I'm on the roof. "What happened?" I ask. But I know what happened. I must have dissociated. "Did Kyung see me?"

"I don't think so," Jesse says. He's staring at me with a look of wonder on his face.

"Why are you looking at me like that?" I step back away from him.

"I saw Rose."

"What does that even mean?" I ask.

"At first I was just so relieved you were safe that I didn't notice, but then when you spoke, when I stopped to really look at you, I could tell it was her."

Jesse is still staring at me like this means something major, but I'm not sure if I like the idea of him thinking he can identify my alters. It feels so . . . intimate. What if he starts insisting I'm not being myself whenever he doesn't like what he sees?

What if he just knows you well enough to know us?

"We should get out of here," I say. "We're probably on camera."

"Good idea." Jesse unties the rope from where he anchored it on the railing of the roof. We head for the door leading back into the building.

"Let me check to make sure no one is in the hallway." Jesse

hands me the rope and ducks into the building. He returns about thirty seconds later. "The coast is clear."

We return to the penthouse Baz rented and Jesse coils up the escape rope and replaces it in its basket. I grab my computer and configure the bug in Kyung's phone. We won't know if it's working until he actually makes a call.

I turn to Jesse. "How did you know?" I blurt out suddenly. "How did you know it was Rose?"

"Well, I could tell by your voice. It changes," he says. "But even before then, there was something . . . different in your expression." Jesse is talking animatedly, using his hands for emphasis, like the fact that I'm actively dissociating is a good thing.

"Different good, or different bad?" I ask lightly, a whole new anxiety settling in on me. What if Jesse *prefers* Rose to me?

"Just different," Jesse says. If I can learn to recognize Rose and Lily, then maybe I can help you learn to live with them."

"Maybe," I say. But I'm not as excited as Jesse about this new development.

Back at the apartment, I play the ViSE I made at UsuMed today and try to figure out whether I know the man I saw with Kyung, the one whose name I think is Alec. Going through the footage doesn't give me any new information, so I switch over to my computer.

I open up a window on the tablet to a Google search box. In it I type "Alec" and "UsuMed." I'm not really expecting to get any results. But I do. Over thirty, almost all of them involving a freelance neurotechnology consultant named Alec Kwon. I skim through the results until I find a picture. Sure enough, it's the other man I saw at lunchtime with Kyung.

I click on a page with basic information about him. Apparently he was born in Korea but moved to London at a young age. He's done work for UsuMed as well as other large pharmaceutical and biotech companies.

Jesse leans over to see what I'm looking at. "Do you know him?"

"I'm not sure. I think so. I remembered his name from somewhere." I switch ViSEs and play the recording I made when Baz and I broke into Kyung's suite, pausing on the scrap of paper that was in his pocket to verify the three names.

Jesse wanders off toward the kitchen while I switch back to my tablet. When I search for Nai Khaing, I find what looks like a profile for a Burmese military leader. This must be the man Baz said was part of a group of rebels in Myanmar. When I try to search his name with Usu and Kyung, nothing comes up. There are a lot of people named Cristian Rojas, including a soccer player from Chile and a researcher at the Massachusetts Institute of Technology, but no one who seems to be affiliated with Usu or Kyung. I flip to image search and scroll through a couple of pages, but none of the images stands out.

I'm expecting the same result with Erich Cross, and for the most part, that's what I get. There's a musician from Ohio and a realtor with that name. No connections to Kyung or Usu as far as I can tell. The image search turns up a wide variety of white men and one African American who works for a TV news channel. Just as I'm about to give up, a picture at the bottom of the screen catches my eye. It's a somewhat grainy still made from a security camera, and the man is wearing sunglasses, so I can't see much of his face, but something makes me click on it. I suck in a sharp breath as the larger picture appears on the screen.

Erich Cross looks a lot like Sebastian.

I wouldn't have noticed it back in St. Louis, because Baz always shaved, but the beard is definitely similar, as is the shape of his nose and jaw. I tap the screen to open the web page that's hosting the photo and I'm not surprised to find out that Erich Cross is wanted by Interpol for questioning in multiple robberies, as well as a car explosion that happened six years ago in Karachi.

I start to call Jesse over but then change my mind. I trust him completely, but if I tell him I think Baz might be communicating with Kyung under an alias, he's going to think I'm losing my mind again. Even if he humors me, he'll probably say something to Baz, and if Sebastian is somehow working for Kyung, I don't want to tip him off that I know.

As if I summoned him with my thoughts, the door to the apartment swings open and Baz enters with a giant green duffel bag. He sets the bag on the floor and slips out of his shoes. Bending down, he unzips the bag and starts unpacking a bunch of black cases.

"What's all that?" I ask.

"Guns," he says.

"Guess what we did?" Jesse says proudly, striding back into the living room with a bottle of cider and a package of cookies.

Baz smirks. "You really want me to guess?" He stacks all of the cases on the floor next to the sofa and sits down.

Jesse snickers. "We bugged Kyung's cell phone."

I watch Baz's expression for any kind of tell that he's worried, but his face remains neutral, with a hint of curiosity. I pull up the audio surveillance program on my tablet and show him the fifth feed.

"This is excellent. Do I want to know how you accomplished this?"

"He was vising," I tell Baz. "But it wasn't the headset that was stolen from me. He's already got his own prototype. But Jesse and I hurried over there and I sneaked in while he was . . . distracted."

Jesse arches an eyebrow at me.

"Well, it was a little more complicated than that," I admit. "But the important thing is that he didn't catch me."

"Good job. Has he gotten any calls?"

"Not yet," I say.

"Let's hope it pans out." Baz opens a black fiberglass case and snaps together three long, black pieces to form what I think is an automatic rifle. "A little showy for our purposes probably, but I couldn't resist the offer." He sets the gun on the coffee table and reaches for a softer neoprene case with a zipper. It's another rifle, this one with a mounted scope.

"Which one do I get?" I ask.

Baz and Jesse exchange a look. "Actually I was thinking you should stick with your throwing knives. It's best if we work to our strengths." Baz opens the two remaining cases, which are both handguns. He and Jesse each take one.

I frown. "I see your point, but if I hadn't used a gun back in St. Louis, both of you might be dead right now," I remind him.

"True," Baz admits. "But come on, Winter. You know guns are dangerous in the hands of . . . troubled people."

I clear my throat. "You mean *crazy* people?" Inside my head, a little voice whispers something about how if Baz is working for Kyung, of course he wouldn't want me to have a gun.

I shush it. He just gave Jesse a gun and I know that Jesse would never betray me.

"Don't get mad. I think it's great you're not hallucinating anymore, but you killed a guy in Los Angeles and don't remember it. Then you called Jesse, talking about how you were someone else and someone else had done it." Baz pauses. "I don't know much about psychology, but if you don't have control over your actions, then I don't feel comfortable giving you a gun."

"But what if I—"

"I have an idea." Baz rises from the sofa and pulls something out of his backpack—a small silver gun. It doesn't look like any gun I've seen before. "It shoots tranquilizers," he says.

I scoff. "What good is that going to be up against someone with a real gun?"

"I'm not expecting there to be too many people with real guns, since they're so hard to come by here. This has got a strong sedative. If you got a shot off first, there's very little chance someone would be functional enough to accurately fire a real weapon." Baz sets the tranquilizer gun on the coffee table. "I know it's not the same as a real gun, but I also know you'd never forgive yourself if you killed someone you didn't want to kill because you were dissociating."

I pace back and forth across the wooden floor. "I saw Kyung at work today and I didn't lose control. It's not like I'm the Incredible Hulk, Baz."

Jesse clears his throat. "No, but you did just—"

I silence him with a glare. "That's different," I say. And it is. Dissociating as Rose is not the same as dissociating as Lily. Rose protects me. I . . . trust her.

"Fine. Prove it," Baz says.

"What do you mean?" I ask.

"I want to try to talk to Lily."

"I can't just call her up on command," I snap.

"Maybe I can." Baz's gray eyes are predatory. He turns to face me. One hand loosely encircles my arm. Without warning, his fingers tighten and he pins my wrist behind my body.

"What are you do—"

"Baz. Stop," Jesse says.

Baz pushes me against the wall of the flat, gently first, and then harder. "Where is she? Where's Lily? Let me talk to her. Let me talk to the part of you who's so anxious to end someone else's life."

"Stop it," I say. "This isn't going to work."

Baz grips a handful of my hair and pulls my head back so that I'm looking up at the ceiling. "Isn't it?" He yanks harder on my hair, until individual strands start to snap loose from my scalp. "This is how you like to be treated, right? You like when men rough you up."

"Shut up," I rasp. My eyes are watering from the pain.

"Dude. This is seriously not okay." Jesse's words are soft and unclear, like they're coming from a radio in another room.

Baz presses the barrel of a handgun against my temple. "I could kill you right now and no one would care. No one would even notice. You are less than worthless."

I don't respond. His words have brought back a flood of memories from another time. Another life. A life I thought was over. My breath sticks in my throat as I swallow back a sob.

"Aww, are you going to cry, you little bitch? Guess what? Some guys like it when you cry. But you know that, don't you? You know just what guys want. Want to hear what I want?"

"No," I say hoarsely. "Shut up, Baz. Just shut up."

"Sebastian. You are way out of line." Jesse's voice is louder now, but it still sounds so far away. Where is he? Why isn't he helping me? *You are less than worthless.*

"Get her headset," Baz says. "She needs to see this."

Darkness swirls beneath my skin. I fight it, but it's too strong. Baz spins me around so we're facing each other. He slaps me and I taste blood. He grasps my throat with one hand.

"Stop," I whisper feebly.

"We've come too far to stop," he says grimly, tightening his grip on my neck. I try to beg him again to let me go, but I can't choke out the words. Suddenly the room goes black.

CHAPTER 33

LILY

I snarl, struggle, lash out. This one doesn't stink of evil like the other men. But his words. They cut Winter. And so they cut all of us.

We are tired of being cut. It's our turn to draw blood.

I am teeth and claws. My hands rake against his face. My fist feels the softness of his mouth.

"Who are you?" he asks, pinning my arms.

"I am Lily," I say.

A second voice. Gentle, a lighthouse, a swarm of fireflies in the endless dark. "Why are you part of Winter?" Someone slips something over my head, tightens it gently.

"She needs me. I am the one who doesn't feel pain. I do the things no one else is strong enough to do."

"Like what?" The first man again.

As I struggle to escape his hold, more words fall from my lips. Red and black words. Death words. I tell them some of the things I've done. I tell them what I'll do if they get in my way.

I try again to break free. A clock ticks in my brain. Fast. Slow. I'm not sure. Time passes, or does it? Someone else inside me is fighting for control.

Both men are on me now.

Holding.

Confining.

They are snakes wrapped around my heart, squeezing. Squeezing until I can't breathe. Squeezing until I can't see.

All I can do is feel.

And be.

And destroy.

CHAPTER 34

I wake up on my stomach with my hands tied behind my back. Not tied. Zip-tied. The hard plastic cuts into my skin. There's a heavy weight on my legs that prevents me from moving. I struggle to turn my head. Jesse is sitting on the floor next to me, a look somewhere between concern and awe on his face.

"Winter?" he asks.

"What happened?" I croak.

"Lily happened," he says.

The weight slides off my legs. It turns out to be Baz. He rolls me over and leans my body against the side of the sofa. There's blood on his mouth and what looks like claw marks under his right eye.

"Are you calm?" he asks me.

"Yes," I say. And then, "Did I do that to you?"

"Well, it sure as hell wasn't Ramirez."

"What exactly happened?"

"I grabbed you. I threatened you. I said horrible things," Baz starts. "Then you turned into a tiger and said you were going to kill everyone who got in your way, even Winter."

"Well, that's reassuring." I twist my wrists back and forth. "Any chance you'll cut me loose?"

Baz pulls a knife from his pocket and cuts through the plastic tie.

I sit up and massage my wrists. "How long was I . . . out?"

"You were Lily for about five minutes. Then I forced you to take a sedative and you went another twenty without speaking and another fifteen where you appeared to be sleeping," Baz says. "What do you remember?"

I press my fingertips to my temples. "I remember you pushing me up against the wall, saying something about how some guys like making girls cry. And then, nothing. It's like I lost consciousness and woke up on the floor."

Baz hands me my headset. "Check it out."

Jesse is still staring at me like I'm a sideshow freak. Something tells me seeing Lily wasn't quite the same for him as seeing Rose. My breath sticks in my throat and my chest starts to feel tight. I slide the headset over my ears.

"Maybe you shouldn't . . . I mean, you've had a rough enough day already." Jesse looks nervously at Baz.

"I need to see," I say.

Baz shrugs. "You can't protect people from themselves."

I rewind the footage and then lie back on the apartment floor. It's not ideal for vising. The hard wood digs into my hips and shoulders, making it difficult to empty my head of sensations. Still. I need to know.

"She needs me. I am the one who doesn't feel pain. I do the things no one else is strong enough to do," I say. Heat courses through my blood. My muscles coil in anticipation.

"Like what?" Baz asks. Three diagonal claw marks are beginning to swell on his face.

He's got my arms pinned. I twist and turn violently in an attempt to break his hold. Beyond him, Jesse stands. He's not saying anything, but his mouth hangs slightly open.

"Like kill you, kill both of you if I need to, if you stand in our way," I rasp.

"What do you mean, our way?" Baz asks.

"The hated man. He dies. Only after he's dead can Winter live."

"Kyung? What if you can't kill him?" Baz asks.

"I can; I know I can. And I will, even if it means killing Winter."

I struggle in his arms again and Jesse steps forward to help hold me. His grip is hesitant and I easily shake him off. I spin around, kicking out with one foot, teeth snapping, saliva flying from my mouth.

My body is forced against the wall again. "Hold her like you mean it," Baz barks. "Help me get her on the ground."

Jesse and Baz force me to the hardwood floor. I am facedown, with all of their weight on me. It's too much weight. I struggle to take a breath. My arms are yanked roughly behind me. The zip tie engages with a harsh series of clicks.

Then I can breathe again, but I can't move. I wriggle back and forth. "Let me go," I bark. Tears form in my eyes.

"No chance," Baz says. "Ramirez, get her sedatives from her room, will you?"

A couple minutes later a pill is forced in my mouth and a cup of water is pressed to my lips. I spit the pill out twice before Sebastian forces it down my throat. He clamps one hand over my nose and chin to hold my mouth closed until I swallow.

I fight it until I start to choke on the water. Then I give in and swallow the pill.

Then for a while, I just lie there, my chest aching, tears dripping silently down my cheeks. Then everything starts to go numb.

I rip the ViSE headset from my head and toss it onto the coffee table. A slight shock moves through me. "I need to get out of here," I say. "I'm going to go run some stairs." Without waiting for a response, I hop to my feet and head to the front door, stopping just inside to pull on my running shoes.

"Do you want company?" Jesse asks.

"You mean besides the crazy people who live in my head?" I ask. "No. We'll be fine." I yank the door open without even taking the time to finish tying my shoes and let it slam in Jesse's face. I hit the stairwell already running and take the steps two at a time on my way to the top floor. I touch the handle of the door that leads out onto the roof and turn, heading down to the ground floor at full speed. I hit the bottom and turn back without even stopping to rest. In no time, I'm at the landing of the top floor again. After the third lap, the pain in my chest starts to dissipate. My extremities tremble from the exertion.

I blink and find myself out on the roof.

I blink again and find myself at the edge.

I look down on the street below. So many people.

Whole people.

I blink again. The wind makes deadly promises to me. I could fly. I could fall. Why look whole if it's all a lie? Why not break my outside to match my inside?

Pain is not the answer.

I reach up to touch the pendants around my neck. A rose and a snowflake, side by side. "Then why do I have so much of it?"

Because you don't share it.

"Share it? Everyone I have shared it with is dead. You think I should put this on more people?" I climb up on the ledge of the building. I hold my arms out, dare the wind to take me. "I have a better idea. Maybe you should let me go." It would be easy. Too easy.

Don't let your sister's death be for nothing.

I sigh. That argument always works. Rose—the real one—would be so angry if she saw me now. For that matter, so would Gideon. As much as I miss them, as much as I want to see them again, I don't want it to be like this. I don't want to dishonor their memories.

I drop my hands to my sides. "Are you really talking to me? Or am I just imagining this?"

Does it matter?

"Kind of. I'm trying to figure out how screwed up I am."

Exactly as screwed up as you're supposed to be.

"Funny. Look, I need your help," I say. "Lily—can we fight her?"

We are her.

Lily, I think. *I need you to talk to me. I need you to trust me.* No answer.

"Please," I whisper.

"Winter?"

Slowly, so as not to lose my balance, I spin around. Jesse is standing a few feet away from me. He rubs his scar. The wind blows his hair forward. "Are you all right?"

"Your hair is getting long," I say.

He steps closer to me. "Is it? I hadn't noticed." He reaches out one hand. "Come here. Come down from the ledge."

"Why?"

"Because you're scaring me."

I shake my head bitterly. "I remember when *I* was afraid of *you*. Before we met, I used to see you at Krav Maga and you scared me. You always looked so . . . intense." A tear leaks out of my left eye. "And then we were friends, sort of. But then in Miami I found out you were lying to me and you scared me again. I was afraid of you, and at that time it felt like one of the most terrible things ever."

"Winter—"

"But now you're standing here saying you're afraid of *me*, and I can't decide if that's even worse."

"I'm not scared *of* you. I'm scared *for* you," Jesse says. "Please come down. You could fall, and I don't want to lose another person I love."

"How can you love me, Jesse? How can you even stand to be near me?" I hop down from the ledge but turn away from him, back to the street below, back to the wind that wants to claim me.

Jesse's hands encircle my waist. He pulls me back from the edge. "How can you even ask that question?"

"I know you *think* you love me, but why? I'm so broken. I have to be the most broken person you know." I still can't bring myself to look at him.

"You think you're broken," Jesse says. "What I see is someone unbreakable." He bends down and rests his chin on my shoulder. "The shit you've been though could've wrecked you so many times, but somehow you're still functioning."

I lean back into him, grateful for his warmth. "You're really not scared of me? Of Lily?"

"No."

"I'm scared of me," I whisper.

"I know," he says. "But that won't always be the case. I promise."

I want him to be right. For a second I don't say anything. We just stand there, two people wrapped together as one, looking out into the lights of the city.

"How can you promise something like that?" I ask finally.

"I don't know. Faith, I guess."

"In God?"

"In you," Jesse says. "Though if God wants to help, I won't turn him away."

I don't believe in God. I didn't go to church as a child and even if I had found religion growing up, the things that happened to me in L.A. would have driven it out of me. It's hard to imagine a benevolent higher power who would allow innocent girls to suffer the way we did.

"What time is it?" I ask abruptly.

"Around ten p.m.," Jesse says. "Why?"

"I'm going to try to reach Dr. Abrams before she starts seeing patients."

"Good idea." He bends low and gives me a kiss on the forehead. "But let's go back inside where it's warm."

I follow Jesse back inside and we take the elevator down to our apartment.

"I'm sorry I clawed your face," I tell Baz. I study the angles of his nose and jaw and the shape of his lips while I pretend to examine the damage I did. There's no way for me to be certain he and Erich Cross are the same person.

Unless you ask him.

It's too risky. Right now Jesse and I are depending on him.

"No worries," Baz says. "You're not the first girl to draw blood—I assure you."

Jesse and Baz start talking about how to assemble one of the guns, and I shut myself in my room and call Dr. Abrams. It's only a little after seven o'clock in St. Louis, but maybe she'll do an early morning session.

She picks up right away. "Winter, are you all right?"

"Yes. Did I catch you while you were driving? I know I said I was going to wait and make an appointment with you when I return to St. Louis, but I just have one question."

"I'm getting ready to leave for my office, but I have the time. Go ahead."

"You said there's no medication for my condition, no drug that will prevent my alters from taking over at times, but what about nonmedicinal tricks for suppressing them? Meditation, hypnosis. Something like that?"

Dr. Abrams exhales slowly. "Not really. They're essentially highly complicated defense mechanisms. If they take over, it's because some part of you thinks you need them."

"But sometimes I feel like there are varying degrees of control. Like I know that Rose has taken over my life for hours at a time, but other times I swear I just hear her voice in my head. Like she wants to impact me, but in a less aggressive way." I pause. "And then sometimes I'll zone out, just for a few seconds, and come back and wonder if maybe that was an alter too, like maybe they just needed a tiny moment of control for some reason, so small that before I knew about my DID, I probably didn't even notice it. Is that possible?"

"Sure," Dr. Abrams says. "I have to be honest with you, Winter. I've seen episodes of dissociation in some of my other patients, but you're the first full-blown DID patient I've ever treated. When Mr. Seung told me he suspected it, I did a lot of research into clinical case studies. Everything you're saying here has been reported—feeling like you're not yourself, hearing voices, blocks of lost time, losing the moment for just a few seconds and then coming back to feel like some small thing has changed."

"So maybe if I try to stay calm and focused, they'll be content to stay in the background, whispering suggestions instead of taking control themselves?"

"Perhaps," she says. "But keep in mind that healing is not about suppressing or weakening your alters, but about accepting them and trying to get to know them in a safe environment."

"But what if one of them tries to hurt me?" I ask.

"If you're worried you might hurt yourself while you're dissociating, then you really need to be in an inpatient facility," Dr. Abrams says gently. "Are you afraid of that?"

"So it's possible? That could really happen?"

"DID patients have committed suicide in the past, yes. We have no way of knowing if they were dissociating at the time."

"All right. Thank you for the information." I don't want to go to an inpatient facility. That sounds like a fancy term for prison. I remember the hospital again—being pinned down, people yelling, people injecting me against my will. What if I get better and they don't let me leave? What if they isolate me from the people I care about and I actually get worse instead of better? Or maybe they'll medicate me so heavily that I lose myself completely. There has to be a way for me to help myself without giving up all my control to a bunch of strangers.

"Winter. My job involves more than just giving you information. If you tell me where you are, I can call someone to come get you and take you someplace safe."

"I can't," I say. "Not yet. But I promise you that once I've finished dealing with a few things, I'll find a safe place to go. Right now I trust my friends to look out for me."

"So these friends—they don't leave you all by yourself?" she asks.

"They don't," I say.

One more way that Jesse is helping me. He thinks he's not doing enough, but he probably just saved my life up on the roof. I'm so tired. I need to figure out a way to do what I came here for, and soon.

I can feel the darkness inside me growing.

CHAPTER 35

Yoo Mi and I are leaving work the next day when I notice one of the security guards from Baz's list heading for the smoking area.

"I need to get a present for my sister. Do you want to stop by Kyobo Books with me?" Yoo Mi tosses her pigtails back over her shoulders. Today she's wearing dark-purple tights and lavender ribbons in her hair. She looks more fairy than human.

"Sure. But I need to make a quick phone call. Meet you over there?"

"All right. I'll be in the English books section."

I reach into my purse to activate the badge cloner and stroll into the smoking section. I find a place within clear view of the guard and frown as I go through my purse, pretending to look for my cigarettes. He takes the bait and holds out his pack. "Would you like a smoke?" he asks in Korean.

"Thank you," I say. "It's been a rough day." I'm close enough now for the device to start copying. I sneak a quick look at his badge. His name is Jason Choi. That name was definitely on the list Baz showed me.

Jason pulls out a lighter and it suddenly occurs to me I'm not even sure *how* to smoke. Do I put the cigarette in my mouth before he lights it? I have no idea. I try to remember how Gideon used to do it, but I always thought smoking was kind of a foul habit, so I never paid much attention. I settle for holding the cigarette between two fingers the way I've seen people do on TV. My fingers tremble slightly in the cold and Jason has to hold my hand steady to get the cigarette to flare up.

"Thank you," I say again. I hold the cigarette to my lips and pretend to inhale. "I'm Jae Hwa. It's nice to meet you."

"I'm Jason. You're new, right?"

I nod. "I'm from Cheonma Staffing. What about you?"

"I've worked here for two years," he says. "Ever since I got out of the military."

The cherry at the end of my cigarette is getting quite long and I do my best to flick off some ash in the receptacle. I take another fake puff, but this time I inhale for real and smoke pours into my throat. I nearly drop the cigarette as I start coughing.

Jason laughs, and then when I keep coughing, he starts to look worried. "Are you okay?"

I extend the fit out a few extra seconds to give the badge cloner time to copy Jason's credentials. "I'm fine," I say. "I actually quit smoking when I started college, but this job . . . it made me want to start up again."

"Ah, so that's it." He grins. "I was hoping maybe it was all a ploy to come talk to me."

"Well, I have enjoyed talking to you," I say somewhat demurely. *Rose?* Once again I feel like maybe she's helping.

Jason's cheeks color slightly. He glances at his phone. "I should get back to my post, but it's been a pleasure. Have a nice evening."

"You too."

Jason grins again. "See you around."

"I hope so." I grind out my cigarette and place it in the trash bin. Then I head for the bookstore.

Jesse texts me while I'm browsing the shelves of Kyobo Books with Yoo Mi.

Jesse: Are you headed home yet?

Me: Soon. I'm actually hanging out with a friend.

I wonder if Jesse thinks it's strange that I'm making friends at UsuMed.

Jesse: Okay. Be careful.

Me: I will. See you in an hour or so.

Yoo Mi looks up from a display of meditation coloring books."Everything all right?"

"Yes." I slip my phone back into my purse and pretend to check out the stack of books.

"I like this idea," Yoo Mi says. "My younger sister is in her junior year of high school and all she ever does is worry about her college placement exam. Do you think coloring would be therapeutic for her?"

I flip through some of the intricate designs. "I don't know. The drawings are beautiful, but they look like they'd be hard to color in some places. I'd probably get anxious about what the end result would look like."

Yoo Mi selects one with illustrations based on the children's book *The Little Prince*. "This one seems a bit more forgiving."

"Good choice," I say. My sister loved *The Little Prince* when we were young. That's probably the reason she chose the name Rose for herself. I think about the Rose from the story. She was fierce, yet vulnerable. She never wanted anyone to see her cry.

As much as I don't want to regain my lost memories about some of the abuse I suffered in Los Angeles, what if other things have slipped away too—images of who my sister really was? Would it be worth it to accept the bad memories if I could have all the good ones back as well? I lift my hand to my chest and trace the petals of the rose pendant with my index finger, the snowflake flash drive nestled behind it.

I follow Yoo Mi to one of the registers, where she pays for her purchase. Then together we head for the subway station. Yoo Mi pauses between the sets of stairs leading down to opposite platforms. "I'll see you tomorrow," she says brightly.

As I start to reply, a kid running for his train bumps into

her and Yoo Mi's shopping bag and purse both fall to the floor of the subway station. The top snap of her purse has come undone and part of the contents have spilled out. Yoo Mi sweeps everything quickly back into her bag, but not before I see a flash of something I recognize—it's a scarf, green wool trimmed with silvery threads, just like the scarf the woman watching me was wearing at Namdaemun Market.

CHAPTER 36

My jaw tightens as I consider Yoo Mi's height and the shape of her face. They definitely feel like a match for the woman at the market. I couldn't tell how young she was that day because so much of her face was covered.

"Jae Hwa, what is it?" Yoo Mi furrows her brow.

I'm not sure what to do, if I should accuse her or pretend like everything is fine. My breath catches in my throat as I take a step away from her. I can see by the look in her eyes that she realizes something is very wrong. There's no point in lying about it. Just once I wish someone would tell me the truth. "Have you been following me?" I ask, accusation hardening my voice.

"Following you?" Yoo Mi tosses her pigtails back from her face. "What do you mean?"

I pull her out of the path of a wave of disembarking passengers. "Don't play dumb with me. I recognize your scarf from Namdaemun Market."

"I got this scarf from a shop at Gangnam Station. A hundred other women probably have the same one."

"Let me see your arm, then." Before Yoo Mi can even protest, I grab her left arm and push up her sleeve. Sure enough, she has a tiny black tattoo of a butterfly on the inside of her forearm. "At the market I thought it was a bird, but that's just because I wasn't close enough."

Yoo Mi tugs her sleeve back down. "I think I know what's happening—"

"I thought you were my friend. Are you actually working for Kyung?"

She tilts her head to the side. "Who is Kyung?"

"He's the only one who could possibly be paying you to follow me. I hope you know he's a terrible man who is responsible for the deaths of two people I loved." I spin on my heel and start to walk away from her.

"Jae Hwa, wait." She hurries after me.

Tears well in my eyes. I spin around. "Wait? Why? So you can lie to me some more? No thank you."

Yoo Mi sighs deeply. "I won't lie. You're right. I was following you that day. But not for anyone named Kyung. For a man called Mr. Faber. He told me he's a friend of yours."

"Baz? Unbelievable," I say through clenched teeth.

But nothing is really unbelievable to me anymore. From the very beginning I questioned Sebastian's motivations for involving himself in my plans. Then his words and behavior convinced me he was on my side, but maybe he just manipulated me. But why? Is *he* the one who's working for Kyung?

"Do you know if he goes by any other names?" I ask Yoo Mi. "Like Erich Cross, perhaps?"

"I don't know. I've never heard that name," she says.

I sigh. "So your job at UsuMed is a total setup? You're just there to spy on me?"

"Not spying. Watching out for you. Mr. Faber hired me to keep an eye on you and your brother. It was just for—"

"My brother?" I say with a gasp. "Wait. You know where my brother is?"

Yoo Mi goes pale. Either she wasn't aware Baz had been keeping this a secret from me or she wasn't supposed to tell me. "You really need to talk to Mr. Faber about all of this," she says.

"Oh, I intend to," I say grimly. "How well do you know him?"

"Not at all," she admits. "He's a friend of a friend of a friend—that sort of thing."

"And he told you not to tell me about Jun, didn't he?"

She nods. "I wasn't thinking. It just slipped out."

"Did he tell you anything else specific? Do you know about the ViSE tech?"

"I know UsuMed stole something from you, but I don't know what. I'm protective detail only. I don't get any information unless I need it to do my job."

"Protective detail?" I ask. Yoo Mi is thinner than I am and about three inches shorter.

"I've trained in martial arts since I was little and I've worked as security personnel for some of Korea's minor celebrities." She grins. "I may be little, but I'm tough. A friend told me an American was looking for someone to keep a girl safe. When I met Mr. Faber, he told me about your condition, but not much else. I think that's the main reason he wanted someone keeping an eye on you at UsuMed, so you didn't end up blowing your own cover."

"How thoughtful." I grit my teeth. "And my brother?"

"Supposedly, he comes to UsuMed every Friday night for the Science Scholars Program."

"You've seen him?"

"Not there, because I just started watching him a couple of days ago. I watch his apartment sometimes." Yoo Mi taps at the screen of her phone and a picture pops up. "Mr. Faber gave me this picture."

I suck in a sharp breath. The boy is tall and thin, with high cheekbones and distrustful eyes. "He reminds me of me," I whisper.

"Me too," Yoo Mi says.

"Where does he live?"

Yoo Mi shakes her head, her thin lips hardening into a

straight line. "You have to talk to Mr. Faber about it. I can't give you that information."

"I could just follow you, you know."

She shrugs. "You could try, I suppose. But I'm not watching tonight anyway. Someone else is on duty."

"Will you at least tell me who he's living with? Is it my mother?"

"According to Mr. Faber, it's your aunt."

My aunt—just like the boy in Los Angeles said. Maybe everything he told me was true. "Will you send me that picture?" I ask. As Yoo Mi nods, I add, "And don't say anything to Baz about me knowing, all right?"

"Why not?"

"Because I'm not sure if I can trust him."

"All right," Yoo Mi says. "But he seems to have your best interests at heart. And I know it doesn't look like it right now, but I swear you can trust *me*."

They're nice words, but she's right. I'm not sure I can trust her either.

I return to the apartment in Itaewon, where Baz has Kyung's latest phone call queued up for me to listen to. I never catch the name of the person he's speaking to, but I can tell from the conversation that it's a specialized engineer from the Singapore office of UsuTech whom he's asking to consult on a classified project. The man is scheduled to arrive on Monday.

At one point Kyung tells the person on the other end of the line that he'll send a car to the hotel with a company representative, who will personally escort him down to Lab 6.

"Down sounds like B-1 or B-2, just like you thought," Baz says.

I nod. I'm dying to confront Sebastian about Erich Cross and about my brother, but I still feel like Jesse and I won't be able to steal back the tech without him. We might need his explosives in order to break in to wherever it's being kept. I might need his help with documents that will get me back to the US. I have to keep playing along until we've gotten everything we need from him.

"Winter?" Baz arches an eyebrow. "Are you still with me?"

"Yes. Sorry. Down, like you said." I rise from the floor and walk a lap around the living room, stopping to turn down the heat and then in front of the wall of glass to open a window. My insides are simmering from sitting on the warm floor, and every time I look at Baz they threaten to boil over from rage. How could he keep Jun a secret from me? "Where's Jesse?" I ask.

"He said something about getting food," Baz says. "So now we just need to clone a badge from that list. Maybe I can follow—"

"I have one. I got it today. Jason Choi." I hand the badge cloner with Jason's clearances on it over to Baz. "I think you should make one for each of us. Just in case one gets damaged or we have to split up." *Just in case it turns out you're working against us.*

Baz nods. "Good idea. I think we should plan for Friday night. Do you know what time the building is usually empty?"

"Not Friday," I say. I don't want Jun anywhere near the UsuMed building when we break in. "What about Thursday? I heard one of the girls at work talking about a K-pop event for Valentine's Day being held near the building. That could make for nice cover."

Baz looks up the event on his phone. "It's an amateur sing-off contest being held on a platform outside of Gangnam Station from nine p.m. until midnight, hosted by some of K-pop's hottest new stars. Good idea. If we need to make a quick escape, it'll be easy for us to get lost in that crowd."

"The coffee shop closes at ten. Most of the UsuMed staff are gone before then."

"Perfect. Unless the components I need are delayed, Thursday is go night. We'll take my bike and park in the garage.

Ramirez will take the subway and meet us. We can enter the stairwell at B-3. We can just walk up the stairs to B-2 and B-1 and find Lab 6. Then all we have to do is blow open whatever case or safe the tech is being kept in, grab it, and get out. Sound good?"

"And Kyung?"

"Well, he's not going to be in the building at ten p.m., so we can go back to the SkyTower and deal with him there."

I nod solemnly. There's still no tug of guilt or shame at the idea of executing someone.

"So that's it, then. Can you think of anything else we need?"

"I don't think so. About Jason," I say. "He's going to end up being implicated in the theft."

Baz shrugs. "If he can prove he was somewhere else when the badge was swiped, maybe he won't get blamed."

"But he might."

"He might," Baz agrees. "This is war. There will be collateral damage."

CHAPTER 37

The next night, Baz, Jesse, and I decide to move all of our stuff out of the Itaewon flat and into a hotel close to the UsuMed building. Baz is going to stay in the penthouse suite at the Seoul SkyTower but suggests Jesse and I get a suite elsewhere, just so there's no danger of Kyung recognizing me.

Once again, it seems a little suspicious. More and more I'm realizing that Baz is saying all the right stuff but acting like a solo operative. "Why don't we *all* stay someplace else?" I ask. "I don't like the idea of splitting up."

"I need to do some work on the explosive charges," Baz says. "It's technical work and it's not exactly safe. I don't want you guys with me if anything goes wrong."

"Goes wrong?" Jesse asks. "Like what? One blows up in your face?"

"It's not likely, but you can never rule it out when you're working with explosives."

"Okay, then," Jesse says. "Separate it is."

The two of us end up getting a room at the hotel next door to the SkyTower.

The desk clerk gives us each a key and we drag our suitcases to the elevator. I feel a small rush of pride when the doors open on the sixth floor and I realize I made it all the way without even feeling anxious.

Jesse takes the bed closest to the door. "We can push the desk in front of it. That way if you try to leave in the middle of the night, I'll hear you."

"All right." I sit on the edge of my bed.

Jesse paces back and forth. Finally he goes to the window and looks out at the skyline. "This is weirder than I thought it would be."

"Do you want me to get my own room?"

"No, because I don't want you to have to sleep in a headset." He flops down on his bed. "It's just hard, you know."

"What is?" I perch on the very edge of my bed.

He rolls onto his side and looks over at me. "It's hard not to think about what sleeping next to you felt like. Holding you." He swallows hard. "Kissing you. It's hard to accept it'll never happen again."

"Jesse. Come on. I told you I'm still attracted to you." I lie down on my side so we're facing each other. "It's not that I don't want to kiss you. I thought about it on the plane. I thought about it the day we sparred up on the roof. I think about it a lot." I sigh. "I think about *you* a lot."

Jesse blinks rapidly but doesn't say anything. He reaches out across the space between us. I scoot closer to the edge of the bed so that when I reach for him, our hands touch. My fingers slip easily between his, pale next to his naturally dark skin.

He massages my palm with his thumb. "You think about *me*?"

"Yes. You have no idea."

He moves from his bed to my bed. I scoot back into the center to make space. A tremor races down my spine as he lies down next to me and takes my right hand in both of his. He lifts my hand to his mouth, pressing his lips gently against my palm. Heat blooms inside me.

Jesse rests my hand on the side of his face. "If you want to kiss me, why don't you, then?"

Beneath my fingertips I feel the ridge of his scar and the almost imperceptible prickle of freshly shaved skin. I lift my other hand to his right cheek, cradling his face between my palms. His eyelids fall shut. "Because I shouldn't take what I want from you if I can't give you something meaningful in return."

Jesse lifts his hands to my face. I rest my forehead against his. "This is meaningful," he says.

"It's not enough," I choke out.

"It's enough for me." He exhales. His breath is warm on my lips. I need desperately to close the gap between our mouths, to erase the cold space between our bodies.

But I can't.

"No, it's not. You want a relationship," I say.

"What we have is already a relationship." His nose grazes mine as he angles his head just slightly. "I know there's no one else for you."

He's right. I love him. But when has love ever been enough? My lower lip trembles. "I'm not healthy. Even if we get out of this and go back to St. Louis, I'm not sure if I can do it." Tears form on my eyelashes at this confession. I've known this—I've known this the entire time I've known Jesse, but I never admitted it so frankly. "You shouldn't wait for me," I continue. "Because what if I never get better?" The tears cut smooth pathways down my cheeks, colliding with Jesse's hands.

His eyes flick open. He presses his thumbs to my eyelids, traces the tears all the way down to my jawline like he's trying to erase them. "You don't need to get better for me. I love you exactly the way you are. I want you to work on healing, for you. But the person you are right now is enough for me. More than enough."

He's said things like this in the past, but that was before he knew everything. That was before he saw Lily, before I killed a man and started plotting to kill another one. "You mean that, don't you?" I ask softly.

"I mean that," he says, looking into my eyes.

"Jesse." I bury my face in his chest. "You're doing that thing again."

"What thing is that?"

"Making me smile when it seems like there's nothing in the whole world to smile about."

He lifts my chin and wipes the last remains of a tear from my face. His other hand strokes the back of my neck, fingertips lost in my hair. "Here's something to smile about."

Our lips touch, just barely. Heat races through my veins. I turn his head and kiss my way up his scar. Still soft. Still innocent. "If we start, I might not be able to stop," I whisper.

"I can live with that." He grins. "But seriously, there's no rush here, okay? I just want to hold you and kiss you." He repositions us so that I'm on top of him, and our bodies settle together like they were made to fit. I stare into the deep hazel wells of his eyes, letting go, letting myself fall.

And then, of course, someone knocks on the door.

CHAPTER 38

Jesse reluctantly rises from my bed and goes to the peep-hole. "It's Baz."

"Of course it is," I mutter.

"Awkward." Jesse smooths some wrinkles from his shirt. "You think if we ignore him he'll go away?"

"I can hear you in there," Baz says. "And I'm not going away."

I snicker. Jesse undoes the dead bolt and opens the door.

Sebastian holds up two white plastic sacks. "I come bearing delicious takeout. I thought we could go over a few last-minute details while we have dinner together." He smirks. "Like a family."

"Most messed-up family ever," Jesse mutters, rolling his eyes at me.

Baz slides out of his shoes as the door closes behind him. He scans our room. "Cozy."

"I thought you were making bombs," I say.

"Explosive charges, not bombs. And I am, but I've still got to eat." He drops the sacks of food on the desk and shrugs out of his coat. "I can't believe we're finally going to do this. Feels good, doesn't it? This is what we've worked for."

"Actually I was feeling pretty go—"

I clear my throat meaningfully and Jesse falls quiet. "I feel like we've been here forever," I tell Baz. "I'm ready for everything to be over with." *I'm also ready for you to tell me the truth.*

The three of us are quiet as he unpacks the food he bought and arranges it on the desk. *"Chap chae* and *galbi,"* he says. Glass noodles and beef short ribs. Baz fixes himself a plate and sits at a little table in the corner.

Jesse and I make our own plates and sit on our separate beds. I try not to think about what it felt like to be pressed against him, to be ready to completely surrender. I can't decide if I'm disappointed or relieved that Sebastian showed up. A little of both, perhaps.

"So." Baz's eyes flick from Jesse to me, a faint smile playing at his lips. "You two are awfully quiet. Did I interrupt something?"

"No," I say, just as Jesse says, "Yes."

Baz laughs. "I hope after tomorrow you guys figure out your shit. You're both annoying as hell on your own, but together you're kind of cute." He pulls two ID cards from his pocket. "Here are your badges. I made them look like Cheonma Staffing badges, just in case one of us gets stopped by a security guard. But be warned, they won't hold up to much scrutiny. Speaking of tomorrow, we need a contingency plan in case everything goes sideways."

"Run like hell?" Jesse suggests.

"Always a good idea if shit hits the fan," Baz says. "But I'm talking about after everything settles, just in case we get separated."

"Why would we get separated?" I try to keep my voice level as I slide the badge into my purse.

"Well, we only have the motorcycle as a getaway vehicle, so we'll have to split up temporarily. Plus, these things just happen sometimes," he says. "There's an unaccounted for variable in your plan and everyone has to scramble to survive. We need a time and a place to meet up. If we all don't show, then we'll know the missing people . . . got arrested."

Or killed, I finish in my head.

"We're all going to show," Jesse says. "But what do you suggest?"

Baz pulls up a picture on his tablet. I see white sand and blue water, with mountains in the background.

Jesse squints. "What is that? Hawaii?"

"Jeju Island," Baz says. "We can get there by a bus and a ferry. If we pay cash, we won't leave a trail."

"It's similar to Hawaii," I explain to Jesse. "Volcanoes, beaches, ocean, honeymooners. But not as tropical." I turn to Baz. "Why would you want us to meet there?"

"If you have to ask, then you've never been there."

I scoff. "No. I grew up in an orphanage, remember? Our excursions were a little more local."

Baz scrolls through a few pictures on his tablet and stops on a beachfront resort. "This is the Sunrise Hotel. We'll meet here on Friday if we should happen to get separated. Let's agree to stay until Monday morning, just in case one of us should get detained. Jeju's airport has less security than Incheon, so it'll be easier to head back to the States."

"We'll still have to transfer through Incheon," I say.

"Yes, but we'll be on the other side of security." Baz produces a pair of American passports from his back pocket. He hands one to Jesse and me. "I had these made for you two."

"I'm more worried about getting into the US than getting out of Korea." I turn the dark blue passport over in my hands. I hope it's a good forgery.

"That's because you haven't committed any felonies yet, right?" Baz says. "If anything goes wrong at UsuMed, the whole country is going to be looking for us."

It's a fair point. We all fall silent at the thought of becoming fugitives, or worse. I flip open the passport and rub my thumb over the picture of me.

"I'll handle things on the other end if any issues arise. I

know people who can get us back into the States, no questions asked," Baz says.

I nod as I slip the passport into my pocket.

Baz picks at his noodles for a few more minutes, dragging his fork through them and making patterns instead of actually eating them. Then he pushes back his chair and stands. "I have a few last-minute things I need to take care of."

Jesse hops up from his bed. "Is it anything you need help with?"

"No. It's personal stuff." Baz slides back into his coat and shoes. "I'll see you guys here tomorrow night at eight p.m. sharp. We'll go over the plan one last time."

"Tell your mystery girl we said hi," Jesse jokes.

Baz stops, turns back, looks at me. "You didn't tell him."

"It didn't really seem like my story to tell."

Jesse looks back and forth between Baz and me, surprised that we've been keeping something secret. "Tell me what?"

"Do you *want* me to tell him?" I ask.

"I don't care. You can if you want." Baz's eyes meet mine for a second and then look toward Jesse. "It's just interesting. You two are thick as thieves, and yet you protected my privacy."

I shrug. "Some thieves are known for their discretion."

Baz smiles slightly. "You're all right, Winter Kim. You know that?"

"Thanks." These words would mean more if I trusted him, if I weren't so angry about him keeping Jun a secret. I keep hoping he'll tell me everything, that he'll have a valid reason for waiting so long.

"What am I missing?" Jesse asks.

Baz pauses inside the door, looks back at us. "You two should get some sleep tonight," he says meaningfully. "Big day tomorrow."

"What was all that about?" Jesse asks after the door closes behind Baz.

"His mystery girlfriend is Chung Hee."

It takes a few seconds for this to sink in. "You mean the hacker? You mean Baz is . . . gay?"

"Bisexual, apparently."

"Huh." Jesse sits on the edge of his bed. "How old is Baz? Didn't he say that hacker guy was barely out of college?"

"I think he's in his midthirties? I guess he likes younger men." I shrug. "I don't judge. But I have a question for you. Do you trust him? Completely?"

"Why wouldn't I?" Jesse asks.

"Because Gideon was his friend, but maybe we're not. Do you ever think that maybe he came with us for some other reason, that he's been lying or setting us up?"

"No," Jesse says. "He wouldn't do that."

"Explain this, then." I pull up the picture of Erich Cross on my tablet and turn it so Jesse can see. "Doesn't this look like Baz?"

Jesse squints. "Possibly. Though I never would have thought so before I saw him grow a beard. Is there a better picture?"

"No. This is the only picture Interpol has of fugitive Erich Cross, wanted in connection with multiple thefts and a car bombing in Pakistan."

"That does sound like Baz," Jesse muses.

"Yeah. And this guy's name was on a piece of paper in the pocket of Kyung's suit."

Jesse's eyes widen as he realizes the implications, but he quickly recovers. "Oh, come on, Winter. There's no way Baz is working with Kyung. He wouldn't do that to Gideon."

"Gideon's dead," I say sharply. "And Sebastian has always been rather practical, wouldn't you say?"

"Still. If he were working against us, we'd both be arrested or dead by now too, wouldn't we? Kyung might have written his name down because Baz has been using that alias here and someone tipped him off to our presence. Maybe that's the name he flew under. Or that might not even be Baz," Jesse finishes somewhat unconvincingly.

"Maybe," I say slowly. "But he knows where my brother is. He's even been having him watched. And he's never bothered to let me in on this secret."

Jesse rakes a hand through his hair. "Are you sure?"

"Fairly certain. I had an interesting conversation with one of my coworkers today. Apparently he's been having me watched as well." I give Jesse a sideways glance. "Did you know about that?"

"Uh, well, he might have mentioned he got another girl hired who could act as backup for you at UsuMed."

"It turns out she's the same girl who was following us that day at Namdaemun Market."

Jesse coughs. "That I didn't know. But come on. There's no way Baz would hide the existence of your brother from you forever. I'm sure he'll tell you once we've done what we came to do."

"Maybe." That does seem like something Baz would do. "So you absolutely trust him, even after what I just told you?"

"I do," Jesse says. "Hurting you means hurting Gideon. And even though he's dead, I still can't believe Baz would betray him."

I lie back on my bed and cover my face with my hands. "I don't know what to think," I say through my fingers. "Maybe I'm just paranoid."

"Given everything you've been through, no one could blame you. I'm surprised you can trust anyone."

"I trust you." I roll onto my side so Jesse can see me. "But I want you to know you don't have to go through with this. You don't have to be a part of tomorrow night."

"Yes, I do."

"No, you don't. My alter pulled you into this mess. I'm pulling you out, if you want. You had a life before you became a recorder and started working for Gideon. You have parents and cousins and people who love you. You can go back to them."

"I don't want to go back to them," Jesse says. "I mean, I do, but right now I want to be here, halfway across the world with the girl I love, helping her seek vengeance against the man responsible for her sister's death, helping her keep safe the only family she has left."

"Jesse . . ." My shoulders slump forward. I want to tell him that I love him back, but it's hard. It feels like a contract and contracts are things that should only be made by people who are sane. I don't want to say those words and then take them back later. Jesse deserves better than that. "You know I care about you too, right?"

"I know." His eyes brighten suddenly. "Hey, there's something I want to show you." He hops up from the bed, fishes around in his suitcase, and comes up with a headset and a ViSE.

"Seriously?" I ask. "You want to ViSE now?"

"It's not a ViSE," Jesse says. "Not really, anyway. It's something I put together—some clips from my old recordings."

Giving him a skeptical look, I take the headset and the memory card. I lie back on my bed again. Jesse turns off the lights and lies next to me. I close my eyes and press PLAY.

I see myself hanging on to a crag of rock at Yosemite's Half Dome, my slender limbs stretched out in all directions, a look of complete concentration on my face.

"You got this." I smile.

Jesse's words feel strange coming from my lips. It's odd to smile his smile. But I remember this moment. We spent three days at Yosemite with Gideon. This is during the first one. We were just practicing but we always wore the headsets in case we happened to capture something amazing. Jesse is a better rock climber than I am, so his main job was to be my second climber and support me. As the better climber, he would normally climb first, but Gideon wanted the ViSE to be from the lead climber's point of view, so I was above him. It was such a hard day, but I loved the challenge of climbing. I felt so empowered when I finally got the hang of it.

The scene flips without warning, going from sunny and warm to snowy and cold. The jarring change in sensation makes my stomach twist a little.

"Whoa," I say.

"Yeah. Sorry. Some of those transitions are a little rough."

I see myself standing at the top of a small mountain, studying a red-and-black snowboard. Thick, fluffy snowflakes swirl through the air. I watch myself clip my boots to the board and look nervously down the hill.

"You're going to rock this," I say.

Jesse's words again.

I marvel at how supportive Jesse is, how beautiful I am in his mind.

The next ten minutes are recordings of me learning to snowboard. I'm a better climber than snowboarder, so this ViSE took even more training. The only similarity between the two clips is the feeling welling inside the recorder. It's hard to explain. Affection isn't a sense and therefore can't be conveyed directly in a ViSE, but somehow I feel it anyway. I feel it when I string together all the neural sequences—the rapid heart rate, the rushes of heat, the smiling, the laughter.

The scene changes again, this time to Jesse and me walking across town. I remember this day too. It was Christmas Eve. He asked me to go sledding with him on the big hill in front of the art museum.

We're strolling side by side down a snow-covered sidewalk in the Lofts. "Sledding? Like for a ViSE?" I hear myself ask.

"I mean, I guess—if you want to. I was just thinking about doing it for fun."

My face lights up and for a second the way I'm smiling at Jesse makes me wonder if maybe I loved him even before he and Gideon staged Rose's death. Maybe these new feelings have been present for weeks and I'm only just now beginning to recognize them, or accept them.

The ViSE skips forward to the two of us on Art Hill.

We're both crouched at the top of the hill on slick fiberglass sleds. "On the count of three," I say.

I see myself kneel down, my hands flat against the icy snow, ready to push off.

"One . . . two . . ." And then I'm moving. I'm laughing.

"Hey!" I hear myself call from the top of the hill. "You big cheater!"

I'm still laughing. My eyes water from the headwind. I wince as the sled hits a bump and goes airborne for a second before reconnecting with the hard ground. I bail off the sled at the end of the hill, just before I would've crashed into the bales of hay that are set up to keep sledders from ending up on the pond.

I pause the recording and open my eyes. "That day we went sledding was so fun," I tell Jesse. "I had almost forgotten about it. I wish I had made a recording too."

"It's one of my favorite memories of us," Jesse says. "You looked so happy—even though I beat you every time."

"Because you cheated." I poke him. "I'm still waiting for you to say 'three.'"

I close my eyes and press PLAY again. The recording continues, all these little snippets of my life over the past few months—Jesse and I playing video games at Escape, Jesse watching Gideon and me spar on the roof, the three of us white-water rafting and cliff diving in Tennessee. Well, only Jesse and I jumped off the cliff. Gideon was afraid. I remember teasing him about how a guy afraid of heights could live on the top floor of a fifteen-story building. He always used to say he wasn't afraid of heights, or even of falling. He was just afraid of landing. Experiencing these moments through Jesse's body is a roller coaster of feelings and sensations.

"Can I have a copy of this?" I ask.

"Of course. This is the girl you are to me," Jesse says. He

holds up a hand. "I know that you are not only this girl, but sometimes I think you like to pretend this girl doesn't exist at all. She does, Winter. Maybe right now your world feels like this happiness-sucking black hole, but you still have the capacity for joy inside you—to feel it, to bring it to other people."

I remove the headset from my head. "I don't know what to say."

"Sorry. I guess it's a little creepy. I just wanted to be able to relive those moments, to feel the happiness radiating off you, to hear you laugh." He pauses. "Are you mad?"

"No," I say. "I was just thinking of how that's such a positive use for the technology, capturing memories. Like photographs, only better. Like, what I wouldn't give to have some recordings with my sister, so I could hear her voice again." I shake my head. "I can't believe you have all these moments of me looking so happy. I never realized how happy you made me. I guess I was always so focused on my own pain. Happiness seemed like something for normal people."

"You make me happy too," Jesse says. "I hope you could feel that."

I blush. "I could." The problem with ViSEs is that they're not real, not anymore. They're just bits of time trapped on memory cards. Maybe I should have embraced those moments back before I knew about Lily. "But what about the girl who killed someone in L.A.? The girl who threatened you and Sebastian? Where does she fit into all this happiness?"

"That part of you exists because you needed it for protection. But you're stronger now and slowly realizing you can protect yourself. And I can help protect you too, if you want. Maybe when you quit needing her, she'll fade away."

"What if she doesn't?"

"I don't know. You should talk about that with your therapist," Jesse says. "A lot of people have dark, angry sides and still manage to live normal lives. All I know is Lily or no Lily, to me you're Winter, and I'll never stop loving you."

I remove the headset and curl up beside him. I drink in the warmth of his embrace. For a few seconds, I think that's all it's going to be—the two of us cuddling. But then a yearning builds within me. I focus on the heat, the desire. I nuzzle the place where Jesse's neck meets his shoulder. "So anyway, before we were so rudely interrupted . . ." I run my lips across the flesh of his throat and then pull his sweatshirt to the side. I kiss his collarbone all the way out to his shoulder.

He groans. I kiss my way back to the center of his neck. "And I'm done," he jokes.

I grin. "Too bad. I was just getting warmed up."

"You feel pretty hot to me." He tries to roll me on top of him again. I don't want that. I don't want this to be about me getting to make all the moves and the decisions. If anything is going to happen between Jesse and me, I want it to be something that both of us are controlling. I settle for lying side by side with him, just kissing him softly, over and over. Part of me thinks tonight should be the night.

I pull back from him. "Do you want to?"

He laughs lightly. "Yes, obviously. But I messed things up last time by moving too fast, so like I said earlier, there's no rush."

"I was just thinking, if things go badly tomorrow, we might not get another chance."

"We'll get plenty of chances," Jesse says. "And there's an entire world between where we are right now and being together like that." He runs one hand up the bare skin of my arm. "I don't want you to miss out on anything."

"An entire world?"

"A world of kissing." His lips brush against mine. "And touching." He drags one fingertip down the ridge of muscle in my neck. "Of getting to know each other, mentally and physically," he finishes.

Our faces are so close right now that I'm seeing double. Two perfect smiles. Three eyes swimming with brown and green and gold. He's right. There's no hurry. "Getting to know each other does sound nice," I say. "In fact, I have an idea."

"What's that?"

"I know you've wanted to see some of the city. Let me take you somewhere special."

Jesse grins. "Are you asking me out on a date, Winter Kim?"

"Yes. My very first date, in fact, so you'd better not say no."

"I would love to go on a date with you," Jesse says.

I grab our headsets and a couple of blank memory cards. "Put this under your hat. This is going to be a night you'll want to hang on to forever."

CHAPTER 39

We barely make it to the subway station before Jesse starts bugging me about where we're going. People mill past us in both directions as he fishes around in the pockets of his warm-up pants for his T-money card.

"It's a surprise," I tell him as I slap my own card down on the reader. We're both dressed warmly—sweatshirts, coats, hats—but neither of us has gloves. When he passes through the turnstile and reaches for my hand, I let him take it, glad for the feeling of warmth around my cold fingers.

"Is it a good surprise?"

"No, it's terrible." We reach the bottom of the stairs and turn toward the platform. I pull Jesse down a few car lengths from the crowded center area. He wraps an arm around me and I lean into his body, my head fitting neatly beneath his chin.

"We're not going to eat puffer fish, are we?" he asks. "Or little pieces of octopus that are still moving around on the plate?"

I snicker. "Have you been watching some sort of Korean *Iron Chef* without me?"

"I've been walking around some while you're at work. There's a lot of weird food here."

"There's a lot of weird food in the States too," I say. "But I'm actually not taking you out to eat, so relax."

"I was only kidding. You can take me anywhere you want." Jesse bends down and kisses me on the forehead. "This is fun."

"More fun than back at the hotel?" I tease.

"Um, I'm not sure how to answer that, but I like getting to have a normal night with you." He squeezes my hand. "A date."

"It is fun," I say. "Let's make the whole night normal. No talk of anything serious or sad."

"Deal." Jesse holds out his hand and I shake it, but he doesn't let go. He twines his fingers through mine and pulls me tight against him, nuzzling the bit of bare flesh above my collar.

Almost without thinking, I tilt my head to expose more of my skin. And then the bell chimes to alert us that a train is approaching and I remember we're not alone. Nearby, an older man clears his throat. I pull back a little. I try to give Jesse a stern look, but I end up collapsing into giggles.

"Sorry," he whispers. "I felt like I'd never be able to touch you again, and now that I can, I kind of want to do it all the time."

The arrival of the train saves me from having to respond to that. We enter the car and find seats at the end of one of the benches. Jesse keeps his fingers wrapped tightly around mine while we're sitting. A month ago this would've made me feel uncomfortable, contained. Tonight I like the feeling of being connected to him.

We swap trains and get off at Myeong-dong Station. As soon as we duck out of the exit, we can see the mountain Namsan looming, with the observation tower perched at the top.

"What is that?" Jesse asks. "Namsan Tower?"

I smile. "Yes. How did you know?"

"Sometimes when I can't sleep, I research stuff online." Jesse is still looking up at the tower. "It kind of looks like a couple of doughnuts threaded onto a spike. Can you actually get up into the round areas?"

"Only you would compare our most famous landmark to doughnuts," I say. "But yes, you can go up inside it."

"So how do we get up there?"

I glance around at the various walkways. A few flakes of snow are falling and street vendors parked up on the sidewalks are covering their wares with plastic and in some cases packing up to go home. "There's supposed to be a trail we can follow painted on one of the roads."

"We're walking up there?" Jesse's voice rises in pitch.

"Maybe," I say coyly. "Unless you don't think you can keep up with me."

"Oh, I can keep up," he says.

I find the painted yellow line we're supposed to follow and the two of us start up the steeply angled streets. Jesse struggles a bit with the altitude change, so we keep a slow and steady pace. But then the snow starts to come down harder, making the concrete under our feet slippery and difficult to navigate. It'll take too long for us to walk up the mountain in these conditions, and by the time we get there, we'll be too frozen to really enjoy it.

So after a few more minutes of carefully following the yellow lines painted on the roadways, I pull Jesse off to the right where a concrete building says NAMSAN CABLE CAR.

"How do you feel about a shortcut?" I arch my eyebrows.

"A cable car? This late?"

There's a dusting of snowflakes on his cheek. I reach out and touch his face, feeling the snow melt under my fingertips. "Yes. It runs until eleven, so worst-case scenario is that we have to walk down the mountain."

"What's inside the tower?" he asks.

A smile plays at my lips. "Puffer fish."

Jesse pokes me in the shoulder. "Funny."

"It's a surprise."

"All right. Cable car it is." A snowflake lodges itself in Jesse's eyelashes and he blinks it away. "After you."

The two of us climb up a flight of steps that leads from the street to the building's entrance. Once inside, we get tickets and wait in a glassed-in area for the car to arrive. The area quickly starts to fill up with tourists, college kids, and the occasional family. I pull Jesse from the bench where we've been sitting so we stay close to the front of the line.

"Trying to get a good seat, huh?" he asks.

"I don't think there are seats," I say. "But I've actually never done this before."

"Why not?"

"We never had money for stuff like this."

"So then we're doing something new together." Jesse wraps his arms around my waist.

I rest my head against his chest. "We are." Even though his coat is wet with melted snow, he still manages to feel warm next to me. And safe. Why did I fight this for so long?

When the cable car arrives, Jesse and I are two of the first to board. We find spots at the back of the enclosure, right up against the glass. I reach out with my sleeve and wipe some smudges away. I pull my phone out and take a picture of the view. The snow is coming down heavier now, bleaching the city a ghostly silver and white.

The operators manage to fit about sixty people into the small car, which isn't much bigger than two elevators side by side. Jesse has apparently adjusted to the Korean standard of personal space and doesn't seem fazed by the family of four pressing up against us, not even the little girl who is hanging on to the knee of his track pants for support.

He makes a slight *ulp* sound as the car starts to move, like it's faster than he was expecting. Then he reaches down and takes my bare fingers in his hand. He lifts them to his lips and blows on them, the heat from his mouth warming my whole body.

Again, I am overwhelmed by the urge to touch his face, to touch all of him, to kiss him. "I'm trying to get pictures," I say sternly, taking back my hands and turning to face the glass.

"What for? You can barely see the city."

"But you can still feel it." Beyond the snowy trees, the endless high-rises of Seoul have faded to a blurry gray shadow, but their presence hasn't dwindled. Even in the poor visibility, there's no denying that the city feels like the walls of a fortress, a fortress that is both protecting us and trapping us.

"And we'll both have ViSE recordings for that," I add.

The cable car shimmies a little and Jesse rests a hand on my lower back to support us both. "Sometimes it's nice to relive something without even relying on pictures. Just embracing the actual memories, you know?"

"You're better at memories than I am," I say, snapping a picture down the mountain. It's mostly snow and trees, with a ridge of buildings at the edge of it, but it captures what I'm feeling right now.

Jesse pulls me completely in front of him and wraps his arms around my waist, bending down to rest his chin on my shoulder. "I want to make a whole bunch of new memories with you," he murmurs.

"I'd like that," I say. And then, as the car begins to slow, I add, "I'm going to make you plan our second date."

Jesse presses his lips to my temple. "I don't know. This one is going to be tough to beat."

The cable car shudders to a halt and I press my palm against the glass to steady myself. We wait for everyone else to get out before making our way onto the exit platform. My feet feel unsteady on the slick wood and I grip Jesse's hand tightly.

We stand there for a few moments as everyone else hurries off in different directions. A floodlight shines down on us, flecks of snow twisting and writhing in the white light.

"I love snow," I say.

"Good thing, as much of it as we've seen this winter." Jesse's face brightens. "Winter. That's a good name for someone who loves snow."

I smile. Behind us, the cable car loads up to go back down

the mountain. I guide Jesse toward a path leading up to the tower.

"More stairs," he says.

Ahead of us, two high school girls are holding on to each other tightly as they try to climb the icy steps in high-heeled boots. They pause halfway up to take selfies with the tower in the background.

"It'll be worth it," I promise.

We take the stairs together slowly, Jesse gripping the railing and me gripping Jesse. My face feels like ice by the time we reach the paved area at the top of the hill. There's a raised platform here with benches and a big circular display where people have locked tiny locks everywhere.

"Love locks, huh?" Jesse says. "Wow, thousands of them."

The locks are all kinds of vibrant colors—reds and greens and teals. The snow is just starting to cover them. I take my phone out and snap a picture. "Rose and I used to talk about coming up here when we were little, leaving a lock for the two of us. But we never got the chance."

Jesse sits on a bench and I sit next to him. "They do this in the US too, on bridges mostly. In some places there are so many that they're weakening the structural integrity. Local governments have had to start cutting them off."

"Well, that's romantic."

"It's a cool gesture, but I never really understood," he says. "I feel like love is the kind of thing you have to nurture and care for. You can't just lock it up in some faraway place if you want it to last."

I look over at him. "So then you've been in love before?"

Jesse smiles. "You mean besides you?"

My cheeks, already flushed from the cold, go even redder. "Besides me."

He thinks for a moment before speaking. "I'm not sure," he says. "There was a girl in high school. Amy. We dated for a year and a half. I thought I loved her. But what I feel for you is different."

I pull my feet up on the bench and hug my arms around my knees for warmth. A family of four stops to take pictures of the love locks. The older daughter leans in close to read the inscriptions some people have written in marker.

"Different how?" I ask.

Jesse exhales a cloudy breath into the cold air. "Caring about her was stressful. I was always trying to keep her from leaving."

"And me?" I'm almost afraid to ask.

"You're always leaving, but you're never gone, you know?" He slouches down on the bench and rests his head on my shoulder. "I think everything that's happened recently has helped me be less selfish when it comes to love. I'll be okay if we don't end up together the way I want. I'm just glad to be part of your life right now. I'm glad for the moments we've had."

"Really?" I wish I felt like that about Gideon and my sister, like it's all right that they're gone, like I'm lucky just to have known them.

"Really," Jesse says. And I can tell by his voice that whether or not it's actually true, he believes it.

I hop up from the bench and turn to face him. His black coat and hat are lightly dusted with snow, his face red from the cold. I pull my phone out of my pocket. "Say *chijeu*."

"What is that? Cheese?" He strikes a pose as I take a picture of him.

I laugh as an unfamiliar feeling envelops me. It reminds me of how I felt when I was playing Jesse's ViSE. I think it might be happiness. I spin a slow circle and then open my mouth to catch a snowflake on my tongue.

Jesse rises up from the bench. He grins wickedly as he approaches me.

"What?" I say. "What are you doing?"

"I was just thinking that I want that snowflake."

My grin matches his. "Come and get it."

He leans in and kisses me, sweet at first, our faces cold against each other. Then his tongue tastes my bottom lip and my bones go a little wobbly. I grip the fabric of his heavy coat as our kisses grow more intense, the heat of our breath warming our cheeks.

"All right. I've seen enough," he says between kisses. "Time to go home and do this for the rest of the night."

I punch him in the arm. "We're not finished yet." Shaking my head, I pull him toward the actual tower, where we buy tickets to the observatory deck.

We take an elevator to the top and step out into a small observatory area. Below us, the mountainside is rapidly being covered by the snow. Off in the distance, the entire city has disappeared. It's almost like the tower is in the clouds. Still, there's something so beautiful about the way the giant flakes of snow take refuge in the feathery green trees, about the way our breath fogs the smudgy glass.

"So. I was wondering," Jesse says. "Will you be my girlfriend?"

I giggle. "I can't believe you're asking me that now."

"Is that a yes?" He grins.

"Yes, I'll be your girlfriend."

Jesse kisses my forehead and then my eyelids and then both of my cheeks. I bury my face in his chest, embarrassed but happy. I don't want this moment to ever end.

"*Saranghae*," he says, which is "I love you" in Korean. He slightly mangles the *reul* sound, a mix of *r* and *l* that foreign speakers struggle with.

"I lo—"

He reaches out and presses his index finger to my lips. "Shh. Don't say anything."

I furrow my brow. "But why not?"

"Because when you eventually say it back, I don't want to have to wonder if you just said it to be nice."

I feign indignation. "When is the last time I did something just to be nice?"

"Good point." He laughs. "Still. I can wait."

I slide one hand inside the collar of his coat, my fingertips resting on his chest, the rapid beat of his heart evident through the thick fabric of his hoodie. "You're my family," I say. "I didn't realize it until you got shot, but I think that you've been part of my family for a while."

"See? Now that means even more to me."

"Good." I smile. "I like that you learned to say 'I love you' in Korean."

He reaches down and tilts my chin so we're looking into each other's eyes. "How bad did I mess it up? Did I accidentally tell you I wanted to kill your pet monkey or something?"

I shake my head. "You did just fine." I lift a hand to my cheek. My skin is blazing. "And your kisses warmed my entire face."

Jesse grins. "Good. After we make it through tomorrow, that's going to become a regular thing."

I blush at the thought, but a shadow falls over everything at the mention of tomorrow. "Tonight is only about tonight, remember?" I murmur. I turn back toward the view of the city, but it's too late—the spell is broken. Jesse and I might as well be caught in a snow globe. Tonight is just a single perfect moment trapped in glass.

Tomorrow our protective bubble will be shattered.

CHAPTER 40

The next morning I crawl reluctantly out from between Jesse's arms when my phone alarm goes off. We spent the better part of two hours kissing after we got home last night, and I wish I could stay locked in his warm embrace all day.

But I can't. Today is the day to do what we came here for. Or should I say the night? My fingers are trembling as I dress for work. The fabric of my skirt swishes gently against my legs as I slip into the bathroom and start applying my makeup.

My phone vibrates, making a sharp rattling noise as it collides with something else in my purse. Back in the room, Jesse shifts in his sleep but doesn't wake. I peer at the screen.

Baz: Are you sure you want to go today?

Me: No, but if I don't go, it might arouse suspicion.

Baz: Only if someone knows who you actually are.

Me: Or suspects who I am. Besides, what if I don't go and something changes?

Baz: What if you do go, and something changes, but you don't know about it?

Me: Then we're not any worse off than we currently are. If I show up as usual, at least they won't suspect anything special is going to happen tonight.

Baz: True. You're a brave girl.

It's exactly the kind of thing I would want to hear from him.

Again, I wonder if he's been playing me from the moment Jesse and I arrived in Seoul.

Me: It's easy to be brave when you're as messed up as I am. It's not like there's a lot to lose.

My eyes flick to Jesse again. Only that's not exactly true anymore, if it ever was.

Baz doesn't respond, so I return to applying my makeup. I slip my headset on and then secure the dark wig on top of it. I arrange my bangs across my forehead. "Last day," I tell myself.

My phone vibrates again.

Baz: I'm in the hallway.

I had almost forgotten his hotel was right next door. I slip into my coat and shoes and then open the door. Sebastian is standing there holding two disposable paper cups from a local coffee chain. Wisps of steam rise toward the textured ceiling.

"Thanks," I say, as he holds a cup in my direction. I take it and do my best to close the door to the room softly, but it still makes a clunking sound when it latches.

"Look. There's something I need to tell you."

"Oh?" I arch an eyebrow. *It's about time.*

"I found your brother." Baz holds out his phone. The picture Yoo Mi showed me is on the screen. "He's fine. He's living with your aunt."

"I know." I sip the beverage hesitantly. It's green tea, with a hint of honey. Just how I like it.

Baz looks surprised. "You know? And you didn't yell at me for keeping it a secret?"

"I was trying to figure out if I could trust you."

"And?"

"I'm still deciding." I'm also waiting for him to tell me he's been in contact with Kyung, or to admit that he's been using an alias here.

Baz leans back against the patterned wallpaper. "Look, my word might not mean much to you, but my word meant something to Gideon, and I swore to him I would look out for you. And I was afraid if you knew about Jun, it might distract you and you could end up getting hurt. I was going to tell you about him and your aunt as soon as we did what we came to do. But I want you to realize what you have to lose. We don't have to do this tonight, Winter. We could pay someone to deal with Kyung. If he dies, chances are the tech—"

"'Chances are' isn't good enough for me, Baz." My voice cracks as my eyes are drawn back to the picture of Jun. "And I think I need to be realistic when it comes to my family. I just don't want them to get hurt—that's all. It's not like we can have a real relationship if they're here in Seoul and I go back to the US."

"Right. If only we had some sort of electronic communication system where people in different places could meaningfully interact."

I frown. "The Internet is not the same."

"No. But it's a start," Baz says. "You can always come back here after things have settled down, right? The important thing is that we keep Jun and your aunt safe. One of my people will be watching them all day. If something goes wrong, I'll call him and give him directions to a safe house. He can watch out for your family as long as necessary."

"Promise me you'll protect them no matter what. Even if it means not protecting me."

Baz grimaces. "Gideon would not—"

"I don't care," I say. "Gideon does not make decisions for me anymore."

"Fine. I promise."

I want so badly to believe him. I don't think I can go through with the rest of the plan if I don't trust him. "Who is Erich Cross?" I blurt out. "Who are all three of those names that we found in Kyung's suit pocket? I'm sure you had your friends at some shadowy agency do a thorough background check." *Last chance,* I think. *Last chance to tell me the truth.*

Baz sighs. "Like I said, the first guy is a rebel commander in Myanmar, the second one is a South American military leader, and Erich Cross is . . . me. An alias I used to use."

I exhale with relief. "Why was your alias in Kyung's pocket?"

"I don't know. I flew in under that name. Maybe he found some link between Gideon and me. Or perhaps he thought I might try to steal the technology. I've . . . engaged in corporate theft in the past."

"Is that how you met Gideon?"

Baz shakes his head. "I wish."

"Tell me," I say. "Tell me the story."

Baz's grip tightens around his coffee cup. "We don't have time for this right now, Winter."

"I need you to tell me," I say firmly.

He exhales. "Fine. We met here. Gideon was eighteen. I was twenty-three, officially an air force NCO but already starting to take off-the-book assignments for various government task forces. I used his mom for an op, got her killed. That was back when I still felt guilty about things. I tried everything to make it up to him, but he didn't want money or guns or drugs or girls, and that was all I had to offer. He just wanted to know how—why—she had died. I told him, even though it violated my security clearance and half a dozen confidentiality agreements."

Baz's voice gets flatter and more emotionless as this story progresses. I feel like maybe he's one of those people who has become so skilled at hiding his emotions that the more he's hurting, the less he shows it.

"Sebastian." I reach out for him, but he steps back.

"Gideon appreciated my honesty and we became friends," Baz continues. "We kept in touch after I left. When he established himself in Los Angeles, he told me I should move there, that he could get me a job that wouldn't keep me up at night. I declined. I was sort of in the thick of things at that point, stationed in Kabul, running ops that wiped bad men off the face of the planet."

"So what happened?"

"Gideon reached out about his plan to escape with you and your sister, and by that point I realized that bad men were everywhere. They weren't just in the desert teaching kids to be terrorists. They were in boardrooms teaching executives to cheat, in classrooms teaching students to hate. They were everywhere, and somehow I had become one of them. Gideon was one of the most honest and righteous men I've ever known. Even though I thought he was crazy, I wanted to help him." Baz pauses. "Maybe I thought some of that goodness would rub off on me." He flicks his eyes toward the ground and then back up at me. "Maybe it has."

I see the sun rising through a window at the end of the hallway. "It's a new day," I say, sipping my tea.

"Yeah. Maybe it is."

There's a rustling sound behind me. "What's going on?" Jesse asks.

I turn at the sound of his voice, take in his broad silhouette in the doorway to the hotel room, the tufts of hair sticking straight up on the top of his head.

"Just talking," I say.

"You've both got the contingency plan memorized?" Baz says. "Just in case?"

"Next stop, Jeju Island," I say.

"Sunrise Hotel." Jesse swallows back a yawn. "But hopefully we won't get separated."

I look back and forth between the two of them. "I'll see you guys tonight." I touch Baz lightly on the arm. "I'm sorry I doubted you." I stretch up on my toes to give Jesse a kiss on the cheek.

"I'll walk you to the elevator," Jesse says.

"I'll wait here so I can go over a couple things with you," Baz tells Jesse.

Jesse follows me down the hallway and stands next to me while I wait for the elevator. "You know, I had this amazing dream last night," he says.

My face flushes. "Me too. Only I think mine might have been real."

Jesse grins. "Thank you for an incredible date. Last night was the most fun I've had in a long time."

The elevator chimes to signal its arrival; I gesture at Jesse's pajamas and socks. "Coming with me to the subway like that?"

He shakes his head. His hazel eyes glimmer with mischief.

"Then what are you doing?" I ask.

The silver doors open with a soft whooshing sound and Jesse sweeps me inside. I feel the usual prickle of dread as the doors close behind us.

And then he kisses me. Soft. Sweet. His lips just barely brushing against mine. He cradles my chin in his hands. Something about the gesture reminds me of Gideon. Something about the gesture reminds me of how it feels to be loved. Jesse kisses his way down my cheekbones and the angles of my jaw. By the time the doors open again, my knees are weak. I stumble out into the lobby.

I look back at him. "What was that for?"

"I read something about phobias the other day, how sometimes it helps to replace a traumatic memory with a new one. Just doing my part." Jesse winks as he presses the DOOR CLOSED button.

The elevator swallows him up before I can even respond.

Jesse's kisses stay with me for most of the subway ride. I'm lucky enough to get a seat, so I close my eyes, lean back against the wall, and imagine Jesse kissing me like that over and over. It occurs to me that I could actually have that life, if I want it. Jesse and I could go home and be together.

But first we have to survive tonight.

As I get off the train and start toward the UsuMed building, my stomach fills with dread. Maybe Baz was right. Maybe I shouldn't have come today.

When I arrive on the fourteenth floor, Mrs. Kim takes me and the other girls down to the twelfth floor, where she says we'll be spending the day sitting in cubicles, listening in on customer service calls completed by other UsuMed staff members.

When Yoo Mi taps me on the shoulder around ten a.m., I am more than ready to go outside for our not-quite-smoking break. I've gotten into the habit of going out with her these past few days just so I can stretch my legs and breathe some real air while she chats with some of the UsuMed boys. To say I'm not used to the office environment is an understatement.

"You seem anxious," she says, as we stroll toward the elevators. "Are you all right?"

"I'm fine." I shift my weight from one foot to the other. "I'm just thinking about many things right now."

"Ooh," Yoo Mi says. The elevator doors open and we both step into the car with a few men in suits who are probably headed to the same place we are. She leans in close to me and hisses, "Is one of them a boy?"

No one turns to look at us even though I'm pretty sure everyone in the elevator heard her. "Yes," I admit, as we hit the lobby and turn toward the revolving doors. "I went on a date with a guy that I like very much."

We step out into the cold and head for the smoking area. Yoo Mi's eyes are bright with curiosity. "Did you kiss?" she asks.

"Maybe," I say coyly.

She giggles. "I want to hear all about it. How old is he? What does he look like? More importantly, what does he kiss like?"

"I, uh—" Luckily I am saved from her barrage of questions as a guy from the sales department asks her for a light. She lights up his cigarette and the two of them start chatting. I step away to give them some privacy.

I pull my phone out and send Jesse a text.

Me: Hi.

Jesse: I was just thinking about you. There's this girl outside the Usu building who looks like you.

Me: In the smoking area? That's me! Where are you? What are you doing here?

Jesse: I'm in the Hyundai coffee shop. Baz told me to stick close to the building today, just in case you need anything. Wait. You're smoking?

Me: I'm not smoking. I just came out with a friend. I was telling her a little bit about our date. I think I just wanted to see your words.

Jesse: Is it safe to call you? I've heard they sound even better than they look.

Me: I should probably get back inside. But this helped. Thanks.

Jesse: Actually, I'm glad you texted. Something happened. Baz told me not to tell you, that it would only make you worry, but given your suspicions about him, I didn't want to hide it from you.

That figures. Less than four hours after apologizing for keeping secrets from me, Sebastian is at it again.

Me: Hide what?

Jesse: Kyung got a phone call this morning. The caller didn't identify himself, but apparently Kyung is having a meeting with someone at 1:15 for a demonstration of the technology. Kyung said all of the laboratory staff would be at lunch from 1:00 to 2:00, so there'd be plenty of time for a demo.

Me: How do you know what he said? Did Baz translate?

Jesse: They were speaking English. The guy sounded British.

Alec Kwon, perhaps.

Me: You think Kyung already has a buyer? Even though it isn't fixed yet?

Jesse: I don't know. I'm going to move to the coffee shop in the UsuMed building around one to see if I can see anyone arriving, maybe get some pictures. I know we're not supposed to be seen together, but I figured you could keep an eye out too.

I reply and tell Jesse that I will, but I have a better idea. A dangerous idea, but one that might finally answer the question of why Kyung wants the ViSE technology so badly. I reach into my purse and curl my fingers around the laminated ID badge that Baz made for me. Time to see if it really works.

CHAPTER 41

Yoo Mi's new friend heads back to work. She returns to my side, her cheeks flushed with joy. "Now about this guy . . ." she starts.

"Hmm?" I ask. I'm working out the details in my mind. If the entire lab goes to lunch at 1:00 and the meeting is at 1:15, that gives me fifteen minutes to find Lab 6 and a place to hide where I can eavesdrop on the meeting.

"Your date," Yoo Mi reminds me. She gestures at my phone, which is still clutched in my bare hand. "Do you have a picture? I know you were texting him."

"I was, but no. No picture."

"I don't know if I believe you." She grabs for my phone as we hit the steps leading up to the front of the building.

I jerk my arm out of her reach and bump into a man just heading out to smoke. Not any man. Alec Kwon. Which means Kyung is probably nearby. The phone slips out of my fingers and falls to the ground. I reach for it, but Alec is too quick.

He scoops it off the pavement and presses it into my right hand, his eyes lingering on my palm for a second. "Here you are, then," he says in British-accented English.

"Thank you." I force a smile at him.

"Have we met before?" It's an innocent question, but there's something teasing about the way he delivers it, like he already knows the answer. He peers down at my ID badge.

Yoo Mi looks from Alec to me, a curious expression on her face.

"I don't think so," I tell Alec. "I have to go. Thank you again." I turn and hurry inside the building, casting a glance back over my shoulder.

Alec is pulling a pack of cigarettes out of his pocket, the interaction seemingly forgotten. But I can't shake the lilting tone of his voice, like he was mocking me, like he knows something that I don't.

YOO Mi and I return to our desks and I grab my phone headset and get to work. It's hard to concentrate, though. Every few minutes I check the time. When we all break for lunch, the other girls get their coats and look expectantly at me.

"Oh," I say. "I think I'm going to skip lunch today. I'm not very hungry."

"You should eat something, at least," Susan says.

"My stomach is feeling a little queasy. Go on without me. I might just get some crackers from the vending machine."

As expected, Yoo Mi says, "Well, if you're not going to lunch. I'll stay with you. I don't want you to be alone if you're sick."

"No, go on," I insist. "I don't want you to starve because of me. I'll just put my head down and take a little nap."

"Okay," Yoo Mi says. She gives me a long look, but she can't really insist on staying with me without arousing Susan's or Minnie's suspicion.

I wait a couple of minutes until I'm sure the girls are in the elevator. Then I take a different elevator down to the second floor, where I duck into the stairwell. I swipe my card to access the level B-1 and peek out into the main hallway. This floor doesn't look anything like the rest of the building. The walls are made of heavy cinder block and the floor is plain concrete. The air is cold and crisp, the scent of some kind of medicine making my eyes water. I start down a long hallway, passing doors on both sides with caution signs and symbols on them.

Luckily the doors are numbered and I quickly realize Lab 6 must be one more floor down. I turn back to the stairwell. Before I can reach it, the door to Lab 2 starts to open. I flail for a hiding spot—a corner, an alcove, a bathroom, anything—but there's no time to obscure myself. I remember something Gideon once told me about hiding in plain sight: the more you act like you belong somewhere, the more people will believe it.

Quickly I adopt a serious expression, striding past an older man in a lab coat as if I have somewhere critical to be. He's busy fishing his phone out of one of his pockets and doesn't even seem to notice me. Whew.

I swipe my badge into the stairwell and descend to floor B-2. It only takes me a couple minutes to find a door marked Lab 6. The door is made of metal with a thick pane of glass embedded in it. I peek through the glass but it's slightly distorted and I can't see much. Glancing around to make sure there are no security cameras pointed in this direction, I lean in and put my ear to the glass to listen for voices. The only sound I hear is the pounding of my own heart.

I check the time. 1:06. Kyung and whoever he is meeting will be arriving shortly. I need to get into the lab and find a place to hide. Fishing one of my throwing knives out of my boot just in case, I swipe my cloned badge and step into the lab.

It looks about how I expect—a big white room full of steel tables and high-tech research equipment. There are racks of supplies between each of the tables, and a long counter along the back wall features microscopes and computers, with rolling chairs at each station. I can tell from the personal items like backpacks and notebooks that at least six people work in this lab.

A clock on the wall reads 1:08. My heart sinks as I realize there's really nowhere to hide in here. And then I see a trash chute in the far corner of the room labeled BIOHAZARD. It probably leads to an incinerator below where medical waste is burned. It's just big enough for me to crawl inside. I squeeze my body into the chute and pull the door almost completely closed behind me. I brace myself against the walls with my feet so I don't fall down into the darkness, grateful to Jesse for teaching me this rock-climbing technique last year when we were recording a ViSE.

I use one hand to hold the chute door open just a hair so I can see out into the room. I can't reach my phone to check it in this position, so I measure the passage of time by counting my breaths. About thirty breaths later, the door to the lab finally starts to swing open. What I see next shocks me so much I almost lose my footing and go tumbling down the chute: Kyung walks into the lab with three other men. One of them is Alec Kwon. The second is an older man in a military uniform. The third man is Sebastian.

CHAPTER 42

Kyung goes to a locked silver cabinet and appears to punch in a security code. The cabinet doors swing open and he removes a couple of ViSE headsets. "Colonel Rojas. Mr. Cross," Kyung says, as he hands each man a headset. I watch Baz's expression carefully. He takes the headset Kyung gives him and turns it over in his hands like he's never seen it before.

I have no idea what this means, whether Sebastian is legitimately trying to buy the tech from Kyung or if he's posing as a buyer just to scope out how to steal it. All I know for sure is that he's still keeping secrets from me, after everything we talked about this morning.

And that means I can't trust him.

Kyung gestures at the nearest table and Baz hops up on it and lies down. Colonel Rojas frowns and says something to Kyung I can't make out. Alec walks right past me to get a chair from one of the workstations at the back of the room. He rolls it up front and Colonel Rojas takes a seat.

"This scenario is just a basic example of the technology's capabilities. We kept it simple for purposes of demonstration, but I'm sure you will both understand what sort of potential we're talking about here, especially once the editor is fully functional," Kyung says.

Both men slip the headsets over their heads and Alec dims the lights to the laboratory.

I wonder what sort of ViSE they're playing. I think again of Kyung in his hotel suite, with the girl. Is he trying to start some sort of digital prostitution ring? But then why would a military colonel want to buy it? There are many covert uses for the tech, but most of them—like spying—are already being done with less complex technology like hidden cameras and listening devices.

I hear the men make occasional noises in the dark as they play their ViSEs. A sigh. A grunt. A muttered curse. But it's not enough information for me to decipher what it is they could be experiencing.

When the lights flip back on, Colonel Rojas's olive skin has gone pale. "That was . . . disturbingly real," he says, his voice wavering slightly.

"And impressive," Baz says smoothly. "How long until you think you'll have a functioning version of the editing component?"

"A few more days," Kyung says. "Two weeks at most."

I swallow back a sigh of relief.

"Have you tested this on human subjects?" Rojas asks. "Can you guarantee there will be no fatalities?"

I nearly choke on my own breath. *Human subjects? Fatalities?*

"Well," Kyung starts, "we're still undergoing testing. But we don't foresee any issues."

Rojas nods, but he still looks shaken.

"The colonel seems a bit reticent about your product," Baz says. "My people are less concerned about the possibility of a few deaths. New technology always has some bugs to work out, right? I can assure you we will be ready to make a deal as soon as you have a complete working prototype. In fact, since the colonel's interest seems so lukewarm, we might be willing to pay extra for exclusive rights to this technology."

"I did not say we weren't interested," Rojas protests. "Let me speak to my superiors and get back to you via secure channels."

I don't know what those secure channels are, but I'm imagining they're probably not Kyung's cell phone. I wonder how Baz has been communicating with him, since we haven't intercepted any phone calls. What if Jesse and I hadn't told Sebastian we bugged Kyung's phone? Would we have caught him red-handed setting up this meeting?

"As will I," Baz says.

Kyung, Baz, and Colonel Rojas chat briefly as Alec locks up the ViSE technology. Something about sports. Something about food. My heart is pounding so hard in my brain that I can barely hear them. Human subjects. Fatalities. What is Kyung doing with the ViSE technology?

When the men exit the lab, I count to sixty to make sure they're really gone and then crawl out of the trash chute. I check the time—1:44. I only have about fifteen minutes before whoever is working in here returns from lunch. I creep over to the cabinet and examine the lock on the door. It requires an access code, and I wasn't close enough to see what Kyung punched in. Still, the metal isn't overly sturdy—some kind of steel alloy most likely. With the explosives Baz made, we should easily be able to blow open the cabinet. Doing so might damage the tech, but I'm not even worried about that. In fact, it might be the best thing for everyone.

And then I remember that I can't trust Baz anymore. I think of the way he asked about a finished prototype, about the way he said his people were unconcerned by the possibility of a few deaths. It sounds like he's back working for whichever government is paying the best this week. Maybe Jesse can manage to shoot open this cabinet with his gun, or we can break in some other way. All I know is we need to figure out a way to steal the tech on our own now.

The clock reads 1:48 as I slip back out into the hallway. Keeping my chin tucked low, I make it to the stairwell without being seen. There, the gravity of what I just did crashes down on me and my muscles go slack. I sink to the concrete steps and pull out my phone. With shaking fingers, I text Jesse.

Me: We need a new plan.

Jesse: What?

Me: I saw who was in the meeting.

Jesse: You did? I've been in the coffee shop since 12:45 and haven't seen anyone besides what look like Usu execs.

Me: They probably entered through the parking garage.

Jesse: Ah, good point. So do you have pix? Should we e-mail them to Baz?

Me: We can't trust Baz.

Jesse: ?

Me: Baz was at the meeting. I don't know if he's trying to buy the tech for a foreign government or steal it or what, but he's lying to both of us.

My phone buzzes with a call. Jesse. I don't blame him for wanting to talk to me. I know I sound unhinged. But now it's 1:55. I need to be back upstairs in a few minutes or Yoo Mi is going to know something happened.

Me: I'm sorry. I can't talk. Text Baz and tell him that you and I are going to grab dinner together after I get off work. Instead of 8:00, we'll meet him at 10:00 to go over everything one last time. Then you and I can steal the tech right after everyone in the lab goes home and hide it. We can still pretend to break in with Baz later if we need to.

I start heading up the stairs back to the office, but my muscles are still weak and on the fourth floor I give up and go out to the center of the building and wait for the elevator.

Jesse: Are you sure you're okay?

Me: Fine, but I have to get back to work. I might have to stay a little later than usual tonight because I haven't been able to focus much today.

Jesse: Maybe you should just leave early.

I'd like nothing more right about now, but if I do, then Yoo Mi will know something happened, and she'll tell Baz.

Me: I can't. Meet me at Gangnam Station, in front of exit 7, at 8:00.
I promise I'll explain everything.

The elevator opens on the twelfth floor and I duck back into the customer service department right at two. Yoo Mi is just settling back into her workstation.

"There you are," she says. "I was just starting to worry."

I smile tightly. "I'm fine. Feeling a little better even."

The rest of the day passes without incident. As the clock ticks past six p.m. and some of the other trainees begin to gather their things, a pair of men enter the room. My insides go cold. One of them is Alec Kwon. The second man is the guy I saw get out of the car with Alec and Kyung on Monday.

The guy with the gun.

"Miss Lee," Alec says in a musical voice. "I'm Mr. Kwon and this is Mr. Yun. Talent Acquisition had a question about one of your hiring forms. If you could follow us, please."

"Sure." I stand up slowly from my chair, looping my purse over my shoulder. Around me, worried eyes start peeking toward me and then back to their work. Yoo Mi's eyes seem to be focused completely on her workstation. I wonder if this is somehow her doing, if Baz ordered her to set me up.

"This way, please," Alec says.

My insides clench into a fist as the men take positions on either side of me. There's no way Talent Acquisition sent a freelance neurotechnologist and a gun-toting security specialist to escort me to their office. Maybe someone caught me on camera on the restricted floors. I glance furtively from side to side as we head down the hallway toward the elevator. There has to be an escape route somewhere.

"So you work for Mrs. Kim?" I ask, trying to remain calm.

"We work where we're needed," Alec replies, pressing the down arrow.

My blood goes cold. Talent Acquisition is above us, on the fourteenth floor.

I glance up at the display. The elevator is four floors away. That gives me just enough time to make a decision. As the elevator button dings and the doors slide open, I take advantage of the millisecond of distraction and race for the stairwell. A pair of executives step out of the elevator and provide me a tiny bit of cover.

But I can't go down stairs very fast in my boots. I hear the door swing open and the sound of heavy shoes on the steps. I push myself to go faster, leaping over the last three or four steps at the bottom of each landing.

But it's no use. The men have sturdier shoes and longer legs. They're only two flights behind me. The farther down I try to go, the faster they'll catch up. I frantically swipe my card at the next door and explode out onto the eighth floor, racing down the carpeted hallway. My head swivels left and right, looking for something, anything, I can use to slow them down. I reach out to jiggle each office doorknob desperately. Some of them are locked. Some of them open to puzzled looks from executives. I need one to be empty so I can lock myself inside. I need a place to hide. I need a few seconds to think. But I near the end of the hallway without finding what I want. Behind me, the men are shouting.

I lean down to pull a knife out of my boot. It isn't going to be much against two men, at least one of whom has a gun, but it's the best I've got. I don't want to actually hurt anyone. I just need to get away . . . somehow.

And then I see a fire extinguisher mounted in a glass box, and next to it an escape rope. There's a metal hook embedded in the wall. Hurriedly, I unlatch the nearest window and push open the glass. There's no time to put on the safety harness. I link the rope to the metal hook, grab onto it, and launch myself out the window.

Quickly, I begin to half climb, half slide down the rope, my hands growing hot from the friction as I get lower to the ground. Seventh floor. Sixth floor. *Keep going.* Fifth floor. I pause for a second. Fourth floor. And then suddenly the rope jerks. I look up to see Mr. Yun hauling me back up toward the eighth-floor window. I slide faster than he can pull me up, but he's taken in enough slack that I'm trapped in the air when I reach the bottom of the rope. I look down. I'm still more than two stories above the ground.

As I rise toward the third-floor window, I make a desperate decision.

I let go.

CHAPTER 43

I've never jumped onto pavement, so I'm not sure which way to land. I end up curling my forearms around my face and bracing my head with my hands. My feet hit the ground first, then my knees. The impact jars me all the way to my bones. My teeth click together, narrowly avoiding my tongue.

I lift myself off the cement, ready to start running again, but a sharp pain spikes through my ankle. I grab onto the edge of a nearby Dumpster to keep from collapsing. I look both ways, desperate for some kind of escape, but I'm not going to be able to outrun anyone. All I can do is limp toward the opening to the parking garage. As I duck into the dimly lit area, I pull the knife from my left boot, just in case. I'm not sure where Alec and his friend have gone.

Inside the garage, I lean back against the concrete wall. I lift a hand to my chest as I try to catch my breath. Right away I can feel that something is different. My snowflake necklace! It must have fallen off me when I jumped. Swearing under my breath, I peer around the corner of the garage. Sure enough, the necklace is lying on the pavement just a few feet away. I have to get it. I limp toward the necklace, but before I can reach it, Alec Kwon appears in my peripheral vision.

"Hello, Ha Neul," Alec says. "You are Ha Neul, right?" He bends down and nimbly plucks the snowflake necklace from the pavement. He holds it up to the light for a moment and then deposits it into my hand, one finger lingering to trace the cross-shaped scar on my palm. "It seems this is very important to you."

I tighten my fingers around the pendant. I can't believe I spent so much effort disguising myself with wigs and makeup only to be recognized by my scar. At least he didn't notice the pendant is more than a necklace. My other hand grips the hilt of my knife. "Get away from me," I say, pointing it at him.

He laughs. "You're on camera. I don't recommend stabbing me." He strokes my cheek with one hand and bile burns in my throat, rank and hot. "Come along. My superior would like to speak with you."

My knife trembles in my fingertips. "What if I say no?"

"Well, then I suppose Mr. Yun would have to take you by force. Or we could call the police if you'd prefer that."

Mr. Yun appears in the opening of the parking garage, his gun drawn. He reaches out and removes the knife from my hand.

"Police? I haven't done anything wrong."

"You know it's against the law to carry that knife, right?" Alec holds up my purse. "Let's see what else you have."

Damn it. I must have dropped that when I fell from the rope.

Alec unzips my purse. "Well, what have we here?" He removes the tranquilizer gun and studies it curiously. "American?" he asks. "I suspect this is also illegal."

I sigh. At least he doesn't seem to know I have a second throwing knife in my other boot. "It's also against the law to hire people to break into someone's hotel room and steal from her," I say. But it's pointless to bring that up. I have no proof Kyung was responsible, and even if I did, that crime happened in the US, not here.

"I'm afraid I have no idea to what you are referring." Alec plucks something else of interest out of my purse—the all-access ID badge. I swear under my breath. Baz put my picture on it, but how hard will it be for Alec to figure out it's actually Jason Choi's clearances? He holds the ID next to the one still clipped to my shirt. "This is interesting. Where'd you get it?"

When I refuse to answer, Alec and Mr. Yun each take one of my arms and we turn toward the entrance to the building. Alec shakes his head in dismay when he realizes I'm limping. "Did you injure yourself?" He wraps one arm around me to support my weight, but I shrug him off.

"Don't touch me," I say. "I'd rather limp."

"As you wish."

The three of us enter the building through the parking garage. We walk down a ramp to the bank of elevators. Mr. Yun presses the UP button and the elevator doors open. The three of us shuffle inside. Alec swipes the fake ID and hits the button for B-2. The elevator begins to move.

"Oh, that's troubling," he says. "Whose badge did you clone?"

"He's not working with us," I say. "He doesn't even know I copied it."

"Who?" Alec repeats.

"Please don't hurt him." I refuse to give them a name. Jason Choi seemed like a nice guy. If there's any way to keep them from discovering his identity, I'm going to protect him.

The elevator doors open and Alec stops at the first door we come to, marked Lab 5. He swipes his badge through the card reader.

"What is this place?" I ask, even though I already know. I'm trying to keep Alec distracted while I figure out a way to escape.

"Just more laboratories." He pushes me inside the room. "Where we do some of our more classified research." Mr. Yun enters behind us and for a few moments the three of us stand silent in the open room.

I still have a knife hidden in my right boot. I might be able to reach it before either man notices, but even if I can take out one of them, I still have to defeat the other and escape with a sprained ankle. That probably means killing them both. Killing wasn't hard when it was self-defense, but what if Baz is right? *Killing someone is different in practice than it is in theory. There are factors you can't prepare for, feelings in the moment where you'll question everything you thought you knew about yourself.* What if I freeze up? What if I can't go through with it?

I can, a voice hisses in my brain. Lily, reminding me she has no problem killing anyone and everyone. Even me.

Almost as if he can read my mind, Alec gestures toward Mr. Yun. "Make sure she doesn't have any other weapons on her."

Keeping his gun trained on me, Mr. Yun pats me down, quick and businesslike, finding and confiscating my remaining knife. Now I'm completely unarmed and in the custody of the enemy. *The most dangerous weapon you have is your brain . . .* All right. Perhaps not *completely* unarmed. I try to decide what Gideon would do in this situation. He would probably go about it in a scientific manner. First, gather information.

"Go get him," Alec tells Mr. Yun.

The stocky security guard disappears out into the hallway.

I pace back and forth, studying the various equipment placed on the counter that runs along the back of the room. There are several computers, along with a high-powered microscope and some machines that I think process blood samples.

Alec hops up on one of the steel tables and sits, his legs dangling down. He watches me with curiosity.

My eyes flick to the door of the lab and back to Alec. If I had the element of surprise, I could probably get to the hallway, but then what? The ViSE tech is in the lab next door, but it might as well be in a foreign country.

"If you're thinking of making a break for it, you should know that the door to this particular lab is keycard-locked from both directions."

"Oh. So it's like a prison."

"We do work with animals in here. Can't have any test subjects escaping, now can we?"

"Is that why I'm down here?" I keep my voice level. "To be some sort of test subject?" Colonel Rojas's words echo in my brain. *Human subjects? Fatalities?*

"You have a vivid imagination." Alec cracks his knuckles. "We're waiting for my superior. He needs to speak with you."

"Kyung?"

"I don't recommend you call him that, but yes." Alec studies me for a moment. "I take it you don't remember me. Pity. I guess it's not true what they say."

I pause in front of a tray of wrapped surgical instruments. I want to ignore him or tell him I don't care who he is, but part of me is curious. "What do they say?" I ask cautiously.

Alec smirks. "That you never forget your first."

The blood drains from my face as I spin around. "Liar."

"I remember it quite clearly," he murmurs, as if he's reminiscing about a fond vacation memory. "Some girls begged for their mothers, some begged for God to intervene, but with you it was *'Eonni, eonni, eonni.'* As if your sister could somehow save you."

"I will kill you," I blurt out. "I will make it hurt." The words spew from my lips like razor blades, sharp, shredding. I can barely understand them because they're not my own. They're Lily's. She thrashes around inside of me like a black ghost.

I shouldn't let go but—

Yes, you should.

Yes, I should.

CHAPTER 44

LILY

The one called Alec steps back, puts a table between us.

I grab the first thing my fingers find—a rack of glassware. Shiny missiles. One, two, three, four, five. I fling beakers and flasks.

Alec dodges them and then backs away. Unhurt. Unharmed. Unacceptable.

My eyes fall on the shards of glass. I reach for another flask, bring it down hard against the counter. It shatters. Success.

"I'm going to kill you now," I say.

There is only the thick pulse in the one called Alec's neck. And the jagged edge of the broken flask in my hand.

I fly.

CHAPTER 45

When I open my eyes, all I can see is a blur of white and gray. I try to sit up, but I can't. I'm restrained, tied down to something hard and flat. Panic swoops in like a falcon. My heart beats its wings in my chest as I try to remember what happened. I blink hard. Gradually, my head clears and the white and gray solidifies into paneled ceiling tiles with silver sprinkler heads. I lift my neck and see that I'm still in the lab. I'm strapped to one of the long metal tables, Velcro around my hands, feet, legs, and chest preventing me from moving. A yawn escapes my lips.

"What did you do to me?" I ask, my voice slow and thick.

"I shot you with your tranquilizer gun," Alec says. "You were trying to stab me with a broken flask, remember?"

I don't remember, but I do remember Lily. I remember letting go.

The door to the lab swings open and I wrench my head to the side to see who is joining us. Bad idea. It's Kyung. His face is stoic but I can sense a bit of glee in his step. He's wearing a black suit with one of his trademark red ties.

"It's nice to see you again, Song Ha Neul," Kyung says. "Though I regret that it's under these circumstances."

"I don't use that name anymore," I say coldly.

"Yes, well. If only we could change ourselves the way we can change our names." Kyung steps forward. "Bold move coming to work here. Even I didn't expect you'd do anything that drastic."

My insides twist and turn at the nearness of him, this horrible man whom I came here to kill because it felt like the only way I would ever be free. Memories crash down on me. Trafficking. Abuse. Assault. My own blood seeping from self-inflicted wounds. "I guess you underestimated me," I choke out, still struggling to keep my emotions in check.

"Perhaps." Kyung pulls the neural editor from the pocket of his coat. "What did you do to this?"

"Doesn't it work? Maybe your thugs damaged it when they broke into my room and stole it." Knowing that Kyung is here because he needs something from me gives me the smallest shred of control. I intend to capitalize on it, somehow.

Kyung leans back against one of the silver tables. "Or perhaps you disabled it."

"I don't know much about the technology," I tell Kyung. "Including how to disable or fix it. Only Gideon would know. Maybe you shouldn't have let Sung Jin kill him."

"Ki Hyun." Kyung shakes his head in dismay. "My brother and I were going to do great things together. Until he developed some sort of hyperactive conscience."

"Your brother?" My voice is shrill, shocked. This can't be true. I would have known. Rose would have known and she would have told me.

Kyung chuckles. "I suppose it makes sense he kept it a secret. Little Brother always was ashamed of me. He and my parents both. I wasn't surprised that my father cut me out of his will. But I was surprised that Ki Hyun thought it was okay to steal even *more* from me."

"It was *his* research," I say. "*His* findings." My words sound hollow. I can't believe Gideon chose Rose and me over his own flesh and blood. To turn against your family, even when they're horrible and wrong the way that Kyung is, can't have been easy for Gideon. I suppose that answers one question I always had about why he didn't go to the police and try to break up the trafficking ring. At the time, I always figured he was worried about being implicated as one of Kyung's clients. But maybe he wasn't protecting himself. Maybe he was protecting his brother.

And then Kyung had him killed.

"Research he only discovered because I set him up with a position after he graduated," Kyung scoffs. "I was a fool to believe he wanted to reconcile after our father's passing. I never should have taken him on."

"He was a decent person," I say. "Not like you."

"He was a lying little weasel," Kyung snaps. "But also an amazing researcher. The kind of man who undoubtedly kept meticulous notes. So where are they?"

The snowflake necklace! I had it in my hand when we entered the lab, but then Lily took over and now I'm not sure where it is. "There might be notes in his study back in St. Louis," I say. "Or on his computer."

"Unfortunately his computer is still in the custody of the local police."

"Look," I say. "I don't know how to make the editor work and I don't know where Gideon's notes are, so if that's what this is about, you might as well let me go."

Kyung smoothes his red silk tie. Only it's not a tie anymore. It's an incision, a giant gaping hole in his flesh. Blood pours from the wound. *We will split him apart,* Lily hisses in my head. *We will show him how it feels to live as pieces.*

I blink hard. The blood disappears.

"Did you search her?" he asks Alec.

"Mr. Yun checked her for weapons."

"You wouldn't lie to me, right, Ha Neul?" Kyung brushes my hair back from my temples and his fingers catch on my wig. He gently lifts the wig from my head and smirks when he sees the recorder headset beneath it. A slight shock runs through me as he removes the headset, collapses it, and hands it to

Alec. "We must remind Mr. Yun to be a little more thorough next time."

Kyung turns back to me. I try to keep from flinching with revulsion as his fingers trace their way across my head and then skim across the fabric of my shirt. He stops at the rose pendant around my neck, leaning in for a closer look. "Please don't," I say, my voice wavering. "It's the last piece of my sister I have left."

"She has another one," Alec says. "In fact, I might not have found her after she went out the window if she hadn't stopped to retrieve it." Alec produces my snowflake pendant from a nearby counter where my purse is also sitting.

Kyung's eyes narrow. He crosses the room and fingers the pendant. He pulls it apart, exposing the drive. "So clever, Ki Hyun was."

"What?" I crane my neck to see what he's doing. "What is it?" I take in a deep breath and exhale slowly, trying to remain calm.

Kyung slots the drive into a nearby computer and frowns at the screen. "What's the password?"

"Password for what?" Maybe I can convince him I didn't even know about the drive.

His lips tighten into a hard line. "Password protection with automatic data destruction. That is unfortunate . . . for all of us."

"I don't know what you're talking about." I try to make my voice sound scared and pathetic.

"Yes, well," he says. "If that's the case, then you won't mind if Mr. Kwon runs a little . . . experiment."

Alec steps forward and begins to unbutton my shirt. Bile surges into my throat. This is the one kind of experiment I might not survive. *Now would be a good time for someone else to take over,* I think. But that's not true. I let go with Lily and only ended up in deeper trouble. As much as I want to blink and wake up on the other side of this hell, I need to stay focused. I need to figure out a way to get free.

"Please," I whisper. "If you have any decency at all, don't do this."

"Relax," Alec says. "We have more important things than pleasure to think about right now." He steps away for a moment and returns with a tangle of wires. He applies electrodes to my chest, above and below my ribs, and then inserts the wires into a computer. A monitor sitting on the table next to me comes to life. I watch the green repeating pattern of my heart rate, the jagged spikes coming closer together as my pulse accelerates. Alec clips a monitoring device to my index finger. A slower blue line that represents my breathing flows across the bottom of the screen.

"It's not going to kill her, is it?" Kyung asks, just loudly enough for me to hear.

Human subjects. Fatalities. Terror rushes through me. My head is suddenly full of voices. *Kill. Wait. Focus. Die.*

"I wouldn't worry." Alec laughs lightly. "That's the beauty of the technology. We can do whatever we need to, with no lasting effects. I just want her vital signs on record so that we can show our potential buyers we've tested the product on human subjects."

"Get it started, then," Kyung says. "I'll be back. I need to make some calls."

I squeeze my eyes tightly closed. I will not give these men the satisfaction of seeing me cry. Pressure builds up in my chest. The monitor beeps.

"Breathe," Alec says softly.

My eyes flick open. I let out my breath in a series of choked gasps. "What are you going to do to me?" I ask in a shaky voice.

"I'm not going to hurt you." He touches my face with one hand. "Not really, anyway. Just do as I say and you'll be fine."

The words trigger a memory. Los Angeles. A hotel room. Alec sitting next to me on a bed as I lay curled into the fetal position. *I'm not going to hurt you. Just do as I say and you'll be fine.*

A tear works its way out of my eyes, and then another. Alec brushes them away with one thumb. Somehow it's even worse that he's being gentle, that he's pretending to be kind. "Don't touch me," I say. "Don't you ever touch me again."

A smile plays at his lips. "Ah, you're remembering."

"You're sick," I say. "I was just a little girl."

He chuckles. "Not that little. I used to help Kyung out with the younger girls, get them . . . acclimated. Something about me seemed to keep them calm. My accent, perhaps."

"I wish she had killed you," I mutter.

"Who?" Alec asks. "Your sister? She wouldn't have killed me. She liked me. Not as much as Ki Hyun, clearly. But I suppose there's no accounting for taste."

My fear morphs into rage. "I am going to kill you twice, once for each of them," I rasp. I don't know if they're my words or Lily's. Right now, I don't know where she ends and I begin.

"Such dark language for such a pretty girl," he says. "Sit tight. I'll be back."

"You're leaving?" I say, and these are definitely my words. I hate the way they sound, like I don't want him to go, like I'm afraid to be alone with his little experiment.

"I'll return shortly," he says. "With a little surprise for you."

The door closes behind Alec with a hiss and a click and I'm left in the lab alone, my wrists and ankles strapped tightly to the metal table. I turn my head, first to the left. I see the doorway to the hall, a line of sinks, a counter with a microscope and other technical equipment. Most of the equipment looks too bulky to serve as a proper weapon, assuming I could somehow get free from these restraints.

I turn my head to the right to see if there's anything more helpful on that side of the room. Broken glass litters the floor.

It looks like someone pushed over a rack of beakers and flasks, but most of the pieces are too small to actually do anything with. Beyond that, just more steel tables like this one, and a cart of surgical supplies. I might be able to find some scalpel blades if I'm lucky. And then I see my throwing knife, tossed casually on top of the cart. Mr. Yun must have left it there. I have to get my hands on it . . . somehow.

CHAPTER 46

There are no clocks that I can see, no windows to the outside world, so I'm not sure how much time passes before Alec and Kyung return. I hear the door open with a soft whoosh and turn my head to see the two men approaching. Mr. Yun is right behind them. I try to steel myself for whatever might happen next.

Alec grabs my ViSE headset from the counter where my belongings still sit. Kyung watches while he slips a memory card into the slot on the back. Alec slides the headset over my ears and tightens the prongs. I shake my head back and forth, trying to make this difficult, but it's no use. If they think they can force me to vise against my will, they're wrong. I'll open my eyes. I'll embrace the overlay and vomit all over this lab before I let them force me to experience something I don't want to experience. But then Alec steps forward with a piece of black cloth. It turns out to be a hood that he slips down over my face.

"I wouldn't want all the light in here to be distracting." I feel Alec's hand on the back of my headset. And then:

I'm in a laboratory that looks a lot like this one. Steel tables, textured white ceiling, tang of chemicals in the air. I'm sitting in a chair, my hands zip-tied together in front of me. My heart races; my skin sweats. I struggle to exhale and nearly choke on something.

Whoever this is, Alec and Kyung have gagged him or her. No, him. The hands are definitely male.

Mr. Yun steps into the room, with Alec at his side. Mr. Yun marches up to the chair and backhands me across the face while Alec watches. A jolt of pain rushes through me. He hits me again, this time straight on, in the teeth.

"Sorry," Alec says. "I realize this punishment might be excessive for your infractions. But in our business, there's no such thing as a minor mistake."

"Stop," I say. "Who are you doing this to?"

"Just a poor unfortunate employee whose ID badge was apparently cloned due to his carelessness."

Jason. Regret courses through me. Of course they found out. By now they might even know that I sneaked into Lab 6 at lunchtime. "Stop beating him. Beat me instead, you cowards. I'm the one who cloned his badge."

Alec clicks his tongue. "See, there are two problems with that. First, you seem to have an extraordinary tolerance for pain. The rope burns on your hands, your injured ankle—those things barely seem to bother you. It's likely we would beat you into a coma and you still wouldn't give us the password. Second, we have it on good authority that you care deeply about other people, even strangers. So this is actually a very elegant solution to our problem. You tell us the password and we'll stop torturing an innocent man."

Alec is right that my hands and ankle aren't bothering me, but tuning out this ViSE is another matter. The pain explodes through me each time Mr. Yun's fist connects with the recorder's body. After about six more hits, I start singing in my head. This is one of the things I used to do back in L.A. when I couldn't convince the man I was with to turn on the television—anything to block out reality.

But the pain of being beaten is almost as hard to ignore as the pain of being sexually assaulted. A couple of the hits make me want to gasp or scream, but I try to swallow back my cries.

I don't want to give them the satisfaction. When Alec pauses the recording a few minutes later, I am sweating and struggling to catch my breath.

The dark hood is yanked up over my eyes. The sharp fluorescent lights make me blink. Two versions of Alec and Kyung gradually coalesce into one.

"Just give us the password, Ha Neul," Kyung says, his voice almost kind. "Your loyalty to Ki Hyun is admirable, but he's gone. No one else needs to die, do they?"

"I swear I don't know," I say. "I would tell you if I did."

"All right. We'll be back." Kyung shakes his head sadly. "Until then, think hard. Maybe you'll remember." The men disappear into the hallway again.

Alone in the room and still strapped to the table, I fight the urge to completely lose control. I struggle against the restraints, but it's pointless. I can't get out of them by using brute force, and the more I attempt to, the more exhausted I'll become.

Tears leak from my eyes. I hate the thought of Jason being tortured just so I can experience it vicariously, but if I want to help him, I have to help myself first.

But before that, I have to survive another round of vising. Kyung and Alec are back with a new memory card.

"Time for round two," Alec says brightly. He slips a new ViSE into my headset.

Alec approaches me. He sticks an electrode to both of my temples. There's some kind of collar around my neck so I can't look down.

A shock pulses through me. It hurts, but not too badly. Gradually, the shocks increase in intensity and duration. My body spasms violently.

"You're going to kill him," I say.

"Just tell us the password, and we'll stop," Kyung says.

I don't believe him. He can't let me go after this. I know too much.

"You'll never stop," I say.

"Yes, I will. You have my word," Kyung says. "I can give

you a swift and merciful death. Or I can make this worse for everyone. The beauty of the ViSE tech is that we can beat you, shock you, burn you, and cut you as much as we want without any worry that you'll die." He pauses. "Of course, without the editor to amplify the sensations as needed, there is the problem that our poor test subject might eventually expire."

I hate the thought that flickers through my mind—that if Jason dies, they won't have anything else they can do to me.

"Rest assured we'll move to a second subject if needed," Kyung says.

I pray that he's bluffing, that he doesn't have Yoo Mi or one of the other girls tied up in some lab.

"You're a monster," I hiss. "I thought I was a monster because I came here hoping to kill you. But you're hurting innocent people. And for what? Money?"

Kyung chuckles. "As if money isn't the number one motivating factor for ninety-five percent of the world. I'm just a businessman. Anything Ki Hyun created while working at UsuMed belongs to UsuMed. It's a very common clause in scientific contracts. The least he could do after stealing my inheritance was to honor his business agreements, don't you think? Give me the password so that I can access the research and no one else gets hurt. It's as simple as that."

"I told you I don't know," I say. "If I knew, don't you think I would stop this?"

Kyung and Alec exchange a look. "Expedite things," Kyung says. "I'll be back." He turns on his heel and strides out of the lab.

Alec bends down so we're eye to eye. "Give me the password, Ha Neul, and no one else dies . . . not even you."

His closeness makes me cringe, as does the kindness in his voice. How dare he speak to me with compassion after the things he's done. "I'd rather die," I say. "And we both know he'll kill me no matter what. Otherwise I walk away from this and go straight to the police."

"You might," Alec admits. "But it would be our word against yours. And we have several employees who would testify that you ran away from building security, going as far as to jump out of a window via the escape rope rather than have a quiet chat about the discrepancies on your hiring forms. And what name would you use to report us, hmm? The name with the falsified Korean documents? The name where you have a long history of mental illness? Your real name, the one where you have no proof that's who you actually are?"

He has a point. Even if I could manage to escape and get to the police, I'd probably end up in jail or a psych ward. I twist my left foot in a half circle. Is that restraint a bit looser than the rest? Maybe if I just had a little more time . . .

"Why would you ask him to let me live?" I ask.

"I find you intriguing. You fended off two of our best men in Los Angeles, you came here and managed to infiltrate the company without anyone knowing, you leapt out of a window and might have escaped if you hadn't twisted your ankle." He pauses. "And then there's your aforementioned loyalty and tolerance for pain. Quite simply put, you're an incredible force and I'd rather see you working for us than in an unmarked grave somewhere."

Tears flood my eyes and I don't even know why. And then I do. I don't want compliments from this man. "You. Ruined. Me," I choke out.

Alec strokes the side of my face with the back of his hand. "No. That's wrong. You're not ruined. You've become something remarkable. Most people who rise as high as we have only do so after experiencing great lows." He traces his index finger around my lips. "It's what motivates us, you see?"

"I am nothing like you," I rasp. "I will never work for you."

"I'm saddened to hear that," Alec says. "I suspect our friend in the next room will likewise be sad."

"Let him go," I say. "Kill me instead. If that's how this

ends, then let's get it over with. Because I will never give you the password."

"We'll see about that," Alec says. There's a mischievous glint in his eyes and it fills me with even more dread.

The instant he leaves the room I push away the lingering panic. I turn my left foot back and forth repeatedly. The Velcro strap loosens just slightly. Not enough to get a foot out, but I keep working on it. My fingertips crawl over the surface of the table, looking for any rough area that I could use to loosen the straps. I flex different muscles, try to turn my body in different ways, inching my way up to the top of the table and then low toward the bottom.

Being tied down is surprisingly exhausting, and for a few seconds I close my eyes and welcome the reprieve from the penetrating fluorescent lights above me. I take a few deep breaths and then do a full inventory of everything on my person, just in case there's something that might be of use. Boots. Tights. Skirt. Shirt. My wig is gone but there might still be a bobby pin lost in my hair. Unfortunately, none of this will help me.

I go back to experimenting with movement. I try small twists and large thrusting motions. The table is too heavy for me to tip over, no matter what. My throwing knife still sits on the cart of supplies, mocking me, taunting me. Again I wonder what time it is, whether Jesse is waiting for me by the subway station or if he's here somewhere, looking for me.

It doesn't matter. Jesse won't stand a chance on his own, not if Kyung and his men are still here.

Alec and Kyung duck back through the doorway again. "I've got a real treat for you this time," Alec says.

A new recording is snapped into my ViSE headset. The hood goes back on.

I'm lying on a metal table. A tangle of wires runs across my bare skin and is connected to a monitor. Alec is holding a throwing knife in his hand. "Recognize this?" he asks.

I shake my head.

This recorder feels different. I can't explain how, exactly. Maybe it's that he's not in so much pain. Yet. I try not to think about what it means if this is someone new, whether they're giving Jason Choi a break or they killed him.

Alec draws near to me. He drags the knife across the skin of my neck. I feel the sharp kiss of the blade. The knife moves lower, beneath the soft cartilage of my throat. Metal penetrates my skin. The pain is sharp, followed by the wetness of blood.

With his free hand, Alec touches part of my rib cage. "If I stab here," he says, "you'll get a punctured lung. Your chest cavity will fill up with air or blood, crushing your lung." He drags his fingers upward. "If I stab here, I'll rupture your spleen. Did you know the spleen is always processing blood? If I rupture it, you'll bleed out in minutes without help. Or I could stab here and with just the right angle and a little luck, I'll hit your heart."

All of my muscles go tense. I try to lean back away from the blade.

Alec laughs. "Don't be afraid. We won't start with any of those." *He makes a second cut, this one into my chest. The pain races through me. My heart rate spikes on the monitor, the number flashing red.*

"You are both twisted and evil," I gasp through my pain.

"Perhaps." Alec removes the hood and pauses the recording. "But I'm not the one prolonging this. Just think, by telling us the password, you can prevent this from happening."

"You'll save lives," Kyung adds, his voice almost kindly. "And help those who are less fortunate."

"How do you figure?" Tears pool in my eyes, but I fight them back. I can't lose it now. I need to focus. Plus, I will die before I let either of these men see me cry.

"If we can fix the editor, we won't have to kill anyone to create the kind of recordings that our clients are interested in buying. We can pay people to be our subjects and just amplify their pain. You'd be surprised how many people would be willing to undergo a few shocks or punches in the name of a pay-check."

"That's sick," I say.

"Is it?" he asks. "I wonder what you'd think of the list of interested clients we've already amassed. Not just terrorist organizations either. A proven interrogation technique that leaves no marks? It's every government's dream."

And now I finally understand what Kyung is doing with the tech. He's trying to sell it to terrorists and government agencies to use for torture purposes. Shock treatments and water-boarding result in accidental casualties. A dead prisoner is a waste. With the ViSE tech, an interrogator would be able to inflict the pain and sensations of those techniques along with even worse punishments right up to death, with no permanent physical harm to the captive.

"Is it proven?" I ask. "It hasn't worked on me."

"Well, as discussed, you are a particularly difficult case. But everyone has a breaking point. Even you." Kyung dials some-one on his cell phone."Bring the boy in here; let's make things interesting."

The door to the lab opens as Mr. Yun wheels in a second steel table. My heart wrenches open at the thought of having to watch someone else being tortured. And then I see who it is.

My brother.

CHAPTER 47

"Jun," I say softly. I don't want to believe it, but he matches the pictures that Yoo Mi and Baz showed me. He has my cheekbones. He has my chin.

"Yes. Ha Neul, this is your brother, Song Jun," Kyung says. "I didn't realize the two of you had already met."

"I'm so sorry," I tell Jun. "I'm going to get you out of this somehow."

Jun doesn't respond. His glazed-over eyes look right through me. His hands are bound in front of his body with a zip tie, but otherwise he's unrestrained. Still, he doesn't look like he's in any condition to fight. His face is soaked with silent tears. If it weren't for the fact that I can see his chest moving and his limbs twitching, I'd think he was dead.

"You'll have to excuse him," Alec says. "I believe he might be in . . . well, shock."

Kyung lifts my throwing knife from the supply cart. "I will kill him with your own weapon if you don't tell me that password right now."

"I'll tell you," I say, my eyes focused on the slow rise and fall of Jun's chest. "But you have to let him go first."

"You're not in any position to bargain." Kyung approaches my brother, brandishing the knife in his outstretched hand.

"Fine, then. Just promise me you won't kill him."

"I promise," Kyung says.

I turn to Alec. "And you?"

He nods. "We won't."

"All right. The password is *sky* with a lowercase *s* and *k* and an uppercase *Y*, and then, um . . ." I rack my brain to remember the formula for the sequence of numbers.

Kyung stares at me. "And?"

"Just a second," I say. "I'm thinking."

"I'm tired of waiting," Kyung says.

"There's a formula where—"

"Here. Let me help you remember." Without warning, Kyung plunges the knife into my brother's stomach.

Jun gasps. His arms and legs spasm.

"No!" I scream. "Why would you do that? I said I would tell you."

Kyung pulls the knife out and holds the red blade against my brother's throat. Jun squeezes his eyes closed, but it doesn't keep the tears from streaming down his face. "You made me wait. And when I have to wait, my clients have to wait. They don't like waiting and I don't like having to ask for something more than once. Tell me *now* or I'll finish him."

I spit out the entire series of letters and numbers that will unlock the drive, praying that I didn't make a calculation error.

Kyung drops the knife next to Jun and returns to the computer. He inputs the password and apparently likes what he sees on the screen. Then he ejects the drive from the computer and then glances at Alec and Mr. Yun. "Kill them both," he says.

"You promised!" I shriek. I turn toward Alec and try to appeal to whatever misguided affection he seems to have for me. "Please. You promised."

Alec pulls Kyung to the side and says something in tones too low for me to hear.

Kyung's response is clear, however. "Trust me. You don't want a pet that might kill you in your sleep."

"Still," Alec says. "She could be useful . . ."

Kyung sighs. "Fine. Then just kill the boy. It's possible I might still need her, depending on what is actually on this drive."

"Don't you dare touch him," I snap. "If you do, I swear I will never help you with anything. You can torture me until I completely lose my mind."

Alec exchanges a glance with Kyung, who shrugs.

"I'm afraid his time is limited already," Alec says. "But if you want him to slowly bleed to death instead of a quick and painless end, we can acquiesce to that."

The three men turn and stride from the room.

"Jun," I say, the instant the laboratory door falls closed.

He doesn't answer.

"Jun," I repeat. "You're not strapped down. You've got to get up. I need you to loosen my restraints so I can help you."

He rolls over onto his side so he can see into my eyes. For the briefest moment I think of Jesse and me on separate hotel beds, reaching out so our hands could meet in the middle. All my brother needs is a connection. Something real, something warm. That will wake him up, strengthen him.

"Who are you?" he asks.

"I'm your sister, Ha Neul."

His face contorts in a mix of pain and confusion. For a moment I expect him to say he doesn't believe me, but then he says, "Imo told me about my sisters."

I nod. Now is not the time to tell him one of those sisters is dead. "I need you to loosen one of these straps."

He starts to sit up but then gasps. His body falls back to the metal table. "I'm sorry. I think I'm dying."

"You're not dying. That's just pain. So much at once can be . . . overwhelming. But you've got to fight it, all right?" I say.

"Why is it so cold in here?"

I watch the blood ooze from his wound—it's a steady bleed, which is bad, but also good because it means his lungs and arteries are probably intact. "That's blood loss, but it's not that bad. Just reach out for me. Can you reach my left wrist?"

Jun flails desperately with his bound hands but doesn't quite make contact with me.

"Scoot a little closer to the edge of your table and try again," I urge. "All you have to do is loosen the Velcro and then I'll take over. You can do it."

Jun reaches out again. His fingers brush against mine, but it still takes him several seconds to find the end of the Velcro strap. "Nuna," he says. "I don't think I can."

"Yes, you can. Just pull back with your fingertips."

Jun manages to pull the Velcro half-apart and I tug sharply with my wrist until it lets go. "Good. Good job," I say. "My turn now."

I have the rest of the straps undone in less than a minute. I sit up quickly and the change in position is almost too much for me. Blackness plays at the corner of my vision, but for once it's because of my blood pressure, not because Rose or Lily is trying to control my body. For once it is all me.

I slide from the steel table, but when my feet hit the floor, my ankle gives out and I collapse to the white tiles in a heap. I swear under my breath.

"Nuna?" Jun says weakly.

"It's all right." I use the edge of the table to pull myself back to my feet. "I twisted my ankle earlier." The rest of my body seems to be working all right, but the ViSE recordings have left my heart rate elevated and my muscles weak and twitchy.

I lean over my brother and twist his wrists sharply to break the zip tie. I press one of his hands over the wound in his stomach. "Hold pressure on it," I tell him.

Jun nods. His face is gray. He looks half-dead. I'm terrified that Kyung's wounding did massive internal damage, that my brother is bleeding out from the inside and I can't save him.

"Do you have a phone?" I ask.

"They took it."

"Mine too," I say. "God, I wish you weren't here. Did they kidnap you or something?"

He shakes his head weakly. "I go to academy here on Friday nights. Mr. Kwon called and said I was needed for a special focus group, something about a marketing campaign to attract more science scholars."

"Were you in a different lab on this floor?"

"Yes. Right across the hallway." Jun shudders. More slick tears make their way down his cheeks. "There was a man in there with me, a security guard. They killed him."

My heart drops. Jason. He didn't deserve to be involved in this. His death is on me, but I can't think about that right now. "Look," I say. "We just need to get you to the street. Someone will call an ambulance for you."

And then I remember we can't even get out of this lab without a badge.

I scan the room, looking for an alternate way out—a heat vent, an air duct. Something. Anything. And then my eyes fall on the fire alarm.

If the fire alarm is activated, all of the badge-coded doors will unlock and all staff must immediately evacuate the building via the stairwells . . .

Perfect. "Saved by the world's most boring training videos," I mutter.

"What?" Jun asks.

I pull him to a seated position. I go pale when I see what he looks like. The splotch of red on his shirt is growing. He's got both hands pressed to the spot now but he looks like he's in danger of passing out. "Keep pressure on that wound, and use your other hand to grab onto me. I need to see if you can stand."

It takes him a few seconds, but Jun gets awkwardly to his feet. He clutches my arm with one bloody hand, his legs looking a bit wobbly.

"Can you walk?" I step back.

Jun steps forward to meet me, his fingertips digging into my skin.

"Good." I tilt my head toward the wall of the lab. "I'm going to pull the fire alarm. Once I do, all the doors will unlock. I'm not sure if the elevators will still work. Do you think you can make it up two flights of stairs to the street level?"

Jun looks at me like I just asked him if he feels up for running a marathon. "I guess?"

"Don't guess. Just keep going, all right? Don't stop. Don't rest. Don't sit down. I'm not certain how long the doors will stay unlocked, but there's no badge reader on the first floor since it's just the lobby and restaurants. So don't panic if the noise turns off."

"Okay." Jun starts limping toward the door. "You're coming with me, right?"

"I've got to try to find Kyung and try to recover something he stole from me," I say. "But I'll find you in the hospital—I promise."

Jun nods and then exhales a deep breath in several shuddery little gasps. "Imo showed me a picture of two girls, both dressed in *hanbok*. My sisters. She said one day she'd help me find you."

Hanbok are traditional Korean dresses. Rose and I only put them on for special occasions. "I would love to see that picture someday." I wipe away a tear. My fingers hover over the fire alarm. "Get ready."

Jun rests his free hand on the door to the lab. "I'm scared."

"Me too," I say. "Just keep going up. Do not stop until you hit the lobby. Ask the first person you see to call for an ambulance."

"What do I tell the medics? What if the police come?"

"It might just be easiest to tell them you don't remember what happened for now," I say. "Making accusations against UsuMed could be dangerous. But if you want to tell the truth, you can. I have resources. I'll figure out a way to protect you—I promise."

Jun nods. "I'm ready."

I pull the fire alarm.

CHAPTER 48

A siren starts to wail. Jun vanishes into the hallway. I grab my knife, still wet with my brother's blood, before following him out. I help Jun to the doorway leading to the stairs and wait until he's disappeared from view before I let the door fall shut. I have no idea where Kyung might have gone, if he's tucked away in one of the other labs or if he took the flash drive with the research up to an office, or back to the SkyTower hotel.

Just as my ears become adjusted to the shrill noise, the fire alarm stops ringing. That didn't take long.

I hear a shout from behind me. "Ha Neul!" It's Alec. "What have you done?"

I spin around. Our eyes meet. My knife is still clutched in my hand. *Kill.* I think of Sung Jin's glassy eyes, of the blond man lying dead on the floor of the K-Town guesthouse. There is something intoxicating about ending a life, about wiping bad people off the face of the earth. But it's also a dark and deadly pull. After all, who am I to decide who lives or dies?

He raped us. He tortured our brother.

True. And what's worse, he didn't even seem to feel bad about it.

Alec is halfway down the hallway now, hurrying toward me with almost a concerned look on his face. "You're going to get us both killed."

I rear back, let the knife fly. It spins end over end. "Just you," I say, as the blade embeds itself in his throat.

He reaches out with one arm as he falls, but he doesn't scream. He can't. All he can do is make a gurgling sound. I go to him, bend down, remove the knife from his throat. He's still alive.

"That was for my brother and sister."

Alec lifts one hand to his neck, attempts to staunch the blood.

"This one is for me." I rake the tip of the blade hard across the side of his neck, severing the carotid artery. He dies in seconds.

I rise to my feet, my bloody knife clutched in my left hand. Now to find Kyung.

But just as I turn toward the stairs, the elevator chimes. Someone is coming. I don't want to hurt anyone else, but if a staff member sees me covered in blood or sees Alec's body, they're going to call the police. I hurry down the hallway and pin myself back against the wall just to the side of the elevator, ready to strike. If it's an innocent person, I'm going to have to knock them out or lock them up somewhere.

But when the silver doors open, Jesse steps out from between them. My muscles go slack with relief and I nearly end up on the floor in a heap.

"Jesse." I slip my knife back into my boot and reach out for his arm, both for support and because I'm afraid he might not be real. He feels solid and warm beneath my touch.

"Winter, thank God you're okay." Jesse throws his arms around me right there in the hallway. "I was so afraid."

"Kyung stabbed Jun," I say. Tears trickle down my face. "They were torturing him. I pulled the fire alarm so we could get out of the lab. I helped him to the stairwell. He only had to go up two floors, but I'm not sure if he made it to safety."

"I'm sure he did," Jesse says soothingly.

"Are you alone?" I ask.

"Yeah," Jesse says. "I told Baz I was meeting you for dinner like you said to, but when you didn't show up and I couldn't reach you, I came to find you. Come on. We have to get out of here. The cops are probably on their way."

"But they turned off the fire alarm."

"It doesn't matter. Someone will still check it out."

"But Kyung. The tech," I choke out. "I can't let him win."

"You can go to his hotel room or something," Jesse says. "If we stay here now, all that's going to happen is we'll get arrested for breaking and entering." His eyes focus on Alec's body, lying at the far end of the hallway. "Or worse."

I glance down at the gun clutched in his hand. He's right. It's hard to leave, though. I feel like I failed at everything—at retrieving the tech, at protecting my brother, at killing the man who ruined my life.

This whole trip has been a mistake.

I try to tell myself what really matters is that my brother is on his way to safety. "Let's take the stairs just in case Jun needs help."

We head down the hallway, passing Alec's body on the way to the stairwell. "Is he definitely dead?" Jesse asks.

"Yes," I say. "It's a long story. One you might not want to hear."

"I want to hear anything you want to tell me," Jesse says soothingly. "Once we get out of here safely." Dim fluorescent lighting illuminates the stairwell. There are drops of blood on the steps and a smeared red handprint on the door leading into the lobby of the building. I breathe a sigh of relief that Jun made it this far.

"You're limping," Jesse says.

"I sprained my ankle. Another long story."

All the main lights are off when we step into the lobby, which means it's after ten P.M. It was only about six p.m. when I went out the window and Alec cornered me in the parking garage. The last few hours are full of rips and holes. But the one thing I'd like to forget keeps replaying in my mind—the sight of Kyung stabbing Jun with my knife.

I turn toward the revolving doors and Jesse grabs my hand.

"Do you have anything under that shirt? You look like a horror movie victim."

I realize the front of me is covered with blood. Jun's blood. Alec's blood. I shake my head.

"Here." Jesse shrugs out of his coat. "Put this on. Keep your hands in your pockets."

I slide his coat over my bloody shirt.

And then the center elevator dings.

Jesse and I turn in unison. The doors open.

Kyung steps out.

Inside of me, dark wings stretch and flutter. Almost without thinking, I grab the gun from Jesse's hand and take aim. "Give me the neural editor and flash drive."

Kyung freezes midstep but recovers quickly. "Put the gun down, Ha Neul," he says smoothly. "You're not going to shoot me."

"Why wouldn't I?" The gun wavers in my trembling hands. "You have taken everything that I love."

"Not everything," he says.

I assume he's talking about Jesse. "You're responsible for the death of my sister and the closest thing I ever had to a father," I say. "You sold me like I was a product."

"Yes, yes, and look at you now. Resilient. Ferocious. We're not so different, you and me. So put the gun away and we can both walk out of here."

"I don't think so. You're a thief and a killer. Do you know how many lives you've destroyed? Do you even care?" I clench my jaw. "Give me back what you stole and maybe I'll make it quick." My finger dances on the trigger.

Kyung sighs deeply. He reaches behind him to press the button for the elevator, and the doors slide open. Mr. Yun steps out. He's half-shrouded in shadow. But I can see he's got his own gun out. It's not pointed at me, though. It's pointed at a hunched-over figure he's holding by the scruff of his shirt.

Jun.

CHAPTER 49

"If I die, he dies," Kyung says. "Do you really want to be responsible for that?"

I swear under my breath. So much for getting away on his own. I can't even tell if Jun is still alive right now. I feel Lily beneath my skin. She's feeding on the darkness. *Do it. Do it,* she whispers.

"Winter, give me the gun. Your brother's life means more to you than vengeance." Jesse's voice is a lighthouse in the blackness, but I wave it away.

"He's already dead," I say. "Look at him."

Kyung glances over at Jun. "It appears you might be right."

Mr. Yun releases his hold on Jun and he crumples to the floor.

My brother.

He crumples.

Like clothes without a body.

Like he's not there anymore.

Like he was never there to start with.

Like I imagined him too.

No. Just because I am sick doesn't mean that nothing is real. Jun is real and Jesse is real and Kyung is real and I am real. I blink hard and then I can see the body on the ground. There's no movement.

Mr. Yun turns his weapon toward me. It's a standoff. If I shoot Kyung, Mr. Yun shoots me.

I remember a time when all I wanted was a gun and to learn how to use it. I thought a gun would make me feel safe. I thought a gun would make me feel powerful. But right now I just feel . . . heavy. Like I live in this world of death and destruction and I'll never escape alive.

The quiet of this moment is interrupted by the shrill cry of sirens approaching.

"We need to go," Jesse says.

"You go. I need to stay here, with my brother."

"I'm not leaving you."

"Then you're going to get arrested."

"Fine, but for what? You think you need this, but you're wrong," Jesse says. "Kyung? The tech? They aren't worth going to prison or dying for."

Lily rises up again, whispering all sorts of things, about how good it'll feel to pull the trigger, how it doesn't matter if I die, because Jun is dead and Rose is dead and Gideon is dead and at least now we can all be together. Her logic makes a strange sort of sense.

"Lily's right," I say hoarsely. "This is the only way."

I close my eyes and surrender to the darkness.

CHAPTER 50

LILY

The hated man waits. Watches me with eyes that are bright and dark, like a serpent's.

I glance down at the boy on the floor. Winter doesn't want him to be dead, but there's so much red, and sometimes nice people die.

Sometimes nice people are made into prostitutes against their will.

I was nice once, I think.

Sometimes nice people quit being nice.

"Winter." The voice is kind, calming, like a ripple in a lake. Soft, but growing. "Winter, you don't want to do this. You want to live. Otherwise all of their deaths have been for nothing."

"I'm Lily," I say softly. "Winter didn't want to do this, so she went away."

The kind voice doesn't miss a beat. "Lily. Winter doesn't want to die for this."

"What do you know?" I snap. "He killed her whole family. Winter is already dead inside. She won't survive this."

"My whole family died too. My military family. I survived. She's stronger than me. She can make it."

The hated man inches toward the back door, like he might turn and run. I start to pull the trigger.

"If you do this, if you die here, then Rose and Gideon died for nothing."

"Gideon." A spark of lightness flares up inside me.

"Yes," the kind voice says. "Gideon died so that Winter could have a life. She *can* have a life, if you let her."

"She needs vengeance for the family she's lost," I whisper.

"There are better ways. She's not a killer. Do you hear me, Winter? You are not a killer."

CHAPTER 51

I blink. My gun is still pointed at Kyung. Mr. Yun's gun is pointed at me. Jesse is talking.

"He's not worth all the good you could do if you walk away from this," Jesse says. "You don't have to shoot him, because he is already dead inside."

The words are tiny fireflies that light up the dark. Jesse is saying the same things to me that Gideon said to me in his ViSE. I can help people. I can be happy. I just have to escape this nightmare. I didn't believe those things back in St. Louis. I thought becoming whole again meant killing the man who broke me.

But maybe I don't need that. Maybe I can put myself back together. With help.

With hope.

I lower my gun. "Fine. Go."

Jesse swallows back a sob. He whispers something under his breath that I don't quite catch. It sounds like a prayer.

Mr. Yun starts to turn toward the back exit. Jun still lies in a heap on the floor.

"You have made a wise decision, Ha Neul," Kyung says. "Ki Hyun would be—"

"Please don't speak his name to me," I bark. "Just go before I change my mind."

"Very well." Kyung heads for the door.

From somewhere above my head, someone mutters, "Enough of this bullshit."

I hear the pop of a gun with a silencer and Kyung grunts and stumbles forward, clutching his chest. A second shot rings out and Kyung slumps to his knees. Mr. Yun looks around in confusion.

I look up. Baz is leaning over the railing of the second floor. "Sebastian," I say with a gasp. "I thought—"

Mr. Yun sees him and squeezes off a couple of shots. Baz grunts in pain and drops out of view for a second. Then he pops back up and takes aim again. Mr. Yun falls just inside the back door.

"Stop thinking and get out of here," Baz shouts. "I'll see you at the rendezvous point."

Baz drops out of sight again and I hurry toward my brother. A police car pulls up outside the front of the building. Red and blue lights ricochet off the lobby walls.

"Winter!" Jesse looks back and forth from me to the doors.

"I can't just leave him." I'm bending down at Jun's side now, my fingers probing his throat, searching desperately for a pulse.

"We have to go." Jesse rushes over to me. "The cops will take care of him."

"What about Baz?" I ask.

"Baz can take care of himself." Jesse lifts me forcibly from the ground.

Two more cop cars pull up in front of the building. Doors slam. There are shouts. Jesse and I run toward the back exit. I pause just long enough to roll Kyung's body onto his back and go through his pockets. I find the neural editor and the flash drive.

He groans softly and I realize he's not dead yet.

I stare directly into his eyes. "I was young when you broke me," I say. "In my head, I made you into a monster—a horrible, powerful monster. But now I see that I was wrong. You're human, breakable, just like me. Except really, you're nothing like me. You killed your brother and I risked everything to try to save mine. I would have died for him."

Kyung's response is just a hiss of air. The second shot hit him in the throat, and blood spurts from the hole in his neck with every heartbeat. His dark eyes are sharp with hate.

"I'm working on putting myself back together," I tell him. "But you're not going to get that chance."

His jaw goes slack. Saliva trickles from the corner of his mouth as his life bleeds out of him. I might not have killed him, but he's going to die now, and that's good enough for me.

I tuck the flash drive and editor into my pockets and then lean low, low enough to smell the cigarette smoke clinging to his clothing. "I hope you remember me," I whisper. "Wherever you're going, I hope you remember me and my sister both."

"Winter!" Jesse grabs my hand as I hop back to my feet. We slip out the back door of the building just as the cops are storming the front.

"Hands up!" a voice shouts. "Drop your weapon."

Jesse and I turn in unison. A young Korean cop is approaching from around the corner of the building, a black baton raised.

Silver flashes in Jesse's hand. Before I can even scream, he's fired off two quick shots. The cop falls, as does a second officer just coming around the corner of the building.

"What did you—" I start. My words fall away as I see Jesse tuck the gun back into his waistband. A silver tranquilizer gun.

"They'll be fine," he says. "But you should probably give me that." He gently removes the loaded gun from my hand. "And this." Jesse pulls the headset from my head, collapses it, and slips it into his pocket. "Now let's go."

The two of us dart across a manicured back lawn, keeping tight to the shadow of the building next door. We make it to the street and duck low behind a parked car. Down the block is the minimetropolis of Gangnam Station, the crowd of people listening to the Valentine's Day K-pop sing-off. Jesse looks in that direction, but I shake my head. "There are cameras."

"There are cameras on the street corners," he points out.

"True, but only the main streets. They'll be expecting us to get as far away from here as possible."

"Sounds like a good plan to me."

"I have a better one." I point up into the hills, to where the big streets fade into cobblestones and narrow alleyways. "Up there."

"Are you sure?"

The adrenaline pumping through me has dulled the pain in my ankle and cleared the haze of sedation from my brain. "I'm sure."

Jesse and I turn away from the main street, pass by a small parking lot, and then duck into another alley that's strewn with trash. Slowly, we work our way up into the backstreets. I limp as fast as I can, putting as much weight as possible on my good ankle.

"Do you need to rest?" Jesse asks.

I shake my head. "I can't stop. If I do, I'll think about things, and then I'll lose it." I try not to think of Jun lying on the floor of the lobby. We walk three more blocks and end up in an area that is mostly private residences with an occasional family-owned shop. Everything is closed at this hour. I pause in front of a glass window with a bunch of saws and drills displayed. Behind it are other power tools. The sign on the door says the shop is only open three days a week and tomorrow isn't one of them. "Here," I say. Beside the shop is an outdoor work area with a Dumpster. I crawl behind it and pat the ground next to me.

"You want to spend the night here?" Jesse asks dubiously.

"It's perfect. No one will look for us. No one will be here early in the morning. We hide, we rest, and then, tomorrow, we run."

"Assuming we don't freeze to death tonight," Jesse mumbles.

That's right. I'm wearing his coat. I unzip it and pull it off, trying not to notice how my shirt is stiff with drying blood. Jesse and I sit hip to hip against the Dumpster and I wrap the coat around both of us. He slides an arm around me and I lean into his chest.

"You saved me back there, you know?" I tell him. "More than once."

"Yeah? About time I did something useful on this trip, huh?"

I smile in spite of everything that's happened. "I guess it makes up for your complete inability to cook rice." I twine my fingers through his. "Seriously, Jesse. I don't know what I would do without you."

"You'd be fine. You're Winter. You always find a way," he says softly. Then, when I don't respond to that, he adds, "We're never going to be able to fall asleep like this."

"I don't mind staying up all night with you," I murmur. Even though the air is frigid, I feel surprisingly warm nestled next to Jesse.

"Me neither." He squeezes my hand.

But the night has other plans for us, or for me at least. My eyelids grow heavier and heavier until eventually the starry sky fades away completely.

My sleep is fitful, my dreams bloody and frantic, but when I wake up, the sun is high in the sky. I'm lying on the pavement now, with Jesse's coat wrapped completely around me like a sleeping bag. He's sitting next to me, staring out into space.

"Hey," he says, as I sit up. "Did you manage to get any sleep?"

"A little. Are you freezing to death?" I start to hand Jesse his coat.

He shakes his head. "I'll be okay. You should keep it until we can find you something else to wear."

Right. I forgot about what I look like. The concrete is damp with frost and I use some of it to wipe the dried blood from my hands. There's not much that can be done about my shirt, though. I zip Jesse's coat closed around me and we head to the bus station, where we get tickets to one of the southern port cities that runs a regular ferry to Jeju Island. While we wait for the bus, I clean myself up as much as possible in the bathroom.

When we're safely aboard the bus, Jesse pulls up the latest news on his phone. Officially, the media are reporting what happened at UsuMed as a break-in and robbery that left dead two executives and two security personnel unlucky enough to be working late. According to the article, the men were killed by an American corporate spy, former military, identity unclear at this point, but Korean officials are working with American officials to learn more. According to the article, this man also died in the attack. There's no mention of my brother.

I know this doesn't mean Baz is really dead. Still, reading that is like unlocking a door inside of me. A door holding a lot of blackness that I'm trying to keep contained, at least for now. Maybe when I get home, wherever that turns out to be, I can find one of those inpatient treatment centers, a safe place to finally let the blackness out. Do like Dr. Abrams said— embrace the dark parts of me instead of trying to suppress them.

"Thank you," I blurt out suddenly.

"For what?" Jesse asks.

"For loving me, even though I'm so screwed up."

"We're all screwed up, Winter. At least you're willing to confront your issues. That gives you a better chance than most people."

"I guess you're right." I don't know what happened to my phone, so all I can do is peer over Jesse's shoulder as he repeatedly checks for any kind of message from Baz.

The bus drops us off in a town called Wando. We eat lunch

at a little café and then board the ferry at two thirty. It takes about two hours to get to Jeju Island. Normally I would love this experience—the waves crashing against the boat, the sea air sharp against my skin. But today all I can think of is my brother and Baz. Are they all right? Are they even alive?

Jesse searches for new information, but it's just a rehashing of the earlier articles. Then he searches specifically for information about Baz or Jun and comes up empty. "This is a good sign," he tells me. "They might have caught Baz on security cameras, but apparently they haven't been able to ID him."

"And Jun?"

"Perhaps they haven't been able to ID him yet either. Or it could just be that he's a minor, so they can't report on him in the newspapers without consent."

"He looked dead, Jesse. I couldn't feel his pulse."

Jesse squeezes my hand. "Whatever the truth is, you'll get through it. We'll get through it, together."

CHAPTER 52

We arrive at Jeju-do and check in at the Sunrise Hotel. Jesse asks if there have been any messages for us, but the desk clerk says no. I spend about two hours in the shower, washing every bit of Alec's and Jun's blood off of me, soaping and rinsing myself repeatedly.

"Are you hungry?" Jesse asks when I finally emerge from the bathroom, my skin bright pink.

I shake my head. "I just want to know what happened to the others, and if I can't know that, then I just want to sleep." I crawl into bed.

"I'll wake you if there's any news," Jesse promises.

The next day, the sun cuts through the miniblinds like a handful of knives, carving sharp paths of light across my face.

I cover my eyes with one hand as I sit up, the soft sheets bunching at my lap. Jesse is sitting on the edge of the other bed. He tilts his head to the side, studies me for a moment. "How are you?" he asks finally.

"Stiff." I inhale deeply as I stretch my arms up toward the ceiling. "Any word on Baz or Jun?"

Jesse shakes his head. "This is only the second day, though, remember? They might both be fine."

"Or they both might be dead."

Jesse winces but then recovers quickly. "There's no point in thinking the worst."

I run a hand through my hair. "Yes, there is. That way when it turns out to be true, it'll hurt less."

"It *won't* hurt less," he says. "Haven't you figured that out yet?"

I mull these words over as Jesse rises from his bed. He grabs a tray of room-service food from the dresser and brings it to me.

We eat our breakfast in silence, the events from two nights ago weighing heavily on our minds. And now here we are. Waiting. I know we're supposed to head back to the US on Monday morning if we haven't heard from Baz by then, but I'm really hoping it won't come to that. He survived military combat. He survived running covert ops for the government. He can survive a break-in at a pharmaceutical corporation.

I wish I were as sure about my brother. I can't get the image of his crumpled body on the floor of the UsuMed lobby out of my head.

"I'm going to be there for you, no matter what, okay?" Jesse reaches out for my hand.

I let him twine his fingers through mine. "I love that you're not filling my head with bullshit right now."

"What do you mean?"

"It's one of the first things I really noticed about you. You don't give people false reassurances. You're not sitting here telling me I just have to have hope, that they're probably okay, that none of this is my fault. You don't say things that aren't true just to make people feel better."

"I want you to feel better," Jesse says. "But not if it means I have to lie to you."

"I love that," I say. "I love you."

Jesse blinks rapidly. He looks away for a moment, bites down on his lip. When his eyes return to mine, he says, "I love you too."

My lashes grow heavy with tears. Jesse doesn't brush them away or attempt to console me. He just lets me be me.

The swelling in my ankle has gone down a lot, so Jesse and I spend part of the day walking the beaches of Jeju. I marvel at the rock formations and the mountains off in the distance, wishing I had a phone so I could take some pictures. We could always go back to the hotel for my ViSE headset, I suppose, but the thought of ever putting that on again after what happened at UsuMed makes me feel slightly nauseated.

It's warmer here than in Seoul, but still quite windy and cool—much too cold for venturing into the water. Jesse and I stand looking at the waves for a while, but I can't keep from scanning the beach, hoping against hope to see Baz approaching. Unfortunately, he doesn't appear.

The next day is Sunday. Jesse and I plan to buy our plane tickets today. We stick close to the hotel and keep Jesse's phone charged. We are ready. We are hopeful. We pack up everything in our room so we'll be ready to leave when it's time.

"Can I stay with you for a few days when we get back?" I ask. "I'm going to make an appointment with Dr. Abrams, talk to her about getting me into a residential treatment facility."

"Is that really what you want?"

"What I want is to be better," I say. "And if I commit myself completely to that goal, maybe I can make some real progress, get to a point where I feel comfortable going to college. Moving on."

"Well, then, of course you can stay with me." Jesse grins. "Under one condition."

My eyes narrow. "You'd better not say I have to cook for you."

"Well . . ." he trails off, his eyes twinkling. "That would be awfully nice. But no, I was going to say that we have to pick up Moo from Natalie's place. I miss that little cow cat."

I smile, probably the first real smile since we made it to Jeju Island. "It's a deal."

"So you ready to book our flight, then?" Jesse asks softly.

"Yes," I say. "But how about one more walk along the water first?"

"Okay."

We head back outside, where the temperature is probably about forty degrees but feels warmer than that because of the sun. Cottony clouds float in the bright-blue sky above our heads. I think about what I'm going back to—the bitter cold of St. Louis, the unforgiving ice storms, the dark memories.

"Hey," Jesse says excitedly. He points into the distance.

Two silhouettes come into view. One of them is tall and broad, with blond hair—Sebastian. The other is smaller, with dark hair. Could it be?

I quicken my stride a little, but pain knifes through my chest as I draw closer and realize the boy with Baz isn't my brother. It's Chung Hee. I try to plaster a smile on my face even though my insides are bleeding.

"I thought you were dead," I say to Baz. "I saw you get shot."

"Only once," he scoffs. "Sorry to worry you. I laid low at Chung Hee's place for a bit until things cooled down a little."

"Hello." Chung Hee smiles shyly at me from behind a pair of dark glasses. "Nice to see you again."

"Do you know anything about Jun?" I ask hopefully.

"EMS took him to Samsung Medical Center. I didn't want to go anywhere near there because there are cops waiting to talk to him when he's feeling better, but Hacker Boy here might have taken a quick peek at his medical records."

Chung pulls out his phone and skims through a file. "Stab wound to abdomen. Massive blood loss. Shock. After receiving emergency volume replacement and four units of packed cells, the patient's vital signs recovered to within normal limits. Prophylactic IV antibiotics and Tdap ordered due to puncture wound. Current status: pediatric inpatient; stable."

"So what does that mean exactly?" Relief courses through me at the word *stable*. Stable is good. It's better than I've been able to manage lately.

"It means he's going to be fine," Baz says. "Thanks to his nuna." He ruffles my hair.

"Is he safe in the hospital? What if someone from UsuMed comes after him?" I bite my lip. "I'm not sure how many people knew what Kyung and Alec were working on, but Jun now has information on classified projects."

"I wouldn't worry about that," Baz says smoothly.

"Why not?" I ask.

He pulls a small card out of his pocket. "It's a recording of the standoff in the lobby, of Kyung basically admitting he ordered Rose's and Gideon's deaths and stole the technology. I even captured him threatening Jun's life."

"But a ViSE won't be admissible evidence," I say. "Just like back in the US."

"No, but I made sure Usu's chairman knows we're not afraid to give it to the newspapers. International ones if the local ones are afraid to run the story. Which means Kyung and Alec Kwon would be responsible for ruining Usu's good name. How many companies do they own worldwide now? Fifty? A hundred?"

"Sebastian, you're brilliant," I say, hugging him.

"I'm just a guy who's always prepared." He pauses. "Should I even ask what the hell happened that night? Or just be glad we're all okay?"

"I thought you were going to betray us," I admit. "That you were trying to use us to steal the tech for yourself. I saw you meet with Kyung earlier in the day as Erich Cross, so I told Jesse and we made a new plan."

"Ah." Baz rubs at his chin. He's clean-shaven again, more like the Sebastian I remember from St. Louis. "You couldn't have just told me? I approached Kyung via an online site as a potential buyer for the tech. I wasn't sure he'd take the bait but figured if he did, I could find out exactly where it was kept."

"You couldn't have just told me you were meeting with Kyung?"

"Touché," Baz says. "I was afraid you'd interfere and end up getting hurt. So you guys broke in without me. That's pretty badass."

"Jesse's the badass," I say, too tired to explain how Kyung and Alec had captured me. It doesn't matter anymore, because they're dead and I'm not. I'm alive, and Jun is alive too. I'm so incredibly grateful for both of those things, and for Jesse and Baz surviving too.

But there's also a heaviness in my gut that I can't shake. I know Baz was right when he said wars always include collateral damage, but I'll never forgive myself for the death of Jason Choi, the security guard. I didn't kill him, but I involved him in our plan without his consent, and because of that he was tortured to death. I hate that his kindness in talking to me brought about the end of his life. I wish the world wasn't like that, that it didn't sometimes punish good people for no reason. Unfortunately, wishing the world was different won't make it so. Life is horrible sometimes. I know that better than anyone.

Baz glances around. "This place is even nicer than I remembered. And the weather is almost bearable."

"It is nice here," Jesse agrees.

"Better than the weather back in St. Louis, for sure." Baz glances back and forth from Jesse to me. "So you ready to go home, or what?"

Jesse grins. "I thought you'd never ask."

"The sooner the better," I agree.

CHAPTER 53

Back in St. Louis, Miso and I move into Jesse's apartment temporarily. Jesse offers to sleep on the sofa so we can have his bed, but we're both willing to share. Still, Jesse and I are sticking fast to our decision to take our relationship slow. Neither of us wants to blow the second chance we've been given.

Gideon's lawyer helps transfer ownership of the apartment building and Escape into my name. He also refers me to a lawyer who can help me apply for a visa, a real one, under the name Ha Neul Song. I still plan on being Winter to everyone in St. Louis, but my real name connects me forever to my sister. It's time I took it back.

Several different companies contact me about buying the ViSE technology. I end up selling the headsets and Gideon's neural mapping notes to a medical school in Minnesota that wants to translate the work Gideon did with sensory neurons over to motor neurons, in an attempt to help paralyzed people regain partial mobility. I donate the money they pay me to a national charity that helps victims of human trafficking. I also send the charity my personal story, including as much information as I can remember about what happened to me in Los Angeles. I don't even know if Kyung was still involved in trafficking before he left L.A., but maybe sharing my details can help free some other girls. I know there will always be evil people in this world. I know I can't save everyone. But I'm hoping the money I donated can help some. It's a start.

I debate selling the neural editor too, but in the end I decide to destroy it. I'm hanging on to Gideon's notes, just in case I ever regret that choice, but right now I don't think modifying the way our brains interpret signals from our environments is a good idea.

Reality is a good idea.

I hold a special service for Gideon at Escape. We close the club to the public for the morning so that all of us who were close to him—Baz, Adebayo, Jesse, me, Natalie, and Isaiah—can honor his memory.

After struggling to decide between a traditional Korean or a more American funeral, I actually opted to go with neither. I came up with the kind of service I think Gideon would have wanted. I set up framed photos of both him and my sister on one of the gaming tables and arranged chairs around it.

The six of us take turns telling our favorite story about Gideon. Some of them make me laugh. Some of them make me cry. All of them make me glad I knew Gideon Seung, aka Cho Ki Hyun.

Adebayo goes last. He tells the story of how when he lost his position at the university for taking bets, he was floundering for a few months. He spent his mornings in the Riverlights Casino, slowly (sometimes not so slowly) gambling away his savings. One night he had a few too many complimentary drinks and found himself kicked out into the cold. Gideon passed by him as he was walking home and asked if he needed medical assistance. When he heard Adebayo's accent, he asked him where he was from. The two men struck up a conversation about what it was like to be so far away from their homelands.

"He could have treated me as if I were a drunk or a homeless person," Adebayo says. "For in that moment, I was perhaps both of those things. But instead of judging, or even pitying me, he bent down to give me a hand. And then he found a common thread between us, the fallen professor and the talented, young upstart."

Tears roll down my cheeks. For once I don't wipe them away. I don't try to stop them. I just focus on the image of the closest thing I've ever known to a father. I wish that my life up to this point had gone a little differently. I wish Gideon were still alive. But I'm glad I got to know him for as long as I did. And I'm glad both he and my sister found love—fierce, unrelenting love—in their too-short lives.

After a few moments of silence, I stand again. "As you probably know, I've sold the ViSE technology, but Gideon left me this club and the building in his will. Adebayo and Sebastian are going to be handling daily operations, but there's a job here for anyone who wants it. And you're also welcome to continue living in your apartments rent-free. Gideon would want me to take care of his people."

"We're your people too," Natalie says. "We're here for you."

"We're all here, for each other," Baz adds. "Let's agree to that. No matter where we might end up, if one of us needs something, the rest will try to be there."

"Agreed," Jesse says.

"Deal." Isaiah gives Baz a fist bump.

"I'm in," Natalie chirps.

"As am I," Adebayo says.

As I look around the table, I realize the way I feel about each of them is slightly different, and the way I feel about my brother and aunt back in Seoul is different yet. But all of the feelings add up to one word—family.

As soon as I finish with business in St. Louis, Jesse and I head to the Echelon Wellness Center in Tucson, Arizona. We make one stop on the way. Los Angeles, of all places.

"Are you sure you want to do this?" Jesse asks.

We're standing at the corner of a certain cemetery that,

according to the Internet, is where all of the ashes of unclaimed bodies in L.A. are buried. As you can imagine, this particular area doesn't get a lot of visitors, so there is no one around who will object if I spread Gideon's ashes here.

"He would want to be with her." I pull a small gardening trowel out of my pocket.

"What if she's not here?"

It's a valid question. I'm not convinced the county of Los Angeles is particularly thorough when it comes to the burials of unclaimed prostitutes. I remove the rose pendant from around my neck. With the trowel, I dig in the dirt until I've made a decent-sized hole. Then I drop the necklace into it. "Now she's here." With a quick glance around to be sure that we're still alone, I dump Gideon's ashes into the hole with the necklace. "I miss you both so much," I say. "But if I can't be with you, I'm glad you'll get to be with each other. Forever."

"Forever," Jesse echoes.

We leave the cemetery and drive from L.A. to Tucson, where Jesse makes a huge fuss over leaving me at Echelon.

"I don't know what I'm going to do without you," he says.

"Take care of Miso, obviously. And help out with the building." Jesse has agreed to penthouse-sit for me while I'm gone. "It's two months. Then you can come visit. I bet the time will fly by."

"Maybe for you," Jesse grumbles. But then he gets serious. "I'm proud of you, Winter."

The old Winter would have shaken off the compliment and said there was nothing to be proud of, but that girl is only part of who I am these days. "Thanks." I smile. "I'm proud of me too."

EPILOGUE

Exactly two months from the day I checked myself into Echelon, Jesse comes to visit me. I take him for a walk around the grounds. We sit on a bench in front of the facility's man-made lake, watching a lady across the water feed leftovers from her lunch to a small flock of mallard ducks.

"Poor ducks." My lips quirk into a smile. "No one wants that food."

"This place seems nice. Look, they even have swans." Jesse points at a pair of white birds swimming side by side in the center of the lake.

"I think I might pay a waterfowl surcharge for those," I say. Echelon is not cheap, but luckily, thanks to the money Gideon left me, I can afford it. I definitely feel like a stronger person since I arrived here.

"Totally worth it if they make you feel better." Jesse blots a bit of sweat from his brow.

A soft breeze rustles a patch of reeds at the water's edge. I take in a deep breath of air and let it out. "I do feel better."

"Good." Jesse pats me on the leg.

"This is a good place for me. There are all kinds of people here, but the women in my building have all experienced dissociative symptoms. There are fourteen of us right now. We all meet for group sessions three times a week and then I have smaller sessions each day with three other women. It's helping me a lot to hear their stories and share some of mine."

Jesse nods but he doesn't speak. I'm overcome by the urge to reach out and touch his long, dark eyelashes, to brush a bead of sweat from the side of his nose. There are so many tiny things about him that are standing out as beautiful to me today.

"I've also been working one-on-one with a therapist every day, a woman who is one of the foremost experts on dissociative identity disorder. Together we've uncovered four alter personas—Rose, Lily, a darker part who calls herself Black, and an older woman who is known only as the Calm One." I pause to let this sink in.

Jesse takes my hand. He massages my palm with his thumb. Above us, puffy clouds part and the sun shines directly down on our bench. I love how warm it is here. "Five of you. That's intense," he says finally.

He reaches out to ruffle my hair, and I drink in the physical contact, the warmth of his touch. This facility is helping me, and I have no desire to leave early, but part of me thinks endlessly about the day I can return to St. Louis.

As if he can read my mind, he says, "Everyone sends their love. Natalie says she misses you. Baz says to get well soon. Adebayo said something inspiring in that mellifluous accent of his, but I forgot exactly what it was."

"Mellifluous, eh?" I nudge Jesse in the ribs. "Did you start college without me?"

"I might be reading a lot of books. But no; I'm excited to take some basic classes with you at the community college this fall. Of course, you'll be in Calculus and I'll be in something like Fun with Fractions, but maybe we can both sign up for Spanish and I can kick your ass at that."

"Porqué eres tan competitivo?" I say with a grin.

Jesse's jaw drops. "How the hell did you pull that out of thin air?"

I blink innocently. "I get bored here sometimes. I found a *How to Speak Spanish* book in the library and remembered there was this one guy I kind of like who speaks it."

"Kind of like, huh? Well, I don't know who that asshole is, but I bet he didn't bring you an awesome present." Jesse produces a small white box from the center pocket of his hoodie.

"You shouldn't have," I say.

"Yes, I should have."

"No, seriously. The nurses will probably take it away if you didn't get it approved."

"I can take it back to the penthouse with me if you're worried. Just open it already." He fidgets on the bench, tapping his feet like he's the one who just got a surprise.

I untie the ribbon and open the box. Folding back the tissue paper, I discover a small glass snow globe. I hold it up to get a better look. It's Namsan Tower and the cable car. I shake the globe gently and the snow swirls. I close my eyes and remember taking Jesse in the cable car up to the top of the mountain. I remember kissing him, him telling me he loves me in Korean. "It's perfect," I breathe. The sun refracts through the globe, casting the reflection of a rainbow on my arm.

Jesse traces the colors on my skin. "I didn't want you to forget our first date."

I glance furtively around and then quickly press my lips to his. We're not supposed to engage in physical affection here. The doctors believe that romance complicates healing, and that when we're here, we should focus solely on our own wellness and that of the other residents. "Thank you," I say.

"I have something else for you too." Jesse removes a plain white envelope from his pocket. "It's a letter, from Jun."

My eyes water. "There is no end to your kindness, is there?"

"Baz helped me reach out to him. I can't take all the credit." Jesse pats me on the leg again.

I rest the letter on my lap. I think I'll wait until my next therapy session so I can read it with my doctor. I hope Jun and my aunt will want a relationship with me even after everything that's happened. But if they don't, that doesn't mean I'll be alone. The last few months have shown me that my family is bigger than I ever imagined, even if most of the members aren't blood relatives.

"Thank you," I tell Jesse. "And thanks for taking care of the penthouse and of Miso too."

"Are you sure you want to move back into the penthouse after everything that's happened?"

I nod. "Everything in that place reminds me of Gideon. And thinking about Gideon makes me feel strong." I pause. "And loved."

"That makes sense, but be warned. Now that the Moo-cat and I have engaged in extensive male bonding, you're probably going to have trouble separating us when you come home. We're talking weeks of guttural wailing and random fits of despondency." He pauses. "And Moo might be sad too."

I laugh. I glance over at Jesse. "Maybe the two of you won't have to separate."

He blinks rapidly. "What are you saying? You want to . . . live together?"

Am I ready to live with Jesse? It feels like a big leap, but I have made so many of those in the past few months. And Jesse has been there every step of the way, supporting me. Loving me. "Well, the doctors here recommend that we stay with a loved one for at least the first six months after we leave. And you're probably going to be around all the time anyway, right? Begging to copy my homework and such?"

"True. And Moo and I do have kind of a regular Friday-night thing where we eat chicken wings and watch Animal Planet." Jesse's voice is playful but then he swallows hard and looks away. I can feel just how much this decision means to him.

It means a lot to me too. Trusting him. Trusting myself.

He pulls up the sleeves on his hoodie. "I know there's no humidity, but I forgot how hot the Southwest could get."

"It is quite warm today." I wave a hand in front of my face.

We turn back to the lake, where the swans have ventured up onto the shore. One of them shakes itself, splashing us a little bit.

"You know the place you're at is fancy when you say you're warm and the swans come to gently mist you with water from their wings," I say.

"Nothing but the best for you," Jesse says.

I take his hand in mine and squeeze it. "Nothing but the best," I agree.

Acknowledgments

Massive amounts of gratitude to the following people:

My family and friends for their endless and unconditional support; Jennifer Laughran, for being tough and real and believing in my work; Kathleen Doherty, for giving this story a chance to live outside of my brain; Melissa Frain, for pushing me to make this book better and for being there for me, especially in Naperville; Amy Stapp, for epic multitasking and fielding lots of frantic author questions; Alexis Saarela, for being a promotional goddess and for the speediest email replies in the industry; Kristin Roth for careful and thorough copy edits that make me look a lot smarter than I am; and everyone else at Tor Teen, for the editorial, design, publicity, sales, and marketing support, and for a cover that is somehow even prettier than the first one. Seriously. You guys are all magic.

Everyone I met while I was living and working in South Korea. Thank you for sharing your stories with me and for being part of an experience that changed my life forever. Thanks to all of my beta readers and experts. The following people were kind enough to provide feedback on elements of story, psychology, technology, medicine, and Korean culture: Marcy Beller Paul; Antony John; Kristi Helvig, Ph.D.; Christina Ahn Hickey, M.D.; Eli Madison; Elizabeth Min; Minjae

Christine Kim; Yun-A Kwak; and María Pilar Albarrán Ruiz. Any mistakes are mine, not theirs.

All of my amazing industry friends and colleagues: the girls at Manuscript Critique Services; the YA Valentines; the Apocalypsies; and all the bloggers, booksellers, librarians, and teachers who interact with me in person and on social media. I couldn't do it without you.

And last but not least, the readers. I said it in *Vicarious* too, but nothing has changed. I couldn't do it without you either, and I will never forget that.